LOVE LESSONS IN STARCROSS VALLEY

ALSO BY LUCY KNOTT

LOVE LESSONS IN STARCROSS VALLEY

Lucy Knott

An Aria Book

First published in the UK in 2022 by Head of Zeus Ltd
This paperback edition first published in 2022 by Head of Zeus Ltd,
part of Bloomsbury Publishing Plc

A CIP catalogue record for this book is available
from the British Library.

ISBN (PB): 9781803281292
ISBN (E): 9781800243330

Cover design: Jessie Price

Typeset by Siliconchips Services Ltd UK

Printed and bound in Great Britain by
CPI Group (UK) Ltd, Croydon CR0 4YY

For Kelly, the Morgan to my Chuck, the Chuck to my Morgan, the Jeff to my Lester, the Lester to my Jeff. For TD, my best friend, to infinity and beyond.

Prologue

'Oh come on, referee,' Marnie mumbled, wanting to get in on the action. The lively crowd were riled up with what seemed to be the star player being sent into the penalty box. The name on the back of his jersey – 'Boeser' – could be the one they were chanting but the pronunciation from the crowd's hollering and grunting blended together. It didn't sound right. Marnie feared she would say it wrong and, therefore, settled with admonishing the referee, albeit quietly. Though a love of ice hockey had been ever present since she was a teen watching it on TV, it had been a while since she had watched a game and kept up with the players and their stats. Not to mention, this was her very first live game and she was by herself, over four thousand miles from home.

'It's pronounced Beser,' came a voice from beside her. Marnie whipped her head to her right, loosening a short strand of brown hair from her messy bun. Her cheeks felt flushed and rosy from a mixture of heat from the bodies in the arena and that cool chill of being so close to an ice rink that made the air tickle the tip of your nose pink.

When she turned she came face to face with startling blue

eyes, eyelashes that went on for days and a wide mouth that was curved up into a grin.

'Thanks,' she said quickly before turning back to the action, suddenly feeling a little disorientated. How was it possible for someone's eyes to be that blue? She appreciated the stranger's help nonetheless. She had been in Canada for four weeks and everyone she'd met so far had been wonderfully friendly, not that she had met an awful lot of people having spent most of her time in her hotel room, but she had waited for this day for a long time, and she didn't want to miss a second of the game being distracted by a friendly Canuck whose eyes were too bright and legs so impossibly long Marnie had had to gaze upwards when giving her thanks.

Gripping her white hoodie, emblazoned with the red Canadian maple leaf – she had wanted to fit in – Marnie followed suit and sat back down with the rest of the crowd.

Five minutes later and a buzzer sounded, signalling the release of the prisoner in the penalty box and the crowd once again rose to their feet chanting his name. Marnie jumped up. It was on the tip of her tongue but she was having difficulty getting herself to say it.

'After three, scream it with me,' came the voice beside her. Marnie turned her head just an inch so she could see the stranger's face, but not so much that she would get hypnotised by her blue eyes. It was to no avail; they pulled her in. Marnie was grateful to see that there was no teasing behind the woman's eyes, but a warmth that made them wide and full of excitement. Marnie gave a subtle nod and returned her own eyes to the rink, awaiting her countdown.

'One, two, three...' the woman shouted.

'Let's go, Boeser!' Marnie hollered with the stranger as the crowd's chants suddenly stopped and people returned to their seats. Instead of looking at them like they were crazy, the crowd raised their beers and cheered but Marnie couldn't help the laughter that erupted from her.

'Sorry, that one was on me,' the woman beside her said with a chuckle. Marnie nudged her elbow as she took to her seat and gave her another glance while Boeser skated smoothly back into the game. Marnie noticed the rosy hue on the apples of the stranger's cheeks and she shook her head.

'That felt good, thank you...' Marnie started and then paused, holding out her hand, in a sudden moment of boldness.

The woman lifted her Vancouver cap off her head, causing her blonde, elbow-length locks to fall into her face, and took Marnie's hand with a gentle grasp. Their eyes locked and both smiled an easy-going smile, relaxing their grips.

'Nova,' the woman said, her eyelashes giving a small flutter, her face a picture of bashful.

'Marnie.' Marnie let go of her hand and returned it to the cosy confines of her sleeve, where it now tingled.

The rest of the game flew by with Marnie having too much fun to feel anxious or insecure. By the time the final buzzer sounded, she was red-faced and sweaty, stray pieces of dark baby hair glued to her forehead and cheeks.

'That was incredible.' She twisted her body towards Nova. She was in no rush to leave with the crowd, instead preferring to wait for the swarm of bodies to disperse before she made her exit. Nova looked around, a little like a meerkat, her eyes darting over the sea of people before she hunched her shoulders and settled back into her chair with her hands in her pockets. She didn't look to be one for crowds either. Either that or she could sense Marnie's unease. The thought made Marnie blush.

'The Canucks are the best in Canada,' Nova replied, with an enthusiastic smile. She then paused and tilted her head subtly to one side, her eyes gently looking into Marnie's. Four weeks ago Marnie would have recoiled if someone had so much as looked her way, let alone made eye contact, but somehow Nova didn't make her feel judged or nervous; after all, she didn't know what Marnie had left behind.

'Do you play?' she asked Nova, relaxing into her own plastic chair, thumb brushing the fabric of her new hoodie, forcing herself not to think of home.

'My ice-skating skills are questionable. I'm wobbly even without a hundred-and-thirty-five-pound human charging at me,' Nova said, with a cheery self-deprecating pout.

Marnie chuckled. She'd always wanted to play but had never had the means back in Orion.

'What about you? Do you play?' Nova returned.

'I've always wanted to but there weren't many ice rinks where I grew up, that is to say there weren't any. Occasionally we'd go into the city, usually around Christmas time when they would set up the festive activities and I'd give skating a go. I'm not bad but I've never wielded a stick on the ice,' Marnie said with a casual shrug, aware that that was the most she had spoken in four weeks. 'It looks fun though, doesn't it?' she added with a crinkle of her nose and excitement in her tone. Nova cocked her head and gave Marnie a considering grin.

'Sure, if you're not scared of pulling a muscle, breaking bones or getting whacked in the face with the puck,' Nova replied, narrowing her eyes playfully, a small smirk at the corner of her peachy lips.

'I'll try it if you try it.' Marnie sat up straighter in her seat, an idea coming to mind that was ridiculously crazy and so out of character for her.

'Whoa, you're not really suggesting that we spend the evening learning how to play hockey?' Nova said, matching her posture and raising a natural blonde brow.

'I know there are at least eight ice rinks in Vancouver. There are none where I live, so...' Marnie started before Nova interrupted.

'It's not a suggestion, it's a plan,' she said finishing Marnie's sentence before blowing out air in disbelief. Marnie couldn't quite believe what she was saying either. Her fingers buried into her palms inside the pockets of her hoodie but she didn't want to go back on her plan. She could do this.

'Exactly.' Marnie jumped to her feet before she could back out, feeling a little more confident to move about the arena now that the crowd had died down. Nova looked up at her dubiously. 'Unless you already have plans?' Marnie said, suddenly worried about her boldness. Brave it might have been to get on a long haul flight and travel across the world on her own but once in the large wide open space that was Canada, her nerves had certainly kicked in and she was very much missing her other half. Going ice-skating had been on her list of things to do, in addition to watching an ice-hockey game. She felt proud for getting to the arena on her own, but it had taken her four weeks to leave her hotel room. It felt comforting having another person by her side and one she felt at ease with, because what if she fell on the ice? And what would people think of her ice-skating alone?

On the plane journey over she had vowed this trip would be her chance to seize independence, to no longer live in fear of standing alone, but it was far from easy. Would Nova think her silly for being nervous to move about the city on her own? That some days it took a lot longer than she liked to leave her hotel room just to go for breakfast? Would she think her ridiculous that some things were harder than others when she was by herself?

'My plans...' Nova started, then stood, making Marnie tilt her head to make eye contact. Marnie's stomach gave a small squeeze of nervous anticipation for what Nova was about to say. Guilty as the thought made her feel, she didn't think she had the confidence to tick ice-skating off her list on her own. Additionally, she found she wasn't ready to say bye to Nova just yet, whatever that meant. '...are not to fall over, not to get hurt and not to make a fool of myself on the ice,' Nova finished, gesturing that they should make a move.

Marnie wanted to hug her, but having just met her, she resorted to a little hop on the spot and a 'yay' before making her way out of the row.

'I feel they should make protective gear a requirement for ice-skating and provide free butt-pads on entry. How do they make it look so elegant in the movies?' Nova whined as she took Marnie's hand for the ninth time in the forty minutes they'd been on the ice. It was apparent extremely quickly that they would not be wielding sticks. Nova needed to learn how to balance without one first.

'I'm not sure about elegant but should the Canucks have a scout watching, I think the tackle you gave that ten-year-old would have gotten their attention,' Marnie said, supressing a laugh. It had of course not been funny at the time but ever since the Dad confirmed the child was OK, a small, awful part of her was battling with a fit of giggles. Nova had been distraught but the Dad had been totally cool. The kid had thought it a blast flying across the ice, being a big ice-hockey fan himself, so there was no harm caused, only to Nova's ego.

'You know that was an accident right?' Nova asked, her bottom lip jutting out, sheer desperation in her blue eyes.

Marnie made her face serious and tone stern. 'Oh of course, absolutely,' she said, her lips twitching at the corners giving away the humour she found in the situation. Nova gave her a narrow-eyed side glance as she reached for the barrier.

'One day I'll come to your town and the shoe will be on the other foot,' she said, attempting to puff out her chest and stand tall but failing when her blades slipped, her movement causing her to bend over and grip the barrier tighter. Marnie couldn't hold it in much longer and laughter burst from between her lips, pushing down the queasiness she felt thinking of being embarrassed in her hometown. Nova was late to the party there.

Rolling with laughter and ignoring the negative voices in her head, she placed a hand on Nova's shoulder.

'Did you just threaten to travel halfway around the world so that you can show me up in my hometown?'

she asked, unable to wipe the smile off her face with the ridiculousness of it all and because Nova had come ice-skating with her even when she was a complete stranger and was clearly terrified. Nova had winced and her cheeks had burned bright red each time she had fallen. There was a small part of Marnie that felt bad. She supposed it would only be fair she return the favour, though it wouldn't take much. She shook her thoughts of home away when Nova looked at her and grinned, her blue eyes sparkling under the fluorescent lights of the rink.

'Yes, yes I did because I'm romantic like that,' she said with a goofy nod of her head. Marnie rolled her eyes and tilted her head towards her. For a moment she got lost in trying to picture Nova in Orion. Would she like Jovi? Would she get on with Antoni? What would she make of her mum and dad's situation or her own for that matter? A loud screech snapped her out of her reverie as a teenager came hurtling towards them. Marnie quickly stretched out her hands to steady the teen and to stop her crashing into them.

'I'm so sorry. Thanks,' the flustered girl said before grabbing the hand of her friend and bravely heading back into the fray of skaters. It took a minute for Marnie to realise that Nova was watching her. There was something about her staring that didn't frighten her but she hastily plastered on a smile. She wasn't in Canada to think about home and the mess she had left behind. She was in Canada to have fun, and besides, the chances of Nova ever meeting her family where as low as the chances of Nova making one full circle around the ice rink without falling on her arse.

'One more go and then food?' Nova suggested, precariously taking one hand off the barrier.

'Sounds good to me.' Marnie gave a cheerful nod before teasing Nova ever so innocently and pretending to rush off without her. But three steps away she gracefully spun around and smirked at her while holding out her hands.

'No, it's fine – you go on without me. Go do your fancy twirls. I don't need help,' Nova mumbled.

Marnie grabbed her hands and helped her fall into a smooth rhythm, ignoring her complaints.

'Nova, you're doing it,' Marnie cried when she slowly let go a few minutes later.

'I am ay, I am,' Nova said, adjusting her cap and returning her arms to an eagle span at her sides to keep her balance. Marnie stayed quiet the rest of the way round, not wanting to distract her. Nova kept her eyes trained on the ice and Marnie looked out for anyone getting too close that might bump her and knock her confidence. By the time Marnie reached the starting point her cheeks ached from smiling so much. It had been hard not to as she watched Nova come full circle.

'If my dad could see me now,' Nova said wistfully as she pulled her cap off her head to scrape back some of her hair that had started to stick to her hot cheeks.

'Can he skate?' Marnie asked, guiding Nova over the step of the rink and onto a bench where they could take off their blades with less chance of causing bodily harm.

'He could. He was a natural, played since he was a boy. He used to get a kick out of me trying. He believed in me with his whole heart but I preferred digging in the mud,' Nova answered, landing heavily on the bench before her skates could slide from underneath her – though there wasn't much chance of that on the rubber mats around the rink.

Marnie raised an eyebrow with intrigue and took the seat next to her, being forced to snuggle in a little tight due to a family taking up the other end of the bench. Nova's black Canucks hoodie grazed against her sleeve.

'Digging in the mud?' Marnie enquired, untying her laces. Nova sat up and crossed her right ankle over her left knee to pull off her skate, but she paused to swivel her cap around so it wasn't shadowing her face as she looked down at Marnie while Marnie was bent over her skates.

'In search of dinosaur fossils of course,' Nova noted, her cheeks rounding into a beaming grin with a hint of childlike mischief.

Marnie stopped messing with her laces to look at her. Her eyes sparkled under the mix of the early evening sun and the street lights, and in them Marnie could clearly see bursting specks of passion. Nova's pearly white teeth bit her long bottom lip, almost like she was nervous to hear Marnie's response and desperate to keep talking at the same time. Marnie couldn't understand her nerves; digging for dinosaurs was the coolest thing in her book. When she realised she was staring at Nova and hadn't spoken for a good ten seconds, Nova's pinched shoulders made sense.

'No way, did you ever find any?' Marnie asked enthusiastically, enjoying the way Nova's body became loose and relaxed once more. Her teeth bit down a little deeper into her bottom lips as she narrowed her eyes at Marnie for a split second before a smile took over her face. It was like Nova really took the time to hear her and take in what Marnie was saying. Nova flipped off her skates and pulled on her black and white vans while Marnie finished tying the laces on her pumps.

'Not in my garden no, but at the digs, yes,' Nova said, getting to her feet and picking up both her and Marnie's skates. 'Were you a muddy child or an indoor child?' she asked Marnie. Marnie stood, coming up to her chin, and they carefully manoeuvred away from the busy skate rink.

'Wait, you can't start asking me about my childhood and not divulge what you found. That's huge. I was an indoor and outdoor child. Anywhere I could craft I was happy, but I never thought to look for dinosaurs. I sound boring compared to you.' Marnie waved her hands, talking fast so she could get to more questions about dinosaurs. Her heart beat in quick succession thinking about her six-year-old niece, whose birthday she had missed due to running away to Canada. Sienna adored both dinosaurs and space. 'So, you're a palaeontologist?' Marnie asked, desperate to know more.

'I hardly think you're boring, Marnie. And you don't think digging for dinosaurs is nerdy?' Nova asked and Marnie could sense a vulnerability in her tone, though she kept her features light.

'Oh absolutely, ridiculously nerdy in the coolest way possible,' Marnie replied, her smile reaching her hazel eyes.

Nova let out a bright laugh, bringing her hand to her chest. 'What do you think about burgers?' she asked as they stepped further away from the noise of the ice rink and back on to the streets of downtown Vancouver.

'Not nerdy but delicious.' Marnie smiled up at her.

'Wait till you try a Wakwak burger,' Nova said, bringing her hands up to her head to twist her cap back around to shield her eyes from the golden sunset.

★

They had been walking in comfortable silence for what felt like hours but what Marnie knew could only have been minutes while they ate their burgers. It was as if time had slowed down to let them enjoy every bite. So mesmerised by the mouth-watering kewpie mayo, Marnie hadn't questioned their destination and wasn't even sure Nova had a destination in mind. They simply walked while trying not to let the juicy sauces from their delectable burgers drizzle down their sleeves and stain their hoodies.

With her last bite of scrumptious beef decorated with seaweed and tempura pieces, Marnie found herself looking at Nova and grinning. Her best friend Antoni would love her. She'd groaned at least ten times while she ate her crispy pork burger layered with cabbage slaw and spicy mustard.

'Do I have something on my face?' Nova said playfully, swallowing a large bite then licking her lips.

Marnie chuckled, for her chin did indeed have a light drizzle of mustard, precariously ready to drip onto her hoodie. Casually, Marnie took a tissue and wiped it without much thought. Nova nodded her thanks as they continued walking. Now that her burger had been devoured, Marnie opened her eyes to her surroundings.

Tall buildings towered over them. They came to a neon blue and white sign with yellow bulbs decorating its edges.

'The Orpheum, where many a legend has played,' Nova noted, gesturing towards the flickering lights.

'I have five more months here and it still doesn't seem a long enough time to see all the cool things Canada has to offer. It would take a mere three days to take in the sites of Orion.' Marnie chuckled and shook her head, trying not to think about the time she had wasted in her hotel room, staring at the list of all the things she wanted to do in Canada, a list she had been putting together for years.

'Every place has its gems,' Nova replied, throwing her burger wrapper in a nearby bin and wiping her hands on a paper napkin.

'Is that palaeontology inspiration?' Marnie teased.

Nova shrugged but she was smiling. 'Something like that.' Nova gave Marnie a wink from underneath her baseball cap. It was a casual wink, a wink that Marnie would never in a million years be able to pull off, but it was also a sexy wink. A wink that made Marnie's knees turn to marshmallows. Her feet felt too light and squishy to feel the solid ground beneath her, but she couldn't look around for a prop to steady herself, not when Nova's blues were studying her so carefully.

Her feet needed to move now. She needed to turn away and walk before the heat of her insides made her erupt like a volcano in front of this beautiful, tall and exquisite stranger. Instead, words flew out of Marnie's mouth without permission.

'So, Boeser huh? You into the ice hockey lads?' Marnie had no idea on God's green earth what possessed her to say those words. The minute she tried to say Boeser's name, she knew she'd butchered it. It hadn't come out like Nova had pronounced it earlier – 'Beser' – it had come out 'Bowser', and when had she ever used the word 'lads'? Her fingers were rubbing hard over the silver of her bracelet under the cuff of her hoodie and her heart was beating manically against her ribcage, probably wanting to abort her body and jump ship to a more put together and less awkward home.

But Nova didn't bark out a laugh or give her a weird or judgemental look, she simply shrugged and turned to continue walking, making Marnie feel as though she could breathe again without her bewitching eyes observing her. Marnie's fingers eased off her bracelet. It was almost as if Nova knew she needed space, a second of air.

'I'm afraid the lads don't do it for me. Now, the women's hockey league, that's a whole other story, ay,' Nova commented causing Marnie to promptly choke on the air she had so desperately needed. Her palms were suddenly sweaty. She wiped them on the insides of the sleeves of her hoodie. Abruptly, Nova stopped walking and put her arm out, gently taking Marnie's wrist. 'I know what we should do,' she said, glancing down at the gold-faced watch with a black strap on her wrist. 'Am I OK to keep you for a little longer, Marnie?' Nova asked sincerely and when she said Marnie's name it was all Marnie could do from blurting out 'you can keep me forever', and so she nodded safely instead, not even bothering to ask the time.

Nova organised an Uber while Marnie managed to calm herself by taking notes. Nova's manner was effortlessly relaxed and carefree compared to Marnie's – always on edge and worried. Her eyes weren't shifty from overthinking the way Marnie did; she simply got on with it. Marnie needed some of Nova's traits to rub off on her if she was actually going to enjoy this trip, make it worthwhile and shed the guilt she bore for being in Canada right now.

'So, of all the delights Vancouver has to offer, what else

have you seen so far?' Nova asked, snapping Marnie out of her self-reflection, thankfully.

They both climbed into the Uber and Nova's pupils grew large under the shadows of the night, like inky pools of inviting yet troublesome treacle. Marnie felt she'd earned her honesty. Maybe it was the four weeks hiding in a hotel room avoiding texts, emails and calls, or maybe it was the feeling that somehow Nova wouldn't judge her. Maybe it was simply those enticing eyes. But Marnie explained her anxiety and spoke of her twin sister back home and how independence, walking through life alone, was not an area of expertise for her. There were things she kept guarded, like her reason for being in Canada alone in the first place, but it was the first time in a long time she had opened up, baring her fears.

The Uber came to a stop when Marnie finished. There was no time for Nova to speak, but before they got out of the car she reached out and took Marnie's hand, giving it a tight squeeze before letting go and opening the door. Somehow, that was all Marnie needed – not words, not sympathy, just an understanding type of squeeze with a layer of 'you got this' that left her palm tingling once more.

When Marnie stepped out of the vehicle she was greeted by a building that resembled Alpha 5 from the *Power Rangers*. Its backdrop: a city of skyscrapers with their tiny windows glowing against the night sky. Taking in the fountain and its sharp crab sculpture, highlighted by the golden bulbs that shone under the water, illuminating its edges and points, she breathed in the spring evening and found herself feeling more weightless than she had felt in a long time. Marnie couldn't quite put her finger on whether it was the Canadian air or the fact that she had opened up her mind, even in a small dose, to Nova.

'We're a little late, but they won't mind if I show you round myself,' Nova said, waving a special-looking key card Marnie's way, her lips curving up, creating a dimple in her right cheek and a thousand flecks of mischief in her eyes. Marnie didn't know if they were about to break and enter, if what they were about to do was breaking the law, or if the people inside really wouldn't mind if Nova showed her around, but it didn't actually make any difference because she walked alongside Nova to the front entrance to the space centre, strangely without a care in the world about anything other than sticking by this woman.

It turned out they were not breaking and entering, as there were staff milling about inside, though the centre was quiet and as peaceful as the night outside.

'I work at the Royal Tyrrell Museum in Alberta,' Nova informed Marnie as they walked through the centre, seemingly following signs for the observatory.

Marnie's thoughts drifted to her niece, Sienna, and how much she would adore Nova. Then they flicked to buying a postcard from this place and sending it back home for the little girl. For a brief second she wondered if Jovi would read it to her or if she would still be angry but then Nova turned around to check Marnie was still walking with her and the way her pupils grew large under her cap, a little like two black holes that Marnie felt if she fell into there would be no getting out, evaporated any thought of back home from Marnie's mind.

'That sounds amazing,' Marnie mumbled, remembering Nova had said she worked at the dinosaur museum.

Nova gave a sort of disarming side smile like she knew Marnie's brain was awash with all kinds of thoughts. It was not exactly a sympathetic look but more kind and considering, like she appreciated Marnie's brain and possibly thought it fascinating while maybe wanting to help her in some way. Their eyes locked on each other's for a few moments as they walked before Nova reached out her hand and grabbed Marnie's to pull her along.

'Oh, the dinosaurs are definitely amazing but this place is pretty spectacular too,' Nova said with a tug, making the tension in Marnie's limbs loosen, yet the cage around her heart tighten.

The next minute, Marnie was being pulled through a large white door and transported into a purple galaxy bathed in golden stars and brushstrokes of the most magnificent swirls of pinks and blues. Both women stood with their mouths open, basking in the space around them. Marnie tilted her head to enjoy the three-sixty views of a galaxy that was supposed to be light years away but tonight felt as if she could reach up and touch it and sweep her fingertips through the silky, shimmering cosmos.

Marnie wasn't sure if the tingles that spread like shooting stars throughout her body were due to the fact that Nova still had hold of her hand, or because she felt as though every emotion she'd been feeling over the last two months threatened to engulf her while at the same time the milky way made her feel like the tiniest speck of stardust capable of the most magical things. How had she been stuck in her hotel room for four weeks when there was a whole universe for her to explore?

When she eventually closed her mouth, licking her bottom

lip to bring moisture back to it, and turned to say thank you to Nova, she was taken aback to find Nova looking at her, her large eyes twinkling almost as brightly as the billions of flickering dots around them.

'Sometimes life hits you like a ton of bricks and throws you completely off course. That new course can be terrifying at first, but then you might come to find that it's all part of the universe's plan to get you on the path that was destined for you,' Nova whispered without taking her eyes off Marnie. Marnie gulped down hard. It felt as though Nova had heard everything she had and hadn't said back in the taxi.

All she could do was nod in return. Yet a moment passed with them not breaking eye contact, which Marnie felt in her bones said more than any words she could or couldn't muster.

Time seemed to move as smoothly and swiftly as the swirls of galaxy that swam around their heads and then suddenly people, who Marnie hadn't noticed before, started shuffling out of seats around the auditorium and heading for the door.

'Time to go,' Nova noted, glancing at her watch and giving Marnie's hand a light casual squeeze, though it didn't feel casual to Marnie. She tried to distract herself from the sparks she felt in her palm by watching the people hum out of the space centre, listening in to their conversations on what they had learnt about the cosmos and making mental notes so she could impress Sienna when she got back home. Home, she thought. She didn't feel ready for home right now.

Nova let go of Marnie's hand when they reached the gorgeous fountain and the Canada night once more. Marnie sucked in a deep breath, enjoying the breeze on her warm cheeks, as a shiver tickled her spine from the fuzziness she felt pumping though her veins that started in her palm. A taxi awaited them, but when Marnie got in Nova rested her arm on the doorframe and stood staring down at her with that sparkle in her eye and dimple in her right cheek.

'Canada is yours for the taking, Marnie. It's waiting for you – you've just got to let it in,' Nova said before giving Marnie another knee-buckling wink that made her feel grateful that she was sitting down this time. Again, words seemed to get lodged in her throat and before she could get anything out, Nova tapped on the taxi like she was in some kind of Hollywood movie.

Marnie instantly felt as though her chest were a vacuum in space, void of matter, empty, as the taxi moved away, but within seconds she felt a burst of light and inspiration explode from within it. She had five more months left in Canada and she had the sudden urge to take charge and see more than just the walls in her hotel room. She wondered if it had everything or nothing at all to do with the woman who was becoming a speck of stardust in the distance.

I

Marnie's long lashes flickered, making her white and oak fireplace come into view horizontally and a little blurry. The breezy late summer air filtered through the open windows and drifted through her apartment. On it sailed a beautiful aroma of something fresh and welcoming. She wiped away a trickle of drool from the corner of her lips that had been squished against her deep navy cushion and pushed herself up, trying to decipher where she was for a moment. Raking a hand through her knotted brown hair, she took a deep breath in, allowing the smell to engulf her as she recognised the familiar walls of her apartment. Empty nails hung on the walls that were once occupied by picture frames. That was no bother though – she had captured plenty of stunning photographs in Canada that could quite happily replace the ones of her ex. Her ex, Josh, whom she'd spent the better half of the last five months not thinking about. She was not about to start now and so she stood on wobbly, jet-lagged limbs and stretched, causing her cream hoodie to rise up and tickle her stomach.

'What are you making?' Marnie called out, turning her head towards the kitchen. She didn't have to speak very loudly; she could see Antoni bustling about from where she was stood in her small living room space. Antoni stopped mixing what looked to be a bowl of white fluffy icing.

'What were you dreaming about?' Antoni countered, quirking his brow. He had picked Marnie up from the airport and hadn't stopped talking the whole twenty-minute car ride back from Manchester to her place in the small village of Orion. There was a lot she needed to be caught up on apparently, but the moment he had walked into her apartment he had retreated to the kitchen and immediately began filling the small space with a delicious smell. Marnie didn't have to question how her pastel yellow fridge was stocked full of ingredients or how her oak cupboards were piled high with food. Neither Antoni nor her sister, Jovi, would allow her to come home to an empty kitchen. A smile of gratitude tugged at her lips as she wandered over to the island that separated the living room from the kitchen.

Marnie looked up at her best friend of way too many years. He knew her inside and out, and the small smile that had been tugging at her lips stretched a little wider. She gripped her oversized cream hoodie at the cuffs and crossed her arms over her chest for comfort.

'I asked you first,' she said, giving Antoni a pointed stare as she tried to think of an answer that nestled under the heading of a white lie that wouldn't break any sort of best friend code.

Antoni's face morphed into a cheeky smirk that brightened his already handsome features and his brown eyes sparkled the way they always did when he was about to talk about food.

'Fair enough,' he started. Marnie appreciated that he was giving her some time to settle before demanding to know the inner workings of her brain and how she was feeling now that she was back in town, but she could see the flicker of concern in his eyes. 'I'm testing out pumpkin rolls for the autumn menu. Your turn.'

Marnie couldn't help but chuckle. She would have preferred more than mere seconds to organise her thoughts, but this was Antoni she was talking about. It was difficult to keep things from him, though that didn't stop her trying. Marnie wasn't always one for being forthright with her emotions.

'I was just wondering if you would be my live-in personal chef and make these pumpkin rolls for me every morning until the end of time?' she replied, swiping her finger in the bowl of white icing and popping it into her mouth. It tasted like heaven and sugar, which were possibly one and the same.

'So, wall up, case closed, we're not going to discuss the millions of feelings that I see swimming around in your brain? Or what had you grinning like a buffoon while you were napping?' Antoni said, ignoring her question as he nudged her playfully before stealing the bowl of fluffy icing away from her hovering fingertips.

Marnie shot him an evil look before slumping against the counter on her elbows, her stomach roiling with a mixture of butterflies and nerves. She'd been having the same dream for the past five months and every time she woke up her cheeks ached from smiling. She wished her brain wasn't so jet-lagged so she could conjure her white lie more quickly, for she wasn't ready to discuss the beauty in her dreams. It would make it all too real, when it couldn't be, so there really was no point in sharing and therefore she couldn't be accused of being a bad best friend when there was nothing to tell.

Antoni crossed the small space in two strides to collect the dough from the oven. The minute he opened the oven door, the room instantly filled with a rich cinnamon scent that carried with it a heavy and bold aroma of pumpkin.

'You don't have to be so modest on my account,' Marnie teased, walking around the counter and relaxing into their banter and returning the favour, ignoring his questions. 'Everything you bake is amazing and you know it,' she said with a smile as she tied her shoulder-length brown hair into a quick bun. 'You could share my room. We could have sleepovers – my bed's big enough, you wouldn't even know I was there,' she added playfully with a casual shrug.

'I'm sure we'd score tons of dates that way. So, where do you live? Oh, I live on Canon Street with my best friend. In those cute town house apartment conversions? Yes. Aren't they one-bedroom? They sure are. So how does that work? Well, the bed's big enough for two; we never even notice one another. You'll have to check it out sometime.' Antoni finished acting out his date scene and handed Marnie a spatula. The two of them looked at each other and giggled at the picture Antoni had just painted but the word 'date' made Marnie's stomach squirm, though she tried not to show her brief discomfort by taking the spatula and turning towards the baked goods now resting on the counter.

'Not there yet, huh?' Antoni questioned. Marnie didn't know why she'd even tried to hide her discomfort. No squirm – no matter how big or small – would get past him. She simply shook her head. Her dreams were certainly telling her otherwise but that's all they were, all they could be. The reality of dating made her feel queasy. Would it only lead to pain again? She shook her head a little more forcefully this time. She had spent the last six months dealing with every emotion and moving past it as she explored and adventured around Canada. She was determined to keep up that momentum and not fall back into the shell of the human she had become when Josh left, but that didn't mean she had to jump back on the wagon any time soon.

'Does Jovi know you're back?' he asked as he scooped a large dollop of icing onto one side of the tray of golden rolls. Marnie copied his actions, adding a large spatula full to the other side.

'From one fun conversation to the next. You're on a roll tonight...get it?' She glanced up at him sideways and elbowed him in the ribs playfully, trying to dispel the heavy direction the conversation was heading. Antoni shrugged and wiped a frosting-covered finger across her nose. Marnie gasped and tried to step out of the way, but the fridge had other plans for her and as her elbow hit the handle she was caught with nowhere to go.

When she looked up at Antoni, he flashed her a 'you can't beat me' smile, one she was accustomed to from their childhood days playing tig, to their teen years playing guess the song, to their more grown-up years playing board games. The man was not born to lose.

'I texted her before I boarded the plane, but she said she wouldn't be able to see me today as she and Jackson were taking Sienna to a sunflower farm and wouldn't be back till late. Day out, summer holidays and all,' Marnie explained, giving Antoni an 'are you happy now?' shrug. 'Can we eat these yet?' she added, licking her spatula. She was about to stick the utensil back into the icing bowl when Antoni pinched it off her and threw it in the sink with ninja-like movements, all the while continuing to perfect his side of the rolls, making the icing smooth. Marnie's side looked like the mountain peaks she had seen in Whistler.

'Give it a minute to let the icing melt and seep into the dough,' Antoni answered, leaning across her and placing his own spatula in the sink, more carefully than he had done with hers. Marnie placed her elbows on the worktop and her head in her hands, staring longingly at the pumpkin rolls.

'I think she's still mad at me for leaving,' Marnie confessed. The words slipped out with ease this time as they crossed her mind. She'd missed being with Antoni in the kitchen. Now she had no idea how she had managed to be without him and his baking for six months. It hadn't been an easy decision to leave. Marnie had never spent more than a week apart from Jovi. Having been womb mates and side by side literally since conception, they rarely went a day without seeing each other, but she'd had to get away. She'd needed to put some distance between her and her ex, between the life she thought they'd built for themselves in Orion, and for the first time in thirty-five years she'd needed to get away from Jovi too.

'But she can't be mad at me forever.' Her words came out soft, like a whisper, as they ticked around her brain.

Antoni's usual cheerful face looked sad for a moment. His eyebrows were drawn, and his eyes glistened but not in the happy way they did when he was talking about cake. Suddenly, he broke into a smile, albeit a forced one.

'Stop by the bakery tomorrow. All will be forgiven when

she sees you. She's just missed you that's all, probably just worried that Sienna has forgotten what you look like,' he said, tearing a roll from the tray. Steam rose from where it detached from the row. Marnie licked her lips. Antoni nudged her elbow, making her face fall off her hands with a jolt.

'Ouch,' she exclaimed through a chuckle, rubbing at her elbow. The thought of her niece forgetting what she looked like made her laugh but also brought with it a wash of guilt. Marnie had missed Sienna terribly while off trying to find herself in Canada. She had prided herself on being the world's best auntie but when Josh had left, that title had been a hard one to uphold. Days spent with the little girl filled her with a longing for what had once been at her fingertips but had disappeared in a flash of naked bodies and lies. Days spent colouring, crafting and playing outdoors, days that had once filled her with joy were wrought with a pain that she couldn't bear to burden anyone with and so she had run.

'Don't do that,' Antoni said, through a half-smile.

'Do what?' Marnie asked quickly, standing up and shaking her head to rid herself of her dark thoughts. Antoni raised the pumpkin roll to her lips; she took a giant bite so that the frosting didn't quite all make it into her mouth and instead smeared across her lips like lipstick. Marnie raised and cupped her hands to catch any crumbs. Then she closed her eyes to savour the flavours. Now that her mouth was full and she couldn't argue, Antoni spoke.

'Don't be so hard on yourself. You needed to get away, you needed to do something for you. We all missed you but you're back now. We survived your absence, so you can stop feeling guilty and punishing yourself for leaving,' he said, matter-of-fact. Having been away from Antoni for half a year, Marnie's body froze with how well he could read her. She had met some wonderful people on her travels, shared stories and anecdotes with them, knowing that she would most likely never see them again, so Antoni's understanding of her inner workings took a minute to readjust to.

When she opened her eyes, he took a bite of the roll, rivalling her big bite. Antoni managed to get frosting on his cheeks and nose, causing Marnie to snigger. 'What? Do I have something on my face?' he asked, wiggling his eyebrows. A sudden flame ignited in Marnie's stomach with his words and when she had last heard them, but she hastily ignored it, taking another bite to put the flame out.

'Stop it,' she said, through her mouthful, her eyes crinkling with laughter. 'Did you, like, thrive survive or survive by the skin of your teeth without me?' Marnie asked through a cheeky grin and a mouthful of amazing food.

'Oh, it was touch and go for a minute there,' Antoni replied with a twinkle in his eye as he popped the last bite into his mouth. 'Please tell me you brought me back some proper maple syrup,' he added, as Marnie stuck her hand in the tray to prise out another roll. 'That would more than make up for my near demise without you here.'

'I knew it. I knew that's all you really cared about. All this time I thought you were on my side, telling me Canada was a great idea, when really you just wanted a bottle of the good stuff,' Marnie cried with fake outrage.

'I could never be so devious,' Antoni replied, faking offense, as he walked past her to switch on the kettle. Marnie couldn't deny the sense of home she felt in her bones, with the easy-going way Antoni moved about her kitchen, his familiar mannerisms, and the way he knew that tonight she would need him and his comfort food. Her travels had been extraordinary – there was no question about that. For someone who had never ventured far from Orion let alone been on a plane by herself before, Canada had been eye-opening. British Columbia had been her favourite spot on her travels, for it was jaw-droppingly stunning and full of adventure. She really had loved every minute, well mostly every minute when her guilt and nerves occasionally subsided to let her enjoy herself, but despite the anxiety of facing the past that now awaited her it felt good to be home.

She licked her fingers absentmindedly as thoughts of hiking in the Glacier National Park drifted through her mind. A smile threatened her features. The trail had been mesmerising. She swore it had taken her triple the time compared to the other tourists as she had walked terribly slowly, not wanting to miss a thing. She had at one point worried that her eyes would freeze open as wide as saucers, for she had dared not blink in case she missed the beauty that had surrounded her.

The image her brain conjured lifted her spirits, but it was brief. Jovi hadn't witnessed the gorgeous landscapes and nor had Antoni, because she'd failed to invite them. The two people she cared most about in the world, who she had done everything with her entire life, and she had abandoned them. She had been selfish to go on such a trip on her own, thinking of only herself.

'Marn, will you tell me about your vacation and stop looking so guilty? You went on the trip of a lifetime, not on a murder spree, so can we embrace that, please? Also, I had better things to do than hike beautiful valleys and kayak crystal-clear lakes for six months.' Antoni paused and waved a coffee spoon around as the kettle boiled. His eyes were narrowed, and a smirk teased his lips. 'You know like fend off a gaggle of men and women who visited the bakery thinking they were going be on some sort of bachelor show and apologise profusely to the fire department for the false tip off they got that the bakery was on fire – things like that,' he finished with a casual shrug.

'Oh my God, she didn't.' Marnie gasped, her sticky hands flying over her mouth in disbelief. Then she snorted, unable to help herself.

'If you're referring to Mrs Higgins, of course she did. I believe someone should take that iPad off her; she's becoming far more creative these days and I can't say I'm a fan of that.' Antoni's eyes twinkled with humour.

Marnie let out the giggle she had been trying to respectfully hold. Mrs Higgins was the town's resident gossip. She'd lived in Orion her whole life and had spent most of it working at the post office and therefore she'd seen and heard a great deal over the years. Antoni was convinced that this is what kept her alive. At ninety-one years young, she didn't seem to be slowing down, except when she had her corn surgery. According to Antoni she had been incredibly irritable and angry when he had been to deliver her fresh bread and a banana loaf one morning and she had not a nice word to say about the doctor who had told her to rest. Since Jovi had settled down and had Sienna, it seemed Mrs Higgins' main goal in life now was to see that both Antoni and Marnie got married.

'I can't believe she did that, though I have to say I'm

impressed,' Marnie noted, washing her hands in the sink so she could pick up her coffee mug.

'You and me both. I could hardly complain about the firemen though and I did get one girl's number,' he said, giving Marnie a wink. She sipped her coffee thoughtfully, leaning against the sink and watching her best friend for a moment. A blush crept up his cheeks.

'Wait, does Jonathan still work at the fire station?' she asked excitedly, standing up straighter. Jonathan had inspected the bakery some time last year and had procured a twinkle in Antoni's eye that NASA wouldn't have been able to miss. He was tall, had sandy brown hair and grey eyes that Marnie was adamant had spent more time inspecting Antoni than the actual bakery.

'Maybe,' Antoni mumbled, his cheeks now glowing a reddish hue.

'Ant, what happened? Did you not get his number?' Marnie practically yelled, her words bouncing off the cabinets in such cosy confines. Antoni gave her a dubious look from under his thick black lashes. 'What? I'm happy to talk about *your* love life,' Marnie said, her smile never wavering. Talking about other people's feelings was never an issue. It was only her own she had problems with.

'OK, so we must have caught each other's eye at least ten times and he was the one to start ushering people out when it was clear there had been some sort of mix-up. He apologised and was the last to leave; he even waited until the girl who gave me her number had left. Forgive me for being a bit callous, but I panicked and wanted to make it clear I wasn't interested in her so when I knew he was looking, I tossed the paper away,' Antoni confessed, his forehead creasing and eyes scrunching up from guilt. 'And then I think we might have had a moment.' At this both Antoni and Marnie let out a squeal, Marnie nearly spilling her coffee over the rim of her mug.

'That's so romantic,' Marnie gushed. 'Oh, Ant, you should try and speak to him.'

Antoni put his mug down and played around with the edge of a pumpkin roll. Marnie wasn't used to him being so reticent, but she knew all too well the fears that love brought with it. Antoni was quite outgoing but with his bakery being his baby, he didn't date much.

'What, and give Mrs Higgins what she wants? Then what would the woman live for?' Antoni remarked in his teasing tone. Marnie rolled her eyes at his more familiar cockiness. He was Mrs Higgins' favourite and could do no wrong in her eyes, nor in the eyes of many. The old lady had been rather disappointed in Marnie when her relationship had imploded. Marnie had tried to explain that she hadn't planned for it not to work out and it had all really been out of her control, but that hadn't seemed to make sense to the old dear. In her day you fixed things, you didn't just throw them away, but Marnie wasn't sure she could fix her brain to want to remain in a relationship with a man who lied.

'True, and while you're still on the market it means all eyes are on you and not me, so no, you shouldn't call him,' Marnie said as she collected a plate from the cupboard and piled it high with the pumpkin rolls. Grabbing her coffee with her free hand, she wandered through to the living room. The sky outside was still a vibrant blue, the sun shining through the window in the late summer evening.

'But what if he's the love of my life? That's going to cost

you,' Antoni said, joining her on the couch and bringing napkins and his own coffee with him.

'I have two bottles of Pure Canadian Maple Syrup for you and a jar of Maple cream,' Marnie answered, wiggling her eyebrows. Antoni squealed and it was his turn to almost spill his coffee, causing Marnie to let out a much-needed burst of laughter. But as she watched Antoni tuck one leg underneath himself to get comfy, her mood turned sombre.

'You're really not mad at me?' she queried, still unable to shake her guilt of leaving her family behind for six months, though Canada had been everything she had needed and more.

Antoni gave her a pointed look, his eyebrows drawing in sharply. 'I'll only be mad at you if you keep on guilt-tripping yourself and not owning your decisions. OK, Marn? The way the gossip mill works around here, I can understand you needing a break, so own it, all right?' He said the last words with a slight wobble in his tone that made Marnie's nose crinkle with curiosity.

'What's been churning through the gossip mill?' Marnie asked, unable to help herself yet not quite sure she wanted to know the answer. She was aware the whole town knew of her split with Josh, her abrupt departure from Cornelia Primary School, and of her parents' separation, but she hadn't made a scene by any means. In fact she had stayed locked up in her apartment until she had boarded her plane to Canada and had very much tried to push it all under the same duvet she had buried her head in. Surely, it was all old news by now? She had been away for six months.

Antoni raised a hand over his coffee mug and gave it a wave as if warding off evil spirits.

'It's late. Don't worry about the gossip mill. You promise me you're good?' he asked, sweetly tilting his head to the side as if about to overanalyse her answer to check for signs of lies.

Marnie squinted her tired eyes firmly. 'Ant, I meant what I said in my last email. I'm a big girl. I know I need to face up to Mum and Dad. I'll do it, I will. I don't want to talk about Josh right now. I spent more than enough time processing and dealing with the hurt while trekking the glorious Canadian terrain. As for getting a job, I'll be back on the job hunt tomorrow.' Though Marnie had felt positive and inspired by the end of her trip when thinking about the 'To Do' list awaiting her when she arrived back in Orion, the slight shake in her voice wasn't to be missed, so she forced a bright teeth-baring smile to emphasise her OK-ness to Antoni.

'And I meant it when I said if you need to talk about anything, I'm here. We can be strong with you and for you. It's OK if you're not OK, OK?' Antoni said, reaching out and placing a hand on her knee.

Marnie smirked over her almost empty coffee mug, 'OK,' she teased at Antoni's overuse of the word. And she was OK, wasn't she? Her big toe spasmed in her left foot and she shifted, suddenly feeling uncomfortable. Life was good and she was strong. She'd overcome her struggles and her heartbreak. Yes, she was OK. She wasn't looking back.

'So, are you going to tell me who or what you were dreaming of earlier that made your cheeks dimple while you were sleeping?' Antoni said, wiggling his eyebrows.

Marnie's chest instantly tightened and she spluttered on her last sip of coffee. No matter the pure glee etched on Antoni's features at the thought of something or someone bringing her happiness, she just couldn't bring herself to open up – not yet. Marnie's eyes drifted around her small home. If she stretched her arm long enough, she could touch the kitchen wall from the yellow couch she was perched on. A cream rug decorated the wooden flooring in front of the fire and her oak coffee table lay upon that, with its countless craft magazine, bits of tissue paper and stickers sticking out from its drawers every which way, so Sienna always knew where to find them. The walls definitely needed a splash of colour.

'Thank you for helping to keep this place tidy while I was away and for clearing it of Josh's belongings,' she said, changing the subject. It was Antoni's turn to crinkle his eyes dubiously, but like the good friend he was, he could no doubt read the jet lag in her eyes and went with the change of direction without questioning her.

'Onwards and upwards, Marn,' he said, getting to his feet and carrying both of their mugs to the kitchen. 'No matter what life throws at you, you got this,' he added as Marnie followed him into the kitchen with the plate. Her eyelids were growing heavy. Her button nose crinkled once more at Antoni's words.

'I hope life gives me a brief pause before it launches anything at me anytime soon,' she said on a yawn.

Antoni's brown eyes wavered, not quite meeting her line of vision. 'I love you,' he said to the apple of her left cheek before dropping a kiss onto her hair. 'Get some sleep and I'll see you tomorrow.'

He was out of the door before Marnie's tired brain could question his shifty eyes. She locked the door and dragged her weary feet to her bedroom, and she'd just flopped onto her bed when slumber overcame her.

2

The next morning Marnie woke as the moon sunk into the horizon. She opened her eyes to the bronzed sun caressing her cheeks and her stomach growling, no matter how many carbs had filled it last night. Her dreams had taken her back to the Great Bear Rainforest where she had spent hours walking across the wet earth, getting lost in the trees and acres of glorious land, and being mesmerised by every beautiful bear her eyes fell upon. It had been one of the highlights of her Canada trip. She had felt incredibly free among the vast forest and free wasn't exactly a feeling she was familiar with in Orion.

As the sun crept a little higher she sat up, raising her hand to shield against its boldness, and swung her legs over the side of her bed. All of a sudden her heart was pounding and her breathing grew heavy. Right now, she felt less than light and carefree. Orion was a far cry from large open landscapes and nature reserves. A sudden wave of claustrophobia washed over her, causing her to whip the duvet off swiftly, for it was making her sweat.

Counting to ten, she took a deep breath and encouraged her eyes to wander over the little things in her bedroom that brought her joy rather than the fear of what lay waiting for her now that she was home. The triangle oak bookshelf that her dad had handcrafted for her two summers ago and she had helped sand down caught her eye. The knots and the bespoke grains in each shelf – and the scatter of cupcake stickers that Sienna had sweetly decorated it with – drew a smile from her lips, allowing her heart to regain its normal rhythm once more.

If Marnie could tackle Canadian dollars and six months without Jovi by her side, she could face whatever the town was gossiping about this week. Getting to her feet, she grabbed her cream fleece hoodie and slipped into it as she made her way over to the small window in her bedroom. The late summer was still gifting her with a subtle warmth. There was no need for the central heating to be on, but she still felt a slight chill moving away from the cosy warmth of her blanket.

The world outside her window was just beginning to wake up, though the sun wasn't yet strong enough to take over from the street lamps. Marnie turned her head as one flickered over the florist. In a few hours its shop window would be bursting with colour, the pavement below its window adorned with potted peonies, anthuriums, kalanchoe blossfeldiana and so many more eye-pleasing delights. She could almost smell the delicate yet confident scents floating along the summer breeze. A smile tugged at her lips as she thumbed the cuff of her fleece.

Five years Marnie had spent working with Jillian at 'Blooming Brilliant'. She had been fresh out of college, in need of a job, and when neither of the two schools in the small town were hiring, much to the frustration of an eighteen-year-old who had just acquired a Diploma in Early

Years Education and was raring to go, Jillian had come to her rescue. Both Jovi and Antoni had gone off to university and Marnie had been desperate to make some money so she could get her own place. That and she needed a little space from her parents during the day, to get out of the house and from under their hair when their arguments had become an everyday occurrence.

Working at the florist had given Marnie the chance to work with her hands and play with colour, which she loved. Jillian had taught her all she knew about creating bespoke bouquets and within her first few months, had given Marnie free rein to create as she pleased. Creativity was the reason she had wanted to work with children. Seeing their faces light up when they passed her window displays had filled Marnie with joy and was the reason she had stayed with Jillian for longer than she'd originally planned. Looking back, going with the flow had served her well then too. It was a mystery then that she was so scared of it and had always liked to plan and map out her life.

From an early age she'd known she wanted to work with children, to help push the boundaries of the curriculum and show them that learning could be fun. She wanted to be a teaching assistant so she could create the most beautiful displays that ignited the sparks in their imagination, encouraging it to roam and explore endless possibilities.

The flower crowns had been her most popular venture at Blooming Brilliant – teamed with a *Secret-Garden*-inspired window display that saw Marnie build an arch of trailing ivy and heathery fern with white roses, every colour peony she could get her hands on and bold, beautiful ranunculi. Every child who wandered past that day had wanted to come in for their crown. They had ended up putting on a workshop, which had been pretty spectacular and had led to Marnie landing her job, as she had originally wanted and planned for her eighteen-year-old self, at the local primary school. Her ex, Josh, was the deputy head teacher at the time and had happened upon the workshop and invited her for an interview. With her dream job and a lovely boyfriend, at twenty-four her plan was taking shape.

Marnie blinked and shook away that last thought. Her grand plan was no more, and she had spent the last six months embracing that fact and was not about to undo all her hard work by allowing herself to dwell on it the moment she was back home, and she was certainly not going to let thoughts of her abandoned plan tarnish the happy thoughts she had of her time spent at Blooming Brilliant.

Today, she would not and could not be deterred. She had people to visit and needed to keep her train of thought positive. Should it get derailed and she chicken out, it would only make matters worse. To start, she would pop in to see Jillian and pick up some flowers and she would fill her apartment with the sweet smell of freesias, which would keep her mood clear and happy, but first she needed coffee. Quickly, Marnie put on her slippers and headed to the kitchen. She couldn't go anywhere yet as it was only half past five and she still had a suitcase to unpack and a load of washing to do. That seemed like a safe thing to tackle first anyhow.

Two hours later and the dryer was on, most of her belongings were back in their places, souvenirs had been given a new home and Marnie was dressed in her burnt-orange trousers, a simple white box tee and had tied her shoulder-length hair into a topknot. The day was set to be beautiful and sunny and she found herself looking forward to it as she nibbled on a leftover pumpkin roll and eyed her living room wall, trying to decide what colour she wanted to paint it. Before her trip to Canada, the thought of making such a decision on her own had been enough to send her anxiety through the roof, but now as the sugary pumpkin frosting delighted her taste buds and the thought of possibly going with a printed wallpaper entered her mind, the endeavour didn't feel so frightening. It was funny what could change in six months; then again maybe funny wasn't quite the right word.

Once she had devoured the two leftover pastries, Marnie sucked in a deep breath, grabbed her backpack and headed out her front door before she could think better of it. The sky had since blended from a rich navy blue and a swirl of orange hues into a light, bright blue and her mood was better for it.

Crossing the road, Marnie saw that Jillian was already pottering around the pavement in front of Blooming Brilliant, with various potted plants in her hands.

'Morning, Jillian,' she whispered, not wanting to scare her or wake up the whole street on a Sunday morning.

Jillian squinted and blinked a few times when she looked up. Marnie was somewhat used to this hesitation as people tried to decipher who they were talking to, with her and Jovi looking so alike. They weren't identical but even they couldn't tell each other apart in their baby photos.

'Oh, hi, Marnie. I thought it was you. It's lovely to see you, sweetheart. When did you get back? We've certainly missed you around here,' Jillian said, standing up straight and reaching for another pot to place in the display.

'Just last night. I've missed you too. How are you? How's Riley?' Marnie replied, picking up two pots and holding them out for Jillian.

'I'm the same old, same old,' Jillian said, waving her words off chirpily as though Marnie was fussing over her by asking how she was. She had always been a bubbly character, more concerned with looking after everyone else. 'Oh, he's fine, thank you. Good as gold. I don't know what I did to deserve him. I did tell him he could watch some TV – it's the last few days of the summer holidays after all – but no, he's helping his dad prepare breakfast and insists that he helps me with this place. He's been in here every day. Mind you his imagination rivals yours,' Jillian told her proudly, turning slightly and pointing at the window display. A rustic tin bucket hung from the top left-hand corner in a tipping motion. A sweeping arch of pink and red roses looked to be falling out of it into a pool of beautiful green foliage at the bottom. It looked stunning. Marnie was impressed but not surprised.

Ever since Riley was around four years old, he'd been studying his mum. Marnie loved passing the shop on her way to work and back, catching Riley buzzing around his mum's feet, a smile bursting from his face as he helped her pick out flowers for custom bouquets. It was no wonder he was following in his mum's footsteps with how content he looked in the shop, and by the looks of the window, at just nine years old, he certainly had an eye for it.

'I'm glad to hear it and he has learnt from the best. That display is gorgeous. Can he come and decorate my apartment?' Marnie said, with a small chuckle, though she was only half joking. Filling her tiny place with such colour and fragrance would certainly keep her mood positive if simply standing outside Blooming Brilliant was anything to go by. 'Speaking of the best, Jill, I know you're not open yet, but I couldn't trouble you for a small bouquet of daisies, could I?' Marnie added, causing Jillian to stop fiddling with the plant pots and draw her attention to Marnie. There was no mistaking the sympathetic look that suddenly adorned her kind face.

'Not at all, hon,' she said, turning away and popping into the shop where the buckets were waiting by the door, ready to be brought out closer to eight o'clock. With Jillian's back turned, Marnie bent down to breathe in the scent of a sweet pea. The look on Jillian's face was one that she'd been afraid of in coming back to her hometown.

'Thank you, I'll call by later to pick up some for home, but I'll just take those for now,' Marnie said, ignoring the look, hoping to continue their conversation as normal when Jillian walked back outside holding aloft of pretty bunch of baby daisies that looked positively cute. 'Thank you so much,' Marnie added with a smile as she spun her backpack to one shoulder to pull out her purse and handed Jillian three pound coins.

'Oh, sweetheart, are you doing well? I mean, it really is good to see you and have you home after...' Jillian's words trailed off as she took the money.

Marnie's guard sprung up. She grinned too much, unable to show teeth, so her cheeks puffed up like a hamster's and her eyes crinkled too thin as the panic she'd felt this morning threatened to overwhelm her once more. Her lips felt like they were PVA-glued together when she tried to speak.

'I'm so sorry, sweetheart. We're all here for you – you

know that. When the time is right, it will happen for you too,' Jillian said, her face serious, her eyes sad.

Marnie could feel a hiccup forming in her throat, making her aware she was holding her breath as her nervous bubbles didn't have an escape.

'Thank you for these. I'll be back later. Maybe Riley wouldn't mind rustling up a bouquet for me for my apartment.' The words tumbled out – much easier than talking of relationships and exes. Marnie tilted her head as she took the daisies from Jillian's outstretched hand, ignoring the statements Jillian had made and instead focusing on the tiny white and yellow flowers that sparkled happily in the morning sun.

'Give my love to Jovi and Antoni this morning, won't you? And of course I'm sure he'll be delighted to put something together, hon,' Jillian said as Marnie started to walk away.

Marnie appreciated Jillian following her change of subject and couldn't help but smile for real at the thought of Riley making her a bespoke bouquet. Jillian and Riley knew everyone's favourite flower in the village. Daisies were Jovi's favourite, not that it would take a genius to know where Marnie was heading so early on a Sunday morning, but for a moment Jillian's thoughtfulness comforted her. There were both upsides and downsides to living in a town where everyone knew everything about each other. Marnie nodded and gave a small thank you.

'Keep your chin up, Marnie. Tim is a lovely guy. I think you'll like him, and everything will work out for you,' Jillian added, before turning away and seeing that her shop signs were all in place.

Marnie stumbled over her next step but recovered quickly, picking up speed, not wanting Jillian to know that anything was wrong. She kept her head straight, looking forward, hiding her confused expression from Gareth the postman as she gave him a small wave and carried on walking. Tim? Who was Tim? She didn't know a Tim; why would she need to like him? And what had Jillian meant by right time for her too? Surely, the right time for Josh to find love was not while he'd been in a relationship with her. Marnie shook her head, the 'L' word sending a shiver down her spine.

By the time Marnie reached the bakery, she had regained her composure and was back to feeling positive thanks to watching the sun find its place in the sky and the birds fly from tree to tree, which she liked to imagine was them visiting family and friends for breakfast and possibly second breakfast with all the happy chirping going on. She'd pushed Jillian's words to the back of her mind. If Antoni had a boyfriend, he would have told her via postcard, letter or carrier pigeon while she was signal-less in Canada, or at least last night. Maybe Jovi and Antoni had hired new staff, or the local pub had acquired a new owner, though that would be sad indeed as Marnie was rather fond of Dennis. He'd been there forever.

She decided there'd been some kind of mix-up. Sometimes people thought they knew all the town gossip and maybe Jillian had just got Marnie mixed up with someone else. That was something Marnie was used to an awful lot. Unable to think of a reason for herself knowing and needing to like a Tim, she concentrated on being present on her walk – something her many hikes in Canada had taught her – and the only love she needed in her life right now: a homemade pastry from the bakery.

The air outside the bakery was like a magic cloud. Though it was sandwiched between the estate agent's and newsagent's, Marnie imagined that when she crossed the line from the edge of the estate agent's that put her in front of the bakery window, she was stepping through a bubble, entering an atmosphere rich with the sweet scent of vanilla, and if you opened your mouth you could almost taste the delectable treats that awaited you inside.

'Are you going to stand out here all day with your eyes closed drooling on my window or are you coming in?' Antoni's voice snapped Marnie out of her delicious daydream. When she opened her eyes, she saw him leaning against the doorframe holding the door open for her, his apron covered in flour and a tea towel over one shoulder, a smirk on his rosy-red lips.

'I'm coming,' she said, giving him a quick one-armed hug as she passed him in the doorway, making up for the time she had missed not being able to do that while travelling.

'Jet lag,' Antoni said, locking the door behind him. The bakery didn't open until nine on a Sunday. Everyone liked their lie-in and then would trickle in for coffees and pastries before their Sunday walk.

'Jet lag.' Marnie nodded, looking around, her eyes landing on the kitchen door nervously. She wasn't going to tell him that it had taken a little longer to get ready due to her anxiety over seeing Jovi today and was grateful that jet lag made a brilliant white lie.

'There's coffee on the counter for you,' Antoni noted, with a nod. Marnie didn't miss him glance at the kitchen door too. She wondered if she would have to go back there to see Jovi or if her sister would come and greet her; he was no doubt wondering the same thing.

'Thank you, should I…' Marnie started, not having to wonder for too long as the kitchen door swung open and her mirror image walked into the shop. There was no stopping the sweat that had begun to form on her brow or the butterflies fluttering like crazy in her stomach. Marnie hated the feeling of being lost for words in front of her sister. The two of them were never lost for words. Jovi carried a tray of cookies straight over to Antoni and placed them in front of him without acknowledging Marnie was there and Marnie's heart sank with a heavy thud.

Marnie was the older twin, by five minutes, which growing up had occasionally worked to her advantage. She would get Jovi to do her chores while she was busy making bracelets or have Jovi ask the teacher to repeat the question when she didn't understand it. She would push Jovi to go first whenever they had to have injections so she could tell her if it hurt, and when she needed to ring the bank or home insurance, she would have Jovi pretend to be her when she didn't understand their jargon, but right now Marnie knew that she needed to be the big sister.

'Hi,' Marnie mumbled, sounding more pathetic than she would have liked. She held out the bouquet of daisies to give her brain some time to remember how to form a sentence.

Jovi turned on the spot sharply and finally met Marnie's gaze, but her face was not friendly. She was looking at her through narrowed eyes, her nostrils flaring. It reminded Marnie of the time when they were twelve and their mum had bought one copy of *Top of the Pops* magazine, telling them they had to share it. There had only been one poster of Five inside and she had been insistent that it go on her side of their bedroom, on the wall next to her bed. Jovi had been distraught, claiming to be the bigger Five fan, but Marnie had been stubborn, swearing that their love for Five was equal and that with her being the older twin it should be hers. Deep down Marnie had known that Jovi loved Five more and she knew that Jovi knew she knew that too, but that day Marnie had simply not wanted to share. For once, she had wanted to be given something without having to divvy it out in equal parts.

'Please don't be mad at me. I needed to go; you know I needed to go. I couldn't stay here,' Marnie said softly, willing herself not to cry. She was not the crier; Jovi was the crier. She lowered the daisies, her arm aching from holding them aloft. Jovi hadn't made an attempt to take them yet. 'Jovi, please, I didn't go because I wanted to hurt you and I'm sorry if you don't understand, but it was good for me. I feel better for it and I'm back now.' Marnie's hands rose and fell at her sides. She didn't know what more she could say. She couldn't take back her trip and she didn't want to; it had been right for her and Jovi would have to accept that.

Jovi let out a sigh. She had one hand on her hip and looked up to the ceiling, rolling her eyes. Her apron rivalled Antoni's in the flour department. She looked every bit like a mother who was about to tell off her child but felt too exasperated to even know where to begin. Her short brown hair, which was about two inches shorter than Marnie's, was clipped back with a large claw grip and a hairnet lay over her frizz. Marnie's stomach turned with guilt. While

Canada had been what she needed, revitalising and soul-awakening, she could see that Jovi was exhausted and that was partly her fault for leaving her to deal with one part of their world being flipped on its head, on her own.

'I'm not mad at you, Marn. It's not your fault everything happened all at once. It's fine,' Jovi said, her features softening a touch, the creases in her forehead smoothing out. She reached out, making Marnie jump, automatically on guard when for a split second Marnie thought she was going to whack her in the bicep, something the three of them often did to show affection or get each other back for a joke, but instead Jovi accepted the flowers in lieu of a hug.

Being twins they were as close as close could be, but hugging and mushy-gushy stuff was not Marnie's thing. Jovi chuckled and shook her head while Marnie glanced at Antoni, who had kept his head down seeing to the baked goods, but in that moment choked on a stifled laugh.

'So, can I help with anything now that I'm back?' Marnie offered, the tightness in her neck loosening now that she and Jovi were speaking to each other. They never did stay mad at each other for long, but it had been a trying seven months and Marnie had feared the worst.

'We're all good on the Mum and Dad front. They are officially separated and honestly better for it, Marn. I know you don't want to hear that, but it's the truth,' Jovi told her, sticking her head in the bouquet of daisies and breathing in the scent, which told Marnie that even though she was acting strong, the thought of their parents not being together anymore stung Jovi just as much as it did her.

She gulped down the lump in her throat and forced a sip

of coffee that Antoni had left her on the counter. She loved the way he made her coffee. No one could make it like him, with the right amount of sugar and the perfect splash of milk. 'Erm, OK, well, that's good to know.' She smiled over at Jovi as the liquid hit the back of her throat.

'Look, I'm sorry I got angry with you when you said you had booked a ticket to Canada. I was mad at Mum and Dad. I was mad at Josh. He hurt you, which hurt me, and then it was like he was trying to hurt me even more by causing you to want to disappear from my life for six months. Everything changed in a matter of weeks and with Sienna and school, with the bakery, there was just so much going on that my priorities got muddled up.' Jovi spoke fast, not one to hide her emotions like Marnie.

When she finished, she made Marnie gasp and Antoni look up when she did in fact step forward to embrace her sister. 'Is there anything at all I can help you with?' she whispered into Marnie's ear. 'Unless Canada acted like a better sister than me?' she added with a chuckle, trying to lighten the outpouring of emotions that were going on at such an early hour on a Sunday.

Marnie stood frozen for a moment and then relaxed into her sister's embrace. Jovi stepped back, assessing the damage to her daisy bouquet that had been squished between the two of them during the unexpected attack.

'It's not you who should be saying sorry. You're allowed to me mad. I don't want you to be, but I left when the going got tough. I'm sorry. Babysitting for the next ten years is on me and if either of you need your houses cleaning, just say the word, I'm on it,' Marnie offered, giving her sister a nod that was reciprocated, which meant they were good.

Marnie's shoulders rolled out and she felt like her head was being lifted by some invisible string. She could stand taller now that all was right in the world, well almost all was right in the world.

'So, you're really OK?' Jovi asked, just for good measure, brushing a cloud of flour off her apron.

Marnie drew her thumb up and down the side of her paper coffee cup. Though the nerves were ever-present and bubbling in her stomach over the thought of bumping into and dealing with Josh now that she was back, her mind did not drift to him upon hearing her sister's question. Strangely, she felt a rush of giddiness bombard her chest with a want to tell her sister all about one specific day in Canada and a woman with a stellar name. As quickly as the giddiness came, so did a reminder of Jillian's words and the pity in her face over Marnie and Josh's demise. Marnie's thrill vanished at the thought of the whole town sinking their claws into Nova. She'd been humiliated once before; she couldn't do it again. Like all supernovas, this one would have to be admired from a distance. It had to be a sign that she lived in Orion and Nova lived in Canada. How much more distant could you possibly get?

'I'm good,' Marnie finally said, with a tight-lipped smile, her chest puffing up as she did so, her arms once again rising and falling at her sides for extra emphasis that she was totally cool, and she really was.

Both Jovi and Antoni gave her a curious once-over making Marnie extremely aware that it had taken her a full minute to express two words. She looked down at her coffee cup, making her go cross-eyed as she took another sip. Then another thought occurred to her.

'So, what are you going to do now you're home?' Jovi asked at the same time Marnie questioned, 'So, who's Tim?'

3

The clock was ticking closer to nine a.m. now. The bakery cabinet was full to the brim with croissants, banana loaves, cinnamon swirls, cookies – both chocolate and oatmeal – and an array of Danishes, thanks to Harry who had just slipped through the kitchen door and handed the trays over to Antoni. Marnie had given him a cheerful wave while not missing Jovi and Antoni exchange a peculiar look. There was something they had failed to tell her via email and were reluctant to do so now.

'Guys,' Marnie encouraged, looking at them with her eyes wide and eyebrows raised.

'I asked first,' Jovi tried weakly, but Marnie could tell Jovi knew she was going to lose to the older twin card.

'No, you didn't. We asked at the same time and I feel my question is more urgent by the looks on both your faces and your reluctance to tell me,' Marnie argued, taking a step closer to the counter where her best friend and sister were rearranging the trays of doughnuts, needlessly. Marnie's stomach rumbled. Her brain threatened to abandon the conversation if she could just go home with a bag of doughnuts, a fresh cup of coffee made by Antoni, and curl up on her couch to enjoy them. It didn't want to have to deal with real life, but she had run away before. Now she was back, she had promised herself she would be brave and face reality.

Jovi let out a deep sigh while Antoni picked up a chocolate doughnut with a pair of tongs, placed it on a napkin and handed it to Marnie. As she took it, she read his expression: 'You might need this.' He gave a small shrug and a hopeful, tight-lipped smile.

'Tim is Mum's boyfriend,' Jovi said quickly, when Marnie had mistakenly taken a bite of chocolatey goodness, unable to resist it the minute she had it in her hands.

'Oh, come on,' Marnie blurted out with a mouthful of doughnut, her free hand brushing over her forehead. She took a few steps away and walked in a circle until she faced them both again.

'Marn, don't make it a big deal. She's really happy,' Jovi pleaded, her face a mixture of annoyance at her sister's response and cheerfulness, trying to make her see that it was a happy thing.

'It's been, what, six and a half months and she's already over Dad?' Marnie showered sprinkles over the floor as she took a lap around the small wooden unit in the middle of the shop that was home to baskets of freshly baked bread and boxes of scrumptious fruit pies.

'Marnie, they had been unhappy for ages – you know that. They were miserable together. It was for the best. It's been good around here,' Jovi said, moving from around the counter to stand by her sister's side.

Marnie tilted her head back in frustration and so that her tears would get the hint and roll back into her head and not stream down her face. Her parents splitting up had been one of the reasons she had jetted off to Canada. She had desperately wanted to get away from the fights, both in their home and her own. She knew deep down that what Jovi was saying was right. With each passing year since the girls had moved out and built their own lives, it seemed that their parents' arguments had grown worse. They disagreed on everything from what to have for dinner to the right way to bring up a grandchild. Visiting them was always a matter of trying to keep the peace rather than enjoying family time.

'How come no one wants to try and fix things anymore?' Marnie whined and gave a small sniffle.

'Marn, look at me,' Jovi said and then paused, waiting for her sister to make eye contact.

Marnie's head lolled as she forced her chin to her chest to look at her twin. It was rare that she looked at Jovi and saw herself. Now though, she could see the resemblance in the dark circles under Jovi's eyes and the wobble playing at her lips. The pout was something they both did when trying to keep it together. Marnie succeeded in keeping her feelings bottled up more times than Jovi. Seeing Jovi's bottom lip jut out strengthened Marnie's resolve. She didn't want her sister to cry.

'You couldn't fix Mum and Dad and you couldn't fix things with Josh – that was on him,' Jovi said.

With Jovi's hazel eyes looking directly into hers, Marnie struggled to keep the lid on her emotions screwed on tight. A tear seeped out, loosening the seal and allowing more to burst through and overflow. Six months she had been without her twin sister and while so much good had come out of that time apart, standing in the bakery, with her sister an inch away, Marnie couldn't quite believe she had done it and didn't know how she had managed. 'I tried to fix it, to fight for him,' she said in between sobs. Jovi pulled her head on to her shoulder and in an instant Antoni was by their sides with a box of tissues.

'I know you did, Marn. I know,' Jovi whispered and Marnie felt her sister's grip around her neck tighten as Jovi hugged her harder. 'But you can't fight for someone who's not fighting for you. It doesn't work like that.'

Those words hit home for Marnie. She had been playing them over and over in her mind during her first few weeks of travelling. She had thought after her many hikes and campfire meditation sessions that she was over it, but coming back home she realised that she was still holding on to a piece of the pain that a sudden change of scenery had not been able to cure, for it was here in Orion that her life had changed dramatically and she needed to accept that, to be OK with it here and face it head on.

'You're right, I know. I'm sorry,' she said, gently pulling away from Jovi but smiling at her in thanks. She took a tissue from Antoni and wiped away her tears and most likely all her mascara, unable to believe that her emotions had betrayed her like that.

'Come on, let's get you some coffee and a doughnut fresh out of the fryer,' Antoni said, putting an arm around her shoulders and guiding her towards the back of the shop. Jovi shuffled along with them, dabbing at her own nose as she sniffled and smiled at her big sister.

'Thank you, Ant,' Marnie said, burying her head a little further in the nook of his armpit where she felt safe.

'Anything for you,' he replied sweetly. 'Plus, if you stand in the front of my shop crying any longer, people will start to think there's something wrong with my pies.' There was a definite smirk on his face. Marnie pulled away and smacked him in the bicep, but just looking at him, and Jovi too, made her feel a great deal better.

Marnie stayed at the bakery until lunchtime, when she knew she had to face the inevitable and go and visit her mum and make a phone call to her dad. She had used the excuse of catching up with Harry and Violet in the kitchen, while Antoni and Jovi did the morning shift on the shop floor, but she couldn't put it off much longer. After her tearful start to the day, it had been lovely to chat about the upcoming autumn menu, discuss Harry's husband's newest addition to his collection of vinyl and run through Violet's must-watch movies of the summer. Violet was single, coming up to thirty and a total movie buff. Whenever she had given Marnie recommendations before, Marnie had enthusiastically added them to her list, for it was difficult not to get excited after listening to Violet review a film, but she never got around to watching them.

With work and Josh not being interested in the same genre of films, they always got put on the back burner in favour of the news or a documentary. However, Violet made curling up alone on the couch to watch a movie that you chose and wanted to watch sound rather idyllic, so much so that Marnie was very much looking forward to a quiet night in with a Sandra Bullock classic. Just as she was about to tell Violet that *My Big Fat Greek Wedding* was filmed in Canada, a movie fact she hoped to impress her with and one she had learnt on her travels, the timer on the oven beeped, letting Violet know that the next batch of strawberry cupcakes were ready and telling Marnie that it had gone twelve o'clock.

'Are you still here and distracting my staff?' Jovi jabbed as she walked through the kitchen door carrying an empty tray. Marnie smiled at her sister's face that, compared to this morning, was screaming contentment now that her big sister was home. The bakery had been heaving all morning. Marnie had offered to help but was waved away by Jovi, who had made a mumbled comment about the town gossip and had sent her to the back to relax with Harry and Violet, yet the dark circles under Jovi's eyes seemed lighter now, her hair less frizzy.

'I am doing no such thing,' Marnie replied, taking it as her cue to retrieve her backpack and make a move. A small stone of anxiety rolled around in her stomach as she did so, which her face must have shown.

'It will be fine. Once you meet him, it won't seem so scary anymore, I promise. Tim's a good guy,' Jovi said, just as Antoni walked into the kitchen to swap with Harry.

'I know, I know, I'm good. I'm looking forward to it,' Marnie lied, smiling at her sister, who clearly wasn't buying her false bravado.

'I wish I was coming with you. If you want to wait, we can go together when we close up?' Jovi offered. 'Jackson's with Sienna so it's no trouble,' she added, refilling her tray with thick slices of vanilla pound cake.

'No, it's OK. I've been back in the country longer than twelve hours. Mum will be wondering where I am. And I'd rather meet our new stepdad indoors than bump into them in the public eye should she decide to come looking for me,' Marnie explained with just a hint of sarcasm. No matter the dysfunction within their family of four, their parents had raised their girls to value and prioritise family above all else. Marnie knew it had been part of the reason she'd wanted to go into teaching. Growing up, Marnie and Jovi were not privy to their parents' arguments or fights. They doted on their girls and did everything together, from cinema outings, camping in the back garden to mealtimes and crafting. Marnie had thought them the perfect, strong family unit. She had parents who loved each other and loved her. It was only when the girls were older they noticed the cracks in the cosy and what Marnie had deemed flawless family dynamic.

Marnie would often picture them chatting about their work days over a cup of tea, doing puzzles together or curling up to enjoy Ant and Dec's *Saturday Night Takeaway* together, laughing at the same jokes and shouting out the answers to the quizzes to see if they could have won the prizes, but the reality was that she would come home from college, the house would be still and cold and Marnie would get the sense that her mum and dad hadn't said a word to each other about what happened at work that day.

Later, she and Jovi would turn up unannounced to surprise them with a bunch of flowers and a cake, only to hear their arguments from the porch. Like Jovi had said earlier, their split had been a long time coming, but with so much of Marnie's life falling apart, them separating almost seven months ago now had been too much to contend with and she hadn't wanted to believe it was happening. She may be an adult, but no kid wants to hear that their parents are splitting up. All that aside, it had been months since she last spoke to her mum. She had been angry with her when she left for the airport. Her mum had taught her better than that. Marnie hated going to sleep when she was angry with her parents, or anyone for that matter, and she very much disliked going such long periods without speaking to them, but it had been a strange seven months.

'Will you come for dinner tonight?' Jovi asked, as Marnie moved towards the kitchen door. 'You can tell me how it goes with Mum and all about Canada. Sienna wants to see the pictures of the bears you were telling us about in your last email.' Jovi offered a hopeful smile.

It had been a long time since Marnie had been to dinner at Jovi's. She hadn't meant to ignore her twin sister, her niece or her brother-in-law. She loved them all dearly, but an overwhelming sense of failure had gripped her when her relationship with Josh had begun showing cracks and then again when she'd walked in on him cheating. Marnie hadn't been able to face playing happy families in her sister's perfect world. Of course, she hadn't told Jovi any of this, which she knew made her a terrible sister, but she knew only she could fix these insecurities; it wasn't fair to put them on Jovi or make Jovi think that she had done something wrong.

'I'll be there too. I'm making apple crumble so you know you can't say no,' Antoni teased, making Marnie's jaw unclench.

The thought of Antoni's apple crumble and snuggling up with Sienna on the couch telling her all about her trip and showing her the pictures of their favourite animal brought a smile to her face. Marnie pushed her negative thoughts to the back of her mind. They were not her thoughts, just brain noise. She wanted to be the free-spirited Marnie who could trek around Canada and get up close and personal with grizzly bears, get back to the happy Marnie, the fun auntie who made papier mâché animals and ate too many Maltesers with her niece – that's the Marnie she wanted to be.

'I'm in,' she said, feeling triumphant as the words left her lips.

'OK, great,' Jovi practically squealed, nearly dropping her tray of cake slices. 'Hope it goes OK with Mum. Text me if you need me and thank you for my flowers,' Jovi called through the kitchen door as Marnie and Antoni walked through it. The daisies were now sitting pretty in a vase by the register thanks to Violet rescuing them from any further squishing earlier that the morning.

When they reached the front door, Antoni leaned down and dropped a kiss on the top of Marnie's head. 'Good job,' he said sincerely, his eyes twinkling when she looked up at him. He didn't have to say much – those two words meant everything to her. Antoni always knew what was going on in her head and she loved him for it. She wrapped her arms around his waist, not caring about the flour and splodges of cake batter that might transfer on to her white T-shirt, and squeezed him tight.

'I'll see you later,' she said, with a joy in her voice that she welcomed.

4

The heat of the summer sun warmed Marnie's skin as she walked along the cobbled streets. Her jangly silver bracelets caught the light with each step and cast sparkling orbs across the path as she walked from the small town centre towards her mum's house. The familiar pathways and children roller skating and skipping in the street brought a wave of nostalgia over her and she couldn't help but long for the days of her youth when she, Jovi and Antoni would spend the entire summer outdoors riding their bikes and building dens in the park behind their childhood homes. Marnie had been the best builder and was rather nifty with a couple of branches and broken logs. She reckoned she could construct a tepee in ten minutes flat.

However, that was all before they entered their teen years when Jovi and Antoni got into baking. Instead of playing on the street, they chose to never leave the kitchen as they honed their cooking skills. If she couldn't build outside, she figured out a way to do it inside and so Marnie had taken to crafting at the kitchen table so she could still spend time with them. It had worked out well for her as she was in prime proximity to taste-test everything they made, and for thirteen-year-olds who had just picked up the baking bug, they weren't half bad.

'Hi, Miss Barnes. When are you coming back to school?' A little voice startled Marnie from her daydream. The bold sun blocked her view up ahead. It took her a moment to realise someone was asking her a question and a further minute to locate the person. Holding her hand up to shield her eyes from the striking sun, she saw that it was a little person who was currently bobbing up and down playing hopscotch.

'Hi, Betsy. How are you sweetheart?' Marnie said, taking a step out of the sun so she didn't have to squint and so she could see the girl better. For a moment she panicked that she might have got her name wrong. It was a wonder how teachers remembered three hundred children's names at the best of times, least of all when they hadn't seen them for ages, but she believed that was just one of the superpowers teachers had, and then Betsy's face lit up and she ran closer waving her bean bag in the air.

'I'm good thank you. You've been gone for so long,' Betsy said, her voice deflated, her head tilted to the side as she stared up at Marnie.

Marnie could feel her cheeks redden and her chest tighten. She smoothed her fingers over her bangles, feeling the ridges in the metal as she thought about how best to approach her answer.

'I'm glad you're well, Bet. I know it's been a long time. I don't work at your school anymore, but I'm happy I got to see you now. Are you having a nice summer?' she asked, squatting down so Betsy didn't have to strain her neck. Betsy had been in her Year One class last year. She was a sweetheart of a little girl, super smart and good at maths and quicker than Marnie at her times tables.

'Oh, I miss you. Mrs Fielding took away my unicorns. She said I couldn't have them back even after I cried,' the little girl explained, fiddling with her bright yellow bean bag. Marnie's stomach sank. Where Betsy was a whizz with numbers, she struggled with her phonics and reading. Marnie had created some small flashcards of unicorns with key words and graphemes on the unicorn's bellies. It had been helping Betsy remember them as unicorns were her favourite. Her mum had even written in her reading record that without fail every night Betsy would read through her unicorn cards before bed and they would play a little phonics game with them. She had been making wonderful progress. The thought that Mrs Fielding had gotten rid of them made Marnie's eyes crinkle in annoyance.

'I'm sorry, sweetheart. I hope you're still working hard with your reading; you are really good,' Marnie said with a smile, trying to keep her voice cheerful.

'I am. I got some new books about unicorns. Mum said you went to Canada to get away from mean people. Is my class mean? I don't like it when the girls and boys aren't kind,' Betsy said, squinting in the sunlight, her black bob shimmering under its glare. Marnie's heartstrings gave a heavy strum at the way Betsy flitted from each thought that crossed her brain and with her heavy words. She shuffled a little in her squatting position to block the sun from Betsy's eyes.

'Oh, not at all, Bets. I loved being in your class. It was so much fun. I just needed a small holiday. I'm sure Mrs Fielding is doing her best to teach the other girls and boys to be kind,' Marnie replied. Betsy's class had been a feisty one for sure with many a strong character. Mrs Fielding was strict, tough and rule-driven, which often meant she missed the emotional side of children's development, telling them to suck it up if someone was being cruel. Marnie felt for Betsy, who had always been as good as gold and sweet to everyone.

'Was it to get away from Mr Beck? He's mean. I don't like it when he visits our classes. I wish he would go on holiday, not you.' Betsy's bottom lip stuck out slightly in protest.

It was difficult to remain balanced when a child hit the nail on the head ever so innocently, but Marnie summoned her strength and remained eye level with Betsy. Though she believed it was good for children to see adults cry, to know that they got upset too and that it's OK to be sad, she didn't want to scare Betsy or for the little girl to feel hate towards her head teacher. He may be the reason that Marnie made the most out-of-character, spontaneous trip to Vancouver, was out of work right now and currently at a crossroads in her life, but she was not about to unload all that information on the child. A small part of her couldn't help feeling a touch pleased that Betsy was on her side in thinking him mean though.

'His job is very hard so sometimes he can get stressed and moody because he is tired. Maybe if you keep being nice to him, he'll learn what kindness is and be kind back,' Marnie explained, not quite able to believe what had just come out of her mouth. Did she really just recommend kindness to the man who had caused her life to unravel? Canada truly had had a profound impact on her. All that hiking had helped, not just in toning her thighs, but in clearing her head and bringing her more peace. She smiled at the thought.

'OK, I will try. A new lady came to our school when you had to go on holiday. She's having a baby,' was Betsy's next statement. In all her years working with children, it was a wonder to Marnie they had this innate ability to sucker punch you but make you smile at the same time. With that, Marnie's legs no longer wanted to support her and so she had to stand and stretch out their wobbles and encourage them to remember how to work. Behind her kneecaps felt clammy and when she stood the sun caught her with its golden rays, making her blink furiously. While Marnie strained to pull herself together and act natural, Betsy added, 'You can't be mean to babies,' which brought a chuckle to Marnie's lips.

'No, you can't,' Marnie agreed, once again raising her hand to shield against the sun, while using the other to dab at the stream of water that the blinding rays had caused to leak from her eyes. When her eyes finally cleared, Marnie looked down at Betsy. Her large brown eyes beamed with innocence. 'Babies often teach people how to be kind and caring to others, so I'm sure all the teachers will be nice to the new lady and be loving to her baby.' Marnie cleared her throat, though something inside her twisted uncomfortably.

Betsy flashed her a cute smile and wrapped an arm around Marnie's hips. Marnie was momentarily caught off guard by the sudden show of affection, having not been used to it for the past couple of months. When working at Cornelia Primary it was an everyday occurrence. She'd missed it.

'Be good, OK, Bet? Now you get back to playing and

I'll see you soon,' Marnie said, patting Betsy gently on her back.

'I will. Bye, Miss Barnes,' the little girl chirped as she ran back to her hopscotch. Marnie watched her for a moment while she collected herself. She wasn't going to let Betsy's inquisition about Josh and talking about him affect her day or let him get in the way of her having fun, which she was sure to have heading to see her mum and her mum's new boyfriend. The thought made Marnie chuckle to herself. She shook her head hoping to shake away the sudden wobbly feeling she felt over hearing of a new pregnant teaching assistant and continued her walk.

Colourful chalk splattered across the pavement leading up to Marnie's childhood home. Rainbows, bike tracks and kids names were depicted on the concrete slabs making Marnie smile. She liked that chalk was still popular amongst kids and that they had been outside enjoying the sunshine rather than in all day on iPads and game consoles. Not that she disliked modern technology – back in the day, she couldn't exactly say how many hours she would occasionally lose to playing Tetris.

Taking a small step up onto the sunflower-printed welcome mat, Marnie raised her finger to the doorbell tentatively. Her brain did a frantic rundown of what she needed to say to her mum, Annabel. Would a simple sorry suffice? Or did she make it more specific? Sorry for yelling, sorry for getting angry and blaming her for tearing apart their family, sorry for fleeing the country, sorry for being a terrible daughter. The apologies mounted up the longer Marnie stood at the door. The sun was beginning to burn her shoulder blades, only adding to the pressure in her mind. Quickly, she pushed down hard on the bell before she lost what little nerve she had that had brought her this far.

Though Marnie and Jovi looked alike and enjoyed similar tastes in music, TV shows and food, their personalities were like chalk and cheese. Jovi was the level-headed twin, the triple checker of all things, organised, neat and very much like the woman on the other side of the door. Marnie and her mum didn't exactly clash – they loved each other dearly – but Marnie was a lot like her dad, Morgan. He was the quirky one who marched to the beat of his own drum and never really took life seriously. Marnie had his creative flair and if the past ten years had taught her anything, planning wasn't their thing or more correctly, their plans didn't always go to plan. At sixty-five, her dad was newly separated and had been ejected from his home. He had moved into an apartment in the next town, Marnie had been informed, and at thirty-five she was single, jobless and struggling for prospects.

A tiny drop of hope, that her mum wasn't home and had gone for a spontaneous walk at one p.m. instead of her usual cup of tea and lunch, evaporated when the door swung open with a hefty pull. Within seconds Annabel wrapped her around Marnie, squishing her tight and pulling her inside.

'You're home, you're home and in one piece,' Annabel exclaimed, shoving Marnie to arm's length so she could assess and clarify her statement. 'How was your trip? I want to know all about Canada.' Annabel's hazel eyes, which matched her daughters', twinkled. It was Marnie's turn now to survey her mum as she stood inches away from her, still gripping her wrists, for fear that she might flee again, no doubt. Her skin looked peachy and had a newfound vibrance to it. She looked less worn out and there was definitely a gloss to her hair that hadn't been there when Marnie last saw her seven months ago.

'Hi, Mum,' Marnie said, finding her voice. Her mum's perfume lingered on her tee and when she breathed it in, her shoulders dropped away from her ears, releasing some of the tension they had been carrying.

'Hi, sweetheart,' Annabel replied, stroking a hand over Marnie's cheek, causing Marnie to smile a genuine smile. She had been expecting a royal telling-off, for her mum to reprimand her for being so selfish and foolish, leaving the country on her own and not calling her every day, but her mum simply stood gazing at her as if she were a precious gemstone, a look that Marnie remembered fondly from when she would read her and Jovi bedtime stories and kiss them goodnight. She would kiss their foreheads, whisper 'sweet dreams' and hesitate for a second, before walking away. The look of pure love written all over her features was, for Marnie, better than any of the stories she ever read.

Marnie cleared her throat and sniffed to keep her tears at bay. She had cried once today, which was her quota for the next month at least. 'Should we go into the kitchen and put the kettle on?' she asked her mum.

Annabel's eyes darted to the floor and she looked nervous. Marnie's stomach flipped in response. This was it; her mum didn't want her in the house. She was mad; she was going to be kicked out just like her dad.

'There's a man in there,' her mum said, putting a stop to Marnie's dramatic thoughts.

'Oh,' Marnie muttered, then thinking back to what Jovi

had told her. She put two and two together and forced a smile. Tim, she had almost forgotten about Tim, but seeing her mum look so healthy and happy, she knew she needed to be good; Betsy had told her to be, after all.

'A man you know at least, I hope,' Marnie said with a small smirk. Annabel shoved her playfully but cracked a smile once more.

'Would you like to meet him?' her mum asked, a hand on Marnie's shoulder.

'Tim? Can you hear us out here?' Marnie said, raising her voice and tilting her chin up towards the kitchen door.

'I sure can,' Tim replied. His voice carried a chuckle and sounded friendly and warm, which put Marnie at ease. She couldn't burst her mum's bubble; she could do this, and she appreciated Tim playing along.

'Well, I can't leave now, Mum. He knows I'm here. How will I ever get favourite twin points if I leave now? He'll think I'm terribly rude,' she said, winking at her mum while spinning her bracelets around on her wrist. Her mum's face practically beamed. Her eyes looked wet, like they were holding back the tears, but she composed herself before pushing open the kitchen door.

When they walked into the kitchen, Tim stood up from the kitchen table, where Marnie noticed there where three plates of ham sandwiches and a couple of bowls of crisps upon it. She couldn't help smiling at her mum's planning. It comforted her to know that there was still a place for her in all this newness. Averting her eyes from her mum's delicious lunch, Marnie looked to Tim who reached out his hand to Marnie. She took it.

'Hi, Marnie. It's lovely to meet you,' Tim said, shaking her hand gently. He was, give or take, four or five inches taller than Marnie, with short grey hair and a five o'clock shadow. His brown eyes crinkled with a kindness that Marnie hadn't been expecting; after all, she'd been expecting to strongly dislike this man.

'Hi,' she replied with a friendly nod.

'So, did you get to any ice-hockey games while in Canada?' Tim asked, breaking the ice with genuine enthusiasm and interest. Marnie smiled in disbelief; it was going to be incredibly difficult not to like this man. She forced the feeling of guilt, like somehow she was betraying her dad, to the back of her mind as she began telling Tim all about her experience seeing her first ice-hockey game. It wasn't like her dad was into sports anyway; in fact it was a mystery where Marnie's love of ice hockey came from, but it was a sport she had always wanted to watch live. In Canada she got to make that small dream of hers come true four times; after her first game, she had become a little hooked and had tried her best to see a game when each stop on her Canada tour would allow.

Suddenly, her palms began tingling so much that Marnie clasped her hands together and squeezed. It wasn't like each time she had been to a game a small part of her wished and prayed that she would somehow bump into a tall stranger, with long blonde hair and crystal blue eyes. It wasn't meant to be and she felt silly now. She prised her hands apart and dived into the crisp bowl to distract herself and focus on the sport she and Tim so clearly loved.

By the time she finished talking she found that she was sitting at the table with her hand still in a bowl of crisps. Her mum was smiling at her and Tim was looking at her with an expression that looked a lot like jealousy. She paused, crisp hovering at her lips. Had she said something wrong? How long had she been waffling on? Then, Tim smiled. 'You must have a favourite team?' he queried, raising a brow, eagerly awaiting her answer.

Some five hours later, Marnie was back on the front doorstep. She had said goodbye to Tim and had genuinely meant it when she had said, 'It was lovely to meet you.' The afternoon had been surprisingly pleasant. Annabel had followed her to the door, a blissful smile permanently on her face since the moment Marnie and Tim had started talking about ice-hockey teams, but as Marnie stepped onto the welcome mat, she noticed her mum's features soften and her smile falter.

'Are you doing OK, sweetheart?' she asked, her voice full of concern. They hadn't discussed what had happened all those months ago – not her parents separating nor the painful break-up that had thrown Marnie's attempt at a plan severely off course. Marnie looked up at the sun, which at gone five o'clock was still centre stage, and then turned to face her mum, fiddling with her bracelets as she did so.

'I didn't want to ask in front of Tim. Canada seems to have brought some light into your life. It sounded like you had an amazing time and I'm so proud of you for doing it on your own. I'm sorry I didn't believe in you before. I'm used to you and Jovi doing things together. It makes me feel content as a mother knowing if I can't help you that she can and will. I feel like a failure when I can't protect you, Marnie, but how are you, sweetheart? You know my door is always open,' Annabel said, her arms crossed over her chest – a habit Marnie had picked up from her. They both hugged themselves when they got nervous or anxious.

For all their differences and for the anger that Marnie had felt before she left, she looked at her mum and smiled. They might not always be on the same page and they would be sure to butt heads again in the future, maybe not like each other's decisions, but there was no denying their love. Marnie wasn't fully OK, but seeing her mum and Tim so jovial together, she knew, or at least she hoped, that she would be.

'I'm fine, Mum. I'm sorry that I got mad and took everything out on you. My anger was misplaced, and I can see that now. I'm glad you're happy and you're right, Canada was good for me. I'm sorry to have worried you but it was something I had to do on my own.' She twirled the silver bangles that jangled on her wrist.

'Sometimes I forget that you're big girls now. And don't apologise for your anger – it was understandable. If your dad and I knew what was happening at home, we would have chosen a better time to tell you, I'm sorry,' Annabel said, reaching out to steady Marnie's fixation on her bangles.

When Josh had left her apartment that day, Marnie had crumbled. It had been a Saturday. Antoni had rung to tell Jovi, who had immediately left the bakery under Harry and Violet's supervision and raced to her side. Marnie hadn't been able to form words as she tried to digest what had happened. She'd spent two days curled up on her couch as Jovi and Antoni took it in turns whipping up batches of brownies, trying to entice her to eat something, and then Monday she had gotten dressed and gone to work, having to act as if her life had not completely fallen apart.

On the Wednesday, her mum and dad had called a family meeting where they informed both Marnie and Jovi that they were separating. Marnie had yet to tell them her news and couldn't bring herself to do so after that bombshell. By the following Monday, Marnie had been called into the head teacher's office, which was the first time she had seen Josh since the incident, only to be informed that the school no longer had a position for her as of the upcoming Friday. The week counting down to that Friday had been trying. Seeing boxes of her dad's things stacked up by the door of their family home had been heart-wrenching; the once warm and loving house having been ripped apart from the inside.

Jovi had insisted she come for dinner every night but surrounded by Jovi's happy family of three suddenly made Marnie feel hopeless and so after a thoroughly awful day at school saying bye to the kids she had grown to love, she had spent Friday evening filling up on way too much sugar, thanks to all the leftover brownies, and dissecting her bucket list with Antoni. With no job and her life plan up in flames, her once-upon-a-time dream vacation with Josh to Canada had seemed like the most reasonable thing to do. Saturday, she had jumped on a plane.

'I don't think there would have ever been a right time, Mum. I should have told you what had happened between me and Josh, but I promise I'm good now. Fresh maple syrup made for the perfect medicine,' Marnie said, giving her mum a lopsided grin.

'I think Tim will be going with you next time.' Her mum chuckled.

Marnie laughed, her brain considering showing Tim

around Canada, like Nova had done with her that one incredible day. Then she blinked quickly, scolding her eyes for the vision of Nova they had just given her. She should not be thinking about Nova, not when she was in the process of getting her life back on track.

'Hey, Mum,' she started softly, taking a step closer. 'I'm proud of you too. Tim is great and I can see that you're happy. I'm sorry for acting like you should be miserable for the rest of your life. I don't want you to be miserable; I want this for you.' Marnie wrapped her arms tightly around her mum, breathing in her scent once more for comfort.

'It was OK to be scared. It's still OK to be scared, but don't devalue your hopes and dreams sweetie. Don't give them up to Josh. They're yours – please remember that,' she whispered into Marnie's hair.

Marnie squeezed her a little tighter and whispered 'OK' before stepping away with a little more confidence than she'd had standing on the doorstep earlier.

5

'He likes ice hockey. Can you believe that?' Marnie asked Jackson, her voice coming out high-pitched and ringing with utter shock. 'Ouch, do you have to stick your elbow there?' she added, when Antoni's elbow found her hip.

'It's not my fault. Does Sienna need to repeat the rules again? I do as she says,' Antoni said, twisting his neck awkwardly to flash her a cheeky grin. Marnie rolled her eyes.

'His favourite team is the Canucks,' Marnie continued, her voice muffled as Jovi's bottom suddenly appeared far too close to her face for comfort. 'Sienna, is it my turn yet? I need to move.'

'Auntie Marnie, stop talking so much. You will be distracted.' Sienna gave her a pointed glare. She looked so cute in her planets and space rocket print pyjamas, but she was taking no prisoners in the game of Twister they were playing. Of course, she was the spinner. No matter how many times Jackson suggested that she would have more fun on the mat, she would not give up control. He'd even tried to entice her by saying she would win and get a prize because she was so good at gymnastics, but to no avail.

The grown-ups were currently being put to the test by a six-year-old.

'He's a cool guy and hey, you now have someone to talk to, who's not us, about teams and players,' Jackson said, cueing sniggers from both Jovi and Antoni. Marnie knew Jackson was smirking, but she couldn't see his face, for Jovi's bottom was still very much in the way. She knew her love of ice hockey was random around these parts, but she liked what she liked. Jackson usually got the low-down on games when she came for dinner because Josh had not been a fan either. Now, none of them had to put up with it because she had Tim, her mum's new boyfriend, to discuss the sport with, which was a far more bizarre turn of events than her liking a sport that wasn't hugely popular in the UK.

'Auntie Marnie, your turn: left hand blue,' Sienna said, after putting a finger to her lips and telling her dad to shush, which made Marnie chuckle. As Marnie lifted her left arm, she made sure to tickle Antoni's armpit, causing him to jolt and fall to the mat.

'Oops looks like Antoni's out, Sienna,' Marnie noted innocently. Both Jovi and Jackson tried to twist to see the action, but limbs were everywhere, making it difficult.

Antoni got up with a tut and bent down to whisper something to Sienna that Marnie made out to be: 'Keep a close eye on your auntie,' before he settled down on the couch and returned to his plate of chocolate cake, making Marnie wonder if she didn't in fact just do him a favour. From the smile he gave her after taking a bite, she had no doubt that was the case.

'Has Dad met him?' Marnie questioned, turning away from Antoni, the question suddenly popping into her brain.

'Yes, he likes him too. You should see Mum and Dad when they see each other now, much more civil. They actually talk to each other instead of shout. Tim's been a good influence,' Jovi told her, panting a touch as she tried to get her right foot across to green. Marnie had to move her head out of the way, so she didn't get kicked in the face.

'Hmm.' She had given her dad a quick call on the way to Jovi's after visiting with her mum, just to let him know she was home safe and that she would ring him tomorrow so they could arrange a time for her to see his new place. He was a lot more easy-going than her mum, and had said whenever she had time worked for him. It seemed that not all things in her hometown were bad and that lots of good had occurred in the months she had spent travelling.

'Mummy, concentrate or you will lose,' Sienna said with a mouthful of chocolate cake that Antoni had just fed her. She'd been eyeing his up after finishing her giant piece. She had a healthy appetite thanks to her mum being an excellent cook. There were always fresh bakes in the house. Marnie didn't think Sienna knew who Mr Kipling was.

'Red, Daddy,' Sienna added, well and truly distracted now by the cake. Marnie's arms were vibrating with trying to keep herself from falling and she was starting to lose feeling in her right thigh. 'Your hand.' Sienna pointed.

Jackson did as he was told but made an overexaggerated attempt to reach for the furthest red square giving Marnie and Jovi a look as he did so. It had come to the part of the game where the grown-ups realised they had some control over how long it lasted and worked together to end it. Marnie and Jovi both played along falling dramatically and the three of them landed in a heap, the last one to hit the matt being Jackson by a hair.

'Daddy won.' Sienna cheered, none the wiser. Marnie shuffled out of the pile of limbs and reached for her own cake. All that playing and she was hungry again, even after devouring a roast dinner with all the trimmings and a healthy bowl of apple crumble for dessert.

'Right, bedtime, little one,' Jackson announced, throwing Sienna up in the air as Jovi plonked herself onto the couch. Sienna squealed with glee. Marnie shoved cake into her mouth and swallowed down the lump that crept up in her throat when her niece's eyes lit up and Jackson cuddled her to him, her tiny body fitting perfectly snug against her dad's large frame. She looked so safe and content cradled in his arms that Marnie's heart gave a sharp spasm.

'Can Uncle Ant and Daddy read me a story?' Sienna asked, making her eyes large when she looked up at Jackson. He smiled and Antoni leapt up off the couch.

'Sure can, kiddo,' he said with great enthusiasm. The three of them headed out of the living room, leaving Marnie and Jovi with some sister time.

'So, I take it today wasn't so bad?' Jovi said, grabbing a cushion and twirling it around lazily in her hands. Marnie sat up straighter, leaning against the couch, her plate on her knee.

'No,' she said thoughtfully. 'I guess not. It was definitely a shock to the system and will take some getting used to, but you were right earlier – Mum's happy. All those years playing pretend, jeez, and now I know what truly happy on her looks like.'

'It wasn't all pretend, you know. She loved our family

unit; she loved that Dad gave her us. We're still a family,' Jovi said, not looking at Marnie but staring off towards the empty brick fireplace. 'And your life isn't over.' Jovi said, kicking her in the shoulder in the process. 'I know there are things you're not telling me, Marn, but you do know I'll always be here for you, right? I missed you when you were gone. Talk about having to get used to stuff, it was like I was missing a limb.' Jovi nudged her sister for the second time.

Marnie smirked, trying to ignore the guilt that was settling next to the cake in her stomach.

'I missed you too, but I needed it, Jovi. I needed to figure myself out, to just do and see the things I wanted to see. Away from everything that was going wrong. It just felt like I could breathe and absorb life better.' Marnie put the chocolate cake on the table and turned to face her sister. She pushed Jovi's foot out of the way and placed her forearm on the seat of the couch, where she then rested her head. 'It was like without Josh I was nothing. I didn't want to sleep in the same bed we slept in together for ten years or wake up knowing that I couldn't just walk around the corner to go to work to see my kids. I couldn't be around Sienna feeling so defeated and miserable. Everything just reminded me of the person I didn't know how to be anymore. I was petrified getting on that plane but somehow staying here felt scarier than that.'

Jovi was looking at her now. These were the moments when Marnie knew they looked alike, when the night drew on and their eyelids began to droop, the skin underneath puffed out slightly from the late hour. Whereas Jovi's tiredness came from working all day and looking after a six-year-old, Marnie's sprouted out of stress and worry. There was also their tell-tale sign of thought, when their Cupid's bows got a touch closer to their noses and their red lips formed a small pout.

'I get it, I do, but you're not nothing, Marn. You've never been nothing. Please don't base your worth on him. You're so much more than how he made you feel,' Jovi said, sitting up and releasing the cushion from her grasp to pinch the rest of Marnie's cake.

'I know that now. I do,' Marnie noted uncertainly. 'It was like doing something I never thought I could ever do made me feel like I still had some control over my life, like I was the one who wanted to go to Canada, and I went. I don't know how I ever believed that Josh even liked the idea. But hey, a plan actually panned out in a funny sort of way.' Her eyes fluttered as she leant her cheek against her forearm. Jet lag was starting to kick in along with the many roast potatoes she had enjoyed earlier. Her stomach was content, and she felt quite ready to curl up and fall asleep.

'I hear what you're saying, and I can't pretend to know how you feel, but when you start to panic, just remember that Mum never planned for Tim, OK?' Jovi offered, giving the top of Marnie's head a stroke with the tip of her toe. Marnie knew that Jovi meant for that to sound hopeful and exciting, but it made her blood rush to her ears with a horror-like theme tune, dun dun, dun dun. With no offence to Tim, he had turned out to be a nice guy after all, but she didn't want a Tim. Did she? She wasn't ready for a Tim. Was she? Marnie closed her eyes tight, forcing her brain not to drift to a warm Canadian accent.

'Did you just stroke my hair with your foot?' she queried,

desperately ready to move off the topic, her tired eyes still pressed tightly shut, forcing thoughts of Nova away.

'Maybe,' Jovi replied. 'Hey, speaking of control, and my question that went unanswered earlier about what you are going to do now you're back, there's a job going at Sienna's school. They need some one-on-one support for a child and they're getting desperate. She goes back on Thursday, but I know the teachers have an inset on Wednesday. You could try ringing tomorrow or fill out an application online. If teaching is still something you'd like to do.'

Marnie jolted herself awake with a soft snore as Jackson and Antoni returned from story time with a tray of coffees. With her ankles trembling from pins and needles, she pushed herself up onto the couch and gratefully took the mug Antoni passed to her.

'I'll look into it, though I'm not sure they'll take me after my sudden and hasty firing at Cornelia. I'm sure they'll consider that suspicious. And I don't suppose Josh will write me the most sparkling reference,' she replied, with a small shrug, before taking a sip of coffee, the rich aroma instantly bringing life back to her weary body. From over the top of her mug, Marnie couldn't help noticing her sister, brother-in-law and best friend glance at each other. She widened her eyes at Antoni, giving him a look that he knew to mean, 'What?'

'I think you should go for it,' Antoni encouraged her, dismissing her look innocently, but the twitch in his right eye made Marnie think something was off. Though she was far too tired to think what.

'Everyone knows you at Sienna's school. They know how amazing you are at your job. And, you know she'd love to have you there,' Jovi said, crossing her legs and snuggling up closer to Jackson now that he was sat beside her but not looking Marnie in the eye. Marnie's brain threatened to overthrow the positive thoughts she was feeling due to the joyful events that had made up the day. She'd had a pleasant afternoon with her mum and her mum's new boyfriend, a delicious dinner with her family and playing games and sharing giggles with Sienna. She wanted to hold on to them, so she concentrated on the robust smell of the coffee and the comforting taste on her tongue and not the idea that her family was acting suspiciously or the fact that she needed to get a job.

'It's just something to think about,' Jovi said.

'Then I will think about it, thanks,' she replied. Considering there were only two schools in their town, Marnie didn't have a whole lot of choice. It made sense. She had loved her job as a teaching assistant and unless someone was going to pay her to trek across Canada, or any of the other parts of the world that were on her bucket list, she needed to get back to work. 'But hey, enough about me. How've you been, Jo?' Marnie asked, realising her sister had been nothing but focused on her since she got back.

'Same old, same old,' Jovi said with a contented shrug and a smile that made her eyes glaze over. The image tugged at Marnie's heartstrings. Marnie was aware she'd left Jovi to deal with a lot while she was away but she was happy to see that Jovi's family life was still going from strength to strength and that she still looked at Jackson with that same dreamy expression on her face that she'd had twelve years ago when they first started dating.

'I was thinking Sienna and I are long overdue a sleepover,

so if you and Jackson fancy a date night just say the words,' Marnie offered, her lips dancing with a grin as Jovi was still lost in her daydream.

'That would be nice,' she replied, not looking at Marnie but studying Jackson for a moment, who caught her looking and sent a wink her way like he knew what she was thinking.

'So, you really liked Canada ay?' Jackson said with a confident cock of his head, causing the three of them to burst out laughing. Marnie had always liked Jackson. This tall, muscly and dark-skinned man had entered Jovi's life when she and Antoni had been away at university. He'd hit it off with Antoni when Antoni and Jovi had visited a local restaurant and he was competing in a 'Man versus Food' style challenge. With Jackson's love of food rivalling Jovi and Antoni's combined, he had smashed the competition. Then he had proceeded to win over Marnie the first time they met by accepting that the twin life had chosen Jovi first and that he could not change that, nor had it ever felt like he wanted to.

Marnie swallowed a large gulp of coffee, having to suddenly push a silly sliver of jealousy deep, deep down into her gut where she hoped it would stay until it shrivelled up from lack of air and died. Her jealousy did not belong in the room now, not with the three people whom she loved most in the world, in addition to her parents and of course Sienna. Jealousy had no place in her and Jovi's relationship though Marnie would be a fibber if she didn't occasionally feel it when admiring the family her sister had.

'It's hard to find the right words. It was breath-taking.' Marnie sighed, letting her mind drift back to the nights spent camping under the stars. The night sky in BC had not simply resolved to a pitch-black. It lit up with a deep, rich navy that blended into a gorgeous purple. Upon that colourful canvas it was as if someone had taken a paintbrush, dipped it in a jar of glitter and swirled it around the sky, leaving specks of twinkling stardust.

It was something she never thought she would ever do but had dreamt about fiercely. She wondered if it had been those dreams that had been vital in making it happen eventually. Granted she hadn't experienced it with Josh like she'd planned, but she'd made it happen. Could the same be said for her dream of one day having a family of her own or was it time to let that dream go? As a familiar rush of nausea swept over her body when a little voice inside her brain told her that that particular dream had expired, she grabbed her phone off the coffee table and opened up her picture album from her travels.

'The pictures don't quite do it justice but look,' she said her voice a little unsteady at first. But when the purple-pink hues filled her screen and her family all crowded around her, the niggling voice quietened, and her thoughts floated back to safer, happier territory.

6

Through the open window rose the scent of warm maple syrup brownies. Marnie removed her gaze from the dust particles that danced on the ray of light that bounced off the windowpane. How long had she been staring at the ghost-like grains that became non-existent every time she reached out to catch them? She chuckled to herself and shook her head, shuffling off the couch where time had obviously gotten away from her. She snuck a glance at the silver clock on her wall. Lunchtime had crept up on her when she took a gander out of the window, to find Antoni staring up at her, waving with one hand and wiggling a box enticingly in the other.

'Don't hurt the brownies,' she shouted before racing to her door to buzz him up. It was the fastest she had moved all morning. She opened the door to wait, the smell of the freshly baked goods getting stronger as she could hear Antoni taking the stairs two at a time. He need not do this, for his long limbs made quick work of the short flight anyway, but she appreciated it all the same. Her stomach growled impatiently. Antoni appeared in his signature work attire of black, slim-fit jeans and a plain, white tee in a matter of seconds. No matter the weather his skin always had that summer bronzed glow about it, but now in the late August sun it was a deep golden. It was only when a line grew between his eyebrows that Marnie registered her outfit.

'Have you been out today or eaten?' Antoni asked, bypassing a hello and a hug as he walked straight past her into her apartment.

Marnie's bird's nest, fluffy slippers and fleece attire clearly gave him the answers he was looking for, not to mention that her stomach was now growling ferociously with the brownies in close proximity. The fact that Antoni was already rummaging around the tiny kitchen told her that he knew the answers too and asking had been his way of showing his worry and disappointment. Marnie's Cupid's bow rose as she cupped her sleeves with her fingers and avoided eye contact with her best friend.

After having a such a lovely evening at her sister's house, ending the night talking about her travels, she had gone to sleep feeling positive, like she could do anything and take on the world. Then her alarm clock had rung out this morning and when her eyes had opened and she'd remembered she had no job to go to and that she was alone in her room, she felt a hollowness in her stomach as if she were a pumpkin and someone had just scooped out all her seeds. And taking on the world hadn't felt so important or appealing after that.

Pushing her slippers across the wooden floor she edged towards the brownies. Her leaning on the kitchen island while Antoni made use of her kitchen was a typical scene in her apartment. As she reached her hand into the mint-green box it was met with a smack.

'Ouch, what was that for?' she said snatching her hand away and rubbing the top of it soothingly. Being hangry meant that her words came out cross and she was aware her face had turned to thunder. She desperately wanted a brownie. Antoni matched her furrowed brow and thin glare.

'Those are for dessert after you've had a healthy lunch, which I am making because you seem have to forgotten that you need food to survive,' Antoni snapped, causing her face to soften into a smirk.

'What if I told you I had a healthy lunch and I cleaned up just before you got here?' Marnie tried, the smell of the chocolate teasing her now that the box was inched open a tad.

'I wouldn't believe you.' Antoni waved her towards the small oval dining table that seated two comfortably. He placed a frying pan on the front right-side hob and then proceeded to crack eggs one-handed into a bowl. Marnie would be worried about slivers of eggshells with the speed at which he was moving and the fact that he was barely looking at what he was doing if she hadn't seen him do it a million times before.

'What?' she questioned as she tucked her knees up underneath her on the dining room chair, sensing Antoni's glare from the heat on her neck. She had half a mind to take down her hair just to give her vulnerable neck some protection, but she knew it would be no use.

'I think you should go to Apollo Primary and talk to them. See if you can get an interview today or tomorrow,' Antoni said, getting straight to the point. They didn't beat around the bush in their relationship. Marnie didn't look up; instead she sat tracing the wood knots on the table with her index finger. Her nails really needed doing, maybe a bright orange colour to match the summer season, though it would be fall soon, her favourite time of year, so maybe a deep maroon would be preferable. Now, her nails just looked sad, the skin around them dry and sore from where she had picked at them.

'I said I'd think about it,' she mumbled. And she had thought about it – or more specifically dreamt about it. Meeting new staff, listening to staffroom drama, having to answer questions about her and Josh. Did she want to deal with all of that again? If the tossing and turning last night had been anything to go by, then no she didn't. But what else was she going to do? Bills were still marked for her address and after her six-month stint in Canada her savings were minimal. She didn't have the luxury of being picky in the job hunt department, not at her age. There was that hollow feeling again, like she was an Easter egg being cracked open to reveal nothing inside. She shifted in her seat and wrapped her fleece tighter around herself.

'Marn, don't let Canada go to waste,' Antoni said as he placed a plate in front of her with a napkin and a knife and fork. Suddenly the smell of a Spanish omelette with grilled tomatoes, parsley and grated parmesan was competing with the sweetness of the maple and chocolate that was still screaming her name from their pretty box. Marnie automatically sat up straight. She couldn't help the curve that tugged at her lips. Antoni's food always looked so elegant. How did he make an omelette look so beautiful?

'Thank you,' she said with a genuine smile as she met his eyes for the first time since he arrived. They were beaming their usual sparkly brown since he'd just been cooking and was now presenting his creation to another human and getting to feed them. It was one of Marnie's favourite things about Antoni: how he showed his love through food. Not least because his love was delicious but also because so much care and thought went into it.

She sliced into the omelette, savouring the perfume of the parmesan as her knife cut through it. As she did so, her head tilted while her first bite hovered by her lips. Antoni was looking at her open mouth expectantly, waiting to see if she liked it.

'What do you mean about Canada not going to waste?' she asked, confused by Antoni's odd words seconds ago. Then she took her bite and Antoni closed his mouth too, almost mimicking her. He wasn't making fun; this is just what he did sometimes when watching people eat, like he was eating with them. When she made a satisfied moaning sound, he leant back in his chair.

'You had all these incredible experiences out there. The pictures you showed us – you looked alive and radiant and happy. You've been cooped up in this small town. Jeez we've been hanging out since we were three, always around the same people. Now I love you, Marn, and I love this town, but I get it. I get why you did it. People always talk about doing big things, about seeing the world and you actually did it. I'm not saying there's anything wrong with our lives here because there isn't, but heaven knows how many times I've said I'll go on holiday and then changed my mind, too scared to leave the bakery. Jovi too, she and Jackson have been talking about taking a holiday forever, but it can be expensive with kids and she feels guilty about leaving your mum and dad and me.' Antoni sounded wistful. Marnie couldn't quite make out if this was supposed to be a pep talk or make her feel more guilty, but Antoni was smiling.

'What happened sucked or more accurately Josh sucked and I know at first taking that trip was so you could get away from everything but by the looks of it, it became so much more than that. You didn't dwell on your fears or hardships; you explored, you created new memories and bloody hell, Marn, you did it on your own. I never thought you'd ever do anything as big and as crazy as a six-month holiday across the world on your own – no offence,' he added with a cheeky smirk and a nudge to her elbow, which caused her next bite of omelette to fall off her fork. She stabbed it again, rolling her eyes and then chewed thoughtfully. It's not like she could be mad at Antoni's words. Being a twin, she never thought she would do anything to that scale on her own either – she'd never had to before. It had been a relief when Jovi had finished university and moved back home. Though their lives had been different in many ways with Jovi getting married, settling in with Jackson and having Sienna, living close by and seeing each other most every day was always a comfort.

'You might not have planned this for your life, but those experiences wouldn't have happened if you were still with Josh. Maybe Canada was always supposed to be yours. I know Orion doesn't quite possess the stunning scenery, the diverse culture, bears or exceptional maple syrup that Canada has but there is still a world to explore. Yes, it's going to look different now, but different is good. It can be exciting. Don't lose that spirit that took over when you were there. Don't shy away from what it gave you. Don't come back here and cripple yourself over who you were and what you had before,' he said, laying a hand on her forearm and giving it a gentle squeeze.

'So, you're saying I need to stop being a miserable cow and wallowing in self-pity, that I need to channel my inner grizzly, be strong and make things happen. Hmm. Can I have chocolate now?' she said, pointing at her clean plate with a huge grin on her face.

'Exactly,' Antoni replied shaking his head as he got up to grab the brownies. He brought the box and two small plates back to the table after flicking on the kettle. The minute the box hit the wooden tabletop Marnie reached in, scored a brownie, and took a giant bite. If the smell was heaven, then the taste itself was paradise. They were still warm in the middle, there were delicate crumbs, there was melt-in-your-mouth goo and the chocolate was devastatingly rich – Antoni only used the best 70 per cent cocoa – but the swirl of maple syrup gave it that lip-licking scrumptious sweet pop.

'Shall I leave you two alone?' Antoni questioned, snapping Marnie out of her chocolate daydream. Her eyes pinged open to see Antoni staring at her with one of his dazzling smiles, which were saved for when he knew how good his bakes were and he was somewhat trying to be modest about it. She swatted him, nearly making him drop his brownie.

'Hey,' he said through a laugh.

They ate their brownies in silence, not wanting to distract from the enjoyment and so they could relish every morsel. When Marnie was done, she washed her hands and saw to pouring them each a hot water. Once Antoni returned to the room after delighting in the last bite of his creation, he joined her on the couch and picked up his mug. Antoni had taught her to cleanse her palate with hot water after such treats, so one didn't dilute the flavours on their tongues with coffee.

For a moment Marnie sat watching the birds glide on the summer breeze, her eyes glazing over as the rhythm of their wings calmed her.

'Thank you,' she whispered, then she blinked and turned to face Antoni, pulling one knee to her chest, her cosy cream sweatpants feeling soft against her skin.

'What for?' Antoni asked, quirking his left eyebrow, making the one-centimetre scar above it dance.

Marnie looked away from the scar and into her friend's warm gaze and shrugged casually. 'Thank you for what you said just now. I have to admit, I'm slightly terrified. I can't run away to Canada every time I want an adventure, or every time life gets rough. I can still be the me I found there, the one who holds some confidence in who she is, is at peace with where she is at and who tries new things. At least I hope I can be. Canada may have answered some of my questions, but it doesn't hold all the answers.' She paused thoughtfully. 'I do,' she added, the words not quite coming out as boldly as she would have hoped just yet.

Antoni scooted up on the couch, making the middle sink in, causing Marnie to fall into his side hug. She laughed and wrapped her arms around his waist.

'That's right and next time you do run off, you're taking me with you,' he said dropping a kiss on the top of her head.

'Deal,' she replied.

'I've got to get back to the bakery but make sure you eat tonight and think about what I said about school,' he noted, letting her go and standing up. Marnie flopped on her side when he moved. Antoni laughed. 'I'll let myself out, but don't stay there all afternoon,' he added.

'Don't worry, I won't. The brownies are over there,' Marnie called out waving her hands lazily in the direction of the kitchen, sending Antoni a wink and in return receiving a full swarm of butterflies attacking her stomach thinking about how terribly uncool she probably looked in comparison to Nova. Immediately she jumped up off the couch just as the door closed behind Antoni, and shook her head vigorously causing her bobble to loosen and her hair to tumble in front of her face. She would most definitely not be spending the afternoon crushing on someone she had no business crushing on.

From her position standing in the middle of her small living room, Marnie harrumphed at the empty spaces on the mantel and the walls. She was a picture person. She loved capturing memories, scenic views, moments in time where something looked so peaceful and stunning that she wanted to remember it forever. Then she would dot them around her little apartment, occasionally making her own frames or sprucing up the ones she found in the shops. Antoni had done a great job of whizzing around and taking down any that had her ex in them while she'd been away, with Jovi's help. Together they had safely stored trinkets and pictures in a box that was now under Marnie's bed.

It was a strange feeling having all her memories confined to a box, memories of a person she had known and loved for ten years were now nothing more than a blip in time. But ten years didn't feel like a blip. Ten years was a long time. It was easy to dislike Josh now, now that he had become a whole new human, but what did she do with the human that he had been for ten years? Sure, he had flaws, just like she did, but they'd had good times too. Marnie pursed her lips and narrowed her eyes, feeling at a crossroads between looking back on all that she'd had and forward to visions of Nova and the hopeful feelings the woman had given her. Could she really start again? Could she give her love to another person?

Deciding not to dwell on those thoughts, Marnie crossed the room and pulled out her metallic silver laptop from her backpack. She then placed another brownie on her plate and returned to the couch. Taking small bites as she waited for her laptop to load she encouraged her brain from wandering to anything but the present and the delicious flavours satisfying her tongue.

Half an hour later, Marnie was rummaging through the trinket box to reclaim those frames that she didn't wish to part with or keep in the dark. She avoided looking at the pictures in them for too long but when she did catch a glimpse, she felt a mixture of fear and excitement when she didn't quite recognise the woman in the photos. A tiny shiver ran through her veins as she spun the bangles around on her wrist to calm her anxious mind. Grabbing the frames she had made with Sienna, which she had painted purple and then covered in planet and twinkling star stickers, and a larger frame that they had hot-glued beads and gems to, she hastily pulled out the pictures of her and Josh and stuffed those back into the box and then shoved it back under the bed. She had new pictures to fill the frames with and it was that thought that motivated her to jump into the shower and make quick work of freshening up.

Still very much in comfort mode, Marnie threw on her brown linen trousers, simple white flip-flops and a white tee and teased her hair into more of a stylish messy bun than a bird's nest. She then paused in her haste to keep her momentum going, just to add some fresh water to the lemon-coloured freesias she had picked up the other day, before exiting her apartment.

The world around her felt very much in half-term mode. She knew not all people had the same hours as teachers and didn't get the luxury of a five-week summer holiday, yet there was a calmness to the atmosphere. Fewer cars drove up and down the streets, children laughed as they chased each other around the park. Marnie could see the climbing frame and crowds of people through the narrow alley next to Blooming Brilliant, where parents were stood enjoying coffees and catch-ups as they pushed their kids on the swings. That sudden feeling of emptiness threatened to squash her newly energised mood and so she snapped her head away from the park and breathed in the overall relaxed vibe that pulsated around her as she passed Jillian at the flower shop and headed to the bespoke craft store at the end of the street.

The bell tinkled as she pushed open the pale pink door where she was then greeted with the aromatic sweet scent of marzipan.

'What are you making?' she shouted into the shop, knowing full well that Cameron would be hunched over her workshop-style bench at the back when she didn't see her behind the register. The register stood to the left of the door and was atop a gorgeous wooden counter that was simple in structure, just a plank of wood across two thick log frames. Cameron had left the logs natural so you could see every knot and line in the bark, but she had painted the plank a pearly white. It was beautiful, as was the rest of the shop. The theme of pearlescent white mixed with the natural furnishings ran throughout the small quarters, with pops of colour jumping off the shelves in different craft forms. There was a section for crocheting and so the vibrant colours of the wool added warmth while the shelf of sprinkles and cake decorations added sparkle and glam.

Marnie walked past the shelf of stickers and scrapbooking materials, making a mental note to purchase the holographic rocket stickers she saw in her periphery as she did so, and ducked behind it to find Cameron gently spinning a cake plate as she airbrushed golden glitter over two marzipan numbers. When she saw Marnie, she waved her index finger in the air, signalling for her to give her one minute. Marnie stepped back recognising Cameron's concentration face from school and from the many times they had crafted together over the years. Her shoulders relaxed as the sugary smell of the cake wafted around the room with every spin and Cameron's hypnotic grey eyes danced around her project, cheeks puffed out and lips pouting.

It was difficult to take her eyes off Cameron. She had light ginger hair, a smattering of freckles and though she hardly ever wore make-up, her lips were always a natural bright pink shade. Today she wore battered white Converse and a long white tee underneath a pale olive green and well-worn overall. When Marnie had first met Cameron back in Year Seven, she had been so in awe of her beauty that Antoni had physically had to close her gaping mouth with his knuckle softly. While she and Jovi were going through their awkward teenage phase, occasionally still dressing the same as they tried to figure out their styles and how to use straighteners, Cameron had been pretty flawless even then. There had been a little sizzle between them, but it had only ever amounted to being good friends, who occasionally teased each other.

Shortly after high school, Cameron met Esme at a scrapbooking event. Marnie thought the world of Esme. She was a photographer, a craftswoman like her and Cameron, and the two of them treated each other like the queens that they were.

Cameron stopped working and was looking at her. 'I'm not for sale,' Cameron said, oozing cheek as she caught Marnie's eye. Marnie rolled hers and chuckled.

'Oh please. I'd have way more fun with the glitter glue,' Marnie teased in return as she walked over to the photo-printing station and placed her backpack on the chair.

'Good to know you've still got that spark in your belly,' Cameron noted with a soft side smirk. She placed a lid over the cake as Marnie turned around to look at her. They could give as good as they got when it came to banter.

'I don't want sparks. Sparks cause fires and fires are dangerous,' Marnie informed Cameron, her own lips curving into a teasing grin over their well-rehearsed conversations. It was hard for anyone to infiltrate the circle that was the three musketeers, but if anyone could do it, it was Cameron. Marnie and she had always been close and when Antoni and Jovi had been away at university it was nice to have another friend to turn to, especially one who owned a craft shop. Cameron had known that she wanted to own her own place, be her own boss, right out of high school. She had started selling bespoke pieces here and there during Year Eleven and had saved a small sum, so her parents had helped her set up 'The Glitter Emporium' around thirteen years ago now and she was still going strong. Antoni and Jovi weren't huge on decorative pieces, neither enjoying fondant work all that much, and so they often worked together – with them making the cake and Cameron doing the more elaborate decorating.

Between that and her many workshops, classes, and all-round ability to make anything, it was no surprise her shop was doing well. It was a beloved staple in Orion.

'So, have you come to tell me of your whirlwind Canadian romance with a ridiculously gorgeous female hockey player?' Cameron asked playfully, swivelling her chair from side to side. Marnie choked on air and held her stomach as she laughed. Somehow Cameron made her feel less terrified when talking about relationships, though she couldn't help the nerves that rapidly filled her stomach as visions of Nova danced in her head, but she remained tight-lipped. It felt like Nova had been an apparition, a blonde vision in a baseball cap or a tall, blue-eyed spirit guide sent to encourage her to live in the moment and enjoy her vacation and that's exactly what Marnie had done. Nova was neither a whirlwind romance or a potential relationship option.

Cameron winked in response as Marnie pulled out her memory stick from her bag, grateful that she had managed to sneak her whizzing thoughts past Cameron and play it cool.

'No such luck. I've come to print off pictures of gorgeous grizzly bears and beautiful scenery. I'm doing a bit of redecorating,' Marnie replied, as the machine loaded her pictures and images of starry nights filled the screen. Her stomach jolted as she was immediately transported back to the Bella Coola Valley with its breath-taking mountains and sapphire creeks.

Cameron snuck up behind her and gasped. 'Wow. Esme would love these.'

Marnie flushed. She was no photographer but as she scrolled through each picture, she couldn't help feeling proud of her shots while also being totally flabbergasted that they weren't stock photos and she had actually been in Canada to take them.

'Way better than some romantic fling, ay?' she said, nudging Cameron in her side. Her voice may have sounded playful, but Marnie 100 per cent had to believe what she'd said or she would drive herself crazy. Romance was not on her agenda, especially not with someone whom she'd had no contact with and whom she had spent one day with five months ago.

'Have you been out much since you got back?' Cameron then asked, moving her eyes back to her work as the printer kicked in, drowning out Marnie's thoughts. Marnie blinked away the stream of colour flooding the white photo paper.

'Only to the bakery, and I popped into see Jillian. How's the summer been? How's Esme?' Marnie replied, taking to the stool by the printer and looking over at her friend.

'So you've not seen anyone?' Cameron asked bypassing Marnie's questions, which Marnie thought odd – she loved talking about Esme.

'Not really and I can't say that's a bad thing,' Marnie answered with a chuckle. She wasn't sure if she was quite ready to face the townsfolk. Josh and her breaking up had been quite the BBC drama. It had shaken the town, then as the news had begun to spread about Marnie's mum and dad's separation, Marnie had felt like her family were cursed in the love department – well, except for Jovi.

'So, have Jovi and Ant got you up to speed on the last six months?' Cameron further questioned, still not meeting Marnie's gaze. Marnie straightened her back on the stool.

'Nothing out of the ordinary, just Mrs Higgins up to her usual antics, the bakery's doing well and Sienna's now six – can you believe that?' Marnie said her mind wandering to her beautiful niece and how much she had grown in six months. Her heartstrings strummed. Suddenly, Marnie's heart began picking up speed. 'Is there something they haven't told me? Oh my God, are you engaged? You did it when I wasn't here! Cam, tell me everything?' she yelled jumping off her stool and punching her friend in the bicep.

Luckily, Cameron wasn't decorating at that exact moment. Marnie stared at her, her eyes wide with anticipation for her friend's news. But Cameron simply gave a nervous laugh.

'No, no surprise engagement Marn. I could never do that to you.' Cameron gave her a toothless grin.

Marnie's shoulders sagged, though part of her felt grateful that she hadn't missed that important moment in Cameron's life. She returned to the stool, taking a quick glance at the computer screen to see how many pictures there were left to print, when Cameron turned to face her. 'You're good though, Marn? You're in a good place?' she questioned, suddenly solemn.

However, Marnie's attention was otherwise occupied when a particularly stunning shot of the Vancouver skyline at sunset shot out of the printer, making her lips curve up into an effulgent smile. 'Yeah, I'm good thanks, Cam,' she said slightly dazed as the photograph captivated her. 'Though I'm more than ready to be your maid of honour. Hurry up already,' she added, teasing her friend again, but registering Cameron's not so bright features she said, 'Are you OK, Cam?'

'Yes, yes I'm grand,' Cameron said without skipping a beat. 'Now show me these pictures and let's gather the ones that will make Esme jealous,' she said, making Marnie laugh and feel a flutter of pride at the same time.

7

Stepping back towards the dining table with her hands on her hips, Marnie surveyed her work. She had spent Tuesday morning so far decluttering her bookshelf, getting rid of bits and pieces that she had grown out of, things that reminded her of the last ten years, and adding a fresh touch of paint to her walls in a wave-like pattern either side of the light wooden structure. The bottom half of her living room walls were white with a pale turquoise on top. The swirl of peach gave it new life and made her cheeks dimple with a smile, as did the frames that now held the most stunning pictures of Vancouver skies and lush green mountains. The summer sun meant that her windows were wide open and the flowers she had bought over the weekend from Jillian were still working their magic in the air. Tidying away the paint supplies, Marnie assessed the cushions on the couch, and decided that they needed re-covering. There was a reason the peach, pale blue and lilac fabric had been calling her name at The Glitter Emporium yesterday.

She rummaged through the pile she had made by the fireplace of yesterday's purchases. She liked to place everything out where she could admire it when she had been to visit Cameron – glitter sparkled cheerfully, paint pots made her heart happy and the bag of colourful pom-poms made her feel like anything was possible. Keys jangled in the lock. For a moment, her body tensed wondering who it could be, then she heard giddy voices on the other side of the door and remembered there were only two people with a key to her apartment.

'Auntie Marnie,' Sienna shouted enthusiastically as she burst through the door first, Jovi following with her hands full of turquoise boxes carefully balanced as she closed the door behind her with her toes. Marnie jumped up and matched Sienna's small skips until the little girl was in her arms, both giving the other a massive hug.

'Hello, my little space mascot,' Marnie said, squeezing her niece tight and twirling her around. She had certainly missed these hugs while travelling. Sienna squealed and immediately sat by Marnie's pile of craft supplies when Marnie returned her feet to the floor.

'That's a pretty colour. I love it,' Sienna said, pointing at the paint pot and then at the wall.

'I would have to agree,' Jovi concurred from the kitchen where she was collecting plates and setting the table. 'Have you taken your shoes off, Little Miss Rocketeer?'

Sienna met Marnie's gaze with a finger on her lips as she quickly whipped off her galaxy-patterned pumps. Marnie chuckled and sat down next to her. 'Of course she has,' she shouted back to her sister, giving Sienna a wink. 'You know, I don't think I emptied the bag. Why don't you check inside and help me unpack the rest?' She delighted in Sienna's face lighting up with curiosity. The bag rustled as her niece found the space stickers, Styrofoam spheres and small pots of paint that Marnie hadn't been able to resist yesterday.

'I thought we could make a solar system,' she told Sienna, clapping her hands together, excited at the thought. The little girl's face scrunched up. She glanced over at her mum, her eyes shuffling a little anxiously, her chin tucked into her chest. Marnie followed her gaze to Jovi who was smiling and nodding at her daughter encouragingly, but Marnie didn't miss how wide her eyes became and how tight her lips where.

'Yes, we can. That will be fun. I know how to do it,' Sienna said slightly hesitantly at first but then her tone changed to that of excitement, before she threw her arms around Marnie's neck. As Marnie squeezed her back and played with a strand of her curly, dark, fluffy hair, her mind clicked, and she couldn't help a small laugh. The pang of sadness that had hit her in the chest over missing out disappeared. Of course Sienna would have already made a solar system with Jovi and Jackson. She'd been away for six months, Jovi and Jackson were amazing parents and if Sienna liked something, they encouraged it and supported their little girl. But there was no rule book to say that Sienna couldn't have two solar systems. It wasn't a competition or anything, but Marnie had an inkling that she would have the edge over Jovi's design and in Sienna's starry eyes it would be a no-brainer as to whose was the best if theirs was covered in galaxy glitter.

'I bet your mum didn't let you use glitter though,' Marnie said, wiggling her eyebrows at Sienna who was now no longer pretending to be enthusiastic but beaming with genuine joy.

'What's that?' Jovi called out, but now it was Marnie who was in on a secret and both she and Sienna giggled with their fingers on their lips.

'Lunch is ready you two,' Jovi said, standing behind the couch, her hand resting on the cushions as she eyed Marnie suspiciously. Sienna got up and ran to the table as Marnie walked slowly past her sister. 'You can try and win with glitter but just so you know, we used neon glow-in-the-dark paint,' Jovi whispered, shoving Marnie in the shoulder before striding back over to the dining table and helping her daughter cut up a vegetable pastie.

'Darn it,' Marnie said, smirking at her sister and rolling her eyes. Her tongue went to her cheek and her brain began whizzing through ideas of how she could make her and Sienna's solar system even more epic. Neon paint was impressive, but crafting was her department – she wouldn't be outdone. The homemade vegetable pastie and cheese and onion pie spread that covered her small dining table was Jovi's area of expertise. The warm, comforting aroma that rose from the table along with Sienna's satisfying grunts were proof of that. Marnie smiled listening to the noises her little niece was emitting to let her mum know that she was enjoying what she had made, and her heart leapt. She wanted Sienna to react like that when they made their solar system.

'Are you going to work at my school?' Sienna asked, crumbs falling from her lips as Jovi picked her up and put her on her knee so that Marnie could take the other chair. It wasn't often that Marnie had the whole family round. Whenever they had family get-togethers over the last ten years it was always at Jovi and Jackson's house, Jackson's parents, or the girls' parents' house. Marnie and Josh had been saving for a house – at least that had been what Marnie thought. Any time the topic came up it would be swept under the rug rather quickly. Marnie couldn't argue that the apartment was convenient and more than enough for two people. It was close to schools, in walking distance from everyone she loved and the shops that she frequented, and she did love its cosiness, but it had been her dream to move somewhere and build a home suitable for kids with Josh, a dream that never materialised for them.

'I would have to apply for the job and go to an interview first and see if they liked me,' Marnie explained, not wanting to get Sienna's hopes up or lie to her. She was old enough to understand that. Jovi popped a bite of pie in her mouth, not saying a word. It crossed Marnie's mind that her sister might have encouraged her daughter to sweetly remind Marnie that school started on Thursday and there was a job vacancy, to save her the trouble of nagging. By the innocent look on Jovi's face and lack of eye contact, this was most definitely the case.

'Everyone likes you, Auntie Marnie. You're the awesomest,' Sienna replied, her large brown eyes piercing Marnie's like she had magical powers that could manipulate minds in the sweetest and most innocent of ways. Marnie wavered and cursed her sister for having an advantage in a ridiculously cute daughter who could now do her 'I'm your twin sister and I know what's good for you' bidding for her. Marnie could hardly argue with a six-year-old, nor did she want to in that moment as she appreciated the confidence boost. Her awesomeness wasn't something she allowed herself to own or truly believe, no matter how many times Sienna, Antoni, Jackson or Jovi had tried to remind her of it over the last seven months. She chewed thoughtfully on a piece of cheese and onion pie, the cheese melting on her tongue, the buttery pastry flaking in her mouth. She glanced behind her at the new peach wave on her wall and the frames that she had made with Sienna that now held pictures of promise and adventure and what she was capable of on her own.

'You know, you're my favourite niece,' Marnie said, tapping Sienna's nose.

Sienna scrunched her face up and laughed. 'You only have me.' She leant forward as though she was telling a secret. Jovi held on tighter around her little waist, so she didn't slide off her knee while Marnie copied the little girl, so their noses were nearly touching. 'I'm the only one.'

'And I love you with all the stars in the galaxy,' Marnie whispered, trying not to choke on a lump that was forming in her throat. Her niece's unconditional love could overwhelm her sometimes and her mind drifted to thoughts of being a mother and what that love must feel like for Jovi.

'Have you had enough, sweetheart?' Jovi asked her daughter, bouncing her a little on her knee, while she was still small enough to do so.

'Yes, thank you,' Sienna replied politely. Marnie sat back in her chair and admired her sister for a moment as she stroked the beads on her bracelets. From the minute they were born they had shared that undeniable twin bond. It didn't happen for all twins but for them there was an instant twin spark that grew brighter and brighter the older they got. Of course, their relationship wasn't without its complications and troubles, which are only natural when you spend 95 per cent of your time with a person, share the same face and are often being compared by others, and on dreaded days by yourself. 'Who's the evil one?' 'Who's smarter?' 'Did you not want kids at the same time?'

But there was no one Marnie loved more on the planet. She had thought watching Jovi cook over the years and live out her passion was one of her greatest joys but seeing her be the best mum to Sienna had completely surpassed and overpowered that joy, transforming it into something unbelievably extraordinary.

'I swear I didn't put her up to that,' Jovi noted when Sienna was happily settled by the fireplace, moving the sheet of rocket stickers around the air so the holographs caught the light. Then Jovi finally saw to eating some lunch herself, taking a few bites of Sienna's leftovers, before cutting into another pie.

Marnie ripped into a veggie pasty, the crispy flakes getting stuck to her fingers, steam and tasty vegetable goodness bursting through the hole she had created. She licked her fingers. 'I guess I should take it as a sign then,' she said with a casual shrug. Nerves still jolted around in her gut at the thought of going back to a school. The stares she had put up with at her old school during her last week had been enough to distort her friendly, happy school image, but it was the children, like Sienna, who helped restore her pixelated vision. She knew Jovi and Antoni were right: she had to at least apply for the job. It would be a new environment, different kids, and a host of possible budding friends in the staff. Jobs were few and far between in such a small town, so unless she wanted to sell her apartment and move in with Jovi and Jackson, she didn't have much choice.

When Jovi and Sienna left just after one, Marnie had stepped out of her paint-splattered overalls and into her white linen trousers, which she paired with a relaxed olive tee. Her hair was now loose and wavy, her middle parting crisp and smart, and she was standing outside Apollo Primary turning over her CV in her hands. The flame-orange sun was nestled high above the building, directing light upon it like it was a saviour, a beacon of hope for Marnie. There were a few cars parked outside, which gave her pulse the go-ahead to speed up, disobeying her brain's signals to stay calm. She knew one or two of the teachers from this place with the town not being huge, but this had been the rival primary school growing up and so Marnie felt the beads of sweat form as if she were walking into the home of the foe.

Gently, she pushed open the iron gate, only to find that of course it wouldn't budge. There may not be children in on an inset day, but safety was safety and routine was routine. She looked around, gripping onto the pale-yellow straps of her backpack, until she spotted the buzzer.

Her nerves made her index finger tremble. She hated these intercom-style communicators; they always made her overthink her words. A few seconds after she had pressed it, a friendly voice came through.

'Hello, Apollo Primary School. How can I help you?' the voice said.

Marnie placed her finger on the button once more, her shoulders relaxing ever so slightly.

'Hi, I'm Marnie Barnes, Sienna's auntie. My sister said

you have a job vacancy.' There was probably more than one Sienna in the school. Marnie squinted her eyes as the sun glared off the silver metal box and she shook her head at her own silliness. She heard static from the other side and hastily pressed the button again. 'Sorry, Sienna Reynolds, her mum's my twin sister.' Did she just cut the person off? Had they been about to speak? Suddenly, there was a click from over by the lock and when she released her finger from the silver button, it crackled with the end of a sentence: '...come through.' Marnie rushed, not wanting to miss her chance.

Right, now she had gotten past that part, she needed to calm down. She was much better at face-to-face interactions where she could see the expressions on a person's face and where they could see her arm movements and her own nuances, which could be lively when she was passionate. She didn't always feel they translated over the phone and it often made her anxious.

Marnie crossed the small concrete drop-off bay and was greeted at the door by a young man in blue jeans and a relaxed sports jacket. He had to be younger than her, for his face was fresh and the only crinkles were around his mouth where he was smiling warmly at her.

'Hi, Miss Barnes, it's lovely to meet you,' he said, sticking out his hand, which Marnie shook. He was the voice from the intercom. 'There's only a few of us in today but you're in luck as Mrs Thomas is in and said she would be happy to meet with you, so if you'll just follow me...' His sprightly, cheerful manner instantly put Marnie at ease.

'Thank you. Can I ask your name?' she said to the back of his head as she followed him through the reception area into a small corridor with doors either side, one with a plaque saying *Head Teacher*, the other *Reception*. It was a brightly lit area, all light oak wood, and pale grey flooring. Children's work was displayed on two colourful boards in between the doors and one above the photocopying area and Marnie found herself smiling as her eyes wandered over the summer artwork made from all sorts of materials from sticks, vibrant green leaves, orange tissue paper, gold glitter and sky-blue paint.

'Oh, so sorry, getting back into the swing of it an all and it's only my third term. I'm Connor, or Mr Lasek. My niece goes to Cornelia and she always spoke highly of you, Miss Barnes,' Connor said, turning around to face her, gesturing for her to take a seat on one of the two chairs outside the head teacher's office. His face had turned a light shade of pink that made Marnie flush in response. She was certainly no one to get flustered over but Connor was looking at her like she was some sort of celebrity. At least his words had been positive, she acknowledged, as she took a seat and gave him a smile.

'And just for the record, Miss Barnes, I don't believe the rumours. You look far too classy for a stock cupboard,' he added, sending a cold sweat over Marnie's forehead and chest but before she could question what on earth he was talking about, the head teacher's door opened.

'Thank you, Connor,' a tall lady said, waving him away with a smile. She was wearing jeans and a beige sweat-shirt, with her greying brown hair tied back in a low bun and purple glasses perching on the tip of her nose. Marnie had forgotten how to breathe and prayed the head teacher hadn't heard that. What had Connor meant by a stock cupboard? She held on to her backpack tighter and stood on shaky legs.

'Hello, Mrs Thomas, I hope you don't mind me calling by. Jovi mentioned you needed one-on-one support and with time being sensitive I thought it best to pop in and introduce myself,' Marnie managed, determined to forget Connor's comment, and not fluff up this opportunity. Now that she was inside the school and had locked eyes on the children's work, she knew this was where she fit. This was the job she was supposed to do and as she couldn't go back to the other primary school in the area, this first impression mattered one heck of a lot.

'Afternoon, Miss Barnes, please come in,' Mrs Thomas said. Her face was friendly, and her brown eyes were kind. Her soft wrinkles became more prominent when she studied Marnie's features. There was no denying the subtle reading of Marnie's character. Marnie tried to steady her hands to stop them fiddling with her bracelets.

Inside, Mrs Thomas' office was further adorned with pictures and letters from the children, which once again calmed Marnie's anxious stomach. A beautiful cuddly tiger, crisp white polar bear and shiny brown rabbit decorated the top of a shelving unit and a large desk bore a computer and plenty of paperwork. The space was inviting. Marnie liked it. After taking it all in, she sat in the chair opposite and handed over her CV. Mrs Thomas caught her wandering eye, again with a suspicious one of her own. Then she offered a smile and jumped straight into the questions that Marnie still remembered answering at Cornelia some ten years earlier.

Why Apollo Primary? What could she tell Mrs Thomas

about British Values, her own ethos? Who would she report to in case of an accident? How would she handle a child being bullied? After ten years working with children Marnie occasionally stammered, worrying a little if she was veering off the professional path. Having had to adapt many rules and guidelines at times to be sure she treated all children as individuals over the years – some rules or guides that worked for one, simply did not work for others – she prided herself on remembering and acting on that.

Mrs Thomas, though kind in her manner and tone, was not giving anything away in her facial expressions. She sat, back straight, in her chair. No more than ten minutes had gone by before Marnie saw her shoulders relax and she leaned forward across her desk.

'Miss Barnes, you would be working with a child in Year Four who requires help with her work and going about the daily school routine. We have been having a few problems with her not doing as she's told resulting in anger issues. She can become obsessed with things, which needs monitoring and guiding in order to open her up to the world. Is this something you think you can handle?'

Marnie's fingers found her bangles as her back stiffened. She couldn't say she liked Mrs Thomas' turn of phrase, not believing that 'handle' was the right term to use when talking about a child, but she had never met the child before so maybe in this instance it was appropriate. She happened to love when children were passionate about something. It was all part of them figuring out who they were and it was something she did herself. Her brain ticked over with how best to answer.

'I believe there must be a reason for her anger and yes,

I feel that I can create a stimulating environment and one that she would then be able to thrive in,' Marnie said, confidently. She didn't wish to demean what the school was doing now, but a little something deep in her gut told her that they weren't quite going about it the right way. Mrs Thomas' jaw gave a slight twitch.

'Right, Miss Barnes, thank you for coming in today. Though it is short notice, I still must run everything past the governors and therefore I will give you a call tomorrow. I do hope that is OK?' Mrs Thomas said, shuffling a few papers around on her desk. Marnie couldn't tell if the interview had gone well or not and found herself doubting Jovi and Antoni's positive pep talk from the other day. Mrs Thomas certainly wasn't grovelling at her feet throwing the job in the palm of her hand and begging for her to take it, which was unfortunate. Now that she had made the brave move of stepping foot in a school again, she was feeling confident that it was where she belonged. She had been satisfied with her own answers considering it had been a long time since she had been in an interview and despite the bills that needed paying, a want had settled into her mind. The place was colourful, bright, and fresh for the fresh start she needed, and she liked Mrs Thomas enough, thus far.

'That's great and thank you for seeing me. I do appreciate it,' Marnie said as she stood up. Mrs Thomas' eyes locked with hers for a few moments, then the head teacher squinted and laced her hands together, leaning forward on her desk, with a tiny sigh.

'Miss Barnes, I do have to mention that here at Apollo Primary we don't encourage staff dating. In fact, we would much prefer they didn't. That extends to parents and any outside agencies that work with the school.' Marnie froze as she went to step towards the door. Her stomach gave a nasty lurch and any confidence she'd had for getting the job vanished as quick as the air that had just gotten knocked out of her. Connor had said earlier that he didn't believe the rumours and now she was getting a lecture on dating etiquette, but Josh had been the one to break up with her and then fire her, she hadn't been the one to cause a scene. What was happening?

Marnie could feel the corners of her eyes sting as they held tightly onto the water that she would not allow them to release. Her mind flashed back to her days wandering the streets of Nelson, in all her anonymity, the sky above her a happy blue, sailboats bobbing along the Kootenay Lake, with no one around to judge her or make accusations other than, 'You're not from around here?'

But she couldn't spend her whole life running and certainly not because of a man. Besides, whatever these rumours were, she knew the truth and that's what mattered most. Wasn't it? But what if they meant she wouldn't get the job? She felt the soft curve of her silver bangle and forced a smile.

'Of course,' she said with a nod as if she knew what was going on. Mrs Thomas' comment hadn't been snarky but simply matter-of-fact, like a rule you tell a child who has just been punished and you're allowing them to play again, under certain circumstances. But as Marnie walked home, she couldn't deny the feeling of dread in her gut. She loved it in Orion. She'd always been the good kid, along with Antoni and Jovi. There was not a whole lot of trouble two wannabe chefs and a budding artist could get into bar setting the house on fire when experimenting with crème brûlées or cutting a finger when sneaking a turn with dad's saw when he wasn't in his shed.

Everyone knew everyone, which had never been a problem except of course, when your twin sister is getting married and having a baby and everyone wants to ask when it will be your turn. However, those were the things Marnie could handle, especially since she always had Antoni by her side to crack a joke or Josh to nod charmingly and say 'oh in due time'. At least then the town was on her side wanting good things to happen to her. Now, it felt like she was the bad kid and considering she had done nothing wrong, it hurt.

Checking her watch, Marnie realised she hadn't been at school too long. The sun was still high in the cloudless sky and she could hear the children playing in the park. She avoided that way home, choosing to wander through the narrow streets, bypassing the main road and the bakery and steering clear of Cameron and Jillian. She needed a moment to collect her thoughts. She'd never been much of a reflecting type. There were always people around her. Life was busy and sometimes chaotic. Her days were spent with kids, which meant no time to her own thoughts. Between Jovi, Antoni, her parents and Josh, evenings were wonderful and by the time she laid her head on her pillow at night, her brain would be too exhausted to think.

Her sabbatical had given her peace and a place in her mind to escape to when things became overwhelming. However, when surrounded by the familiar faces, cobbled streets, and occasional claustrophobic houses of her hometown and not the vast, epic scenery, snow-capped mountains and waterfalls of the British Columbia, it was proving a tad difficult to escape to that calm nook she had carved out in her mind.

Unlocking her apartment door after climbing the short flight of stairs, Marnie breathed in the smell of fresh freesias mixed with drying paint, her shoulders easing some of their tension. When you're younger people always tell you not to care what other people think. For Marnie that had always been a battle. Some days it was as easy as pie. She had Jovi and Jovi's opinion was the only one that mattered, plus, having Jovi meant always having someone by your side who had your back and would stand up for you no matter what. With them against the world, Marnie felt safe, secure, and understood. Occasionally though, a monster would rear its head on the other side of the battlefield. People's words could seep into their contented bubble. 'Who's the good one? Do you fancy the same boys? What do you think of Jovi getting married? Wouldn't it have been nice if they had a joint wedding and got pregnant at the same time?'

What people thought swam around in a loop in Marnie's head, a loop that she couldn't switch off. There were times when she wanted to scream, 'Why does there have to be a good one and a bad one? I like girls too. I think it's wonderful Jovi's getting married – that's a stupid question, she's my sister. I'm happy for her. Sure a joint wedding would be great, but I haven't been asked and my partner doesn't want kids yet.'

Before when these thoughts arose, she would suppress them. She knew she had people who loved all of her and that most of the questioning was innocence and intrigue about the life of twins. After all, they were the only twins in the town. But Connor and Mrs Thomas had thrown her off with talk of stockrooms and unprofessionalism. When she found out that Josh was cheating, she had thought she'd remained calm. She didn't shout or scream or throw his things through the window and onto the streets. She had stayed indoors, hadn't spoken to anyone but Antoni and Jovi.

Then she had given him space to clear out his things by flying halfway across the world. She hadn't aired his dirty laundry on social media or put posters up around town that he was a cheat, so why did it suddenly feel like she was the bad guy? Whatever rumours Connor and Mrs Thomas had heard, was she strong enough to ignore them?

8

Marnie swung her backpack off one shoulder and pinched the zip with her index finger and thumb. Then she paused, shaking her head.

'I'm sure they'll call, pet. It's not even lunchtime yet,' her dad said reassuringly. It was ten-thirty Wednesday morning. Marnie had been up in the early hours doing a touch of feng shui in her apartment and looking up jobs online. The job hunt had only lasted ten minutes before her stomach felt uneasy and her self-worth dipped, and she gave up. Sure, she knew her way around social media for the most part – she could tweet and post a picture – but she couldn't keep up with the younger generation in the technology department. She had panicked and applied for two start-ups that were two towns over and would mean an hour commute on buses each morning and sitting behind a desk, and another job at one of the retail giants in Manchester city centre that would take her almost two hours to get to and where she would have to provide customer service. None of her local shops were hiring, so she had been checking her phone nervously every few seconds since she had rolled out of bed, already frazzled from her lack of a decent night's sleep, for Mrs Thomas to ring.

Taking her dad's advice, she gave her shoulders a jig, shuffling her strap back onto her shoulder and resisting the urge to check for missed calls or messages for the millionth time.

'Sorry. Thanks, Dad. So, do you like it round here?' she asked, blinking away her foggy thoughts and actually looking up to take in her surroundings. The neighbouring town of Gemini was more rural, dainty and serene than her hometown. The houses were further apart. They were handy to two corner shops, a coffee shop, a giant park and their pride and joy, the Museum Borealis. It was thanks to the museum and of course the names of the towns, that people often referred to Orion and Gemini as Starcross Valley. It had taken Marnie thirty minutes on the bus and then a half-mile walk over a large hill to get to her dad's new place.

'It's great, Marn. I like the space and it suits me not having neighbours on top of me. I can work into the night or start in the early hours without complaint that my drill's too loud and menacing,' he answered with a satisfied shrug and pleased smirk. His short-cropped greying hair, strong jawline, emerald green eyes and slim jeans and slim-fit tee made him look every bit a young fifty-nine despite being sixty-five. His strong forearms, with their fading tattoos, and his calloused hands gave hint to his age just a touch. For the longest time, Marnie couldn't understand how her mum could find fault in him or dislike anything about him. It made her angry and frustrated that she would argue with her kind, caring dad who could build, fix and make anything. So angry that a mere four days ago she had been nearly five thousand miles away from the confusion and heartbreak.

However, while she'd been in Canada, she'd had time to reflect, to weigh up the pros and cons. Since getting back and seeing her mum with Tim and talking to her dad now, she could see how happy they both were. Two good people did not a successful relationship make. In some cases, opposites attracting made for an exciting partnership, but in her parents' case, it simply did not. Their lack of shared interests, after the girls had left the nest, had sent them in two directions. Marnie had always been a fan of one direction. Having an underlying mismatched common ground and outlook had in the end not boded well for her either.

'That's good, Dad,' she replied, staring across the green fields at a horse that was grazing. Its silky brown coat glistened in the sunlight. 'Do you get lonely?' The words found their way to her lips before she had chance to overthink them or feel embarrassed by them.

'I suppose everyone feels lonely sometimes, pet,' her dad replied after a moment's hesitation. He squinted, following her gaze across the fields. 'But people in relationships feel lonely too you know. Things are good. I've still got my family and friends – it's not like I've been banished to Mordor to spend eternity on my own.' He chuckled, nudging her with his elbow. 'Besides, lonely is a state of mind. You're pretty awesome to hang out with, you should try and enjoy you more,' he added.

Marnie cast him a side glance and gave him a sweet one-sided grin, his words resonating with her. While she had made friends on her travels, she had enjoyed time on her own. There had been the odd, lonely wave but that had quickly dissipated when she stopped her brain wandering to negative territory and took in the world around her.

'Ten years is a long time to be with someone, I know, but instead of focusing on what you don't have, focus on what you do have and get excited about what the world is making room for, pet,' her dad said.

'Dad, did you really just get all spiritual on me?' Marnie asked, chuckling herself now as they walked through the park past the families enjoying picnics on the grass – some kids still zooming around on their bikes ignoring their parents pleas to come eat, clinging onto the freedom of the last day of their summer holidays.

'What? Your mum likes to plan and she's good at it, but sometimes *che sera sera*.' He beamed.

'You're like a new man,' Marnie said, shaking her head with suppressed laughter. She couldn't quite believe how calm both her parents had been since she got back. They were practically glowing. As they reached the line for the coffee shop window, where they had planned to get a takeout cup and keep walking, her chest began to spasm. 'The plans never seem to work out for me either, Dad,' she mumbled. She and Jovi had had the same general goals growing up: work a job they loved, get married, buy a house, a car, have kids, but somehow only Jovi had accomplished the entire checklist, leaving her behind. Her job had brought her such comfort and so had her ex. Josh being by her side at least filled her with hope that everything else on the list was possible. Two green ticks she could look down at with pride, but now she didn't know if she would have that job security again and her hope in the love and kids department was dwindling.

'Marn, don't do that. You are two different people. What's right for one person might not be right for another. It's easy to look at other people and want what they have but you forget to look back on their journey, what it took them to get there. Jovi and Jackson went through their struggles to get Sienna. They had their share of heartache and derailed plans – just different to yours, OK? The pain sucks, and I know it might sound a touch wishy-washy coming from your old man but this, this is a clean slate, a fresh start. I wouldn't say I'm a new man. I'm still me except with a new outlook, a new chance at life,' her dad told her, placing a hand on her shoulder while they waited. Marnie often thought by not expressing her emotions with words she was quite nifty at hiding them but it seemed her family had grown used to reading her face. The smell of coffee grounds soothed Marnie's erratic nerves that were making it hard for her to accept what her dad was saying and the fact that he had read her mind. She watched the coffee beans bounce and whizz around the grinder as she pondered his words.

'You do know that you travelled across the world without your twin sister, right? That took guts kid,' her dad replied, looking over the menu on the chalkboard propped up against a large flowerpot containing a vibrant green neatly pruned shrub. Marnie's lips twisted into a small smile. She guessed her travels had finally been her rite of passage into adulthood or normal hood or newfound singledom, maybe? She appreciated her dad understanding that even at thirty-five she would not be winning any Miss Independent awards. Not everyone understood how weird it often felt for her, being out and about on her own. To others, a simple trip to Blooming Brilliant to pick up some flowers on their own was considered natural. Shopping independently, walking up and down aisles on their own was regular.

But for Marnie, whenever she was on her own, she would hum to herself, play with her bracelets, occasionally feeling shifty, like she didn't know where to look. The feeling of being on her own could engulf her and she wouldn't know how to act.

Of course, she had gotten used to many independent tasks, but her anxiety always lurked. The first few weeks in Canada had been intense and she had beaten herself up mentally for having been so stupid, fleeing her hometown alone. But she had prevailed and conquered and bumped into Nova as a result of facing her fears. Just the thought of Nova sent a static shock through her fingertips. She squeezed her hands tightly into fists, pressing her nails into her palms until the vision faded.

'You know, there were moments when I was terrified, but you're right, Dad, part of me enjoyed the not knowing, the abandoning my list.' She rested her head briefly on his arm.

'I'm proud of you, Marn,' her dad said, kissing the top of her head just as her phone started ringing from the depths of her backpack. She whipped her head up and swung one strap off her back, diving inside. Her dad waved her away signalling he'd get their order and Marnie walked to a quiet spot on the street under a small conker tree that would be getting ready to blossom soon.

'Hello,' Marnie answered enthusiastically, cupping the phone around her ear to drown out the chatter from the street and the occasional car that drove by.

'Hello, is this Miss Barnes?' the voice asked.

'It is yes,' Marnie replied, a nervous rattle in her voice.

'It's Lesley Thomas from Apollo Primary School. We'd like to thank you for yesterday's slightly unconventional interview,' she began, making Marnie's stomach tighten with nerves. Didn't a thank you only come first if you hadn't got the job? 'And we'd like to offer you the position starting tomorrow.'

Marnie's knees bent as her body flooded with relief. 'Thank you, Lesley, that's wonderful news,' she said, spying her dad looking over at her and sending him a thumbs up. Marnie stayed on the phone a while longer as Mrs Thomas went through tomorrow's requirements – things she needed to bring with her and so forth – and when she hung up Marnie practically skipped over to her dad, feeling over the moon. At least now, bills would be one thing she need not fret over; parents, staff and town gossip would of course still be high on that list. As her dad handed her a frothy cappuccino with a dusting of chocolate, she decided she would think about that tomorrow and for now she could celebrate with her dad in a town that didn't know all her secrets.

The late summer sun was still heating up the evening with its delicious cosy rays when Marnie got off the bus in Orion. The stroll around her dad's new home and an afternoon crafting a mini library box, which the park had commissioned Morgan to make, in his workshop had helped take her mind off the butterflies that strutted cockily in her stomach over the fact that at thirty-five she was starting a new job and her life had changed dramatically over the last couple of months. Her parents were separated, her boyfriend had left her in a telenovela-like fashion, her biological clock was a ticking and she had left her heart in Canada, but she was fine.

The treacly smell of liquid gold maple syrup lingered in the air as Marnie pushed open the door to the bakery. Inside Jovi was serving the last of the day's customers, who were picking up dessert for their evening meal. Many residents of Orion had their traditions when it came to dessert. Jillian at Blooming Brilliant loved picking up chocolate chip cookies for her son, husband, and herself to enjoy after their evening meal. Mrs Higgins always called by on a Wednesday for her small apple pie and on the weekend it was banana loaf. And Cameron and Esme liked a box of chocolate-glazed doughnuts to celebrate getting through a Monday. Marnie herself was fortunate, for she would often receive a mixed box of leftovers, though she was partial to a Bavarian cream doughnut, she wasn't picky when it came to all things sweet.

The inviting and scrumptious smells lent themselves to Marnie's celebratory news, and forgetting the list of somewhat anxiety-inducing huge life changes of recent months, she allowed herself to breathe them in and fill her veins with the heavenly scent of sugar and spice, making her body tingle with excited goose bumps.

'I have news,' Marnie announced, resulting in Antoni bursting through the kitchen doors as if he had radars for ears.

'Good news or bad news?' he asked, taking two strides until he was practically nose to nose with her. Jovi chuckled. Marnie took a small step back and waved her arms out to her sides, enjoying the fact that she was getting to share this happy moment with her two biggest cheerleaders.

'I got the job at Sienna's school,' she revealed, grinning broadly, allowing pride to engulf her for a moment. Getting a new job was a big deal for anyone; she could and should feel proud.

Jovi let out a squeal and ran around the counter while Antoni scooped her up in his arms and spun her round. Marnie let out a laugh. This was a fresh start, a new opportunity and she had done it herself, albeit with a gentle shove from Jovi and Sienna. When Antoni put her feet back on solid ground, Marnie didn't miss the relieved look that he had subtly tried to send Jovi's way. She scrunched up her nose.

'Hey, I thought you guys said I was a shoo-in,' she said when Antoni let go and after Jovi gave her a small squeeze. 'You didn't actually think I was going to get it, did you?' She eyed them dubiously.

'Of course, we did – that's why we're so happy. It's a cause for celebration,' Jovi exclaimed with a beaming smile that Marnie could tell was half-forced. Her skin was slightly pale. Marnie eyed her curiously for a moment.

'Come on, Marn, after everything that's happened, you deserve to celebrate this. We knew you could do it,' Antoni said, backing up Jovi. He then walked around the counter, collected a box and began filling it with the window's leftovers.

'This is exciting. It's a fresh start, Marn, and the kids are going to love you. Wait until I tell Sienna. She'll be on cloud nine,' Jovi said, rubbing Marnie's bicep and then retrieving a custard doughnut from the box that Antoni had only just put in. She held it out for Marnie to take. When she did, Antoni grabbed two more and handed one to Jovi before raising his to theirs in cheers. Marnie hesitated before forcing her shoulders to loosen with a roll. They were right. Getting this new job was a relief, an accomplishment and a new beginning. The last couple of months hadn't only been filled with heartache but adventure, magic and joy. It was time to put the past behind her and celebrate all the wonderful moments and moving forward, but could it really be that simple?

She took a bite of the fluffy cake doughnut and savoured its sweet flavour, licking the dusting of powdered sugar off her lips – not wanting to waste a crumb, but there was still something niggling in the back of her mind.

'The receptionist – Connor, I think he said his name was – said something about me being too classy for a stock cupboard,' she noted, thoughtfully chewing on a bite. 'Do either of you know what that's all about?' She raised an eyebrow.

Jovi didn't miss a beat and started waving her arm frantically. 'Oh God, Marn, probably just some dark receptionist humour or plain nonsense. Ignore it. I know you're nervous about tomorrow, but I promise you it will be great. Don't let anyone's silly jokes get inside your head,' Jovi finished, wiping her fingers on her apron, and bustling back around the counter to finish cleaning.

Marnie paused before taking her last bite. Her sister wasn't telling her something. Marnie knew the signs of Jovi lying to her – not making eye contact, her voice coming out a higher pitch, busy hand movements – but Antoni's cheeks had turned pink and there was a distinct knot between his brows as he looked at Jovi.

'Jovi, you do realise we shared a womb for nine months?' Marnie said, her doughnut still hovering mid-air.

'And?' Jovi tried and failed to close the box of treats, the flaps not aligning with the paper-thin slits down the side. Antoni looked between the two of them, licking his fingers nervously.

'So, our brains were this close...' Marnie demonstrated how close by holding her thumb and index finger mere millimetres apart with her doughnut free hand '...for those nine months. I could practically see the inner workings of your mind. I always know what's going on in there.' She didn't exactly but it was worth a shot. Jovi succeeded in closing the box and then looked up, her identical hazel eyes staring directly into Marnie's.

'Oh yeah, and Ant here says you've been grinning in your sleep and every time you talk about Canada you get this dreamy look on your face that screams more than just enchanting waterfalls and magical mountains, so are you going to tell your favourite wombmate any more about the people, or person, you met in Canada?' Jovi asked with a coy smirk. Touché, Marnie thought, shoving the last piece of her doughnut into her mouth immediately.

'Can we just get back to celebrating me?' she mumbled through her mouthful.

9

Like with any major event in her life that involved Marnie taking the first steps on her own – no Jovi or Antoni by her side – she felt the tornado of nerves swirling around in her gut as she weaved past the cars in the car park and pressed the buzzer on the gate. The sky above Apollo Primary School was a beautiful pastel blue and the sun illuminated the bricks of her fresh start. She dug her nails into her palms to centre herself and thought back to what her dad had told her yesterday: that she was brave, she had guts, she could do this.

Connor buzzed her in and greeted her with the same enthusiastic and cheerful smile from the day prior and then took it upon himself to abandon his post behind the reception desk and walk her to the staffroom, which Marnie quietly appreciated. Upon entering the room there were at least twelve teaching staff already gathered and conversing. Connor's youth and bouncy personality were not to be intimidated and so he announced Marnie's arrival to the fray, which garnered a hand raise and: 'Thank you, Connor. I can see to introducing Miss Barnes,' from Lesley. Not to be fazed, Connor beamed at the room before returning to his office. Marnie wished he could stay; she enjoyed his positive aura and non-judgemental eyes.

Turning back to the room, Marnie gave a tight-lipped grin and nodded, acknowledging the several eyes on her. Her audience was a mix of older teachers – classic suits and ties, pencil skirts and blazers with greying hair, laid-back awaiting the head teacher's instructions; those who looked to be her age sat with their planners on their knees going over the day's curriculum, heads down in their work; and lastly the younger teachers whose fresh faces and bright eyes merrily engaging with each other gave away that their foray into teaching was new. They lacked the bags under their eyes that no matter your love of teaching, no amount of heavy-duty eye cream could make disappear; Marnie had experimented over the years.

Lesley gestured to a comfy-looking brown cushioned chair, which Marnie took, placing her backpack by her ankles. When she sat down and took another look around, she couldn't help her brows from furrowing and had to force her eyes not to squint in confusion. To the left of her, an older man and woman looked to be sitting quite cosily side by side, and if Marnie had heard correctly, they were discussing whose turn it was to make dinner that evening. Across from her a younger lady in a fuchsia floaty dress subtly held hands with a man who looked to be a little older than her, with his black polo shirt and flecks of grey in his hair.

'Morning, Lesley,' Marnie said, clearing her throat and straightening out her fingers. Her palms had started to pulse from where she'd been digging her nails in so tight. She laid her hands over her navy pinstripe trousers and tried to shake off the puzzlement of why Lesley would have warned her about the rule on staff dating when there were clearly staff mixing and mingling.

'Good morning, Marnie, welcome to Apollo Primary. Right, everyone, we'll begin.' The chatter in the room died down while Mrs Thomas welcomed everyone back after the summer holidays. She ran through schedules, ensuring all TAs knew where they had been placed and she explained Marnie would be in Year Four with Paislee and that she wished everyone a wonderful first day back.

As everyone began leaving Lesley stood and greeted Marnie with a more relaxed and encouraging smile before waving over the young lady in the floaty dress. Up close her porcelain skin fit her into Marnie's fresh out of university category.

'Marnie, this is Amber, Miss Olsen. She's the Class Nine teacher you will be working alongside. This is her second year with us. She knows all about Paislee and has spoken with her previous teacher, so follow her lead and have a great first day. Connor will get a copy of the policies to you at some point today and we will go through anything else before you leave,' Lesley informed her.

'Nice to meet you, Amber,' Marnie said smiling. 'And thank you, Lesley, that sounds perfect.' She nodded at Mrs Thomas before the head teacher turned to leave.

'Come on, follow me and I'll show you my classroom. Oh you can pop your bag in one of those lockers on the way out,' Amber said, her tone of voice not quite matching the cheerfulness of her outfit. Marnie picked up her backpack and quickly thrust it into a locker so she could keep up with Miss Olsen. 'You have a twin, right?' Amber asked as they walked along the main hall, through a set of brown double doors and on to a colourful corridor full of eye-catching displays. There were four doors along the right-hand side. Amber headed into the third.

'Yes – Jovi. She has a little girl – Sienna. She's starting Year One today,' Marnie replied, taking in the classroom as she did so. Amber liked her positive affirmation posters, which Marnie thought sweet, but again they didn't quite match her severe tone and expression when asking questions. There was a spot on the wall where a mirror hung with quotes around it, which Marnie thought a wonderful idea. The backing paper was clean and held no work yet, the borders crisp and neat. It was a space Marnie thought she could get used to. She didn't want to judge Amber too quickly by her cold tone.

'I've seen her on the playground at home time. I thought your face looked familiar,' Amber explained firing up her computer and the whiteboard. 'OK, so Paislee will be sitting with Mason. When she's completed her work, she can take breaks, but she's expected to join in with assemblies and follow the rules like everyone else. There are toys, Lego and blocks, in that cupboard over there and you can just keep an eye on her and time her breaks so she knows when it's back to work. If she gets angry, she can sit in the library where we have bean bags and soft toys,' Amber noted. 'Her files are in my stockroom; you can refer to them and have a read when you get time. Any questions?' Marnie's brain tried to process the manner in which Amber was speaking, without much compassion and more matter-of-fact than Marnie would have liked. Marnie cleared the tickle in her throat for the second time already that morning.

'I've read her EHCP – Lesley sent it to me – but it would be great to see her files. You mentioned her getting angry. Is there a reason for that?' Marnie asked, feeling like between Amber and Lesley and Paislee's EHCP, she'd heard and read the words *angry* and *behaviour* a lot but had not heard or read of reasons as to why.

'She's autistic and she has learning delays,' Amber commented with a look that suggested she thought Marnie had two heads. Just before she could try again with her questioning, the bell rang out and Amber pulled up the register before getting out of her seat and walking towards the door. Marnie watched her and though she really did hate to judge there was a coldness to Amber that didn't quite match the bubble-gum exterior. Marnie felt a prickling in her gut that told her that something was off in how people were treating this child.

Where moments ago, the corridors had been as peaceful as a museum, now they hummed with life as every child tried to tell their friends what they had been up to over the summer holidays. They all talked over each other, trying to get a word in edgeways as they stuffed their too large backpacks into their too small lockers. Marnie couldn't help but smile at their excited faces. She placed herself near Paislee's table – Amber had placed name plates on each table so the children knew where they would be sitting in their new classroom – as the children greeted Miss Olsen and then skipped into the room.

'Good morning,' Marnie said enthusiastically to a few confused faces. 'I'm Miss Barnes, it's lovely to meet you all.' Slowly, the uncertainty on their faces was replaced with smiles as they each took their seats. Suddenly, a ball of energy rolled into the classroom and headed her way. Marnie's smile reached her ears.

'Hi, I'm Mason. Are you Sienna's Mum?' Mason asked while taking his seat. Marnie noticed he pulled out Paislee's chair next to him a little, ever so casually.

'Hi, Mason, I'm Miss Barnes. It's nice to meet you and no, Sienna is my niece. Her mum is my twin sister,' she explained, squatting down a little. She'd have to find herself a chair. She didn't think her knees could handle squatting all day and it might intimidate Paislee and Mason if she hovered in a squatting position by their table all day.

'Wow, that's cool. You look just like her. Sienna's nice. Do you like space too?' Mason asked, joy dancing in his eyes. Before she could answer, Amber turned around in the doorframe.

'Everyone should have their reading books out, including you, Mason. I shouldn't hear any talking,' Miss Olsen said, her stern voice silencing any noise. Marnie felt her cheeks burn. Amber hadn't made eye contact but she had just completely belittled Marnie as a colleague. She was having a conversation with a child and had passively been told to stop. She was gobsmacked. As she picked her jaw up off the floor, she noticed a petite girl walking into the room. She had shoulder-length brown hair and bright blue eyes, which were trained on the tables scouring for her name. The little one didn't look up until she made it to her table and sat down.

Marnie stepped back to give her a little space and time to get settled. Paislee gave her a brief glance before her fingers intertwined and she played with the edges of her reading book. Mason looked like he wanted to say something, his eyes side-glancing at Paislee, but he couldn't seem to get the words out. After a few more moments, Marnie bent down.

'Hi, Paislee, I'm Miss Barnes,' Marnie said with a warm smile. 'Space is my favourite and I love dinosaurs too,' she added, recalling Paislee's 'All about me' sheet. At this Paislee met Marnie's gaze and her eyes lit up.

'Class Nine, that will be enough chatter, thank you.' Miss Olsen's voice made both Paislee and Marnie jump. It was only ten past nine and Amber had already raised her voice twice. Marnie had a sinking feeling that when it came to teaching, her and Amber were on two extremely different pages.

Paislee's hands were shaking as she scratched her head for the second time in two minutes. Marnie had secured a chair and was sitting just to the right of her while Miss Olsen stood at the front of the class going through today's maths lesson. There had been a brief chat about summer holidays, Miss Olsen had allowed three children to tell the class what they had done and then it had been straight to work. Paislee had sat fidgeting with her book the entire time and Marnie could now sense the little girl's agitation. Every time Marnie had tried to speak to the little girl to explain what Amber was saying, Amber had glared at her and said, 'Shush, quieten down,' like it was the children who were speaking out of turn.

'Now, off you go. You will be doing this work independently, which means I don't want to hear any talking. When you have finished you can read your book,' Miss Olsen announced.

Paislee took one look at the worksheet in front of her and mumbled, 'I can't do it.'

Marnie leaned forward. 'Why don't we take a little break first?' she said with a smile. Paislee had done so well having to sit and listen for that long when Marnie wasn't entirely sure that she had got anything out of what Amber had said.

'We don't take breaks until we have finished our work,' Miss Olsen said, standing tall over Marnie and Paislee's shoulders, not for the first time today undermining Marnie as a TA.

'I can't do it,' Paislee said. This time frustration was clear in her tone and her voice grew a touch louder.

Before Marnie could speak, Amber opened her mouth.

'You can do it, sweetheart,' she said, her voice coming out slow and, for all Marnie knew, with well-intended encouragement, though it didn't quite sit well with Marnie, nor Paislee for that matter. Paislee pushed out her chair and stood up, scrunching up her worksheet before running out the room. Amber turned to her with a raised eyebrow. Marnie couldn't help the evil gaze she offered in return before she went after Paislee. The clanging of chairs and loud grunts could be heard from a nook up ahead, which Marnie took to be the library.

'Paislee,' she called out, not wanting to suddenly appear in the doorway and scare her.

'Go away. I hate work,' the little girl shouted. Marnie stood back when Paislee plonked herself on a bean bag, wanting to allow her some space once she knew she was safe and couldn't hurt herself.

'Will you let me know when you want to talk?' Marnie

said, sitting down in the doorway so as to not loom over her.

'I can't do it. She said I can,' Paislee cried, punching the pillow and smacking the radiator with a loud clang. A teacher from another room ran out frantically and having been shunned too many times by Amber already this morning, Marnie stuck up her hand to tell them to stop immediately and send them away. The last thing Paislee needed was someone yelling at her for hitting a radiator and acting all manic in front of her. It hadn't been a hard hit and Paislee didn't look in pain; she would be OK.

'I know. I'm sorry,' Marnie replied after a few seconds to allow Paislee to catch her breath and so Paislee knew that she was taking her feelings into account. The little girl looked over to her.

'I don't like it. I can't do it,' she said with another frustrated sigh.

'I know. Do you think we should have a break?' Marnie said nonchalantly, pulling a dinosaur book she could see peeking from one of the shelves. She placed it on the floor and read the title. 'Oh, I've never read this one before,' she said chirpily.

'What's it say?' Paislee asked scooting a tad closer to the book.

'*Ten Little Dinosaurs*,' Marnie replied. 'Ooh I think she's my favourite,' she added, pointing to a purple dinosaur riding a skateboard.

'I like that one,' Paislee said, pointing to a blue dinosaur wearing an astronaut helmet. That would no doubt be Sienna's favourite. Marnie smiled at the thought.

In the library they sat together and read through *Ten*

Little Dinosaurs five times and each time Marnie would pause before the end of the rhyme to let Paislee finish the sentence or say the number as they counted down, taking one away. It made Marnie question the level of the work that Paislee was being given and how much it was causing the little girl to worry.

'Should we see if there's another book like this and take it back to class?' Marnie suggested.

'I don't like her. Why did she shout?' Paislee queried, not moving from her spot.

'I think Miss Olsen is sorry. She just wanted to see how well you knew your numbers,' Marnie explained. 'Maybe we can show her the book.'

Paislee thought it over for a moment then picked the dinosaur book off the floor and hugged it to her chest while they searched for another number book.

Walking back into the classroom with *Ten Little Astronauts* and *Ten Little Dinosaurs* Paislee excitedly went over back to her desk. Marnie nodded at Amber but kept on walking back to her table. While Paislee flicked through the astronaut book Marnie picked up her literacy book and wrote out some sentences about astronauts, just two simple sentences with space in between each word so Paislee could clearly read the letters and have enough space to write the words out, having seen in Paislee's previous books that she ran out of room on each line as her letters were often quite large.

'Hey, should we write about the astronauts while Mason does his writing and then we could tell Mason all about them?' Marnie asked. Though Mason's eyes stayed trained on his work, Marnie could see his lips curve into an excited grin. Marnie then placed the workbook down on the table. Paislee looked at it. 'When you're ready,' Marnie encouraged with a smile and then sat back not to overcrowd her.

Paislee finished looking through her book then looked over at Mason before picking up her pencil.

'What's it say?' she asked, looking up at Marnie. Marnie looked into her crystal blue eyes and read the sentences out loud while Paislee took her time copying the words. No wonder the little girl had been getting frustrated. She was being made to complete worksheets that she couldn't fully read or understand. After finishing her sentences, Paislee went back to flicking through the pages of her book with Marnie reading the rhymes and encouraging her to count out different objects within the illustrations.

At twenty past ten, the bell rang signalling first break and as Marnie oversaw Paislee and Mason retrieving their snacks from their bags, she could feel the skin on the base of her neck prickle.

'In my classroom, we follow the rules, Miss Barnes. We do the work that has been set and we follow routine so that every child is treated equally. I know you are much older than me so if you need help remembering what you learnt in college, please don't hesitate to ask questions.' Amber spoke over Marnie's shoulder in a hushed tone while the children dashed out onto the playground. There was no mistaking the threat in her words. Who was this woman?

For a moment Marnie felt frozen, unable to form a response, but then she saw Paislee with her eyes slightly glazed over while she navigated the busy corridor, Mason staying close to her side seemingly wanting to help but not quite knowing how, and Marnie's words found the atmosphere.

'Don't forget that often the old are wise and surely for such a spring chicken you haven't forgotten that treating people equally doesn't mean treating them the same Miss Olsen,' Marnie retorted warmly, before promptly turning on her navy ballet flats and following Paislee and Mason out onto the playground. Marnie would be damned if she let a twenty-something university graduate tell her how to do her job. In the last year, she had lost many things in her life. She had thought that she might lose her passion too, but the morning had signified otherwise.

She wasn't one for bitching, gossip or meanness but suddenly her blood boiled with a determination to not only stand up for Paislee but for herself too. She was back in Orion and this time no one was going to run her out.

10

When the final bell rang at the end of the day signalling home time, Marnie and Paislee were out on the playground walking along the giant snakes on the snakes and ladders board that was painted on one small section of the tarmac. The afternoon had consisted of more of the same from Miss Olsen, which had caused Paislee to get upset and run out of the classroom. Marnie had followed but when she laid eyes upon Paislee, she had given her some space to organise her thoughts rather than barrage her with questions or possible solutions. After five minutes, she had said the same thing she had said in the library: 'Let me know when you want to talk.'

It had been ten minutes before Paislee looked up and Marnie had wandered closer, and they began their walk around the playground. They enjoyed a comfortable silence before Paislee had noted that she 'hated school and Miss Olsen'.

Marnie thought carefully for a moment before responding.

'I think she's a little scared. There are lots of new children in the class. She doesn't know everyone yet,' she offered.

'No, she's mean,' Paislee countered angrily and though

Marnie wanted to nod and agree, she knew she couldn't and she had to figure out a way to make all the relationships here work for Paislee.

'I understand. It wasn't nice of her to shout. I think she's learning too,' Marnie responded, diplomatically.

'I'm angry at her. I have lots of anger,' Paislee said, picking at a leaf from one of the trees they passed that lined the playground. Marnie smiled inwardly, rubbing her thumb over her silver bangle.

'That's OK, Paislee. Everyone gets angry. It's OK to be angry,' Marnie told her.

'Do you have anger too?' the little girl asked, still staring at the leaf she was breaking up in her hands.

'Of course. Just ask my niece Sienna. One time, we were walking to the shops and she ran ahead and nearly ran into the road. I was so scared I shouted and told her not to let go of my hand.' Marnie remembered the day clearly. Her heart had come extremely close to leaping out of her chest and splattering across the pavement.

'Did she cry?' Paislee asked, looking up with great curiosity in her blue eyes.

'She did, yes, and I said I was very sorry, but I was terrified a car might have hit her. I just wanted to keep her safe.' Though Marnie wanted to keep talking about emotions with Paislee, she was conscious of the time. She didn't want her mum to be worried at the school gate. 'Now, shall we go see your Mum and I can meet her?'

'Yes. Tell her your name. Will you tell her? You tell her,' Paislee said, looking up towards the classroom, her voice a little anxious.

'Of course, let's go.' Marnie beamed and they raced off

towards the classroom to collect Paislee's belongings before heading to the front gate.

When she reached the parents' collection point, the glares she received from Miss Olsen and Mrs Thomas, who were stood chatting with each other by the main door, were glacial. There were but a few parents left, one being Paislee's mum who greeted her daughter with a beaming smile and a hug. Paislee took the hug shyly, leaning into her mum's side.

'Hi, Mrs O'Neil, I'm Miss Barnes. It's lovely to meet you,' Marnie said once mother and daughter had greeted one another.

'Is this your new teacher, Lee?' she asked Paislee who nodded with a smile. The smile warmed Marnie's heart where it had been threatening to freeze by the powers that be who were still monitoring her. 'It's nice to meet you, Miss Barnes,' Mrs O'Neil added, meeting Marnie's gaze.

'Paislee's had a good day today,' Marnie said, then gave pause for thought. 'Paislee, is it OK if I ask Mum about some work?' Paislee nodded, just as Sienna came bounding over. Her little arms wrapped around Marnie's leg. 'Sienna, will you and Paislee have a little play by the tree for me while I talk to Mrs O'Neil?' Marnie asked. She caught sight of Jovi who nodded in her direction, understanding to keep an eye on the girls and not interrupt Marnie and Mrs O'Neil just yet. Paislee followed Sienna a little cautiously. Sienna was giving her space and occasionally firing off questions about space, which Marnie could see Paislee processing.

'Is everything OK?' Mrs O'Neil asked, concern on her face.

'Oh yes, absolutely fine. I just wanted to ask about the work, and how Paislee is enjoying school. Was she anxious at all about coming back?' Marnie said, standing tall and giving Mrs O'Neil her focus, ignoring the icy stares from the main gate.

'It can be a task to get her here, I'll admit, and I've told the teachers that before. I know she can be stubborn. She doesn't enjoy writing or doing work and I know they've talked a lot about working with her on understanding her emotions, so we do a lot of that at home too,' Mrs O'Neil replied, glancing over at her daughter. Marnie could see that same motherly concern on her face that she often saw in Jovi when she watched Sienna from afar – the thoughts that ran through her brain of whether she was doing the right thing, if she doing enough for her daughter.

'I think she simply needs to feel like it's her choice, like she has some control over the work she's doing so she feels safe. Are you happy for her to deviate from the curriculum and do more one-on-one activities?' Marnie asked. She had a strong idea as to what was affecting Paislee's learning and enjoyment of school and that desperately needed to change if Paislee was to get anything out of primary school at all.

'Of course, anything that makes her happy. I know she's behind the others,' Mrs O'Neil started but then trailed off like she didn't exactly know what to say or where to go with that thought.

'Please, Mrs O'Neil, she's not behind; she's right where she needs to be. Now, let us focus on her enjoying learning and everything else will fall into place,' Marnie said with a smile, just as Paislee ran up to her mum, panting a little with Sienna chasing her.

'That would be wonderful, thank you. Is it time for us

to get home? Shall we say goodbye to Miss Barnes?' Mrs O'Neil said, her arm around her daughter's shoulders.

'I'll see you tomorrow, Paislee. Bye, Mrs O'Neil.' Marnie waved them both off and then turned to catch Sienna running at her. Scooping up the little girl and squeezing her tight, she said, 'Will you save me an iced chocolate please?'

Sienna squealed with excitement; it had been a long time since they had shared an iced chocolate. Marnie having disappeared off to Canada for the better part of the year meant they had missed all their summer traditions. After her first day at a new job, she felt she deserved it and was looking forward to celebrating moving forward with her favourite niece.

'We'll meet you at the bakery.' Jovi nodded as Marnie placed Sienna's feet back on the ground. Marnie didn't miss her sister curiously look over to the gate where Lesley and Amber still stood observing her. She raised an eyebrow at Marnie, but Marnie gave her a subtle twitch of her lips and quick nod to tell her that she would explain later. Twin telepathy successful, Jovi nodded and took Sienna's hand and walked away, leaving Marnie to head back to the classroom to plan for the next day.

As she walked back down the corridor towards Class Nine, Marnie heard two pairs of heeled footsteps click-clacking behind her.

'Miss Barnes, may I have a word?' came Mrs Thomas' voice as she entered the room behind her, her tone not even half as friendly as it had been this morning. 'Miss Barnes, we don't have parent meetings without going through me first, so would you care to enlighten me on your conversation with Mrs O'Neil?'

Marnie straightened up from where she was collecting Paislee's books and worksheets. For a moment, her anxiety threatened to make a comeback; her palms felt sweaty. People had a habit of looking down on others in this school. There was certainly some intimidation factor at play. But she wouldn't be deterred. She was aware that she had only known Paislee for a day, but she had been working with children for a little over ten years and she knew to trust her instincts.

'It was in no way a meeting, Lesley. I simply wanted to introduce myself to Mrs O'Neil and to tell her about Paislee's day. I like to work with the parents in order to know how best to help a child – that is all,' Marnie said, speaking clearly and holding her head high, though she could feel her nails digging into her palms.

Mrs Thomas' lips pursed together, but the malice in Amber's eyes was absent in Lesley's. She didn't seem all that mad at Marnie's answer and there was no quick rebuttal or argument.

'Just because you were sleeping with the head teacher at your old school and could swan around like you owned the place, doesn't mean you can do the same here. This is my classroom,' came Amber's rather sharp retort. All of a sudden, Amber's iciness made sense. If Marnie had thought before that her anxiety was making her think Amber disliked her, then Amber had just settled and confirmed her theory. Marnie's fingers felt the smooth edge of her bracelet while her mind raced for a comeback.

'Aren't you dating Mr...' Marnie started before she was cut off.

'That's quite enough, Amber,' Lesley said, raising a hand to cease Amber's attack.

'Friday, Marnie. I would like to meet with you after school on Friday to go through any changes you suggest with Paislee and to discuss anything you wish to report to Mrs O'Neil. And I do hope the two of you will get along otherwise it's going to be a very long year.' Lesley waved her hands between Marnie and Amber and then she turned and left the classroom, taking any spark of warmth in the room with her.

'So, first day and it looks like you and Miss Olsen have become fast friends,' Jovi said with a smirk, her tone clearly dripping with sarcasm. Marnie looked up from chasing her straw with her lips, which scored a giggle from Sienna.

'Honey, will you go and see if Uncle Ant needs any help in the kitchen, please,' Jovi said when Sienna nearly blew bubbles from her nose. She wiped her daughter down with a tissue and took her seat once Sienna had run off through the kitchen doors.

'So you could see her ice daggers too?' Marnie enquired, leaning forward on her stool where she was sat by the front window, which had a high wooden table that stretched across a portion of the window so customers could look out onto the street. She took another sip of her iced chocolate and swiped at the condensation on her glass.

'Call it twintuition but I didn't just see them, I felt them,' Jovi explained with a shudder. 'Do you need me to step in as your protector and tell her who's boss?'

Marnie looked up, her lips curving into a small side smile. Jovi was certainly the more take-charge twin but just like Marnie she wasn't one for confrontation.

However, if someone messed with Marnie she became an entirely different person and nothing or no one could scare her. It was a wonder that Josh was still in one piece, but Marnie had begged that Jovi not do anything rash or draw attention to the situation and her sister had for once obliged and not turned into a vigilante, out for revenge. There was something to be said for growing up and having a daughter and a family to protect, though Marnie knew she would always be a priority in her sister's life, it was different now with Sienna and Jackson and she was OK with that. It was a good thing that Jovi's initial plans had been squashed and that Marnie had been able to talk her down off her 'he won't see the light of day again' pedestal.

'No, not yet anyway but thanks,' Marnie answered whilst twirling her straw around her glass, clinking the ice against its walls. In a few more days she couldn't wait to be sat in the same spot as the windows bore autumn décor of brown and orange sugared leaves and fairy lights and the street slowly began decorating for the autumn months. Orion held the Starcrossed Festival on Halloween and Marnie looked forward to it every year. The whole family did. Thinking about it reminded her that she needed to start planning her costume. It might be a month and a half away but costumes were important. Sienna wouldn't have her slacking. As Marnie caught sight of a few straggling parents with school kids, her mind drifted back to her workday.

'Jovi, do you think it's fair that Lesley talked to me about dating in the workplace when I've already come across two couples? And Amber made a comment today about my getting away with things at Cornelia because I was dating the head teacher. I know how that thinking works – women can never just be good at something and succeed – but I have to admit it stung.' She stared out the window for a moment longer before turning to her sister.

Jovi squirmed on her stool with a slight twitch in her left eye. Marnie watched her sister intently, trying to analyse her reaction.

'Jovi, if something's going on, you know you can tell me. I get that our family has been in the spotlight, what with Mum and Dad separating and me and Josh but you'd tell me if something was off,' Marnie said, touching her sister's forearm to get her to look at her. Jovi turned around and twisted her body to focus her attention. To Marnie, she suddenly looked very much like mother Jovi and not twin sister Jovi, which caused Marnie to squint her eyes suspiciously. Mother Jovi sugar-coated things to protect Sienna, right now sugar-coating was not what Marnie needed.

'Amber sounds quite the peach,' Jovi said through a half chuckle, half scoff. 'You're an amazing TA, Marn. Everyone knows that and Amber will soon enough. Let the town worry about their silly gossip and you focus on your new adventures and allowing for all the magic to find you. Let Lesley worry about who's dating who; you concentrate on this Canada glow you've got going on.' Jovi's tone turned from a touch dazed to bright and cheerful.

Marnie placed her fingers on the bridge of her nose and sipped up a big gulp of chocolate, her mind wandering to the rushing Kitimat River and its calming waves.

'Josh is still with her then?' Surprisingly, Marnie didn't suffer any lack of oxygen or a puncture in her heart when the question left her lips. By the time Jovi shrugged and nodded, she was already smiling at Jovi's words: that she had a Canada glow going on.

'And, what on earth is a Canada glow?' Marnie asked through a snort as Antoni walked through the door with Sienna. Sienna was proudly carrying a tray of large rainbow cookies, which instantly made Marnie's stomach growl. She jumped off her chair and raced towards Sienna who screamed and started running around, nudging and knocking the small table in the centre of the shop, which was now, thankfully, empty of baked goods.

'Are all those cookies for me?' she teased, adoring Sienna's delighted squeals.

'No, Auntie Marnie, you have to share,' Sienna wheezed through her laughter.

'But I already share a birthday. That means I shouldn't have to share anything again ever in my life,' Marnie protested. She saw Jovi shake her head but there was clear concern on her twin sister's face – her eyes glistened and creases showed between her brows. She was looking at Marnie as if she were a Fabergé egg. As impressed as Marnie was by Sienna's ability to run while keeping all the cookies on the tray, Marnie was grateful when her favourite rocketeer made herself comfy on the floor by the counter.

'Thank you,' Marnie said, panting slightly as she took a seat next to her niece and retrieved the cookie Sienna held out for her.

'You can't be sad when you have a cookie in your hand,' Sienna noted, before taking a bite of her own.

Marnie smiled down at the special little creature who was a gorgeous mixture of her most treasured human and her rather wonderful brother-in-law. Jovi and Jackson had explained to Sienna that Josh would not be coming round anymore and that Auntie Marnie had been feeling quite sad. They wanted their little girl to know that it was OK to cry and for people to express themselves. Therefore, she knew that Auntie Marnie had gone to Canada for a little break. Marnie's heartbeat quickened at the simple solution Sienna had come up with to make sure she was happy now that she was back and so she took a giant bite and made a show of how delicious the cookie was with a beaming smile and a loud 'yum'. Sienna's giggle echoed around the bakery and Marnie thought it might just be her favourite sound in the world.

'You are right,' Marnie whispered. 'I'm not sad anymore.' She nudged her gently, not wanting her niece to ever worry about her.

It was then that she heard Antoni mumble to Jovi, 'We should just tell her, then it can all be done with. We're here for her and she's in a good place now.'

'Ant, stop. Just let her get settled with her new job and get used to being home. I'm not letting Josh get into her head or ruin her fresh start. She doesn't need to hear his name or think about him, OK?' Jovi's hushed tone was far more aggressive, but Marnie resisted the urge to look over to her sister and best friend.

'But...' Antoni started.

'No buts, she doesn't need any more drama. I'm not going to be the reason she disappears off to Canada for another six months, Ant. I can't do it,' Jovi insisted, her tone more pleading this time.

The small guilty knot in Marnie's stomach grew. Deep down she had known her stint in Canada had hurt Jovi more than her sister was letting on. Jovi had forgiven her far too quickly even for their twin standards. Whilst she wanted to reassure Jovi that she wasn't going anywhere anytime soon, she couldn't help her blood prickle with thoughts of what they were keeping from her.

11

Marnie fluffed up a cushion on Antoni's fleece beige couch before creating a mini mountain of them around her spot. She would need some to tuck her toes under, some to cuddle across her chest and one loose one in case she got scared and needed protection from whatever TV show Ant was currently hooked on and coercing her to watch instead of their once-upon-a-time traditional Friday movie night; that was back in play now that Josh was no longer in the picture.

Once she was settled and had gotten herself comfy, Ant appeared carrying a tray of all her heart desired. In addition to maple syrup brownies, Antoni had concocted maple syrup churros, which resided by a small bowl of melted chocolate. There was a colourful bowl of peanut M&M's, two tall vanilla milkshakes and a large bucket of buttered popcorn. Marnie's eyes bulged at the display.

'What's the occasion?' she teased as he snuggled up next to her.

'One, it's been a while and two, you started a new job this week. I think that's plenty cause for celebration,' Antoni answered seriously, passing her a milkshake and clinking her class against his.

'Thank you,' Marnie responded sincerely as her best friend took a giant sip of creamy goodness, indulging in a quarter of the glass in one slurp. She hid a loving smile behind an enthusiastic gulp of her own.

'Is there any produce out there unfazed by your charms? That's magic in a glass. God, I've missed your food,' Marnie said on a long, satisfied sigh.

'Is that all you want me for these days?' Antoni asked, making his scar dance above his eyebrow, a smirk dazzling his features. Marnie wiggled her brows in response, feeling fully relaxed and at ease for the first time since being home.

'Maybe,' Marnie teased. 'Any news from the fire station?' Marnie tried to downplay her curiosity by stuffing a handful of M&M's in her mouth like it was no big deal and she was genuinely interested in reports from the women and men in red and yellow on the daily. Marnie knew her best friend and so she knew that he had tried to avoid bringing up all talk of crushes and his own love life since hers imploded, only giving her a snippet the day she had returned home.

'No new news.' Antoni shrugged, taking a page out of her book and shovelling a palm full of M&M's into his own mouth.

'Johnathan still putting out fires?' She tried to dig a little deeper to get more information, incredibly aware that she strongly disliked being put on the spot when it came to her own feelings, but not wanting Antoni to feel like he had to hold out because of her troubles. She wanted him to be happy, always.

'And indulging in triple chocolate brownies every Friday at one p.m.' There it was, Antoni's face practically radiated golden sunbeams, which could only mean he had a crush and that his crush seemed to be reciprocating those gorgeous and giddy feelings. Marnie's own lips contorted into a grin that felt too big to fit her face. Love suited other people. Love suited Antoni and maybe Mrs Higgins had been onto something after all with her grand plan to meddle in Antoni's love life. Marnie let out a squeal in lieu of actual sensible words of advice and wisdom, not that she had any when it came to love.

'Stop that,' Antoni said, though his face remained jolly. 'I don't want to jinx anything. It's early days and that's been a more recent indulgence of his.'

'That's news Ant,' Marnie said when her squeal subsided and she threw an 'I can't believe you didn't tell me that nugget on Saturday' handful of M&M's at him. 'Has he asked you out? Have you asked him out?' she then asked, helping herself to a brownie, but feeling as if she'd already eaten three of the sugary treats with how high and happy she felt.

'Would I be sat here with you on a Friday night if he had asked me out?' Antoni teased, his lips offering a wicked grin before he plunged a churro into the pot of smooth chocolate that Marnie was eyeing up next.

'Ant, if you like him, you should go for it,' Marnie encouraged, a small wobble in her voice, which she tried to hide with a cough and sip of her milkshake.

'That's easier said than done though, right?' he replied, his tone still cheerful. His eyes reflected an advert for some new dating show that flitted across the TV, which they weren't paying attention to.

'Hmmm,' Marnie agreed, suddenly feeling a touch solemn. Then she bit into a chocolate-dipped churro and the explosion of cinnamon and sugar that danced on her tongue obliterated any negative thoughts that were threatening to ruminate in her mind. She sat up straighter, taking in their mound of colourful cushions, Antoni's olive-green accent wall adorned with pictures of his family, Marnie's family and the three of them – Antoni, Marnie and Jovi from since they were three – and the trove of treats laid out before them, and exclaimed, 'Antoni! Any human would be lucky to be with you. If they can't see your awesomeness then quite frankly they don't deserve you. But also, we could sit here thinking about all the scary bits or we could choose to think about the exciting possibilities. I know which would be more fun.'

Antoni looked up, his neck flushing crimson. 'People in uniform,' he said with a cheeky grin, while dusting sugar off his fingertips and catching Marnie's eye.

'That's more like it. You sound just as excited as you did when I gave you the syrup, almost. I mean you could get more creative than a firefighter but...' Marnie teased and gave a playful shrug. It worked and Antoni flashed her one of his trademark grins as they both leaned back into the couch with their hands rubbing their stomachs.

'So, speaking of exciting possibilities, are you ever going to tell me what happened on your travels that's given you this Canadian glow?' Antoni asked, tucking his navy sweatpants underneath him and pushing the plate of churros gently away should he be tempted to eat more.

'What is it with you and Jovi and your suspicions over this Canadian glow? I spent the summer hiking in the sunshine, of course I'm glowing,' Marnie tried with humour, scrunching the cuffs of her beige jumper into her palms in an attempt to calm the waves of anxiety that began rolling around her stomach.

'Oh don't give me that. I've lived through your Jonathan Taylor Thomas and Hilary Duff crushes. I know it's more than sunshine and some grass,' Antoni argued tapping her spiritedly on the knee.

'But really, can you blame me?' Marnie joked. She still adored Hilary Duff. She eyed up the small bowl of dipping chocolate, contemplating drinking it so she'd have a mouthful of velvety chocolate and didn't have to talk.

'Marn, you're allowed to love again. You do know that right?' Antoni said and this time his tone was softer, less playful.

Suddenly, Marnie's heart felt too large for her chest and her lungs too big for her body. She tried to remain relaxed in her seat and not curl up into a ball and her face must have been showing the difficulty.

'Potty break,' Antoni cried, changing the subject, clearly noticing her discomfort.

Grateful for the hasty change of topic and the excuse to stand and stretch her limbs, Marnie jumped up and raced past Antoni. She shot down his small corridor, trying to avoid a plethora of potted greenery and burst into the bathroom, pushing the door to behind her.

'Oi, that was my call. I go first,' Antoni shouted, racing after her down the jungle-like atrium and stopping at the door Marnie had now closed.

'You'll have to be quicker next time,' Marnie called out, breathing heavily but savouring the air in her lungs.

Antoni spoke through the door. 'How did everything go with Mrs Thomas yesterday? And hurry up.'

Marnie used her elbow to nudge the door open as she washed her hands, letting Antoni stride in. 'As well as I expected I guess. They have their way of doing things at Apollo Primary but Paislee is the one I care about. I think Lesley can see that and part of her likes me, but she doesn't want to let me know that she likes me. She's got this hard exterior, like she can't let her guard down and always has to be professional, which makes sense. I've got a reputation around these parts for dating head teachers.' Marnie shrugged and gave Antoni a wink through the mirror. He rolled his eyes jokingly, but there was a slight quiver to his sharp jaw.

'Oh my God, did you meet a hot teacher in Canada? A hot Canadian ice-hockey teacher?' Antoni shrieked, with a small clap of his hands.

The little angel of guilt tutted on her right shoulder for keeping Nova from her sister and very best friend, but then what was there really to tell? It had been one day out of the blue in Canada and she had no way of contacting her. She'd most likely never see Nova again.

'Come on, you. Our milkshakes are getting cold,' Marnie said, flashing a brief playful smirk, wanting to keep the evening light and shake off any thoughts of Nova, before turning on her heel and sprinting back to her cosy spot on the sofa.

On Sunday morning Marnie beat her alarm clock and woke ten minutes before it could scare the life out of her and sing her into a new day. Yesterday had been busy, spent mostly tucked up on her couch recovering from her sugar hangover from Friday night and planning some new activities and worksheets for Paislee. It had been productive and she felt more prepared for Monday. However, today was a strict no-work day. She was meeting Jovi, Jackson, Sienna and Antoni at the farmer's market and she couldn't wait.

Glancing at her pictures on the wall that were being illuminated by the sunrise, she took in a deep breath and exhaled the serenity of Kootenay Lake before making quick work of getting dressed. She could never be late to the farmer's market, not when she skipped her morning coffee at her apartment in favour of the scrumptious market stall brew awaiting her. Tying her hair up with a blue bandana, she threw on a pair of light blue linen pants and reached for something cosy in her wardrobe, knowing that the weather would be breezy for another couple of hours. Her hands fell upon her white cotton Canada hoodie, which she still hadn't washed since getting back. For a moment Marnie hesitated, then conscious of the time, she scooped it up and popped it on. As her head squeezed through the neck-hole, the smell of the Canucks win at the Rogers Arena filled her nostrils, making her stomach feel slightly fuzzy.

A tingle caressed her palms and her feet itched with the need to glide as the memory of her time on the ice with Nova slid full pelt to the forefront of her brain. It had been months since that day but the fizzing and swirling that was currently going in her stomach made it feel like yesterday.

Catching sight of one of her favourite pictures of her and Sienna on Sienna's fourth birthday – Jovi and Jackson had rented a bouncy castle and had been hard pressed to get Marnie and Sienna off it the entire day – the picture showed them both lying in a crumpled heap, Sienna sprawled out on

Marnie's chest in the middle of the bouncy house as the sun set in the background. Marnie shook away her thoughts of Nova, collected her cloth bag and made for her front door.

The farmer's market was alive yet peaceful at six in the morning. The vegetable store, with its green, white and red awning and wooden crates, was heaving. Marnie waved at Tony as he packed a brown paper bag with plump red strawberries and thick pink rhubarb. Michaela and Ethan were already filling the fresh morning air with their rich roast from the back of their sunset orange camper van, which was where Marnie found her family.

'Auntie Marnie,' Sienna called, rushing towards her and wrapping her arms around her legs.

'Good morning, space cadet,' Marnie replied, bending down and picking her up – Sienna was still small enough that she could. Marnie inhaled her comforting scent, nuzzling her nose into her curly black locks and smothering her cheek with kisses.

'Auntie Marnie, stop,' Sienna screamed as she giggled and half-heartedly pushed Marnie's kisses away.

'Morning,' came a chorus of voices as Jovi, Jackson and Antoni caught up to them, bearing recyclable coffee cups with steam bursting from the tiny holes in the lids. Marnie gave Sienna one last giant kiss, before she placed her safely back on the floor so they could retrieve their Sunday morning treat. Sienna had a hot chocolate while Marnie enjoyed a foaming cappuccino with one sugar.

Taking the cup from Jackson, she waved her thanks to Michaela and Ethan. Ethan returned her wave enthusiastically but Michaela not so much. Before Marnie could overthink it, Sienna was pulling her in Cameron's direction and towards the craft stall, where Esme was zipping around taking pictures of the display and Cameron was dusting glitter over something that looked like a cake pop in the shape of a planet.

'It's Mars,' Sienna called out when she saw it. Cameron lifted her head up and grinned. Esme captured a candid shot of the interaction before putting an arm around Marnie's shoulder in a half side-hug and kissing her on the cheek.

'It's good to have you home,' she whispered, sweetly.

'Thanks, it's nice to be home,' Marnie replied while Sienna was busy with Cameron, taking over glitter duty, and the rest of their gang took their time walking towards the stall. Antoni and Jovi needed to get to the produce stands early to get the good stuff. Jovi trusted Jackson's opinion. He had a better eye for happy eggs than Marnie did apparently and so this was Marnie and Sienna time.

'Cam mentioned you've got pictures to show me,' Esme noted, squeezing Marnie's shoulders with excitement. Marnie loved how passionate her friends were about their work. They were constantly inspiring her, which reminded her that though today was strictly a no-work day, she wanted to pick up some crafty things for Paislee.

'They are nowhere near your calibre. Canada just happens to have the most stunning vistas and is a rather beautiful model,' Marnie explained, her cheeks turning rosy. Esme's photographs were exquisite. Her shots were nothing in comparison, though she was pleased with them.

'I'd still love to see them,' Esme said before getting back to clicking away at Cameron's project, which had now somewhat become Sienna's – who was wielding the glitter with great dynamism.

'Can we do this, Auntie Marnie, please?' Sienna asked, not taking her eyes off what she deemed Mars. On closer inspection, Marnie realised the little girl was right. Cameron had made the solar system using cake pops for today's market display.

'Absolutely,' Marnie said, squatting down to observe the project.

'I've put together some bundles, so everything you need to make your own solar system is in here, Captain,' Cameron told Sienna, pointing at a medium-size shoe box that was wrapped in space wrapping paper and tied with cellophane so you could see what it contained.

'We'll take one of them please, Cam, and do you have anything like that for a dinosaur village or world?' Marnie asked with an excited smile.

'If you give me a couple of minutes, I can put something together for you, Marn,' Cameron offered.

'That would be awesome, thank you,' Marnie replied as a lady came over to the table looking for Cameron's attention and carrying a ball of wool. 'We're in no rush. Take your time.' Marnie nodded at the lady. Cameron smiled her gratitude as Marnie went back to squatting near Sienna as she followed the instructions Cameron had given her of sprinkling each planet in their designated coloured glitter.

'Are the dinosaurs for Paislee?' Sienna asked, pausing for a moment, glitter scattering back into the bowl as her fingers hovered, while she gave her auntie a curious look.

'Yes, I think she'd like to do something like that,' Marnie

said, looking into her niece's eyes, which suddenly widened like large chocolate buttons.

'I think she'd like that too. No one ever plays dinosaurs with her and if I go onto her playground, I get in trouble,' Sienna explained, innocently, dipping her fingers in the yellow glitter. 'I wish I could play dinosaurs with her. She's always on her own. I'm glad she has you now.'

Marnie rocked back and forth in her squat position, a touch shaky at hearing Sienna's words. Last Thursday and Friday, she had witnessed a little of Paislee keeping herself to herself on the playground but had not seen the full reality as she herself had wandered around with the little girl, chatting to her. In class, she had gotten a sense of Paislee being isolated, not engaging because she didn't quite understand what was going on and the only time Amber interacted with her was to tell her off if she wasn't doing the right thing. Sienna's words confirmed that Marnie's intention of overhauling the curriculum to suit Paislee was the right thing to do and she would not let Mrs Thomas' trepidation make her doubt herself.

Lesley might have told her to give it another week so that Paislee could get used to her, that her acting out was probably through fear of getting to know a new face, but Marnie didn't believe that was the case at all. She had mentioned to Lesley that the curriculum was not meeting Paislee's needs and that she believed it needed to be adapted and that she would see fit to do so. That's when Mrs Thomas had neither agreed nor disagreed and simply stated that she adhere to Miss Olsen's set work, informing her that the guidance given for Paislee had been to encourage her and teach her to follow the rules, that she needed to know what was expected of her. Marnie had read Paislee's paperwork and something hadn't felt right.

She'd had to bite her tongue when Lesley had said they were doing their best, before dismissing her. She had wanted to retort that their best was not good enough but felt like maybe that was slightly unfair, for she had only been at the school for two days and didn't want to undermine the other professionals involved. However, now hearing Sienna speak, all the jargon she'd read about trying to discourage Paislee from talking about dinosaurs all the time made no sense to Marnie. Paislee was eight and being given an eight year-old's work when she was working at a four-year-old level. Moreover, she wasn't enjoying school. That first and foremost needed to change.

'Please will you help me pick out some crafts you think Paislee would like?' Marnie asked Sienna. Sienna dusted off her hands with vigour and leapt out of Cameron's foldaway chair eagerly. Marnie's heart skipped a beat. Her sister and brother-in-law had raised one incredibly kind human. Marnie could only hope that one day her own child would be just as lovable. With that thought, an all too familiar pang squeezed at her chest.

12

A chorus of 'Good morning, Miss Barnes' echoed around the classroom as the children passed Miss Olsen, who stood just outside the door to greet them, and went to their seats.

'Good morning, Finn. Good morning, Adya,' Marnie replied with a bright smile. 'Morning, everyone. Are we all excited about this week?' she asked them all but keeping an eye on the door for Paislee. Marnie liked to be in her spot by Paislee's desk when the little girl came in to ensure routine.

'Morning, Miss Barnes,' came an enthusiastic voice along with excited footsteps. Marnie swivelled around on her flats.

'Good morning, Mason.' Mason was full of energy, and he shared the same enthusiasm for dinosaurs as Paislee. Though the two sat next to each other, they never spoke or played together. Marnie was hoping she could appeal to Amber's heart and on Thursday she could put them in the same group when they visited the museum on their school trip. Marnie thought it would be a great way for Paislee and Mason to get to know each other and the thought of seeing them experience the dinosaur exhibit together filled her heart with glee. She had been to the museum when she was a young girl and then again when Sienna was four and both times she had been mesmerised by the dinosaur features. As her brain filled with fossils in all shapes and sizes, it unearthed a glimpse of Nova looking up at her in her backwards cap, eyelashes fluttering and eyes glistening under the luminous tube lights of the ice rink as she told Marnie of her days excavating in the mud.

'Is this where we're going, miss?' Mason asked, his voice carrying across the classroom and snapping Marnie out of her musing. He was pointing at the brochure on Paislee's desk.

'It is, yes. I know we're excited but let's remember to use our inside voice, OK?' Marnie said, bending down and putting a gentle hand to Mason's head, not wanting to dampen his enthusiasm or for him to feel told off. She had placed the brochure on Paislee's desk so that they could read it each morning while Miss Olsen took the register and the class did their silent reading. She wanted Paislee to be a little familiar with the look and layout of the museum before they got there on Thursday. 'Will you show Paislee when she comes in?' Marnie asked Mason, encouragingly.

'I will,' Mason exclaimed, his eyes widening a little nervously as he looked to the door. Then he put his coat on the back of his chair. Marnie watched for a moment as he sat looking over the front of the brochure. He paused before opening it and began tapping his fingers over the dinosaur skeleton, choosing to wait for Paislee before he looked inside. Marnie's heart melted. She had a feeling Mason wanted to play with Paislee and was super aware of the little girl's likes and dislikes, but he'd been scared, assuming that she just liked playing on her own.

When Marnie turned back towards the door, she saw Paislee coming in. She walked a little hunched over today, with her head down, and rushed straight to her desk. Marnie could sense she carried a lot of anxiety on a Monday after being in the safety and comfort of home over the weekend and so she didn't rush in speaking. Mason followed suit and didn't ambush Paislee on arrival. They waited a moment as Paislee took her seat and picked up the squishy dinosaur that Sienna had found at the market on Sunday and thought Paislee might like. Marnie took her seat, and when she looked up to meet Paislee's gaze, she smiled. 'Good morning, Paislee.'

'Are we seeing the T-Rex today?' Paislee replied, taking her eyes off Marnie, and leaning towards Mason to see what he had in his hand. Mason looked at Paislee and Marnie could tell he was bursting to speak. His lips were twitching, but he was waiting for Marnie and Paislee to finish their morning exchange and looking at Marnie to know if and when it was OK.

'We're going in three days,' Marnie explained, holding up three fingers. Paislee's mum must have already told her about the trip over the weekend.

'Three weeks?' Paislee said, pulling the brochure a touch closer to her. Mason let her.

'Just three days, Monday, Tuesday, Wednesday and then we go,' Marnie noted. Paislee sat back in her chair quietly, looking at the front cover and playing with her squishy dinosaur as Miss Olsen took her seat to do the register.

'Everyone should have their books out and be doing silent reading. That includes you, Mason,' she said, giving Mason a firm glare.

'He's just reading with Paislee,' Marnie informed her, mirroring her firm stare.

'It's called silent reading, which means we read by ourselves,' Amber shot back. Marnie chewed on the inside of her lip. She was trying really hard to like this woman but it was first thing on a Monday morning and she was making it extremely difficult. Mason's cheeks grew red as he pulled his reading book in front of him, a red cover depicting a flying beast and ancient script – one from the popular *Beast Quest* series – Paislee sat up and leaned in close to him.

'What's that?' Paislee asked curiously, taking in the detail of the creature.

Mason turned to Marnie and Marnie nodded. 'It's a serpent, but it has wings because it's magic,' he told Paislee with a smile. Paislee kept her eyes trained on the book, but her brows were furrowed with great interest.

'Did I not just make myself clear that this time is called silent reading? Unless you two would like to stay in at break time, I suggest you be quiet,' Miss Olsen interrupted.

'Can I have a word outside for a moment, Miss Olsen?' Marnie said standing up and staring Amber in the eyes so she didn't have a choice but to get up and follow her. Marnie's fingers played with the star on her bracelet, her chest vibrating at her boldness.

'I will be right back. Keep reading, you two,' Marnie said, bending down slightly in between Paislee and Mason as she walked past.

Out in the corridor, Amber didn't waste any time. 'I don't know what game you think you're playing but this is lesson time now,' she sternly told Marnie, in a hushed tone.

'I think it's imperative that Paislee has friends. She is

an important part of the class just like everyone else and deserves to be seen by her peers. While I appreciate the tight ship you run and the professionals that have given you a long list of ways to ensure she fits in, I don't believe their way is providing her with the best opportunities to learn. She might be sitting there in silence during silent reading but I don't take it as a win if she's not reading or showing an interest in a book. Talking to Mason is a huge thing for her. Looking at that book is a big deal, so if you are going to give her equal opportunities to learn, then you have to understand and accept that her way of learning is different and encourage that.' Marnie spoke quickly and authoritatively. 'I'm not trying to undermine you, I'm trying to do my job as her one-on-one, so I ask that you please do not undermine me,' Marnie finished and walked back into the classroom.

Her insides were shaky and her mouth felt dry but seeing that Paislee was flicking through the *Beast Quest* book transformed her forced smile into a real one. Mason sat turning the pages of the brochure and the two looked content, giving Marnie hope that she was doing the right thing.

A few moments later Amber walked back into the classroom and went straight to the whiteboard.

'Jade, can you please give out the literacy books and everyone else look this way,' she announced.

Occasionally while Miss Olsen spoke and went through the PowerPoint on the whiteboard Paislee looked up. Marnie had looked through her old literacy book to see the worksheets, the tracing letters and the copying sentences and she saw the uninterest and scared look in Paislee's face when Miss Olsen went around placing worksheets on everyone's table including her own.

'Hey, Paislee, what letter is this?' Marnie asked pointing at the letter B on the sheet.

Paislee's hand moved to her hair where she started scratching the back of her head. 'I don't know.'

'That's OK,' Marnie replied casually. 'Should we get our writing done?' she added, putting a pencil in front of Paislee and opening her book.

'I don't like it,' Paislee replied, her voice riddled with frustration. Marnie felt torn between the routine that she knew had been put in place all these years and the instincts she had just talked to Amber about. Confident as she was in her teaching ability, she still doubted herself at the best of times, especially when she could feel Amber's glare burning a hole in the back of her neck.

'How about we do this later and build some dinosaurs first?' she asked Paislee, while closing the book. The little girl turned to her with bright eyes and great intrigue. 'Should we go and sit in the corridor and use the table out there so we have more space?' Marnie asked. Paislee twisted towards the door, nervously looking around the room and then gave a small nod.

'OK, I'll go and get what we need,' Marnie told her and then got up to go to the stock cupboard. As she walked past Amber, she whispered, 'We're going to be right outside.'

Once she had collected the box, she nodded at Paislee and with some trepidation Paislee stood and followed Marnie out of the classroom, bringing her squishy dinosaur with her.

'Please can you help me get everything out of the bag?'

Marnie instructed. Paislee peeked into the canvas bag, her eyes widening when she saw the goodies inside. As her face lit up, she pulled out the mini dinosaurs, struggled a little with the bag of sand but didn't give up, grinned wide at the volcano that needed painting and was neither here nor there about the plastic trees. The small bag of mud came next, along with different shapes of wood for signs.

As Paislee drew them from the bag, Marnie organised the items so that Paislee could see everything. She wanted this dinosaur world to be very much created from Paislee's imagination. When Sienna was really little and they had first started doing crafts together, Marnie had itchy fingers when it came to sitting back and letting Sienna scribble. She would mix paints – which always made a lovely shade of grey no matter what colours she had – plop glitter in one big mound rather than sprinkle it evenly and attach googly eyes in a way that made Santa look rather wonky and crooked. But over time, she learnt to relax and let go. She loved Sienna's creations and treasured her masterpieces, for they represented her one and only niece and how she saw the world. Who said snowmen couldn't be blue and have strawberries for noses?

When everything was out of the box, Marnie put the bag to one side and placed the cardboard in front of Paislee.

'This is your dinosaur world, what would you like to do first?' she asked, squatting down at the edge of the table. Paislee scanned the crafts and then pointed at the sand.

'They need land,' the little girl said and Marnie handed her the small scissors so she could cut open the bag. Paislee took them eagerly. 'What did you watch last night?' Paislee asked while she concentrated on cutting the top of the bag.

'I watched a show called *Bridgerton* with my friend, but it's a grown-up show,' Marnie answered honestly.

'It's a fifteen?' Paislee enquired, dumping the sand into the centre of the carboard box.

'It is, yes. It's a bit too grown-up for children,' Marnie told her.

'Mum won't let me watch fifteens. You should go home and watch a PG. You're not allowed to watch fifteens,' Paislee replied, picking up a tree and placing it in the sand.

'It's OK for me. I'm allowed to watch fifteens because I'm thirty-five. What did you watch last night?' Marnie said, playing gently with the sand as they spoke.

'*Power Rangers*,' Paislee said, picking up the volcano and placing it in the middle of the pile of sand.

'Oh I love the *Power Rangers*. I used to watch it when I was little, but it's changed a lot now,' Marnie said, eyeing the white volcano.

'You watched it last year?' Paislee asked, turning to Marnie slightly and catching her eye.

'Not last year, back in nineteen ninety-five, a long time ago,' Marnie explained.

'Count,' Paislee said.

'OK.' Marnie began counting on her fingers from nineteen ninety-five to twenty twenty-two. Paislee watched her closely. 'Twenty-seven years ago – that's a long time.'

'Are you still young?' Paislee enquired, looking away again and opening the bag of mud.

Marnie smiled and opened the tiny pots of paint. 'Yes, I'm still young. Would you like to paint the volcano?' she asked.

Paislee looked up. 'No, keep it like that.'

'OK, it looks great,' Marnie said, fighting the urge to try and persuade Paislee that the volcano would look brilliant if it was painted all the right colours. 'What do you think we should call the place?' She moved on casually, collecting some of the pieces of wood and closing the lids on the paint pots only slightly reluctantly. Paislee retrieved another tree but stuck it in the mud this time before reaching for the dinosaurs. She had poured some mud at the base of the volcano on top of the sand and some in the top right-hand corner of the cardboard box.

'Dinosaur Island,' Paislee noted, while she placed the dinosaurs around the island.

'That sounds awesome. It should have a sign,' Marnie said excitedly, grabbing a marker for the wood.

'I don't know how,' Paislee said, her voice coming out a little rough.

'How about I write it first and then you can copy it?' Marnie suggested, writing the words on the wood with enough space in between and underneath so Paislee had room to write.

'We need water,' Paislee announced enthusiastically. 'For here.' She pointed at a spot she had created with trees around it in a circle.

'I'll go and get some water, while you finish the sign, OK?' Marnie said, catching her eye. Paislee nodded. Marnie smiled and got to her feet, shaking out her pins and needles. She walked into the classroom quietly and filled up a cup by the sink with tap water. When she saw Amber looking at her, she smiled confidently and sent her a thumbs up. She didn't wish to make enemies at school and she hoped Amber would understand that and not fight her every step of the way regarding Paislee and her learning. The little girl was engaged, problem solving and, upon returning to their makeshift workshop, Marnie could see her writing. Paislee had not only written the sign but had also put some numbers on two more pieces of wood that she was placing by the dinosaurs' houses that she had constructed out of lollipop sticks. Dinosaur Island looked amazing.

By the time the bell rang for playtime, all the dinosaurs were bathing in the makeshift pool at the bottom of the volcano and the smile on Paislee's face clearly showed how proud she was of her work. Outside, the little girl took to wandering around on her own as Marnie had seen her do many times before.

'Hey, Paislee,' Marnie said, on her third lap around the small grassy area of the playground. Paislee pulled a leaf off a tree and then looked up. 'Have you ever played dinosaurs before?' The little girl shook her head. She squinted at the sun, a look of curiosity on her face before a smile broke out.

'You're the dinosaur,' she said, pointing at Marnie. Marnie smiled and took a tentative step forward with her arms bent like a T-Rex. She watched Paislee's face for a second and saw her take a step back, her eyes still on Marnie, her face crinkled with a grin. Then Marnie let out a 'rawrrrr'. Paislee giggled and ran across the grass.

'I'm going to catch you,' Marnie cried.

'Dinosaur's don't talk,' Paislee shouted back.

'Oh yes, sorry, rawrrr,' Marnie replied, ducking behind a tree.

No sooner had they started playing than the bell rang signalling the end of play.

'Can we play again tomorrow?' Paislee asked, jumping in the line.

'We can play again at lunchtime, if you'd like?' Marnie suggested. Paislee nodded. 'Maybe we can see if Mason would like to play,' Marnie added. Paislee looked around, a little unsure, before following the line and heading inside.

Whilst Amber explained the maths lesson, Paislee sat squishing her toy dinosaur and occasionally looking up while Marnie scoured the classroom for multilink cubes, successfully finding a tray by the time the workbooks got passed around. Marnie brought the tray to Paislee's table, where Paislee looked at her as she sat down.

'I bet I can make a taller tower than you,' Marnie challenged with a smile before getting her tower underway.

From the corner of her eye, Marnie could see Amber looking over. When she reached Paislee and Mason's table she placed two worksheets down and gave Marnie a stern glare.

'We can play later. First we must get our work done,' Miss Olsen said, towering over Paislee.

'We've just got to build our towers first. Mine is going to be the tallest,' Marnie informed Amber. Not to be out-teachered, Miss Olsen placed her hand on top of Paislee's to stop her building.

'Paislee, it's important that we do our work now. You can write your numbers and then you can play,' Miss Olsen said, standing tall so that Paislee would have to look up and meet her gaze if she did in fact look up. But Paislee kept her eyes on the small cubes.

'Not today, I'll do it tomorrow,' Paislee mumbled, her

eyes flickering over Miss Olsen's hand that was still resting on her own.

'We need to do our work now, Paislee, not tomorrow,' Miss Olsen said more firmly.

'We're working hard on our towers, Miss Olsen, don't you worry,' Marnie said lightly and with a warm smile, hoping that Amber would understand, take the hint and walk away.

Out of those three options, Amber did none.

'Let's put the cubes away now and get our work done,' she said, sternly, taking a few cubes and placing them in the tray. Marnie could feel her pulse quickening. Paislee started scratching at the back of her hand. Not wanting to stand up and overcrowd Paislee or cause a scene in class where some of the children had already started to turn their heads, Marnie leaned a touch closer to Paislee.

'Should we go and check on our dinosaur island and we can bring the cubes with us?' she asked. Paislee nodded. She let the little girl stand first, then followed.

'Miss Olsen, we're just going to check on our dinosaurs, but we will take these with us, thank you,' Marnie informed Amber who was giving her daggers, as Marnie picked up Paislee's maths book and the tray of cubes.

The rest of the day saw Marnie and Paislee working in the corridor where they built towers and created houses for the dinosaurs with the cubes, counting out how many blocks were needed for both the bigger and smaller buildings. Paislee kept a check on some of the dinosaurs by writing their names and how old they were next to it in her maths book and she was happy and engaged.

At lunchtime, Mason joined in with a game of dinosaur

tig and it turned out he was a far better dinosaur than Marnie. He could really do the growl, though Paislee much preferred him being on her team – leaving Marnie to be the mean hunting dinosaur. The two of them sat quietly together at lunch and flicked through the museum brochure during silent reading and this time Miss Olsen didn't say a word.

The day ended with P.E. where Marnie and Paislee took to racing around the playground due to Paislee not being too fond of dodgeball, which Marnie could wholeheartedly understand – she didn't like the idea of balls being thrown at her either. She did attempt joining in for five minutes to encourage Paislee but it was not to be.

By the time the bell rang for the end of the day, there were lots of happy faces and Marnie waved Paislee off with a big grin that was returned by both mother and daughter. She let out a contented sigh.

'Miss Barnes, my office please,' came Mrs Thomas' voice, interrupting Marnie's positive thoughts. Marnie's palms were suddenly stinging where her nails had automatically begun to sink in as she nervously followed the sound of the voice.

13

'How are you holding up today?' Jovi asked, handing Marnie her coffee mug after filling it with a fresh decaf roast. Marnie had already drunk her first mug on the walk over to the bakery where she had barely been able to enjoy the first signs of autumn as a few orange and brown leaves scattered the pavement. She felt like today was a more than one cup of caffeinated coffee day, but there would be no telling Jovi that. Jovi would only let her have decaf now she'd had her caffeine fix. Marnie gratefully took her mug nonetheless, the hot ceramic comforting her noisy mind.

'It would be a lot nicer if everyone was on the same page. I think with Amber being fresh out of university she wants to follow the book. There's a part of her that understands all children work differently, of course they still teach that, but it's clouded by her belief that no child should put a foot out of line and that the classroom needs to run like clockwork. I think she's one of those people who feels that with enough pushing and with enough enforcing of routine Paislee will one day fall in line too,' Marnie said with a frustrated shrug, just as Antoni came from the kitchen carrying a brown paper bag and a note.

'Lunch for today and Violet wanted me to pass on this

number,' he said, holding out the brown bag and a small ripped piece of paper.

Marnie's shoulders softened, looking up at her best friend and thinking of the simple bagel with cream cheese she had wrapped up in her bag. Since being on her own, she had to admit that food was something she struggled with. Food for her was family and friends. She was still getting used to cooking for one and finding enthusiasm for it.

As she took the brown bag from Antoni an image of a food truck and a white paper bag appeared before her eyes followed by the memory of strolling downtown Vancouver eating the tastiest burger she'd possibly ever eaten, with company she had thoroughly enjoyed. There was no denying the flush in her cheeks, but this morning she felt that familiar pang of sadness in her chest and a tingle in her nose. She hastily turned away thinking how ridiculous it would be to cry and what excuse she would have to come up with for her sister and best friend.

'Thank you, Ant, I appreciate that,' she said quickly moving on. 'What's the number?' she asked, noticing the note only had a name and a number.

Antoni scratched the back of his head and nervously looked towards Jovi who was eyeing him curiously too.

'A friend of a friend of Violet's. She said she's really cool and thought you might hit it off.' Antoni waved his hands out in front of him. 'She said there's no pressure at all but when and if you felt like dating again, she's a lot of fun and a sweetheart.' It was Antoni's turn to look a little flushed. He was looking at her as if she were a firework that he couldn't quite light but really wanted to run away from. She couldn't blame him. In the two weeks before she'd fled to Canada, it seemed everyone she made contact with spoke of the millions of other fishes in the sea and how there would be someone out there for her. Even Jovi and Antoni had talked of Josh simply not being the one and how if she chose to look on the positive side that this elusive one still being out there was exciting. Marnie did not choose to look on the positive side and it had been the last thing she'd wanted to talk about nearly eight months ago.

She'd thought Josh was the one. How could she trust herself to pick again? Yet as she flipped the note over in her hand all she hoped for was that somehow by the miracle of the universe it would be Nova's name and number waiting for her.

'There's no rush, Marn,' Jovi said, cranking a lever on the giant coffee machine.

'Of course, yeah,' Marnie replied in a slight haze. 'Thanks. Tell Violet thanks, but I best go. Adventure awaits.'

Suddenly, Antoni's arms were around her neck, his watch getting a touch tangled in her loose waves – and he was kissing the top of her head. 'I put a chocolate-covered doughnut in there for dessert. Have fun at the museum,' he said, making Marnie forget about her dating woes. She wrapped her arms around his waist, careful not to squash her precious cargo against her beige knit jumper, and squeezed him tight.

'Thank you,' she said.

She walked out of the door to an echo of 'love yous' and placed Violet's note neatly in her navy trouser pocket. Should she really be getting back out there? Did you really get another chance at the one?

★

'We'll wait for Miss Olsen. She's going to do the register and then everyone can go to the toilet first. Is that OK?' Marnie told Paislee.

Paislee nodded, too busy scanning the cover of the museum brochure now. Marnie smiled and nodded at Mason, content that Paislee was settled and that the two of them would be happy looking through the brochure for a little while. The usual morning routine of everyone making their way into the classroom had been a lot more hectic this morning, with parents chasing after their kids ensuring they had their packed lunches, money for the gift shop and checking with the teachers what time the coach would be back at school. Paislee had come in quite happy, but the noise was certainly up a few notches, giving her a glazed look in her eyes, but once she had sat down and Mason had excitedly pointed out the dinosaurs they would be seeing today, she'd gotten comfortable.

'Paislee, this is where the dinosaurs are. Look,' Mason said, opening the book. 'We can go right up to them,' he added giddily.

'Are they real?' Paislee asked, looking over at Marnie.

'They were real a long, long time ago,' Marnie told her, sitting in her chair just as Amber walked back into the room to take her seat at her desk.

'They died,' Paislee said. 'They are real.' This conversation had taken place every day for the past four days, which had made Marnie have to up her dinosaur knowledge game. She had been doing some research of her own at home. Marnie was beginning to understand that when Paislee loved something, she loved it wholeheartedly and an answer of 'I don't know' would never suffice. Researching dinosaurs was another reason why Marnie didn't have time to date – she was too busy trying to pronounce dinosaur names and remember which one was which. Her lip twitched when she realised she had just thought about dating. She didn't need to think of excuses for not dating, she simply needed to not think about dating full stop.

'Yes, they were real, millions of years ago. We'll learn more about them today. Now, let's listen to Miss Olsen,' Marnie said, encouragingly pointing towards the front of the class. Amber took the register and went over the rules for the day, which mostly covered how the children were expected to behave when in a museum. She answered the children's questions. Five out of the six hands that shot up wanted to know if there was a gift shop, naturally. Paislee and Mason sat quietly, going through their brochure, and it was all smooth sailing getting everyone to the toilet and then onto the coach.

When the children were all buckled up and Paislee was settled with her book next to Mason, Marnie tucked the sick bucket between her feet and buckled herself in.

The short twenty-minute coach ride to Gemini went by without a hitch. Marnie had spent a good ten minutes acquiring a Netflix summer watch list from Mrs Humber, Caden's mum who was volunteering, and the other ten gazing out of the window. Autumn was slowly sneaking in; trees were looking more sparse and flowers had closed their buds for another year. Marnie's eyes glowed bright. Deep in her bones she felt a sense of new beginnings and excitement she hadn't felt in a while. Whenever she found herself feeling overwhelmed about the turn her life had taken and the things she didn't have, she reminded herself of all she had achieved and seen in Canada and it gave her the boost she needed. Spending time with her family and making more time for Sienna again had been filling her heart up in the best ways and how could she possibly get sad about not having a family of her own when her niece was a ball of magic? As for dating, it was the least of her concerns.

Suddenly, Marnie's elbow slipped from where she had it propped up on the tiny black rim of the window. Dating had crossed her mind more than once already today and it unnerved her. She pulled out the tiny piece of paper Antoni had given her that morning, which seemed to be burning a hole in her pocket. Then she scrunched it up and threw it in the bin bag that was hung up on the back of the seat in front of her.

The hills between Orion and Gemini were nothing but lush grass and busy ponds crowded by ducks with mesmerising shiny coats and pretty patterns on their wings. The bike lanes were being put to good use and as they got closer to Gemini there were picnic tables dotted about the meadows. It looked to be a happy town, which made her worries about her dad having to uproot his life here and leave their town behind waver a touch. She made a note to visit him more. It had been a week since she'd seen him last, though they'd since spoken on the phone with her telling him all about her new job.

By the time the bus came to a halt, Marnie's attention was back on Amber, who ran down the group list, the day's schedule and the emergency procedure for the fourth time. Her dark hair was slicked back into a severe ponytail that made her jaw appear harder than usual. Paislee had been contented with Mason, listening to him talk about all the possible dinosaurs they were going to see while also spending a happy portion of the ride gazing across the meadows. She smiled when she saw Marnie stand up.

'We're here,' Marnie said calmly and quietly as the clicking from all the children unfastening their seatbelts resounded around the coach. Paislee took her time and Marnie stepped aside to wait while the other children disembarked first.

'Where are the dinosaurs?' Paislee asked as she stood up and held tightly on to her brown paper bag. She shuffled towards the aisle as Mason joined the end of the line.

'We're going to see them now. They're inside,' Marnie replied, following behind as Mason led them off the coach towards the other now very excitable children and the volunteer parents scattered around the flock of twenty-five kids gathered outside the Museum Borealis. When Marnie was a child, she remembered this school trip fondly and could understand the children's eagerness to get inside. She couldn't wait to experience it all through Paislee's eyes. Once a member of the museum staff had come out to greet the school, Amber called out all the groups and had the children find their teacher or parent leader before each group made their way inside, following the girl in the green-collared top and smart beige trousers.

There were five children in Marnie's group: Paislee, Mason, Luke, Sky and Tommy and they all got on well with each other. Sky's mum, Mrs Oakley, was their group leader so that Marnie could stay close to Paislee.

'Are you excited to see the dinosaur fossils?' Marnie asked Paislee as they stepped through the grand foyer. The tiled floors, stone walls, fabric banners and wooden framing made it feel as though they had gone back in time and were visiting a king's castle. Sky's mum pointed them in the direction of the dinosaur exhibit, with that being the first stop on their group's agenda. Marnie worried slightly that it might be tricky to pull Paislee away when their time to move on was up, but the little girl would only get frustrated if they saved the dinosaurs until last and that wasn't fair. After looking through her files, she knew there was a time when taking her on school trips away from the comfort and familiarity of the school wasn't possible. She was making huge strides and Marnie wanted to keep encouraging her progress and not give her too many challenges all at once.

'We're going to see the dinosaurs. They're real?' Paislee replied, her voice rising with anticipation.

'They were real, a long time ago, yes,' Marnie replied with a warm smile as they followed the arrows through the entrance hall and came upon a banner over large double doors, with intricate engraved details, that had a large picture of a T-Rex roaring and bold words informing them that they'd reached the era of the dinosaurs.

Beside her, Mason squealed, while Paislee shouted and tugged at the hem of Marnie's T-shirt. 'Look, Miss Barnes, it's a T-Rex. Look.'

Mrs Oakley walked through the doors first, with the group following her footsteps, and Marnie walked in last. The room was full of glass cabinets and roped-off areas where life-size replicas re-enacted movements and family photos. But the be-all and end-all of the magical exhibit was the larger-than-life skeleton that proudly loomed over them, nearly touching the ceiling, of a T-Rex.

Mason clasped Paislee's shoulders and bounced up and down on the spot. This wasn't something just anyone could do with Paislee, but it made Marnie excited to see. With the introduction of their dinosaur tig game, both Paislee and Mason were coming out of their shells around each other and had been forming a rather lovely bond. Paislee never got scared when Mason displayed his emotions in this way. She smiled at him and threw an arm over his shoulders, like she could be free to be excited too in his presence.

'This is going to be fun,' Mason said, in a whisper close to Paislee's ear, making Marnie's heart pang. His caring nature and ability to read Paislee, wanting to ensure she was OK in this new situation, was pure childlike kindness and it was the sweetest thing.

Once in the hall, Marnie reminded the children that they must not touch anything or leave the dinosaur exhibit. She told them to make sure they could always see her or Mrs Oakley and to have fun and try to fill out as many facts on their worksheet as possible.

'Miss Barnes, look, you gotta see this,' Paislee shouted, cutting Marnie's speech short before she could tell the group to work together and to find the teachers if they needed the toilet. Paislee had wandered straight over to the larger-than-life skeleton structure and was gazing up at the ginormous beast, with her eyes like saucers, her eyebrows raised.

'What did you find, Paislee?' Marnie asked, while Mason brisked walked around the perimeter of the T-Rex.

'It's the T-Rex,' Paislee replied, all-knowing and not taking her eyes off it.

'Wow, he's massive,' Marnie said, as she took in the skeleton with her adult eyes. The last time she'd visited the museum she had only been a small girl too. She had a whole new appreciation for the creature now and she still felt incredibly tiny stood next to it.

'What's he made of?' Paislee asked inquisitively, tilting her head to one side.

'I'll read the facts,' Mason said helpfully, springing to life once more and skipping to the board that bore the dinosaur's name.

'He's made of bones,' Marnie replied confidently, grateful for an easy answer. 'This is his skeleton; it's made of all different types of bones,' Marnie added, feeling self-assured in giving her extra information.

Paislee tilted her head the other way. 'What are bones made of?' she asked. Marnie opened her mouth before closing it again, totally stumped by the question. Her brows furrowed. She looked over at Mason for some backup, but he was still reading the fact board, completely mesmerised. It looked like she was on her own to come up with a comprehensive answer for this one. Again, she opened her mouth and closed it and when she looked to Paislee, she found her staring up at her expectantly.

'Dinosaur bones are made of calcium and collagen,' came a whisper from somewhere behind Marnie. Marnie glanced around but all she could see was a pillar bearing a large jaw of a T-Rex, but the voice sounded oddly familiar.

'What are bones made of?' Paislee repeated, her brows furrowing now with Marnie's lack of an answer. Marnie turned back around and squatted down a touch, so she was on Paislee's level.

'Bones are made of collagen and calcium,' she repeated a little hesitantly, resisting the urge to look over her shoulder and feeling a blush creep up her neck. One hand went to her bracelet where she rubbed her thumb over the smooth silver.

'What's colli... Say it again?' Paislee asked, screwing up her nose, and putting her hand on Marnie's forearm, eager to know more and without knowing, steadying Marnie's anxious hands.

Marnie didn't mean to look over her shoulder and away from Paislee's intense gaze, when she knew eye contact was important for the little girl, but she couldn't help it. Mason was now inspecting the claws of the T-Rex by leaning over the railing to get as close as he could. 'Mason, don't lean over too far, sweetheart,' she said, momentarily getting distracted, but also buying herself some time.

'Collagen is a protein. It's a tissue that grows.' The voice came again and this time the accent was more prominent. Marnie stood, but kept a gentle hand on Paislee's, not to scare her as she looked around.

'Say it again,' Paislee urged, in desperate need for the information. This was not going to be Marnie's comeuppance. She held her head high remembering what the voice had said and repeated it clearly for Paislee.

'Collagen is a protein, which is a tissue that grows,' she said, smiling confidently, though her palms were growing a touch sweaty as she squatted back down, her stomach flipping with nervous anticipation.

'You know, your teacher is very smart.' The voice came again but this time its occupant made itself known, stepping out from behind the nearest pillar wearing a gentle smile and a green-collared shirt emblazoned with the museum's logo.

Marnie's stomach instantly felt like it had just hit the eighty-five-foot drop on the Jurassic World Velocicoaster that Mason had been telling her about earlier in the week, as she was completely caught off guard by the woman's vibrant blue eyes and silky blonde hair. She swallowed down hard to rid the lump in her throat and quickly spun her attention back to Paislee in order to ground herself and because Paislee wasn't always fond of strangers talking to her. The woman didn't rush forward though; she stayed by the pillar and squatted down on her long legs, so her tall frame was less intimidating. Without a baseball cap securing her hair, her blonde locks fell into her face, which she brushed back casually as she offered Paislee a warm smile that lit up her whole face.

Trying to process the information, Paislee looked back at the dinosaur. Marnie wondered for a moment if the woman would think Paislee rude for not responding to her, but again she didn't rush her movements and neither was she hasty in repeating herself, seemingly letting Paislee take her time.

'She knows about dinosaurs – you tell her, Miss Barnes,' Paislee said, nudging Marnie in the elbow and keeping hold of her hand.

'Did you know that dinosaur bones are made of collagen, which is a protein?' Marnie said with a playful and confident nod. She could see little dots of light in front of her, like her eyes were sparkling with the mischief she felt in her own bones, as she tried to keep it together in front of Paislee and be professional on the school trip. But what she really wanted to do was jump up and give Nova a giant hug and ask her what in the world she was doing in Orion.

'Wow, that's pretty awesome eh,' Nova said, tucking a

lock of hair behind her ear so her eyes were clear without the shadow of her cap, just as Mason came bouncing over.

'Hi, did you see its claws, Paislee?' he asked, looking at the woman and Paislee in quick succession. Marnie sure did love his energy.

'Hi,' Nova said with a small wave. Paislee put an arm on Mason's shoulder tentatively and raised her eyebrows with an excited grin. Then she took a step forward towards Nova.

'Where are his parents?' she asked, leaning in a little closer. Marnie stood up and shook out her legs before taking a step forward, feeling a rush of protectiveness towards Paislee. Occasionally when Paislee's ears pricked up to something Miss Olsen said in class or a conversation between kids on the playground piqued her interest, she would burst forth with a question but it wasn't always met with a simple answer; instead it would be received with either a bemused expression or it was completely ignored. On the playground Marnie would intervene to make sure the kids answered her. She would not stand for them dismissing her and being rude. And if Miss Olsen's vague reply did not satisfy Paislee's interest, Marnie would interject and answer in more detail.

However, Nova's face didn't contort into a confused or humoured grin. Her features remained warm and she was lasting a lot longer in a squat position than Marnie had.

'His parents are in a special box. We look after their bones too,' she answered.

'That's so cool,' Mason exclaimed. 'Paislee, come and see its claws.' He tugged her elbow.

'We must say thank you to the kind lady for answering our questions,' Marnie told both children before quickly glancing around to check that Sky's mum was all right with the others. The museum was quiet today, and it was just their group in the dinosaur exhibit now.

Paislee looked over her shoulder at the huge T-Rex and then back to Nova.

'Thank you,' Mason said with a huge grin, his eager feet bouncing on the tiled floor, ready to take Paislee exploring.

'Thank you, Miss...' Paislee said, her voice quiet and muffled against her shoulder as she looked at Mason, her mind now ready to go and see the dinosaur's claws.

'You're welcome and my name is Nova. What are your names?' Nova asked. Paislee looked up at Marnie and Marnie gave her an encouraging nod.

'I'm Mason and this is my best friend...' Mason started, putting his arm around Paislee's shoulders. She hunched a tad at his touch.

'Paislee. I'm going to see the T-Rex now, Miss Nova,' she told Nova before turning slowly and breaking out into a slight jog towards the skeleton's feet, Mason skipping along by her side.

Marnie watched them close in on the skeleton, Mason pointing at its long, pointy claws and reading the facts on the board once more but this time giddily repeating them for Paislee. She smiled at their passion. When Marnie returned her gaze to Nova to thank her for coming to her *Are you smarter than an eight-year-old?* quiz rescue, she found her looking at her with that warm smile of hers and Marnie couldn't help shake her head with a laugh.

'Well, what can I say, you really are passionate about getting your revenge,' Marnie noted, the corner of her mouth twitching, trying to withhold a grin as she recalled Nova saying she would fly halfway across the world to embarrass Marnie after the many bumps she took on the ice.

'That I am,' Nova replied, straightening her back out and combing a hand through her middle parting to sweep her hair out of her face again.

Marnie glanced over her shoulder to make sure the kids were all right. Sky, Luke and Tommy were busy scribbling on their clipboards while Paislee and Mason now had their noses pressed up against a cabinet containing dinosaur teeth. Content that they were all occupied and behaving, Marnie quickly embraced Nova in a hug, breathing in the sweet scent of her that she'd not forgotten over the last five months.

'Hi,' Nova whispered in her ear. They had never embraced before and suddenly Marnie felt a touch self-conscious that she was crossing some line in their friendship, if she could call it that since they had only met once. But Nova's grip matched hers in strength. Had Nova missed Marnie as much as Marnie had missed her?

'Hi,' Marnie whispered back before letting go. 'So, England…' Marnie started before a shout took her attention.

'Miss Barnes, look, look, you have to see quick.' Suddenly there was a child nudging her in her hip bone and Marnie's question got lost in the atmosphere as her focus turned to Paislee. In her side-eye, she saw Nova smile and swing her hands behind her back like she was about to follow but thought better of overcrowding them or getting in the way of her work. After all, she was working. It had certainly been lovely to see her, an absolute shock to the system, though an incredibly happy one, but she had kids to look after and Nova had a museum to attend to.

'What is it, Paislee?' she asked, as Paislee pulled her wrist in the direction of a family of dinosaur statues. They were incredibly well done. Every detail from the wrinkles around the eyes, delicate hairs on their backs and intricate spikes on their tails gave them an impeccably lifelike vibe. It looked to be a Triceratops family – two large Triceratops standing by a pool of water with a smaller one playing nearby.

'Are those his parents?' Paislee asked. 'What are their names? Are they going to eat us?' the little girl fired off.

Marnie found herself looking around for Nova, but she had disappeared. The thought crossed her mind that she would rather like her being their museum guide. With her gone she was on her own to satisfy Paislee's queries. She could use her dinosaur expertise.

'Yes, those are his parents, and look, he's playing,' she said, as she glanced around to see if there were any signs of a name plaque. Coming up empty, she squinted in thought, trying to think of the best dinosaur names that would suit a Triceratops family.

'The dad is called Milo and the mum is called Stella. The baby is called Troy,' Marnie said happily, pleased with the names. The baby was cute and looked like a Troy.

'Troy,' Paislee repeated. 'They won't hurt us?'

Marnie looked down at Paislee's curious face. Her eyes were scanning over the baby dinosaur, watching it in mid-play. The innocence in her eyes was beautiful and Marnie could tell that Paislee was picturing them quite vividly running around, splashing in the water and playing together.

Paislee spent five minutes looking at the family of dinosaurs while Marnie helped Mason answer some questions on his worksheet. She checked in with Sky's mum and the others and they spent a few minutes looking over fossils and trying to show Paislee the cavemen and cave drawings that were hung up on one of the walls. Paislee was happily mesmerised with the Triceratops.

Twenty minutes went by where Marnie weaved in and out of the pillars and cabinets with the children, keeping a close eye on Paislee in the corner, trying to fill out any unanswered questions, while trying not to think about finding Nova behind one of them. She wasn't sure how long she was in town for. The uniform looked promising but maybe her job here had only been a summer job and she would be leaving soon. Another piece of paper flapping in her face signalled another question that needed answering from Tommy, and so Marnie reminded herself that the school hadn't signed up for a guided tour, neither had she signed up for a distraction.

'Paislee, we have five minutes OK? Then we're going to go into the next room,' Marnie told the little girl.

Then she gathered the group by the door and answered any questions they had about the dinosaurs, ensuring too that everyone had their belongings. Luke had to run and retrieve his lunch bag from the bench by the cavemen tapestry and then they were ready.

'I don't want to go. I want to stay with the dinosaurs. You go,' Paislee said, coming to stand with the group. Marnie squatted down to make eye contact.

'I know we like the dinosaurs but it's time to go and see the other parts of the museum,' Marnie explained. Mason suddenly appeared by her side and put a comforting arm around Paislee.

'Come on, Paislee, there's more cool things to see and

then we get to see the dinosaurs in the gift shop,' he said, his voice full of excitement. Mason had a special way of comforting her and making her laugh and at ease. It was like he'd always wanted to be friends with her but his own doubts and shyness had stood in the way. Simply asking him to play had given both children a friend. Marnie stood to give Paislee time to process the instructions she had given and Mason's words. Then casually Mason took his new best friend's hand and started walking with the group.

'See you later, Troy,' Paislee shouted over her shoulder towards the baby Triceratops. This sweet action once again tugged at Marnie's heartstrings and she found herself smiling and waving back at the baby Triceratops and its family too.

14

With the Ancient World exhibit complete and lunch coming to an end, they had one more room to explore before the gift shop. Paislee had done well looking around at the large maps and Marnie had thoroughly enjoyed her mozzarella and tomato sandwich and chocolate doughnut that Antoni had prepared for her. As she popped her brown bag in the recycle bin, she smiled at the thought of stopping by the bakery after work to catch up with Antoni and Jovi to tell them about her day rather than rush through or making an excuse to head straight home to see Josh. There was nothing wrong with being giddy about getting home to see your other half but Marnie was beginning to realise how often she'd cancelled plans with her family to be with Josh because Josh hadn't been one to make an effort with them.

'Right, we've got one more room to look at,' Marnie explained to Paislee and Mason as the group stood to gather by Mrs Oakley at the door.

'They have toys?' Paislee asked. 'They have dinosaurs?' She looked up at Marnie with her big blue eyes full of intrigue.

'No, this is the Egyptian room. We're going to see the

pyramids and the mummies, like Miss Olsen has shown you in class. Then we'll see the toys,' Marnie informed the two friends.

'I want to see the dinosaurs,' Paislee expressed. Marnie could hear the frustration in her tone and with a gentle wave of her hand down by her hip, encouraged Mason to keep walking, hoping that the pyramids would be enough of a distraction to keep Paislee interested for ten more minutes before it was their turn in the shop.

'We'll see the dinosaurs after the mummies. Ten minutes, OK?' Marnie said.

'Oh whoa, cool. Look at this, Paislee.' Mason said when the Egyptian tombs came into view. Marnie couldn't exactly fault Paislee for not caring for the mummy exhibit; she wasn't really a fan herself. The mummies and bodies had scarred her for life as a child. Now she was grinning and bearing it, while trying not to look at the objects for too long. She kept her eyes on Paislee to avoid looking at the bandaged relics of humans. She had shown Paislee books in class to prepare her for this exhibit. Paislee wasn't one to get scared and would happily watch a T-Rex munch on a carcass, so she wasn't too worried about her reaction to the mummified people. The children were a lot braver than her. Horror movies, zombies and the like, were not Marnie's thing.

Mason's enthusiasm seemed to grab hold of Paislee for a moment as her eyes scanned over the new room. However, the moment they landed on the mummy lying down in a class cabinet, Marnie saw the little girl's face morph into panic.

'I don't like it,' Paislee shouted. She had remained glued

to the spot by the door, but she turned to face Marnie who in trying to be encouraging was standing two metres ahead by the pyramid display.

'That's OK, Paislee. Don't look at those, come and see the pyramids,' Marnie urged, but Paislee's face was turning red.

'I want to see the dinosaurs. I hate this.' Paislee's voice rose with anger and fear. Marnie walked calmy, but quickly to her side.

'OK, Paislee, we can sit on this bench for five minutes and then we can go and see the dinosaur toys,' Marnie said, keeping her voice neutral and soft.

'No, I don't like it. It's too scary,' Paislee replied. Her brows were scrunched up and her cheeks were rosy.

Marnie sat down on the bench behind her to give Paislee some space. She didn't respond straight away as she knew Paislee had to get out her anger and frustration. Two members of the public, not with their group, looked over and gave Marnie a disapproving look, probably thinking that she should control her child better and tell her that shouting in museums was not allowed. If Paislee wanted to use a label to explain herself to people when she was older, then she could, but the little girl didn't owe them anything. If they wanted to be judgemental people, that was their prerogative and it looked far less appealing than a child who was simply expressing themselves. Marnie smiled and waved them on, not wanting them to share their unpleasant faces with Paislee.

'Would you like to join me on the bench?' Marnie offered.

Paislee turned around to face her. 'No, I don't like it in here. I want to get out. I hate it.' Her little voice reverberated off the walls. Mrs Oakley looked over and gave Marnie a subtle nod to see if she needed any help while the other children knew not to crowd around or fuss over Paislee, as that would only heighten her discomfort. They continued about their business of filling out their worksheets. Paislee didn't like people looking at her when she was trying to express her feelings. Marnie had learnt that on Tuesday when handing in her maths book to Miss Olsen. Amber had made a big production of Paislee completing her work and got the class to clap. Paislee had run out of the room, retreating to her safe space in the library. After a moment's pause Marnie spoke again.

'We're going to get out of here in five minutes,' she told Paislee.

'It's too long. I've been waiting ages,' the little girl screamed. Marnie's calm approach this time did not help and before she could get to her feet to try and distract Paislee with a cool picture or interesting object, the little girl dashed right out of the Egyptian exhibit door in a blur.

Panic gripped at Marnie's chest, but she forced herself to remain calm. She shot up to her feet and jogged over to Mrs Oakley. On a whisper, she told her she was going to look for Paislee and that could she please ring Amber and tell her what had happened. There was no need to alarm the others. Once they had finished their worksheets, she could gather the children together and go on to the gift shop.

Then Marnie broke out into a run, breaking the museum's no-running rule and leaving Luke and Tommy with their jaws on the floor as she flew past them.

Running past the classrooms where they had only just had lunch, Marnie paused briefly to look inside. Though she had an idea where Paislee had run to, she had to check everywhere just in case. Her heart pounded in her chest and she could feel tiny beads of sweat forming in her hairline. This was every teacher's worst nightmare when it came to school trips. Not having a child in your line of vision, not being able to place them was agony. She thanked God that the museum was quiet today so that Paislee couldn't get tangled in groups of people coming and going from the museum entrance. When Marnie ran through the foyer, she noticed there were museum staff stood by the front doors and the tightness in her chest loosened a fraction.

She raced straight over to them, breathless now from fear and jogging.

'Has a little girl left this building on her own?' she asked hurriedly, while bouncing on her tiptoes.

Both the museum staff member's faces morphed into expressions of sheer horror, which only made Marnie feel worse than she already did.

'No, gosh no, we would never let a child leave alone. They have their uniforms on, so we know what groups they all belong to – that's why they're a requirement on school trips,' the younger of the two staff explained to Marnie, making Marnie feel rather daft and extremely inadequate at her job.

'OK, thanks,' Marnie said, running backwards, feeling a touch relieved that Paislee had not been able to get outside but full of guilt for letting this happen. It didn't bear thinking about what would have happened if Paislee had left the museum. Her stomach twisted with nausea as the thought flitted through her mind. She pushed it away upon seeing the tapestry for the dinosaur exhibit and took a deep breath, trying to steady her queasiness. Greeting Paislee in a frantic state with sweat all over her face and tears threatening to fall from her eyes, would only cause Paislee to get upset. Paislee didn't like other people crying, especially if she felt that she had been the one to make them cry.

When she entered the prehistoric exhibit, Marnie shouted out hello, not wanting to scare Paislee by creeping in and out of the pillars and posts. When she received no reply, her stomach flipped. She had to be in here, Marnie thought as she wiped at the sweat on her brow. Just then she heard quiet voices coming from one corner of the room by the low table that held a miniature model of the Jurassic era. Mini Allosauruses roamed the hills, Stegosauruses drank water by the lakes, Diplodocuses nibbled on the tall trees and Nova and Paislee sat playing.

'What's his name?' Nova asked, pointing at a hungry Diplodocus.

'Dippy,' Marnie heard Paislee say after a short pause. She felt like she had just escaped Jurassic Park with the stitch in her side and the fear that had caused her heart to attack her rib cage, no doubt leaving it bruised. Hearing the little girl's voice, Marnie fanned her face and rolled out her shoulders.

'I like that name,' Nova replied softly.

'What did I say?' Paislee asked her sweetly, the anger and frustration in her voice having vanished.

'You said it's called Dippy,' Nova told her with a cheery tone. 'That's a perfect name for a Diplodocus.' Marnie giggled. It really was a perfect name she thought. She hated to interrupt the dinosaur-naming party, but she had to get Paislee back to the group. She didn't want her to miss her slot at the gift shop as Marnie knew she would enjoy picking something out – that and they had a coach to be on time for. Quickly, before making herself known, she pulled out her phone and texted Amber to let her know she had found Paislee and that she was OK.

'Hi, guys,' Marnie said, quietly, testing the waters and stepping forward. Paislee looked up and Nova turned her head to face her. Paislee's eyebrows furrowed slightly, remembering that Marnie had made her angry. Nova seemed to notice this change. She looked away from Marnie and back to Paislee.

'Let's tell Miss Barnes the names of the dinosaurs. I think she'll like them,' she said.

With her words Paislee's eyebrows relaxed once more and she began pointing at the dinosaurs. A smile grew wider on her face when each time she forgot one she would look at Nova and Nova would tell her its name. Marnie had crouched down now so she was squatting in between the two of them.

'I think those names are wonderful. Definitely cool dinosaur names,' she said enthusiastically. 'Which one is your favourite, Paislee?' Paislee looked over the model world.

'Trixie,' she said, pointing at a baby Triceratops that looked to be rolling around in a puddle of mud.

'Good choice,' Nova noted. Her long legs were tucked to the right of her as she sat on the floor against the small table. She looked completely at ease in Paislee's company. Marnie felt a stir in her stomach and brushed it off as her stomach settling after her marathon around the museum.

'She looks cute,' Marnie said, taking her eyes off Nova.

'OK, Paislee, we have five minutes and then we're going to go to the shop, OK? We can see what dinosaurs they have.'

'We won't see the dead people? They won't get us?' Paislee asked, her big blue eyes looking up into Marnie's eyes. Marnie held back from letting out a sad sigh. She hadn't thought the mummies would have made her this frightened, but the fear in Paislee's eyes was evident and Marnie hated that she had put it there.

'No, they won't get us. They were just pretend people. They weren't real – just like Play-Doh,' Marnie told her.

'I was mad. I got scared.' Paislee took her hands away from the dinosaur and sat back on her heels, her lips turning into a frown.

'I know you did, and I am sorry they scared you, but it's OK to be scared,' Marnie told her.

'They sometimes scare me too. I like the dinosaurs way more,' Nova chimed in. Marnie offered Nova a small smile.

'What do you do when you get scared, Nova?' she asked, hoping Nova might read her mind and understand where her brain was heading. She smiled in return, that earnest smile of hers, and fiddled with her ear and the silver earring that Marnie noticed was a small dinosaur footprint. She then crossed her long limbs and leaned forward, across Marnie, so she was closer to Paislee. Marnie's breath hitched.

'When I get scared, I tell someone. I think Miss Barnes is nice. I would tell Miss Barnes and stay close to Miss Barnes,' she whispered, like she and Paislee were in a secret club. Paislee smiled.

'That's a good idea right, Paislee? We mustn't run away. You can tell me, OK?' Marnie said, her voice a little croaky as she leaned in, like she was a child and didn't want to be left out of their secret gang. Paislee chuckled, looking back and forth at the two of them.

'Is Miss Barnes your girlfriend?' Paislee asked, her face turning serious and full of curiosity. Marnie's stomach immediately flipped like she was back on the same rollercoaster as before. She had no idea what her face looked like, probably like she had seen a ghost. Fear enveloped her for the second time in thirty minutes. It was extremely uncomfortable and she wasn't sure why. Nova was giving her a soft smile and there was a twinkle in her crystal eyes. Nova didn't scare her but the term *girlfriend* was giving her the heebie-jeebies.

'No, she works here at the museum and now she's going to show us the way to the gift shop – right, Nova?' Marnie said rather briskly while getting to her feet.

'We're going to see the dinosaurs,' Paislee said, jumping up excitedly, all the action of the last thirty minutes forgotten. Marnie knew she would have to talk to the little girl more about running away and its dangers when they got back to school. She would of course tell her mum later when she picked her up too, so that her mum could talk with her and reinforce Marnie's lesson.

'Right,' Nova agreed, pushing herself up and towering over the two of them once everyone was standing. 'To the gift shop,' she added in a sing-song tone, raising her fist.

'To the shop,' Paislee copied.

Marnie let Nova and Paislee walk in front as it was lovely to see Paislee engaged and comfortable around a new person. She was asking Nova about dinosaur bones and how they were made, repeating her questions a few times, and asking Nova to start from the very beginning of where they came from every time she finished talking. Nova's enthusiasm each time she answered never wavered. Though her heart rate had returned to normal Marnie felt exhausted with anxiety. She kept a smile on her face, wanting the last bit of the trip to be enjoyable for the children and wanting Paislee to have fond memories of the place.

The noise level picked up as they edged closer to the gift shop. In contrast to the dimly lit and moodier atmosphere in the foyer, the shop was bright with fluorescent white lights and coloured trinkets filling the shelves. When they entered, Marnie was immediately greeted by Amber who asked if everyone was OK. Marnie smiled and assured her that it was, not wanting to draw attention to the situation in front of Paislee. The little girl was happy now, reunited with Mason and busy pressing buttons on roaring dinosaur figures.

Having chosen a mini Triceratops that looked like Trixie from the small Jurassic world in the dinosaur exhibit, Paislee followed Marnie to the counter where Marnie encouraged her to pay for the toy. Though a little shy, Paislee was excited to play with Trixie and followed instructions, placing Trixie on the counter, then she turned to Marnie when it came to paying and speaking with the lady. Marnie happily demonstrated what to do as Paislee excitedly watched the exchange, eager to get the small plastic dinosaur back in her palm.

In the midst of the mayhem in helping children pay for their treats, Marnie had lost sight of Nova. She did a quick scan of the room before she was being pushed in the direction of the exit with her group.

As the children clambered onto the bus, the worry lines

on Marnie's forehead smoothed out ever so slightly. Once everyone was accounted for and safely buckled in and the bus was in motion, her shoulders moved an inch away from her ears and she felt like she could breathe a little lighter.

This time as the rolling greens and picnic spreads passed by her, her mind drifted to Nova and how wonderful it had been to see her again. She let out an 'I can't quite believe it' sigh and shook her head as her lips eased into a sincere grin. Her Canadian friend had made it to her side of the world and she had failed to get her number again. Pursing her lips, she looked up to the wispy clouds in the blue sky. The blue was beginning to mix with a dash of grey now that autumn was here, and she figured that another trip to the museum was in order very soon in hopes that she could catch her friend before she had to leave again.

15

The crisp autumn leaves that sprinkled the pavement on Monday morning tempted a smile from Marnie, but she was having difficulty getting her lips to curve. The weekend had been enjoyable – getting to spend time with her dad in his workshop and then with her squad at the market – but she couldn't help brood over the fact that she hadn't been able to bring herself to head back to the museum to catch Nova. Nerves had very much gotten the best of her and now it was taking all she had not to think about those blue eyes and peachy lips that had dazzled her once more, when their eyes had met mere days ago, after some six months apart. She wished the weekend would start all over again in a hurry but this time with a confident her so she could go back to see Nova. Just the thought made her palms tingle.

She buzzed herself into the school building where she gave her lips no choice but to lift with a grin – albeit toothless – but a grin nonetheless. She loved her job and it was time to focus. For all she knew, Nova could have been working for the summer and Thursday could have been her last shift. She could already be back in Canada right now, Marnie thought as she wandered the quiet halls to Class Nine.

She had made it to work before Amber and so began

setting out Paislee's table: her squishy dinosaur, a book and a piece of paper with a few coloured pencils, in case Paislee fancied drawing. She squished the dinosaur a few times, using it as her own stress relief this morning before placing it next to the paper. Paislee wasn't a huge fan of paper and pens but over the last two weeks Marnie had been drawing a lot of dinosaurs and writing down their names and Paislee watched with great intrigue. Marnie wanted to make learning fun and accessible without always saying 'it's time to do this now'. She wanted to provide Paislee with an array of tools and encourage the little girl to want to try new things without so much pressure.

When she had finished, Amber walked in, looking a whole lot more glamorous than usual, Marnie couldn't help but notice. Marnie tended to save her favourite outfits for the weekends, knowing how messy she could get at work with being prone to crawling around on the floor when pretending to be an alligator or supporting kids in their slime and painting adventures. Not that she was judging Amber's skater dress and four-inch heels – she looked great whereas Marnie looked practical in her wide-leg brown gingham trousers and white box tee. Maybe Amber was celebrating.

'That dress is beautiful,' Marnie noted honestly, aware that she and Amber never really engaged in talk that wasn't to do with work and suddenly feeling a tad shy about what she had just said.

Amber stood tall against her desk. After switching on her computer, she looked up. 'Thank you. We've got Maths and English first thing this morning, which I want to get through quickly to free up the afternoon. Every Monday and Thursday for the remainder of September and for the month of October, we have someone coming in for part of our science and history topics. You can let Paislee know of the change in routine.'

So, the topic had quickly turned back to work but had Amber just considered Paislee's needs and taken Marnie's compliment without snapping at her? Marnie nodded with a smile.

'Sounds great. I'll do that. Thank you,' she said to the back of Amber's head as Amber sat down at her desk and went on with her morning routine and her usual act of pretending Marnie wasn't there.

'That looks amazing, Paislee, I love it,' Marnie expressed, as she sat on a small chair outside the classroom looking at Paislee's Blu-Tack creation. The little girl had made a small T-Rex out of some Blu-Tack that they'd found lying around. Though the table was littered with boxes Marnie had been collecting for a junk modelling session, Paislee had been drawn to the Blu-Tack.

Whilst Paislee busied away adding scales to her dinosaur, Marnie eyed the boxes and tried to think of which would be best for her own model.

'How about I make a T-Rex with these boxes?' Marnie voiced, picking up a long kitchen roll tube and grabbing some green card. For a few minutes she flipped the paper over in her hand, placed it up against the roll and surveyed the table. Then she reached for the scissors and Sellotape with an idea.

'OK, but don't make it terrible,' Paislee cautioned.

Marnie smiled and got to work. Ten minutes later and Marnie had what she believed to be an impressive dinosaur model. Into the green card she had cut out triangles to give her dinosaur a spiky back, she had then wrapped the card around the kitchen roll, fastening it with a touch of tape. Using a thin strip of more green card she had attached a long tail before cutting out small T-Rex arms and gluing them to the front. She had then drawn a T-Rex head onto card, leaving the neck a little long when she cut it so that she could attach it to the top of the tube where she stuffed the middle with newspaper so it looked 3-D. Last but not least had been claws for the feet, which she secured with more tape.

Once completed, Marnie placed it in the middle of the table with a satisfied 'ta-da'.

She sat back and admired her work while Paislee used a pencil to make a hole in the middle of her Blu-Tack dinosaur's mouth, to give it depth; the thing looked incredible.

'We need more Blu-Tack,' Paislee said before looking up and doing a double take at the creature before her. Pulling her pencil out of the T-Rex's mouth, she placed both the Blu-Tack and the pencil down and grabbed Marnie's toy and immediately started swishing its tail and giving it a voice.

Just then, a familiar voice carried down the corridor.

'That is an extremely cool dinosaur you've got there, Paislee,' Nova said with a broad smile and a slight bend in her knees. Marnie narrowed her eyes at Nova, feeling that all too familiar rollercoaster of nerves and excitement in her belly, but before she could speak Amber came scurrying out of the classroom.

'Miss Clarke, right this way,' Amber said, her voice as sweet as a cherry drop. As the two shuffled past, Paislee looked up.

'What's her name?' she asked, her eyes still focused on the classroom door.

'Nova. Nova from the museum,' Marnie answered, standing up and moving towards the door, where she could hear Amber announcing to the class that Miss Clarke was here to teach them about the prehistoric age and fossils. Seven months ago if someone would have told Marnie that she'd take a solo trip to Canada, make a new friend and that one day that new friend would end up not only in Orion but working at the same school as her, a school that she had only just started working at herself, she would have shaken her head and politely told them that her life was most definitely not some rom com. Now, she had to stifle a laugh as she shook her head in disbelief. 'She's got something to tell us about dinosaurs. We should go and sit down,' Marnie said casually but with excitement in her tone, looking down at the little girl standing at her side, peering into the room.

'I can bring him too,' Paislee stated and Marnie nodded as the two walked through the door and back to their classroom table, Paislee holding her new junk model T-Rex.

Nova made the next hour fly by with a whir of lively activity. Dinosaur noises were made, drawings were sketched on whiteboards and posters of incredible beasts were shared. Paislee listened and occasionally piped up with a question: 'Is that the jaw?' Nova would answer and then Paislee would get back to her own dinosaur noises as she played with Marnie's T-Rex. The rest of the class were on the edge of their seats and Marnie couldn't blame them – she had been fully enthralled by the lesson too. Nova certainly had a captivating way of teaching, what with her cool accent and passionate approach.

Once the children had all departed for home time, it was just Marnie, Nova and Amber left behind in the classroom. Marnie concentrated on tidying away leftover boxes, scrap paper and glue before settling down to write up Paislee's 'plan, do, review' and mark her work. Heat flooded her cheeks at the thought of talking to Nova in front of Amber, so she kept busy. Would Amber see the heat in Marnie's cheeks or hear the rustling of the butterflies in her stomach? That was all purely from seeing her friend again after so long, but still Marnie couldn't let Amber confuse it for something else, not after she had been given a lecture on dating people who worked in the school. Amber would no doubt run to Mrs Thomas right away and try and get her fired. Marnie shut the workbook in front of her, urging her brain to shut down the topic of dating that seemed to be ruminating in her head a lot lately.

She certainly didn't want to get fired and she really wasn't looking to date so she had nothing to worry about. Besides, her feelings were imprisoned securely in her chest. Liking someone was not something she would be setting free ever again. It was far too dangerous to be on the loose in the big wide world. As far as she was concerned, making decisions on love and being so bold and courageous in that department was way out of her skill set and she should leave it all well alone.

'Hi.' Nova's voice snapped her eyes away from the words she was scrawling on the page. Marnie looked up to see her with her hands in her pockets, shoulders slightly hunched and that welcoming grin on her wide lips.

'Where's Amber?' came Marnie's abrupt question as she suddenly felt extremely aware of her surroundings and the way her heart was beating fast. The playful tone in which she usually spoke to Nova had not made it into the air and her shoulders tensed painfully.

Nova cocked her head ever so slightly. 'The phone rang,' she said, then tilting it towards the direction of the door. Marnie had been so in her head that she hadn't even heard it ring. The easy banter that often came to her in Nova's presence had left her brain. She looked around the room casually and then her eyes landed back on Nova's and Marnie wondered for a moment if this is what it felt like in an interrogation room. Was she about to start sweating?

'Any chance you'd like to go for a coffee while I'm this side of the pond?' Nova asked, her cheeks brightening with a touch of colour that accentuated the gold highlighter on the top of her cheekbones.

Marnie's head shot towards the door. Why was she feeling so on edge, like they were being watched? It was just coffee with a friend. Yet it felt like there were at least ten police sirens blaring in her head.

'Erm, coffee,' she mumbled. Now her brain was playing the *Countdown* theme, like she was running out of time to answer. 'There's a market here on Sunday. Meet me there?' she hastily stammered.

'I can do that. Should I give you my number this time? Three times bumping into each other is a charm, but just in case,' Nova said, rocking on her tiptoes slightly, her blue eyes shining in the sunlight that caught her face through the window.

Just then Amber walked back through the door.

'No no, it's fine. I'll make myself a Corythosaurus and grunt,' Marnie replied and immediately cringed that she had just told Nova she would grunt to get her attention. But it had felt like desperate times. She couldn't let Amber see Nova pass on her mobile number. Nova snorted at Marnie's words, causing Marnie's stomach to leap with some sort of jovial win. Marnie wanted to shout 'stop it' to her misbehaving organ when she caught Amber looking her up and down.

'I'm all done for today. See you tomorrow, Amber, and I'll see you on Thursday, Miss Clarke. I know Paislee will be looking forward to it,' Marnie said, closing her books and shooting to her feet, before marching out of the door in haste.

'I have to tell you something,' Marnie noted desperately, leaning across the counter to Jovi, who was collecting the last few unsold chocolate doughnuts from the window and boxing them. As she put one into the box, Marnie immediately took it back out and took a giant bite, the chocolate calming her nerves. Jovi narrowed her eyes at her sister, then shrugged her shoulders and claimed her own doughnut. Marnie didn't miss the way her sister's cheeks grew a tad pale.

'Wait, I'm here, I'm here,' came Antoni's voice through the kitchen door. Like he was a dog and Marnie had just blown a whistle, he could sense the gossip and didn't want to miss out. He cast his tea towel over his shoulder, strode over and picked up a doughnut, concern etched on his striking features. Marnie couldn't help wonder what both Jovi and Antoni thought she was about to say but right now it didn't matter, because she didn't think she could hide a blonde-haired Canuck from them at the market on Sunday.

'I made a friend while I was in Canada,' Marnie started and instantly regretted it as Antoni's eyebrows wriggled up and down and she could see wedding bells chiming in her sister's mind.

'No shi…' Antoni blurted out, waving his doughnut around like he knew all there was to know in the world, but Marnie interrupted before he could finish.

'I said friend. Please stop.' She sighed before shoving another huge bite of doughy goodness in her mouth. Jovi started squirming, impatient for Marnie to finish chewing.

'Fine, fine, tell us about your friend,' Jovi urged while waving away Marnie's moan.

Marnie glanced out of the window and took a deep breath, trying to ignore the squirms in her stomach. Nova was a friend, nothing more. She had no reason to be making such a fuss over coffee. At work she had simply panicked about Amber overhearing them talking about hanging out away from the school.

'Her name is Nova. We met at a hockey game and hung out for a day in Vancouver. She's a budding palaeontologist and is currently over here working at Museum Borealis and teaching classes at school. She's cool,' Marnie explained, increasingly aware that with each word she knitted together,

her smile grew bigger just thinking and talking about Nova so openly.

'So, what's the problem?' Jovi enquired, her brows stitched together in confusion.

'I guess, I just panicked at work. She asked about catching up over coffee and wanted to give me her number. I hated the thought that Amber would hear our conversation and do that "oooh" and wiggly eye thing you both just did if she thought we were spending time together and then she'd snitch on me to Lesley. They have a no-dating policy, though I'm certain Amber is dating Mr Gonzalez, and Mr and Mrs Harrison are a couple, obviously, and so I invited her to the market on Sunday.' Hearing it out loud now, Marnie sucked in some air and plonked herself onto one of the stools at the high table, needing to catch her breath after talking so quickly. What had she just gotten herself into?

'Oh, yeah OK. Introducing her to your family is way better than spending time alone with her over coffee,' Antoni teased with a devilish smirk.

'Don't. I'm serious. I'm not ready to date.' Just saying the word made Marnie shiver. 'And you of all people know that. So be kind. This is not a date.' She gave Antoni a stern stare.

'Well, considering Sienna came bouncing in after school today talking about her new favourite teacher, who is the coolest and knows everything there is to know ever about dinosaurs, I'd say she's more than welcome,' Jovi noted, her face regaining its usual rosy hue that was her permanent make-up when at the bakery and rushed off her feet.

'Hey, I thought I was her favourite teacher!' Marnie whined.

'But are you the coolest?' Antoni teased, scrunching up his nose and giving her a faux sympathetic look.

'Get away. You know that means she loves her more than you too,' Marnie shot back with a winning grin.

'Children, such fickle creatures.' Antoni sighed before finishing his doughnut.

'Yeah, but I birthed her so I'm safe in the knowledge that she'll always come back to me. So, you guys enjoy your fifteen minutes of favouritism,' Jovi joked, pulling a wet cloth out of a nearby bucket and beginning to wipe down the counters.

Marnie chuckled but it wasn't a hearty chuckle. She knew her sister hadn't meant anything by her words and that they were merely good-natured fun but ever since Josh had left, Marnie was aware that her emotions were a touch sensitive when it came to baby talk. The mother-daughter relationship that Jovi and Sienna had was beautiful and Marnie had admired it the moment Sienna was born, but over the years she had also secretly envied it.

Jumping to her feet to squash down her emotions, Marnie grabbed her bag and noticed Antoni looking at her. This time the sympathy on his face was genuine. Marnie shook her head with pursed lips to tell him that she was fine. She didn't keep much from her sister but telling Jovi how she felt about her married life and wonderful child was something she hid from her behind locked doors. If she expressed her feelings to Jovi, Jovi would only feel guilty over something she couldn't control and that twin guilt was something that Marnie would never wish to put on her sister. She knew all too well how painful it could be and that had only been when they were teens and she had won a signed picture of their movie idol. Marnie had had no control over who won the competition but the guilt she felt over beating her sister and having something that was specifically hers, with her name on it, when it was something they had both wanted had very much ruined the joy of receiving it.

She couldn't imagine the damage that would be done should she share her silly jealous feelings with Jovi. Anyway, she had been working hard to heal those feelings and these days they were few and far between. Focusing more on what she did have in her life instead of what was missing was helping tremendously. Learning to control her breath on mountain hikes had given her the skills to catch herself when she felt her mind spiralling into overwhelmed territory.

Jovi eyed her sudden movement.

'Calm down, Marn. It will be lovely to meet your friend,' Jovi said, smiling widely.

'Yeah, she's just a friend. It's all fine – everything's good.' Marnie swung her hands behind her back and averted her eyes from Jovi and Antoni. She cast them over their window display that was starting to take shape. Antoni had now painted the autumn leaves on the window and the box of fall decorations lay beneath the bar. 'She showed me some beautiful places in Vancouver; now I get to show her around Orion.' Marnie took a deep breath and rolled out her shoulders. 'Right, yes. I can do that.'

'You can so do that,' Antoni concurred, licking the powdered sugar off his lips.

'OK, I'm off. Have a beautiful evening. I love you both,'

Marnie said, grabbing her bag and rushing out the door. Thoughts of babies had quickly turned into thoughts of where she could take Nova on Sunday that could blow Wakwak Burger out of the water.

16

Marnie barely got chance to talk to Nova on Thursday afternoon when she arrived for Class Nine's lesson, which wasn't necessarily a bad things as she was still wary of being seen talking to her. The morning had been a glorious hive of experiments, or one could say mess. As Paislee wasn't confident with the alphabet and the more Marnie was getting to know her and her frustration when it came to writing, they had spent some time at her desk looking at pictures of her favourite toys and movie characters with Marnie repeating the names that Paislee told her, sounding them out and saying the first letter. 'A for Allosaurus.' 'J for Jurassic.' Paislee had been quiet but content. Marnie had then written their names on a small whiteboard and placed the strips in front of Paislee with a pencil.

'Please will you write them for me so I don't forget?' she asked. Paislee gave her a curious look. 'Just one,' the little girl said.

'That would be great. We can do the other one tomorrow,' Marnie encouraged with a smile.

The two of them had then snuck into the corridor where Marnie had made bowls of jelly, each hiding letters of the alphabet in them. They had spent the morning digging them out with different tools with Paislee asking what the letters were when she found them and Marnie making it into a fun game.

'S for Sonic. S for Sausages. S for Sand.' She had scored a few giggles from Paislee in between the mouthfuls of jelly the little girl was gobbling up.

In the afternoon, the kids all sat on the edge of their seats with eager anticipation for Miss Clarke to make her grand entrance. Marnie left Paislee looking at a dinosaur book with Mason while she saw to the sticky table and clearing away the empty containers.

'Good afternoon, Miss Barnes.' She heard Nova's voice before she saw her and Marnie couldn't help grin at the enthusiasm and cheer in her tone.

'Good afternoon, Miss Clarke,' Marnie replied as she turned around to greet her. Though Marnie had recently seen her on three occasions, compared to the one occasion with her donning a baseball cap, she kind of missed it and there was a part of her that sensed the cap was to Nova what Marnie's bangles and bracelets were to her. Nova stuffed one hand in her beige trousers and the other tucked her signature wavy locks behind her ear.

'There you are, Miss Clarke. The kids are all waiting patiently,' Amber said as she came rushing out to guide Nova the one final step she needed to take into the classroom.

'Sorry, got a little held up talking about whether dinosaurs would survive in space with Class Four,' Nova explained with a soft chuckle.

Marnie snorted, guessing the culprit behind that question. Dinosaurs and space had Sienna's name written all over it.

She definitely was going to have competition on Sunday when it came to cool points with her niece.

Marnie had settled on breakfast at 'Made with Muffin but Love' and delighting Nova with their famous breakfast muffin that melted in your mouth with its buttery, cheesy, bacon bits – goodness that made your tongue come alive first thing in the morning. That's where she would take her and depending on how the day went and everyone's endurance, lunch would be a vegan sandwich masterpiece from 'Grahams'.

Nova was already there when Marnie arrived at the entrance early, beating the family. The cap she'd been wearing that day in Canada was fixed on her head, her blonde waves cascading down the back of her oversized soft olive-green hoodie. As Marnie made her way over to her, hoping to give her a rundown of her family so she didn't feel ambushed, she heard a holler from behind her.

'Auntie Marnie,' Sienna called out. Too late. She was going to have to wing it. Nova's head turned following the sound of Sienna's voice and Marnie's name and their eyes connected. Nova's sparkled a crystal water blue while Marnie's deepened, turning a greyish hazel, slightly cautious about today. But once Sienna's arms were wrapped around her thigh, her shoulders unknotted a touch.

'Hi, Miss Clarke,' Sienna said cheerfully. 'Will you come and see Cameron? She has all the dinosaur tools,' the little girl added innocently and excitedly when Nova reached them. Sienna clearly didn't want to waste a moment of time.

'Morning, Sienna. Hello, Marnie,' Nova said, gripping her

baseball cap and tilting it down. 'That sounds awesome.' Her tone was that of genuine interest, friendly and warm.

'Shall we let Mum and Dad catch up before we go?' Marnie noted. It wasn't really a question and more of a statement as she watched Jovi, Jackson and Antoni walking through the crowd nearing the spot where they stood. It hadn't been hard for Sienna to race ahead when Jovi and Antoni tested every fruit at the grocery stall.

For the five minutes they waited, Sienna picked Nova's brain about the best places in town she recommended digging for dinosaurs, to which Nova had suggested she visit the museum and they could research on her dinosaur map for where they could start.

'Good morning, Miss Clarke,' Jovi said, snapping Marnie out of watching and listening to the new and fast friends' dinosaur exchange. Marnie looked at her sister. Jovi was beaming, her eyelashes touching her eyebrows, with all her teeth on display. Marnie had to raise her hand up to her face due to the blinding sunrise when she caught sight of Antoni who looked a little flushed. Jackson was his cool, easy-going self, offering his hand, which Nova took with a bright smile.

'Call me Nova. It's so great to meet you all,' Nova said, reaching her hand to Antoni next, who caught himself and smiled.

'It's lovely to meet you too,' Jovi expressed. 'We've heard lots of wonderful things.'

'Mostly from Sienna,' Marnie teased, nudging Nova's elbow and instantly falling back into her easy banter. Away from the classroom, her chest didn't feel so tight and she found herself giddy at Sienna's suggestion of craft shopping with her favourite rocketeer and Nova. Now that the introductions were done, Sienna tugged at Marnie's hand and pointed in the direction of Cameron's stall.

'You don't mind if we leave this fizzing ball of energy with you this morning while we pick up supplies?' Jackson asked Nova politely, patting his daughter on the head and giving her a 'be on your best behaviour' look. Sienna stared back with perfectly large brown eyes.

'Not at all. I think she can teach me a thing or two about dinosaurs while I'm here,' Nova said with a smile.

'Come on,' Sienna said, bouncing forward and waving Nova in the direction of Cameron. With Marnie one step behind, she felt Antoni sneak up behind her before they parted ways.

'She's beautiful. Have fun on your date,' he whispered, a mischievous grin lighting up his whole face.

Jovi whacked his bicep while Marnie's stomach flipped out.

'It's not a date,' she muttered back, before shaking her head to dispel any thoughts of how beautiful Nova looked on a Sunday morning from taking up residence in there.

It didn't help that Cameron nearly gave Marnie and herself a glitter shower when she wandered out of her small trailer and her eyes fell on Nova. Nova was squatting down next to Sienna as Sienna named all the planets in the solar system that were spinning around in a diorama at the front of The Glitter Emporium table. Her blonde hair was shining in the sunlight, her lightly powdered cheeks were rosy with the passion in which she engaged with Sienna and with her tight leggings and oversized vintage-print olive jumper, she looked simultaneously striking and snuggable.

Marnie coughed, as though it would help clear her thoughts, and quickly picked up the stray rolling bottles of glitter from the ground to draw Cameron's attention away from Nova. She didn't like the way other people's attraction seemed to be rubbing off on her today. She couldn't see Nova like that. Nova was her friend.

'Morning. Everything OK?' Marnie said, placing the bottle back on the tray Cameron was carrying.

'You do see the Greek goddess talking to Sienna, don't you?' Cameron asked, blinking a couple of times. Marnie did not follow Cameron's gaze. She stroked her bracelet and focused on the tiny flecks of glitter in the bottles. 'Do you know her? Does Sienna have a nanny I don't know about?' Cameron added. Marnie couldn't help but chuckle at that suggestion.

'Now, why would Sienna need a nanny?' Whenever Jackson had to stay late at work or Jovi was busy at the bakery, Sienna would always have somewhere to go in this town. If she wasn't with Marnie or their mum, she was with Jillian or a neighbour or Cameron and Esme.

'Oh I don't know, it seemed like the only liable option considering she's wearing a Canucks cap and my very dear friend failed to mention anything about meeting anyone on her travels,' Cameron fired back, finally meeting Marnie's gaze and giving her a pointed mock-annoyed glare.

'We hung out for one day, that's all. She's a friend, she's cool and that's it,' Marnie explained speedily to Cameron, wanting to get on with the day and enjoy it with her Canadian friend without all the inquisitions and pointed looks.

'And now said "just friend" is in Orion that just so happens to be over four thousand miles away from Canada,'

Cameron noted, suspiciously, placing the bottles of glitter on the table.

'She's here working at Museum Borealis if you must know,' Marnie noted.

'I must and how convenient.' Cameron smirked, dimples appearing in her freckled cheeks.

'Are you done now?' Marnie asked, feeling a little like a child when she was unable to stop from rolling her eyes. Was everyone determined to make her feel awkward today? And why couldn't everyone understand that she was no way near ready for a relationship of any sort?

'Hi, you must be Cameron.' Suddenly Nova's voice sounded from right next to her and Marnie had to snap out of the foot stomping that was going on in her brain, wipe away her pout and slap a smile on her face. It wasn't hard to smile when Nova's accent rushed her ears.

Cameron seemed to choke on air, spluttering her introduction. 'Yes, yes, that's me and you are?' she asked, her usual cool demeanour faltering slightly. Nova looked from Marnie back to Cameron, probably wondering why Marnie hadn't given her name before. Marnie shook herself into action, shaking off her nerves and the silly thoughts others were putting into her mind this morning.

'Cameron, this is Nova. Palaeontologist in training and die-hard hockey fan.' Marnie grinned at her friend. Somehow in her presence, when her blue eyes rested on her, Marnie's brain relaxed. It was everyone else who was throwing her off today.

'It's a pleasure to meet you, Nova. If I can help you with anything, just let me know,' Cameron said, finding her regular voice.

'Thanks, I think you have a crafting connoisseur in the making. Sienna knows a great deal about everything in your shop eh,' Nova said, smiling broadly. Just then, Sienna appeared at their sides with a small armful of bits and pieces. Two bright, eager and large eyes looked up at Marnie over a stack of card, Styrofoam straws and a large bottle of glitter that would make Jovi wince.

Cameron swiftly helped her drop them all into a small basket. 'I'd gladly have her if NASA wasn't calling her name,' Cameron said, nudging Sienna's shoulder and making the little girl beam proudly.

'Should we leave our stuff with Cameron while we show Nova around? Is that OK, Cam?' Marnie suggested to Sienna. Sienna nodded and took her hand.

'No problem. Have fun. I'll catch you all later,' Cameron said, waving them away. Marnie ignored her mischievous stare and hoped Nova didn't catch it. Thankfully, Nova was busy looking around the market stalls and listening to Sienna talk about the candy floss stand.

'Breakfast muffins first, candy floss later,' Marnie said. Sienna didn't argue.

The girls walked either side of Sienna, Marnie pointing out different shops and giving Nova notes on their history and how long they had been around. She wasn't sure if her memory was off since having been away for six months but she was missing some of the usual banter she could recall from a few shop owners. She could have sworn Ted and Minnie from the jewellery shop had been friendlier before she left. Today there was no small talk or compliments about her jewellery, just two unenthused waves.

Conversation about whether dinosaurs would like

ice-cream distracted her from overthinking as they reached Made with Muffin but Love. Marnie ordered her and Sienna's traditional order while Nova scanned the menu.

'It's your choice – you can pick from the mighty menu or have me and Sienna surprise you with the best muffin you never knew existed but will be oh so glad you uncovered thanks to yours truly.'

'Well, I can't exactly say no to the best muffin in existence,' Nova replied, readjusting her cap with one hand and meeting Marnie's gaze before raising her eyebrows excitedly at Sienna. Marnie could feel her own excitement bubbling as her brain thought back to the streets of Vancouver and her Wakwak burger. This was fun. She was happy that dinosaurs had roamed the planet and vacationed all over the world.

By the time their muffins were ready, Jovi, Jackson and Antoni had joined them and were now awaiting their own. The muffins needed warming in the oven so they were just the right temperature to soothe the soul.

'So?' Marnie said, turning away from Antoni, who was trying to grab at her muffin, too impatient to wait for his own, to Nova. Nova's eyes were closed as she chewed the muffin slowly and suddenly Marnie didn't want to interrupt; she just wanted to watch her as Nova's smile grew wider. When she opened her blue eyes, she tilted her head from side to side and pursed her lips in thought. Marnie raised her brows, eager to find out what Nova thought.

'It could do with a little maple syrup,' she said, a light smirk playing on her lips.

'Oh my God, don't let Eva and Lionel hear you say that,'

Marnie said overdramatically looking over her shoulder at the van and shoving Nova.

Antoni stepped forward and leant between the two of them and said, 'She's right you know. Speaking of Maple goodness, Nova, you don't happen to have…' But Marnie stuffed a piece of her muffin into his mouth before he could finish.

'Stop harassing my friend for maple cream; I brought you back one jar of the stuff,' Marnie said, mock annoyed.

'Ooh, one jar of maple cream – you should have run that by me, Marn. One is just not enough. I would have told you to bring back at least six,' Nova said, playing along as the friends teased each other.

'When would you have told me that? While men were smashing each other over the head with sticks or when you were focusing ridiculously hard on not twisting an ankle on the ice?' Marnie responded jokingly as Jackson handed Antoni and Jovi their muffins and Sienna stood distracted, taking small nibbles to finish up her own.

'I suppose either or would have been appropriate. Rookie mistake when making friends with a tourist. Always tell them about the maple cream first,' Nova said, shaking her head and then giving Marnie a wink. Marnie felt the laughter flutter in her stomach first and then leave her lips. Antoni pointing at Nova and proclaiming 'she gets it,' reminded Marnie that she and Nova weren't the only two at the market, and she quickly averted her eyes from Nova and looked across the stalls. Something achingly dangerous happened in her chest whenever Nova winked at her like that and she wouldn't allow it.

For a few moments, the only sound was her family

munching on their morning muffins and wiping their hands on hard paper towels, in between hollers and shouts from different stands. Marnie went around collecting rubbish from the group and felt another tug at her chest with how seamlessly Nova was fitting in with them all. Nova had shown no signs of irritation at Sienna for holding Marnie's attention or for asking Nova a million questions and she hadn't been fazed by Antoni's humour or irked by them making group decisions.

Marnie knew she shouldn't have been doing it, but there was a tiny part of her brain that couldn't help compare Nova in this situation to Josh. Josh had attended the market one Sunday with Marnie and her family. He'd spent a lot of time on his phone saying it was 'work stuff' and then never went again. Marnie had kept it up until Josh had complained that Sunday morning should be their morning together, which was why she had missed the markets for so long.

'We don't have any famous sports teams out here but if your dad is anything like our dad, there is a cool woodwork shop if you're looking to get any souvenirs for family and friends,' Marnie told Nova, shaking away her thoughts and forcing herself to be present. It wasn't difficult when she was surrounded by her favourite people. For a split second Nova's clear blue eyes glistened as though wet, then she secured her cap, messing with the visor and when she met Marnie's gaze they were clear once more and a wide smile appeared across her face.

'Why don't you two go and do a little shopping. I need Sienna for some taste testing,' Jovi said, taking Sienna's hand and whispering something about chocolate bark. Sienna squealed with pure joy and so Marnie thought nothing of it, nodding at her sister and agreeing to meet back up around lunchtime.

'Sounds great, I'd love to see it,' Nova replied to Marnie before bending down a little and whispering to Sienna, 'Candy floss later, if Mummy and Daddy say yes,' then giving the little girl an 'it's our secret mission' kind of nod, which Sienna reciprocated.

Nova was definitely not Josh, Marnie found herself thinking as she led the way to the wood shop. Marnie's hands fiddled with the straps on her backpack; her back felt warm underneath it. Though the autumn weather was slowly nudging out the summer's scorching sun, today the sun was putting up a tough fight, reluctant to give up its spot to the billowy clouds. It was the perfect crisp autumn day.

'So, you get your love of crafting from your dad?' Nova asked, rolling up the sleeves of her jumper and revealing her two delicate wrist tattoos, Marnie's favourite being the geometric Triceratops on her left wrist.

'I do. He's always making something. He was a joiner but since he retired he's been selling bespoke pieces and I've never seen him happier. What about your dad?' Marnie enquired but promptly felt her stomach twist as that flash of sadness flickered through Nova's eyes once more. 'I'm sorry, you don't have to talk about your dad if you don't want to.' Marnie gently reached a hand out to Nova's forearm without thinking. Nova shrugged her shoulders and then gave Marnie a gentle shoulder check.

'He'd grab me in a headlock and ruffle my hair if I missed an opportunity to talk about him and his awesomeness,' Nova said with a chuckle. 'He passed away ten months ago – that's why I was in Vancouver. I was visiting my mom, trying to help her organise a little more of his stuff. It's hard to visit as often as I'd like when working at the museum in Alberta. I was trying to get back to some normalcy at the game. I think he was looking down on me that day,' Nova explained, a light flush tickled her cheeks pink with her last words.

Marnie felt her chest tighten. She couldn't imagine not having her dad around and it sounded like Nova had been especially close with hers. And, what did Nova mean by he was looking down on her that day? That the Canucks won? Probably that.

'I'm so sorry for your loss,' Marnie said. 'Gosh, I know that probably doesn't help or make anything better but I truly am sorry.' Marnie wanted to give Nova a hug but at the same time didn't want to be awkward as they were still walking. She let her hands fall to her sides and accidently brushed her fingers against Nova's swinging limbs. Nova laughed.

'Yeah, me too. Don't worry I get it. I don't think anyone has the right words to say in these kinds of situations,' Nova replied, not moving her arm away from Marnie's, instead letting it continue to sway and occasionally bump against Marnie's again. The familiar tingle that ran through Marnie's fingertips made her shoulders roll out with ease and comfort. She liked having Nova close and friends were allowed to offer each other warmth and contentment. Antoni provided her with both, minus the tingles, but Marnie chose to ignore that fact. She loved being at the markets and it was extra special today getting to witness Nova exploring it for the first time.

'Would your dad say that he needed a pencil pot carved out of wood in the shape of a DeLorean, like mine would?' Marnie asked with a gentle smile that grew wider when Nova barked with laughter.

'Absolutely, oh I have to get that for my mom. She'll think it's ridiculous,' Nova said, taking the object carefully from Marnie and turning it around in her palm, studying the detail.

The two of them lost track of time between the tables of the wood shop talking about their families, Marnie telling Nova about her parents' separation, Nova telling Marnie how her mom and dad had been soulmates meeting in their thirties and having Nova quite late by society's standards at the time. Nova had loved school, worked hard and gone to college to get her doctorate and then in her second year studying to be a palaeontologist, her dad had fallen ill and she'd ceased her studies, wanting to be there for him and her mom.

With her dad having put up a tough fight, he'd encouraged her to get back to work and when the museum job came up he wouldn't let her turn it down. She'd made the day trip from Alberta back to the British Columbia so many times, always anxious to get home to see him, and he treasured hearing about her work. Fortunately, she'd been home when he passed and she'd gotten to say bye. Knowing how happy the museum had made him, she'd stuck at it but hadn't quite found the motivation to get back to her studies yet.

They'd discussed their favourite pieces in the stall and come away with a gift for Nova's mom and a small carving tool for Marnie's dad.

Halfway round the candle stall, they heard a shout from across the market.

'Miss Clarke, Auntie Marnie, candy floss time!'

17

It had been quite some time since Marnie had spent an entire day at the market with her family. By the time her watch told her that it was five p.m., she was all candy-flossed out and had bags full of glitter and craft supplies courtesy of Cameron and because Sienna kept adding more things to her shopping basket that she thought Paislee might like. Nova had picked up a bag of ground coffee beans from The Sweet Latte so her mom could try a new blend of coffee, though Marnie had noted Canada had some great brands that were hard to beat, and failing to choose anything for her friends this time, Nova said she would have to come back again before she left to decide on what trinkets she would like to take back with her. Marnie had smiled at the thought of bringing Nova back to the market again.

'OK, but pink icing with colourful sprinkles or chocolate icing with chocolate sprinkles?' Marnie asked Nova as they walked side by side towards the exit of the market, the others right behind them. Though Marnie had a stomach full of candy floss, she found herself dreaming of a cosy evening that involved doughnuts and coffee while she curled up on her couch.

Nova tilted her head and narrowed her eyes, a serious

expression etched on her face. Marnie could feel her lips flutter as she supressed a smile, not wanting to distract Nova from her thinking and because she felt pleased that Nova was taking the question so seriously.

'Neither. Cake doughnuts filled with custard or Bavarian cream. But if I'm craving doughnuts and need them right this instant, chocolate icing with chocolate sprinkles. If I'm to sit and take my time, then definitely a cake doughnut with some kind of cream filling,' Nova said with a confident nod. This time Marnie couldn't hide her smile.

'Oh my God. You've just given me the most brilliant idea,' Antoni exclaimed from behind them. The girls twisted their heads around, still walking to keep with the flow of pedestrians leaving the market, and raised their eyebrows, intrigued.

'Antoni, if you say what I think you're going to say, then you are a genius and I will not take no for an answer at being your number-one taste tester.' Nova said, her eyes wide with excited anticipation. Marnie smiled at her best friend and her new friend getting along so well and felt amused that Nova knew what Antoni was thinking before she did. She might have felt a touch jealous if she didn't find Nova's matching love of doughnuts and the delight in her face when thinking and talking about them so cute. It was rather distracting, so much so that Marnie failed to spot the man and woman walking towards her before it was too late and the man's elbow bounced off her bicep, sending her bags crashing to the floor.

'Oh gosh, I'm so sor...' The words were halfway out of Marnie's mouth but got stuck the moment her eyes met the man's. Suddenly Jovi was at her side gathering all the glitter that had broken free from the brown paper bags and was throwing them back in with great haste. Antoni had taken a step forward, seemingly trying to block the person whose hand the man was holding from view and usher them both on but the man wasn't moving and it took Marnie a minute to straighten herself. 'Josh,' she mumbled.

'Marnie, is that you? Hi,' Josh said. He always had an aura of confidence about him, oblivious to what others might be feeling, but today there was a little tremble in his voice. Marnie had no doubt it was due to the posse that surrounded her. Both Jovi and Antoni's expressions were hard and Jackson stood tall, towering above him, impressive even when holding a little girl in his arms. Even Nova looked ready for battle and she didn't even know who he was.

Marnie bent down to collect the remaining scattered glitter bottles to clear her head. She was not doing this. She was not going to feel vulnerable and flustered in his presence. It was nearing nine months since their relationship ended, she was so much stronger than that now, or at least she had thought she was. 'Er, yeah, it's me,' she said assertively, claiming some control over her voice when not looking at him.

'You look great,' Josh mumbled.

'You really do.' Without looking up, Marnie knew the woman had spoken, her voice sweet and innocent, making Marnie's insides flip. Marnie took a deep breath, staring at the glitter that sparkled from within the bottles, her brain flashing with images of glittering planets, then abruptly disturbed by the pairs of feet that belonged to Josh and the same woman she had caught him in bed with. Then she stood up, wobbling slightly.

Antoni stepped forward. 'She doesn't need your compliments or approval, mate. Maybe you should get a move on,' he said, but Marnie caught his arm and pulled him back, revealing the not so flat stomach of Josh's other half. The birds stopped chirping, the patter of pedestrian footsteps ceased and all Marnie could hear was the painful thumping of her blood whipping around her body straight to her ears. Her skin felt cold, prickling with sweat that felt increasingly uncomfortable the longer she stood there.

Images flashed before her eyes. Words fought through the swishing sounds of blood in her brain, conversations she and Josh had had during their time together: 'I'm not ready for kids.' 'We look after kids all day at work, can't it just be us when we come home?' 'We have all the time in the world to have kids.' 'Kids will be too much work.'

Marnie's mind felt void of a response. Surely there were things she should say, things she should scream at Josh right now? Remind him of the words he had spoken, make him aware of the pain he had caused her, admonish him for the hurt, yell at him for having been so cruel, question him, demand answers. Why was this woman worth a baby and her not? But no words, no sentences formed. The only thing that formed were tears that were beginning to pool in the corners of her eyes.

Suddenly, a warm tingle shot through her fingertips, making her turn her head away from the baby bump and Josh. She looked down at her hand where Nova was relieving her of her heavy bags. Marnie's eyes wandered from the closeness of their hands and up to Nova's face where she could see a slight furrow of confusion in Nova's brows, mixed with clear concern in her blue eyes. When their eyes met, something passed between the two of them. Nova leaned forward, breathing into Marnie's ear, making Marnie's inside fizz. 'You got this,' Nova whispered, underneath Marnie's hair, her lips grazing her ear.

If Marnie hadn't fainted before at the sight of Josh and his baby-bearing girlfriend, she was afraid she might now. Her knees felt dangerously light and unable to support her weight. When Nova leaned back, a smile curved at her peachy lips and Marnie forced some air into her lungs with a sharp breath. Aware that Jackson and Sienna had continued walking to the gate and that Antoni's fist were curled tightly into balls, while Jovi was giving Josh the death glare, she knew she had to speed up this interaction.

'Erm, have a nice evening both of you,' Marnie managed. No matter Nova's confidence in her and pep talk, Marnie's voice betrayed her a touch. The old feelings of hurt that bubbled in her gut over Josh, the nausea that stirred upon seeing his new girlfriend pregnant mixed with the very new feelings that somersaulted around her stomach at Nova's proximity were an odd combination.

Before Josh could reply Jovi grabbed Marnie's hand and led her away. Air seemed to return to Marnie's lungs by the time they reached the gate.

'OK, you three have some serious explaining to do,' Marnie said suddenly finding her voice as anger slowly started to zip through her veins at what had just happened. She looked from the ground up to her sister, brother-in-law and best friend in a slight daze. 'What's going on? I take it that's what you've been keeping from me? But then, please tell me why I'm the one who has been getting filthy looks from the town? That's the bit I don't get, also I'm stumped at why none of you thought it a good idea to warn me.' Marnie was not one to make a scene but she became aware that she had stopped walking, her feet like lead, carrying the heavy weight of her questions.

'Marn, let's go back to mine and I can explain,' Jovi said, her face pale as she caressed Sienna's face while the little girl yawned. Marnie felt a sudden rush of guilt. This wasn't a conversation Sienna needed to hear, yet she couldn't help herself; her body was in shock. When she thought the past couldn't hurt her anymore, it had come out of nowhere and surprised her when that could have been avoided if her family had been honest with her.

'Funnily enough, I'm not really in the mood for Sunday dinner or family affairs, Jovi. You let me look like a complete fool,' Marnie noted, her voice stern and dripping with hurt.

'We didn't mean for you to find out like this, Marn. Come on, please let us explain.' Antoni held out his hands, trying to reach out to soothe Marnie by gently touching her forearm but she stepped backwards, nearly bumping into Nova. Looking at Nova only intensified the tears that stung her eyes. There were too many emotions spinning around her body.

'It seems like you didn't mean for me to find out at all,' Marnie said feeling all the air deflate from her lungs. She gasped, trying to refill them. Her mind zoomed back to the day she had walked in on Josh and his new woman. The lies, the betrayal, the fact that it had been going on for months and she had been none the wiser. 'I'm going to go,' she whispered, her voice strained. Jovi and Antoni having kept this from her was too much.

'Marn, don't do this. He isn't worth it. Please forget about him. You've been doing so well moving on, we didn't want to bring up the past and damage your healing. You don't need to think about him anymore,' Jovi protested, frustration knotted between her brows.

Marnie's stomach twisted painfully. When she looked up she caught Jackson nodding at Jovi. He gave Marnie a brief nod and walked in the direction of home with a sleepy Sienna in his arms. It was early evening, getting to six p.m., but the little girl had had an exciting day. The tension in Marnie's shoulders momentarily loosened as she looked at her favourite rocketeer, until Josh's girlfriend's baby bump and the lies flashed across her brain.

'Jeez, Jovi, I'm sorry. Why didn't I think about forgetting the past ten years of my life? All these months, I didn't realise it was as easy and as simple as that,' Marnie retorted, aware her voice was hard, but she had no control over it. Her emotions were erratic. 'I'm sorry that once again my plan didn't quite go as smoothly as yours. I'm the stupid one who can't let go and leave it all in the past. I should just click my fingers and not be fazed at all by this news.' Marnie's cheeks were moist with tears – just another thing she hadn't been able to control.

'She didn't mean that, Marn. We know it's hard. Why don't we go and talk about it?' Antoni asked, again moving to take her elbow but Marnie's legs sprung to action and she moved away.

'No thank you, Ant, I think I'm done talking about it now. Is that better? Isn't that what you want?' Marnie said, looking from her best friend to her sister. Jovi had one hand in her hair and Antoni was looking at the ground. His six-foot frame appeared much smaller. Marnie couldn't figure out if she was more hurt by the baby news or the fact that the people she loved most in the world had kept it from her.

Jovi let out an annoyed sigh. 'No actually, Marn, what I wanted was to be there for you, to talk about it, to help you heal, to keep you in the loop as life changed and we processed it together, but you're the one who fled the country, so don't give me that. Oh and while you're opening up about life being so easy, it sure was easy navigating Mum and Dad's separation alone, helping Dad find a place, meeting Tim for the first time while you hiked the bloody Great Bear Rainforest, so yes please talk to me about how my life is so easy,' Jovi returned, her cheeks red, her face flustered.

Marnie narrowed her eyes at her twin sister. Her chest felt hollow, like all the wind had been knocked out of her. How could Jovi stoop so low and bring up their parents? Wasn't the fact that she didn't have a baby and Josh had one on the way enough to contend with?

'Really? I'm sorry about Mum and Dad but at least you got to home to Jackson and Sienna, to a solid family, people to wrap their arms around you and tell you it's going to be OK. What did I have? My cold and empty apartment filled with nothing but pictures of Josh and Mum and Dad as a happy unit everywhere.' Marnie cried. Her fingers were trembling as that feeling of being so very alone washed over her. She rubbed her thumb over her bangle.

'You had me.' Antoni's voice was so quiet, it was hard for Marnie to hear over the pounding in her head, but Marnie was too angry and upset to feel any sympathy for him after he had helped keep this huge secret from her. 'You know I didn't mean it like that, Ant.' She sighed with frustration. Antoni ran a finger through his hair, not making eye contact.

'I'm going to go and check on Jackson and Sienna. I'll talk to you tomorrow. Love you,' he said quickly and walked off, his head drooping.

Both Marnie and Jovi watched Antoni walk away, then Jovi shook her head. 'You talk about being alone but since everything happened with Josh and Mum and Dad, you shut everyone out. Heck, even when you were with Josh, we were second fiddle. You kept us at arm's length. We didn't even know about Nova until two days ago. I don't know what you want from me. We're trying.' Jovi dropped her arms to her sides, her tone defeated.

Marnie felt a dozen tiny pricking sensations in her chest as the words Jovi spoke stung her heart. She couldn't look at her sister and she most definitely couldn't bring herself to look at Nova.

'You wouldn't understand,' Marnie replied, truth in her words but at the same time she heard the truth in her sister's words.

'It was lovely to meet you, Nova. Please forgive us for our family drama. It happens rarely, so consider this a one-off special Orion event for your holiday scrapbook,' Jovi said, with a half-hearted chuckle.

Marnie's cheeks flamed. She could feel the heat rise from her chest all the way to her ears. Her whole body felt overwhelmed with a heat too hot for her to handle. How could she look at Nova now? Nova had just witnessed the mess that Marnie had been trying to hide. She'd not spoken of Josh or her fears of never having kids. As she stared at the ground, Marnie watched Jovi's feet walk away. She felt the sudden urge to scream at her sister, an agitation rising in her body that Jovi would never understand her, but she was all out of fight and deep down she knew why.

How could Jovi help her if she kept things from her? But by the same token, even if she told Jovi how she felt, how was her sister supposed to help then? Get a divorce? Tell her of Sienna's terrible tantrums? Marnie didn't want any of that. She was happy for her sister, so why did her stupid brain have to feel jealous?

Marnie squeezed her eyes tight and when she opened them she turned to look at Nova. The sky around them had now grown a deeper blue, the moon hiding behind a few late clouds not quite at its brightest glow and Nova stood with patience etched on her features, kind blue eyes staring back.

'I'm so ridiculously sorry about all that,' Marnie stammered, stepping forward to relieve Nova of the heavy bags she'd been holding. As she brushed her hand against hers, Marnie didn't even allow herself to enjoy the pleasant tingle that shot through her veins. How could she have put Nova through all that? She hung her head in shame.

'No need to be sorry,' Nova said, tilting her head to the side, a small smile appearing at the corner of her mouth. 'Should we walk and talk? I do need to bring some life back to my fingers eh,' she added casually. It was then that Marnie could feel the breeze that had picked up around them, which only added to the guilt that was forming in the pit of her stomach.

'Oh gosh, I'm sorry. You really don't have to walk with me. I'm sure you have better things to do,' Marnie said, unable to stop the flames that burnt her cheeks contradicting the cool breeze that grazed them.

'I can walk,' Nova said simply.

But as they walked, there was no talking, just a surprisingly comfortable silence. Marnie escaped her busy overthinking brain by being increasingly aware of Nova's existence. With each gentle but chilly breeze that blew around them came the aroma of Nova's sweet vanilla perfume that eased the tangle of knots that had formed in Marnie's stomach. Despite the tension in her belly shifting, Marnie still couldn't find the words to engage, feeling wholly mortified by the events of the last hour and it was all her fault. She stopped walking when she realised her feet had led her back home and she stood outside her apartment building. She placed the heavy bags full of crafting supplies on the floor by her feet and reached around for her backpack to get her keys.

Once the keys were in her palm, she looked up at Nova. 'I can make tea, or coffee, if you'd like one. You don't have to come in. I can understand if you're tired and want to run far away from me,' Marnie mumbled trying at the end to force a small chuckle to break the awkwardness that had risen since they stopped walking.

'Is this your block?' Nova looked around as though making a mental note of her surroundings. Her eyes scanned the street and registered each shop with a small nod. Marnie nodded in reply to her question. 'Will you give me five minutes?' Nova asked.

Marnie hesitated, suddenly anxious that she was putting pressure on Nova. 'Erm, yeah sure, but please don't think you have to. I'll completely understand if you want to head home. Erm, but just press the buzzer if you did want tea,' Marnie said, her lips feelings dry, 'or coffee.' She turned away slightly and put the key in the lock.

'The buzzer, got it,' Nova said with a closed-lip smile and determined nod before she turned and walked away.

18

Once through her front door, Marnie went through the motions of taking off her cropped wide-leg trousers and replacing them with her navy sweatpants. She then did the same with her denim jacket and tee, replacing them with her favourite matching hoodie. It wasn't until she flicked the kettle on with a 'just in case' feeling that the weight of the afternoon's events hit her. The tears fell first as she gripped the counter, heaving heavy sobs.

Who was she kidding with 'just in case'? Nova wasn't coming back. She'd made an utter fool of herself tonight. She had fought with her twin sister in the middle of the market and her words had been a jumbled mess. Yes, there had been truths. She could still feel the anger and frustration in the base of her stomach. The frustration that everyone acted like this whole moving on thing was easy. The anger that rose when she thought of Josh pregnant with another woman after years of putting it off with her, and the fact that her family had kept this nugget of information from her.

But then the jealously. A word that made Marnie squirm uncomfortably. A word she strongly disliked yet there it sat, like a stubborn leech stuck to her chest, sucking up all her gratitude for the life she had and tormenting her with the things she so desperately wanted but couldn't have; the things her sister had.

And how could she have been so cruel to Antoni? He was right. She had him. She always had him. He hadn't left her apartment when Josh had walked out. He'd taken her to the airport, been on board with her spontaneous plan even when it hadn't included him. She'd needed her space but her adventure had forced Antoni to take some space whether he wanted it or not and he hadn't complained, only wanting to see her happy.

Of course, the cherry on top of the cake was the presence of Nova. The Nova who Marnie had spent one day with in Canada and who she hadn't been able to stop thinking about since. And now Nova was in town and causing all sorts of problems with Marnie's emotions. She, naturally – like Jovi had accused her of – had kept Nova at arm's length, not divulging anything about Josh or work woes during their time together, only to have it all erupt like some school science experiment and explode into the atmosphere all at once. Nova had been so open and honest about her dad and Marnie had buried her feelings hoping that, unlike one of Nova's digs, Nova would never be able to extract them.

Feeling too weak to pick up the kettle or even mix a teabag, Marnie shuttled over to her couch where she flopped herself down and covered herself with cushions. Just as she was pulling a throw over the top of her, her buzzer sounded around the tiny apartment, making her insides jump.

There were a few apologies Marnie needed to make tonight but she didn't know if she was ready. She would need to cool down before talking to Jovi as her head was still pounding and she was scared of what she would have to say to her sister whom she loved so much. As for Antoni, Marnie didn't know if she could bear the thought of seeing his hurt expression anymore this evening, but she took a deep breath in and prepared herself for it anyway as she got up off the couch.

'Who is it?' Marnie said automatically, her finger over the intercom. Her voice sounded forlorn and dazed and she had to force the words but it was the rules of the building not to buzz in strangers.

'It's Nova. Is that coffee still on offer?' Nova said, her voice a lot more positive that Marnie's.

Marnie's legs immediately turned to jelly. Nova had come back.

'Sure, yes,' Marnie choked out.

The next minute Nova was stood in Marnie's doorway with a box of doughnuts in her hand that contained both pink icing with sprinkles on top and chocolate icing with chocolate sprinkles on top. The smile that crept across Marnie's face was genuine and she stepped aside to let her in.

'I was limited for choice as everything is closed for the evening so corner shop doughnuts it is. You guys have really cute corner shops here by the way.' Nova made her way to the kitchen and placed the box on the counter. Marnie followed after her, the smell of sugary doughnuts mixed with the smell of Nova's vanilla perfume, making her feel lighter, though it was hard to un-fuzz her brain with the scent of Nova and her kind gesture.

'You don't think I'm an awful human being?' Marnie's

words came out before she could overthink them. She stood in the doorway watching Nova glide around her small kitchen, plating up doughnuts and flicking on the kettle, and she wanted with all her heart to glide with her but she knew she could not dismiss what had happened tonight. Nova deserved more than that. Nova had given more than that, yet Marnie had hid so much of herself. Maybe it was the lure of the doughnuts but she wanted to let Nova in.

Nova closed the cupboard after selecting two mugs and looked Marnie's way.

'Oh absolutely. You, Miss Barnes, are an awful human being for having feelings and for having a past that wasn't all sunshine and rainbows, and if I'm putting the pieces of the puzzle from tonight together, for having an ex who is a little bit of an insensitive jerk,' Nova said, getting back to the kettle.

For a moment Marnie stood in shock. How was Nova so effortlessly cool and good at being up front and honest?

'I get it from my dad, if that's what you're thinking. He was always so open, went after what he wanted, loved what he loved fearlessly and didn't believe in wasting time,' Nova told Marnie, passing her one of the small plates with two doughnuts on it, one pink, one chocolate. Their eyes met as Marnie reached out for it and Nova's face softened. Her voice grew slightly quieter and less bouncy. 'But that doesn't mean you have to be good at expressing yourself or that you must tell me everything just because I never shut up. You're allowed to tell your story when and if you would like.' Nova's blue eyes beamed sincere and sparkled with warmth.

Marnie pulled the plate back to her chest with one

hand and started picking at the sprinkles on the pink doughnut. She gave a gentle nod, appreciating Nova's words greatly and giving her brain chance to register them completely.

When you have a twin, it's easy to question every move you make, every life choice, every personality trait, when you have someone right beside you doing it better and people asking you the same questions and often trying to fit you into the same box.

You two are so cute. The boys will be lining up to take you on dates. Oh your poor dad, grown-ups would say during the girls' early teen years and Jovi would flush and giggle while Marnie would stand awkwardly fiddling with the homemade beaded bracelets on her wrists.

Oh pastry chefs, that's fantastic. Your parents must be so proud, people would reply, Jovi having answered the question first and them deciding that Jovi had answered for the both of them.

It will be your turn next. I bet you were picturing yourself up there, you and Josh. You've got all this to come, people said waving their hands around the church where Jovi and Jackson got married. Was it wrong for them to assume that Marnie would want the same type of wedding? Was it wrong for them to assume that just because Jovi had it, that Marnie would have it too? And what happened when there were things that Jovi did have that Marnie wanted?

How sweet would it be for you to get pregnant at the same time. Oh just think, your kids will grow up so close and be the best of friends.

You and Josh need to get a move on. Sienna is going to need someone to play with.

What happened when people's words and thoughts matched her own? What happened when she wanted to climb into Jovi's life but she couldn't? What happened when life had other plans for you and there's no proposal, no marriage, no babies and instead ten years of memories washed down the drain? You become a disappointment to yourself and others.

'Jovi's always been a little more carefree with her feelings than me,' Marnie said, walking over to the couch and taking a seat. Nova didn't reply; she simply let Marnie talk while she brought over her plate and then went back for the two mugs of coffee.

'It didn't used to be like that. I told Jovi and Antoni everything when we were younger. I could always talk to my parents. I liked making friends. I could be myself around people for the most part but somewhere after high school between trying to figure out what I wanted to do and Jovi and Antoni going off to college and university, it was like I got stuck. I found my footing with college and I loved it, but it was hard to find work in a school and it was a little harder to be myself without Jovi and Antoni around. It felt like there were parts of me I had to hide and I kind of fell into people's assumptions and just accepted them. Then I met Josh and it was great. He was a few years older and the deputy head teacher back then at Cornelia Primary School. He was smart, focused and we had fun. I was working at the flower shop across the street when a job came up at his school and I went for it. Jobs around here can be a little tricky to come by but a lady was retiring and I gratefully took her spot.' Marnie took a moment to pause and take a bite of her doughnut. Nova sipped on her coffee but didn't break eye contact. Strangely enough, Marnie didn't feel any pressure to keep talking but she wanted to.

Nova offered her a smile as she took a bite of her own doughnut. She was eating the chocolate one first.

'Jovi had met Jackson at university. He was doing hospitality management or some kind of business degree and so he's the brains behind the bakery. He was a permanent fixture in our small circle when they came back and I loved him, but the two of them always made a relationship look so easy. It seemed as they got closer and created this wonderful world of a cosy family business, the less Josh fit. He wasn't as bothered about fitting into to our little unit as Jackson had been. At first it worried me, but then I just got used to it. It was me and him against the world, he used to say, like we didn't need anyone else. Then my parents kind of imploded. It was getting harder to ignore their arguments and unhappiness, so I guess I retreated a little. I believed Josh. I hung on his every word.' Marnie couldn't help the tear that trickled down her cheek as she spoke. The sprinkles before her became blurry as she absentmindedly took another bite and chewed slowly.

'I'd spent my youth trying to figure out my identity, fighting to be seen as different to Jovi around other people. Antoni got it. With him I've always been able to be me. He never treated us the same. Josh was extremely vocal about my being different to Jovi too and how we had different lives, but not in the way Ant was. If I ever expressed the want for a house or marriage and a baby, he turned it into some twin thing, reminding me that I was different and that just because Jovi had them I didn't need them too. Gosh, I tortured myself over that. I kind of just stopped talking.

Never in my life have I been jealous of my sister. I love her more than anything. I love my brother-in-law. I adore my niece, but resentment started to build and for the first time in my life, I was hiding something from her.'

Marnie let out a breath, the words having rushed out of her mouth. Her chest had begun hammering as if there were a hundred tiny hammers attacking the walls of her ribcage. Her body felt too hot and claustrophobic. She needed to calm her thoughts and relax her tense muscles.

Suddenly two hands reached out and rested on top of her shaking ones. Nova's smooth skin was cool against hers and when Marnie looked up into her blue eyes, that were like tiny galaxies with their flecks of white and turquoise, her breath hitched a little differently and the hammering transformed into a more comfortable and pleasant beat.

'You are one of a kind – don't you forget that. Sure you're a twin but you're still your own magical star that's made up of a gazillion specks of stardust. I'm a woman. There are many women out there in the world – many sisters, many moms, many aunts, many wives, many girl-friends, many lesbians, many trans, many bi, many cooks, many skaters – we may all share a label but none of us are exactly the same. It's not possible. We all have different experiences. We all have unique brains that make us who we are,' Nova said, giving Marnie's hands a gentle squeeze, making the tension release from her shoulders and the rigid knots in her stomach turn into a squishy marshmallow flump.

'You're just saying I'm one of a kind because you've never witnessed someone make a dramatic scene in a market before,' Marnie found herself teasing. Having spilled the inner workings of her brain to this beautiful woman before her, who she had technically only known for a handful of days, but felt like she had known forever, she could feel her limbs loosening as well as her tongue.

'It depends if you only consider dramatic to be a bad thing. My parents were plenty dramatic but more in regards to grand gestures and acting like big kids in public with no concern for who was watching,' Nova noted and Marnie took in the way her plump lips curved into a fond grin as her eyes vanished with swirls of silvery specks into a memory. Marnie gave her a moment, enjoying the feel of their hands together. When Nova came back to the room and their eyes found each other's again, Marnie spoke.

'They really loved each other, eh?' Marnie asked, adding the 'eh' to hopefully draw a chuckle from Nova and lighten the heavy load that she had dumped into the room this evening. The marshmallow in her stomach practically melted when laughter burst from Nova's lips.

'They did, very much so,' Nova replied with a smile that reached the second piercing in her ears. As she laughed, Nova released Marnie's hands and sat back in her spot on the couch. 'Now, how are you feeling?' she asked, picking up her other doughnut as Marnie did the same.

'So much better, thank you. For years, Josh told me he wasn't ready for kids and I waited. So to see his girlfriend pregnant, well I think it was all a bit of a shock. Then I got angry with Jovi and Ant for keeping it from me but you know, I'm not even sure I'm upset about Josh, I just don't like being kept in the dark. They should have told me. I could have handled it. I'm happy and focused. I love my new job, in spite of Miss Olsen's vendetta against me.

Mum's new man isn't all that bad. You'll have to meet him. He's a big ice-hockey fan if you can believe that. Sienna and her space-loving ways make me ridiculously proud each and every day and I love spending more time with her and there's this new teacher popping in and out of school teaching the kids about dinosaurs, which I think is slightly nerdy but she's also pretty cool and brings me doughnuts when I don't really deserve them, so...' Marnie said, her words coming out with unaccustomed ease. 'It just felt a bit like an ambush, that's all.'

Nova chuckled again and the sound and the fact that Marnie had caused it made Marnie's cheeks flush.

'I'm always happy to meet a fellow hockey lover. And I think doughnuts are always deserved. And you know, I think you handled yourself well out there today. I've heard of people who swing punches, burn belongings and recite evil rituals to curse the unborn child, so you were pretty tame.' Nova winked. Her blonde hair framed her face now that she wasn't wearing her baseball cap. It hung loosely in waves and made the peachiness in her cheeks pop. It was a face Marnie was beginning to find a lot of comfort in and was growing fond of. After upsetting both her best friends this evening, Marnie felt grateful for Nova's companionship. She might need a new best friend if Antoni decided never to speak to her again. Jovi didn't exactly have too much choice. Sure, Marnie knew she had screwed up big time and was well aware that she would have to apologise, but Jovi was her twin, which meant she couldn't get away from Marnie as easily as others. She was stuck with her for life.

'You've cursed unborn children?' Marnie teased, licking her lips as she finished her second doughnut. The chocolate one had been rather delicious, only slightly superior to the pink glazed.

'I'm not that creative,' Nova started, with a cheeky smirk as she reached forward and placed her plate on the coffee table, collecting her coffee before tucking her feet underneath herself once more. 'I've had my fair share of heartache, been told I'm too serious when it comes to relationships. I care too much or I love my job more. The longest relationship I've been in lasted three years and she left me because she didn't want a family. I made her feel trapped when I talked about marriage and kids. Then she would say that I spent more time talking about dinosaurs than about her and our future. Ultimately, I couldn't win. I loved thinking and talking about her and our future – dinosaurs too – but then I realised that she would get mad because my idea of the future didn't align with what she wanted.' Nova shrugged and brushed her hand through her middle parting to flick her hair out of her face.

'Relationships,' Marnie said with an overexaggerated sigh and a playful shudder.

Nova smiled back but it didn't reach her ears this time. Her lips were pressed together and a thoughtful look flashed across her face. 'You don't believe in relationships anymore?' Marnie didn't miss that Nova's voice came out soft and worried, but she couldn't seem to look her in the eye. Did she really not believe in relationships anymore? She had been quite bold and fierce in telling Jovi and Antoni that she was done with relationships but something inside her was making it extremely difficult to tell Nova. The angst and stubbornness were not finding their way through her lips.

'I guess, it's hard to believe in happily-ever-afters these days, what with Josh, my parents...' Marnie mumbled weakly instead.

When she chanced a glance at Nova, Nova quirked her head to one side and gave a fleeting sympathetic smile, but her words were not sympathetic; they came out with their familiar passionate bounce.

'You mean to tell me that you don't believe in fairy tales and Prince Charming sweeping you off your feet?' There was a hint of sarcasm in Nova's tone but when Marnie caught the glimmer in her blue eyes she also knew that Nova was legitimately asking. Marnie stretched out her legs and relieved herself of plates and mugs and turned to face Nova.

'After ten years of waiting for my fairy godmother to whisk me to the magical wedding ball and listening to my parents argue and supposed Prince Charming sweeping another woman in to his chambers, no I don't believe I do. It's terrifying and that is something Disney failed to share with us if you ask me. You're telling me that you actually believe in forever?' Marnie asked. It was her turn to quirk her head at Nova. The world was filled with dating apps that promoted one-night stands, thrills for married men and women. How could anyone truly believe in love anymore? Marnie was aware that somewhere along the way she had gotten rather cynical and she wasn't sure if that scared her more than the thought of dating.

'Of course I believe in forever. OK, Disney may have got it a little wrong but the thought was there. They meant well. Forevers are not without obstacles. Forevers do not equate to perfect relationships. And forevers are different for everyone. There's no magic formula or timeframe. My mom and dad promised to love each other forever. My dad's forever was cut short. She loved him for his forever and he loved her for his forever. I know my mom still loves him, but who knows, she's hopefully got many more trips around the sun and she might meet someone else she can love,' Nova explained with surprising enthusiasm when talking about such a sad turn of events. Marnie furrowed her brow.

'So, you're saying we meet people we love and we hold on to them for however long our forever together is? And sometimes that forever is a few days, maybe a few months, a couple of years or until one of us cheats, leaves, gives up or dies?' Marnie queried and couldn't help the snort that escaped at the end of her sentence.

'Exactly, what if life is not just one big forever but it's made up of many forevers?' Nova said, her face glowing.

Marnie's nose creased and her eyes narrowed.

'Mind blown eh?' Nova added with accompanying jazz hands.

'My head hurts,' Marnie teased though she was half serious. She rubbed at her forehead.

'That's because it's getting late and we have work tomorrow,' Nova said, catching sight of the clock on the wall and tapping her hands on her knees. It was nearing eight p.m. Marnie was most definitely an early to bed, early to rise kind of person apart from in Canada when she had been a late to bed but still early to rise kind of person because she didn't want to miss a thing.

Nova stood and gave a little stretch.

'Will you be OK getting back to your B&B?' Marnie asked as the darker evenings were beginning to replace summer's light nights.

'Sure. I'll Uber it. If you don't mind me hanging around for another ten minutes?' Nova said, casually and Marnie stood for a moment simply admiring her friend. How effortlessly cool she was. It had taken Marnie four weeks while in Canada before she had found the confidence to 'Uber it'.

'Of course. That's no problem,' Marnie replied, stifling a yawn. She covered her mouth with her hand, not wanting to seem rude.

'Don't worry, it's way past my bedtime too,' Nova said, as if reading Marnie's mind. Though her tone was playful, her lips curved into a sympathetic and warm grin that went straight to Marnie's belly. The thought that Nova understood early nights and rose in the early hours to greet the sunrise as well comforted Marnie, and after the events of the evening, Marnie hadn't realised just how much she'd needed to feel seen and understood.

19

Marnie had tried so very hard to never fall victim to the 'Monday blues'. When she had begun working at Cornelia she leapt out of bed with vigour, ready to dive into a day full of listening to readers, crafting, helping wherever she could and answering the strange and obscure questions often presented to her by primary school kids. Granted, since walking in on Josh cheating and her mum and dad separating, the Monday blues had rubbed their hands together, thrown their heads back and cackled victoriously as they gripped her with hands so fierce and tight Marnie had feared she'd never be able to escape. But escape she did. Vancouver life had been far too alluring for her to stay cooped up in her hotel room all day and the more she roamed the streets, the more she forgot about Orion.

This Monday morning, however, she did not have the luxury of procuring a coffee from Finch's while people-watching the pedestrians on W Pender Street before taking a leisurely stroll to Creekside Park. She had to face the inhabitants of her hometown – more specifically her twin sister and best friend.

Every step Marnie took towards the bakery felt heavy, even though her legs felt as though one gust of wind would blow her down as they shook nervously. It wasn't that she was so worried about saying sorry – that she could do – but owning up to her deepest fears… Was she ready yet? Was Jovi ready?

The familiar scent of vanilla pastries tickled her nostrils as Marnie knocked on the door quickly before she chickened out. It was early, the front of the bakery was dark but she gave it a few beats before she knocked again and Antoni's sullen face appeared at the door. Marnie gave a lips-together 'I'm sorry' smile, making her hazel eyes wide, which she knew wouldn't be enough to earn forgiveness but Antoni did open the door.

'Can we talk?' Marnie asked, playing with the hem of her denim jacket and trying to keep eye contact.

'Yep, back here though. Bread won't bake itself,' Antoni replied, turning away, his voice cool but wobbly. Marnie could sense he didn't want to stay angry but that what she'd said at the market had truly upset him and she wasn't surprised. He had been her other, other half, to Jovi's other half, and she had dismissed him with one cruel sentence.

'Ant, I'm sorry. I'm so very sorry. I've never been alone. I know that but I was in shock and I was angry that you and Jovi hadn't prepared me for a moment like that. What was I supposed to do?' Marnie began rambling as she trailed after Antoni into the kitchen where Jovi gave her a pointed glare and Harry and Violet momentarily stopped kneading dough. She nodded at the two friends but averted her eyes from Jovi. Antoni first, then Jovi she told herself. 'My brain was jumbled. I know there's no excuse to ever mistreat you – I understand that. I never want to hurt you but it was a lot to process in the moment.' Marnie's words were not stopping until Antoni looked at her. When he did, his brown eyes glowing a tad wet, Marnie's heartbeat sped up. He couldn't hate her forever. She'd be lost without him.

'You're right,' he began, throwing his tea towel over his shoulder after wiping his hands down. Marnie gulped. Her palms were sweating. 'You're right,' he repeated and in her periphery Marnie could see that Jovi had stopped mixing and was looking at them both. 'We should have told you. Except you came back from Canada looking all fresh-faced and glowing. You had all these adventures to talk about and it was like you were moving forward. You were in full swing of your new beginning, your fresh start and we were scared. You weren't talking about Josh and so we thought we could just put him in the past and leave him there.'

Marnie nodded her understanding, unable to speak as her mouth had gone a tad dry.

'It wasn't fair, not when we knew about the rumours and of the looks you were getting but we just thought if we ignored it all, it would go away,' Antoni finished and Marnie's stomach tightened. They knew about the looks too. The thought felt like another stab in the heart but she wasn't here to argue. They were getting everything out in the open. She wasn't a child; she couldn't stomp her feet and walk out, not when she'd come here to hear the whole truth and not when she still had another apology to make.

It was then that Marnie heard Jovi sigh to the right of her. Marnie turned as Jovi hung her head and covered her mixing bowl with a tea towel before stepping around the kitchen island towards her, blocking the kitchen doors; no doubt sensing that Marnie was starting to feel overwhelmed.

'Look, Mar.' Jovi closed her eyes and squeezed them

tight. When she opened them again, she rested a hand on Marnie's forearm and looked her in the eyes. 'When you left it gave Josh plenty of opportunity to spin the story of your break-up in his favour. You know what Orion is like. The townsfolk went from well-wishes and giving you both space to being at your apartment door every time Josh went to collect his things. I think there was only so much tutting and 'how could you let that one go' comments that Josh could handle and the next thing you know customers are coming in mumbling about how you had been cheating on him and so he had to break it off. You became the guilty party because you fled. He created quite the sob story for himself. Of course, now the bump is showing, the townsfolk aren't silly. They put two and two together,' Jovi explained before wrapping her arms around Marnie's neck. When she released her, Marnie let out a breath. She could feel tears pooling in her eyes.

Jovi started again. 'We couldn't email you, not when you were having the time of your life in Canada. On top of dealing with Mum and Dad's separation, I felt a little powerless and defeated and just wanted all the hurtful things to go away.'

'I'm sorry for leaving you to deal with Mum and Dad on your own,' Marnie croaked out.

'What is it with you and being alone?' Antoni returned with a small flash of his charming grin as he nudged her in her bicep playfully. Even with the weight of everything Marnie had just heard, she found her lips twinge with a small smile of her own and one of the smaller knots in her stomach loosened.

'I know it can sometimes feel like you're alone, Marn.

Even having you for a twin, I've felt it but I had this one to yell at.' Jovi shoved Antoni playfully. 'Jackson offered to be my punching bag and these two over here worked overtime when I had to be elsewhere. I'm not alone,' Jovi explained softly.

Marnie suddenly found the flour on the floor incredibly interesting.

'It felt like everything was falling apart and no amount of PVA glue could fix it.' Marnie spoke her fear out loud. 'I looked at your lives, the bakery you built from the ground up, the family you have, Jovi, and I got angry, like how could you possibly understand my life.' Marnie wiped at the tears that spilled down her cheeks. 'But you did everything for me without question. Ant, you booked my ticket to Canada and dropped me off at the airport. You both helped me secure a new job and looked after Mum and Dad for me and jeez, all you want is for me to be happy and let you in. I'm sorry for being so ungrateful,' Marnie said, assessing the reality of the last few months.

'You're part of my family too, Marn. Please don't forget that and I'm not going to stand here and act like me just saying "when the time is right you'll have kids", will automatically put your brain at ease because I know that's ignorant of me but you can take Sienna whenever you need her, keep her for a week if you want. It would give me a chance to try and get the glitter out of the carpet,' Jovi said, a lightness to her tone now as she wiped at her own fallen tears and rubbed Marnie's bicep with her other hand. Marnie hiccupped over Jovi's knowledge of her wanting kids. Maybe her deepest fear wasn't such a secret after all.

'How are you feeling about the whole Josh with baby

thing?' Antoni piped up, his voice soft as he tucked a stray piece of hair behind Marnie's ear.

Marnie thought about it for a moment, but each time a vision of Josh and his missus popped into her mind it was quickly nudged out of the way by an image of Nova curled up on her couch animatedly talking about how a Triceratops's frill could reach nearly three feet in length. She shrugged, a smile playing at her lips.

'I think I'm OK,' she answered, a little meekly at first. 'You're right. I don't want to go backwards, I want to keep moving forward. I'm sorry I pushed you away and, Jovi, I'm sorry for acting out of resentment. I guess it's not that easy to stop comparing myself to you, even now that we're older, but I love you and I'm proud of the life you worked hard to get,' Marnie said, and this time it was her that wrapped her arms around her sister's neck with a tight embrace.

'Uh, I'm trying to decide which is worse, twin guilt or mum guilt,' Jovi said into Marnie's ear with a chuckle. 'Don't think I don't get jealous of you either, by the way – you and your cultured adventures while I'm stuck in here with him,' Jovi said ribbing Antoni. When she stepped back he swatted her with his tea towel, making all three of them laugh.

Catching Harry and Violet chuckling in the background made Marnie's cheeks flush.

'So sorry for this morning's entertainment brought to you by family and relationship drama, guys,' Marnie said, cringing slightly but knowing Harry and Violet were part of the family that Jovi had been talking about and it was safe to speak around them.

'No worries, Marn. You know we're here if you need us

too, right? I can clog Josh's car exhaust with sourdough,' Harry kindly offered, making Marnie grin and her shoulders loosen. Not wanting to be mean, she hadn't really allowed herself to speak about Josh in this way. There had been no imagining hypothetical situations like the one Harry had mentioned, no rage-filled stomping around her apartment or coming up with purely humorous attacks on Josh's character like: 'What kind of person hates Oreos?' But just the thought that Harry would do that for her and by simply allowing herself to play it out in her mind made her feel a little more human. It wasn't something she would ever do but it was fun to watch in her mind and it helped release some of her pent-up frustration.

'Thank you, Harry, I appreciate that but hold off on the sourdough, for now,' she replied, with an appreciative smile. 'I best get to work,' she added, not wanting to distract Jovi and Antoni for much longer when they had a serious amount of baking to do.

'It's still early – I can make you a coffee,' Jovi offered, lifting the tea towel she had draped over her bowl and checking on its contents.

'No, thank you. Now that I know about these rumours and what's been going on I have a few people I need to speak to and if I don't do it now, I might never do it,' Marnie returned, walking around the island to give Harry and Violet one-armed hugs before wrapping her arms tightly around Antoni's waist and burying her head in his chest.

'I love you,' she said, squeezing him hard.

'I love you too,' Antoni spluttered, dropping a kiss on the top of her head.

'Are you going to be OK today?' Jovi asked walking her

towards the front of the bakery once Marnie had released Antoni.

'I think so. I love you, Jovi,' Marnie said stepping out into the cool grey morning.

'I love you more,' Jovi replied waving her off.

The school was eerily quiet at seven. Only a few cars were parked out front, two of which belonged to the people Marnie needed to speak to. She buzzed herself in with her key card, bags knocking against the doors as she did so. Rarely a day went by where Marnie was not loaded with supplies for Paislee. She deposited the bags in the staffroom and took a deep breath before making her way to Mrs Thomas' office.

Marnie could faintly hear nails tapping against a keyboard as she stepped up to the door and she realised this was quite the opposite of running away from her problems and that she was, for the first time in her life, addressing conflict and going to face it head on.

'Come in,' Lesley shouted after Marnie had knocked. With sweaty palms Marnie opened the door.

'Morning, Lesley, may I have a word?' Marnie asked, poking her head around the doorframe.

Lesley looked away from her computer screen and waved Marnie in, gesturing to the chair opposite her desk.

'How can I help, Miss Barnes?' Lesley asked, giving Marnie her customary once-over. Marnie didn't sit down; instead she stood forcing her fingers to keep away from each other. She held her arms confidently by her sides rather than fidgeting.

'I think there have been some rumours going around about me that have caused you, and maybe some other members of staff, to think unkindly of me. I believe it affected your judgement of me and my ability to do my work somehow; like I might create drama or flee when things get tough. I also believe that it has led you to treat me unfairly, suggesting one rule for me and another rule for others.' Marnie spoke softly but kept her head held high.

'If I thought you weren't capable of the work, I wouldn't have hired you, Miss Barnes,' Lesley said, her face stony, her voice flat. Marnie got the impression not many people spoke to her this way.

'While I appreciate that and feel that I have more than shown you my work ethic and knowledge, I still feel as though I'm walking on eggshells. I was with Josh for ten years. Yes, he gave me a job at Cornelia but as you now know, I am really good at my job. Back in March I found out that he had been seeing someone else. At around the same time, my parents decided to separate and it all got too much. I needed to get away and so I took a trip I had been waiting and wanting to do for a lifetime. I am not a homewrecker nor am I a cheat. I can promise you I love working with Paislee and I am dedicated to working here. I can also promise you that all staff relationships are perfectly safe and I would greatly appreciate people not making assumptions about me based on town gossip. Gossip that up until yesterday I had no knowledge of,' Marnie finished, feeling her lungs fill with air that she hadn't realised she had been depriving them of as she spoke.

Lesley looked her up and down once more but this time her eyes were not filled with suspicion and the slight hint of dislike but instead there was a sense of awe, which confused Marnie until she opened her mouth.

'I don't suppose it was terribly easy for you to come in here and tell me all that you just did. I have to commend you for such bravery,' Lesley said, making Marnie shuffle uncomfortably on the spot. She didn't feel brave, a little light-headed and somewhat proud of herself for speaking up, but the butterflies in her stomach kept the feeling of being some sort of brave knight at bay. 'I apologise that I have made you feel that way. Josh has spun quite the story while you were away, Miss Barnes, but it was wrong of me to take his side verbatim. If you would like me to address this in a staff meeting then that is something that can be arranged, but the next steps are up to you. I am here to help should you need me.'

'No, that's OK, about the meeting. I'll see if I can handle it from here. Thank you for listening,' Marnie said with a slight bow as she took a step towards the door. That had been pretty simple and Lesley's apology hadn't taken nearly as long as Marnie was thinking it would. Part of her had even thought that she might not get one.

'Oh and, Miss Barnes, I must say I've noticed how Paislee now skips into school each morning. Her mum has been on the phone expressing her gratitude to you and your lesson plans. Her little girl is happy and making progress. I'm sorry that I was too blinded by two decades of paperwork and courses to even consider your way of teaching. Where I looked at her and saw "autistic" you looked at her and saw "Paislee". I may be an old fossil at this but I still have room to learn,' Lesley finished and the butterflies suddenly left Marnie's stomach to perform a dance around her heart.

Knowing that Paislee's mum could see progress and that Paislee was happy meant the world to Marnie. It was hard to wipe the grin off her face as she left Mrs Thomas' office.

This morning Marnie had woken with a dark cloud over her head but after speaking to Jovi and Antoni and clearing the air with Lesley, she could see the cloud brightening. She just had one more person to contend with.

Amber was in her classroom bent over a stack of books, which were open on her desk. Her hand swiftly made ticking motions against each page but stopped the minute she noticed Marnie's presence.

'You're here early,' Amber said and once again Marnie received a suspicious once-over.

'Look, Amber.' Marnie surprised herself by adopting Jovi's matter-of-fact mothering 'there's no messing with me' tone. 'I'm not here to steal your man. Mr Gonzalez is lovely and he's great with the kids, but me and him – never going to happen, not least because he's so in love with you, but also he's way too into football and I'm more of a hockey girl myself.' Marnie's voice shifted at the end. She couldn't help a chuckle at the ridiculousness of what she was having to say. Josh had been her longest relationship. She'd always struggled dating in college and her early twenties and yet here she was defending herself for being perceived as some kind of alpha female, Jezebel of Orion.

Marnie could have sworn Amber's lips curved up at the edges, though she was desperately trying to hide a smile. Marnie guessed this wouldn't be as easy as talking to Jovi and Antoni or even Mrs Thomas.

'I didn't think you were going to steal my man,' Amber said after a brief silence, her eyes still scanning the work books in front of her, 'but don't even think about trying it,' she added, resting the pen against the page and finally looking up to meet Marnie's gaze.

'You have my word,' Marnie said holding up her hands in surrender. Amber stared and it was no less icy than usual. Marnie sighed. It was her word against Josh's but if she didn't let Amber in, how was Amber ever supposed to trust her? 'For what it's worth, Amber, Josh cheated on me. My friend Ant and I walked in on him and his new girlfriend. I don't even know her name.' Marnie harrumphed as she sat down on a nearby table.

'Miss Rose – Sarah,' Amber said, deadpan. Marnie's brow knotted. The name rang a bell. Betsy had mentioned something about a new teaching assistant at Cornelia: Miss Rose. Of course, Josh had hired her as Marnie's replacement.

'Thanks,' Marnie replied, then shook off the negative thoughts that were threatening to dissolve the positives of the morning. 'He was supposed to be at a teaching conference so I had arranged to spend the weekend with Ant. I'd forgotten something – I can't even remember what now – and so me and Ant had gone back to get it when we walked in on them. They were stupidly drunk and had somehow stumbled back to our apartment without thinking.' Marnie was doing a lot of shrugging this morning, her shoulders moved up and down again.

'From what I've heard, she's not the friendliest of teaching assistants. She makes at least two kids cry a day and she doesn't like stickers. Stickers, can you believe that? Even I love stickers,' Amber said and her words were so warm that Marnie feared global warming had some competition. Marnie forced her face into a smile rather than a show of surprise. She had always wanted to believe Amber capable of kindness, she wanted to encourage it now, not put her off by having a face like a goldfish.

'Thank you, I appreciate that,' Marnie replied and for the first time she looked around the classroom and actually felt like she was welcome.

'Seeing as you're here early, there's a bag of dinosaur books in the stock cupboard that I thought Paislee might like, if you want to go through them.' Amber nodded toward her stockroom with a trace of the faintest of smiles on her face. Was this what a breakthrough felt like? Marnie didn't want to get ahead of herself but this felt good. OK, so maybe she and Amber wouldn't be swapping best friend necklaces anytime soon but it certainly felt nice to be able to communicate with her without feeling like Elsa had mistakenly zapped a cold dagger into her chest. Marnie went through the beautiful new books and picked one out that she thought Paislee might like for today and went about setting it down on Paislee's table.

'What is the plan for this morning?' Marnie asked Amber as she took a seat at Paislee's desk after collecting a bunch of Paislee's workbooks.

Amber gave Marnie a rundown of the morning and with an hour to go before the kids were due to arrive, Marnie sat and carefully curated a maths worksheet and a piece of English writing that vaguely touched on the topics Amber had explained she would be doing with the class, but with a bit of a dinosaur twist and that suited Paislee's level. She then prepped an experiment in the corridor using a few bits and pieces she had purchased from Cameron over the weekend.

When the clock declared that they had ten minutes before the first bell, Marnie quickly gave Amber the details of her lesson plans for Paislee and was pleasantly surprised by Amber's positive nods and encouraging reaction.

'It's so much more than exams, ticking boxes and seeing them as a label isn't it?' Amber said, almost to herself. Marnie could sense by her lowered lids, pink cheeks, pursed lips and arms crossed tightly over her chest that Amber felt ashamed. She looked over Marnie's setup out in the corridor where Marnie had placed colourful mats with numbers outlined on them, which were filled with sketches of dinosaurs, on the table. On top of each mat was a bowl each with different sensory items in them, like oats and flour, and hiding in the bowls were small dinosaurs. Paislee would have to match the bowls to the numbers. Marnie had wanted to give her as many sensory opportunities as possible when she had realised she wasn't getting much sat in the classroom all day.

Today it was all dry ingredients. She would introduce wet ingredients slowly; though Paislee loved playing with water, getting things on her hands was not something she cared for. Marnie had noticed this when they made the dinosaur world and the sand got mixed in with the water. When it stuck to Paislee's hands, Paislee had gotten irritable and her breathing heavy until Marnie quickly wiped it away with a wet paper towel.

'Oh absolutely,' Marnie replied, with a big smile. 'Learning isn't a one size fits all; this isn't Build a Bear. They're kids. Feelings are beautiful and messy, reactions are unpredictable and personalities are bespoke. There's no rule book. Even handbooks get it wrong and I'm not saying I don't get it wrong sometimes too, but as long as they are happy, kind, safe and can express themselves and who they are without judgement, then I think we're doing something right.'

20

'Miss Barnes, Miss Barnes?' It took Paislee tugging on Marnie's white long-sleeve blouse, that she had tucked into her navy trousers, for Marnie to snap out of her trance and realise that Nova was looking at her, her blue eyes shimmering with amusement, seemingly waiting for an answer. Marnie blinked and looked around the classroom to give herself some time to rack her brain for the question but she was coming up empty.

Nova had been so animated, her long blonde waves swishing from side to side as she crept low, stretched tall and weaved in and out of the tables, ensuring that every kid from the front row to the back was paying attention and able to hear her, as she told them facts about the mighty king that was the T-Rex.

T-Rex means... T- Rex means... Marnie stuck with the words hoping they would supply her with an answer. All the children were looking at her now, their faces a mix of shock and boredom that one Marnie, a teacher, didn't know the answer, and two that they were having to wait for Marnie's answer before Miss Clarke would be able to continue. Marnie couldn't blame them. Nova's passion for dinosaurs was the reason Marnie was now in this predicament. She couldn't take her eyes off her, watching her whole face come to life, her cheeks glowing and glistening a peachy hue, as she talked about what she loved.

Marnie swallowed and Paislee leaned in to her, her little elbow resting on Marnie's thigh as she played with the ribbon on one of Marnie's bracelets.

'King of the lizards,' Paislee whispered, looking up and into Marnie's face. Her bright blue eyes growing more comfortable looking into Marnie's instantly made Marnie relax. The sweat on her forehead cooled ever so slightly.

'King of the tyrant lizards,' Marnie said, her voice coming out a touch wobbly.

'Correct, Miss Barnes,' Nova said, while the class erupted with a round of applause that made Paislee grip onto Marnie's wrist with a jolt.

'OK, settle down please,' Nova said without skipping a beat and the class hung on her every word, doing as they were told. The room descended into silence and Paislee's grip loosened. 'You don't want the T-Rex to hear us while he's out hunting,' Nova added.

'Thank you, Paislee. You did great listening,' Marnie whispered to Paislee during a brief pause where Nova pulled out some pictures of dinosaurs from a plastic wallet and got herself ready to hold them up.

Paislee didn't speak but gave Marnie another glance as though taking her in. The look wasn't scrutinising or judgemental. There was a calm across Paislee's features. Then Paislee gave a tiny tilt of her head in Marnie's direction before she was back to being enthralled by what was going on in front of her. Nova was now holding up truly epic pictures of dinosaurs, which were so detailed and vivid Marnie pictured a friendly photographer getting up close and personal with the magnificent creatures, like Jia talking to Kong, and capturing the stunning shots. It was hard to believe that palaeontologists had been able to bring to life such concepts, with their feathers, skin textures, teeth, colours, movements and sounds, with just a bone. Marnie was as fascinated as the kids.

Once all the children had been sent home at the end of the school day, Marnie saw to wiping down the table out in the corridor. She was brushing up flour when she heard footsteps coming her way. She looked up to see Nova in her beige trousers and green collared museum shirt, walking her way. She looked like the prettiest nerd Marnie had ever seen and it was hard to fight the smile that spread across her face, but it was a smile that was beginning to make her anxious. She smiled when she saw Cameron and Esme. She smiled when she saw Antoni, like a ridiculous cheesy smile at the sight of him, but this smile – the smile that made her cheeks ache – seemed to only be reserved for Nova.

'Hi, great lesson this afternoon,' Marnie said, forcing herself to be casual. Nova was her friend; she could do casual.

'Thanks, sorry for putting you on the spot with the question. I think it's always fun for the kids to know we're learning too,' Nova said, scraping a hand through her blonde locks and smirking, a hint of teasing behind her sincerity.

'King of the tyrant lizards. I won't forget it,' Marnie

replied, turning back to the table to finish up cleaning away the mess, but not before Nova chuckled and winked at her. Why did Nova have to do that? What was it about her winking that made Marnie's knees buckle? Was it simply out of envy, the way she managed to make it look so effortless and cool? Or was it the way Nova's blue eyes twinkled and pierced straight into Marnie's soul with such a tiny action?

Marnie focused on the grains of oats that decorated the table.

'Hey, are you free tonight?' Nova asked and when Marnie turned to look at her again she was kneeling on the floor sweeping up a few oat flakes and cornflakes with the small brush Marnie had brought out from the classroom. Marnie simultaneously melted at the way Nova was helping her and having heart palpitations at Nova's question. Now that she had cleared up the rumours with Lesley, surely it was OK for her to date? Wait, why was she using the word date? Nova hadn't mentioned a date. They were friends. Plus it was a school night. School nights were for planning and organising and getting activities ready for the next day. She couldn't be gallivanting across town on a work night, there was no time.

However, today, Marnie had been the Marnie she wanted to be: talking to Lesley and speaking to Amber. She was moving forward, being bold, not going backwards and shying away from things, yet panic still gripped her.

'What activities do you have to prepare for Paislee? I can help you with those and then I'd love to show you something, if you are free?' Nova said, as though reading Marnie's mind, which Marnie recognised she did a lot.

Nova's cheeks were flushed pinker than their usual peach and she looked at what she was doing rather than looking at Marnie. Her Canadian accent and the relaxed yet shy vibe she was giving off found its way to Marnie and all she wanted to do was keep listening to Nova talk. Marnie needed to relax. There was no rule to say that she couldn't have friends. But there was most definitely a rule that stated if your friend had travelled over four thousand miles and was only in town until the beginning of November, you should spend time with them. That Marnie was sure of and so she cleared her throat and nodded.

'I'd like that,' Marnie said and the moment the words left her lips she realised they answered not one of Nova's questions. She closed her eyes tight and cringed at her own awkwardness. Nova must think her such a dork.

The October leaves crunched under Marnie's feet as she walked side by side with Nova, chatting about their favourite autumn desserts. After picking up treats and coffees from the bakery, they were feeling festive and inspired. Nova was adamant she needed to make an apple maple poke cake for Marnie and Marnie informed Nova that she wasn't allowed to leave Orion without trying one of Antoni's pumpkin cinnamon rolls.

Marnie's stomach growled with their food talk and with the occasional scent that emitted from their box of doughnuts as they walked to her apartment. She had promised Sienna that they would have a sleepover soon, because Sienna thought it highly unfair that Marnie was getting to hang out with Miss Clarke when she hadn't been invited, and Marnie couldn't help but think about how nice it would be to have Nova there too as the three of them baked together.

'There was one point in time where I was the favourite auntie,' Marnie joked as she unlocked her front door.

'She's just sucking up to me because she thinks I can get her a pet dinosaur,' Nova said, throwing up her hands when Marnie rolled her eyes as if to say 'really?' 'True story, she asked for one earlier today. I did promise not to tell you or Jovi, so if you could be so kind as to not mention it, that would be great. It is kind of fun being the favourite,' Nova teased.

Marnie let out a laugh. 'I won't tell but at least now I have ammo. I can't believe you're lying to a child. I'll be there to swoop in and pick up the pieces when her dinosaur doesn't get delivered and I'll be the favourite once again,' she said, taking her shoes off by the door and loving the feel of her toes against the carpet as she wandered into the kitchen. After a busy day, the carpet beneath her feet always made Marnie feel at home and content.

'You wouldn't dare and who says the dinosaur won't get delivered?' Nova retorted, placing the box of doughnuts and cookies on the kitchen counter and smirking so much at Marnie that a dimple formed in her right cheek. Marnie hastily looked to the floor, heat flooding her belly.

'You have pterodactyls on your socks,' Marnie noted, grateful to the gods of palaeontology for the distraction and the giggles that replaced the heat in her stomach. Nova wiggled her toes.

'A dinosaur for every day of the week eh.' Nova chuckled. 'Are they too nerdy? Did I take it too far?' she asked, her tone going from playful to genuine concern. Nova kept her eyes trained on her socks as Marnie took in her red cheeks and the nervous flutter of her eyelashes. Every time Marnie looked at Nova all she saw was this tall, blonde-haired, blue-eyed, passionate human with an easy-going manner and who managed to make falling on her arse look cool. She wished she had an ounce of Nova's charm, but occasionally, like when Nova had first spoken of loving to dig in the mud back when they met in Canada and now, when she bared her insecurities and doubts when it came to her dinosaur-loving ways, it made Marnie feel seen and less alone in her own vulnerabilities. Everyone had them.

'No, they're cute,' Marnie stated with a nod and then reached for the plate of doughnuts to take to the coffee table. 'I'd say taking it too far would be if you're wearing matching dinosaur underwear,' she added unable to resist the taunt. Nova faltered for a moment as Marnie brushed past her through the kitchen archway towards the living room. Then her face transformed into a beaming grin, the sun from the dining room window highlighting her bronzed cheekbones.

'I'll never tell,' Nova said biting her lip and grabbing their coffees from the kitchen counter before joining Marnie on the carpet where she had left a few craft supplies from Cameron.

Marnie wouldn't put it past Nova to have matching underwear and the thought made her smile, a stupid, goofy smile that probably made her look like she was already on a sugar high when they hadn't even touched the treats yet.

'What are you smiling about?' Nova asked, spreading

out the card in front of her and picking up some dinosaur stencils.

'Nothing,' Marnie replied, but the two locked eyes and for a moment it felt like the whole room had heated up as if they were standing right next to a volcano that had just erupted. All the dinosaurs could have been stampeding around them and neither one of them would have noticed before it was too late. The lava would have encased them and just like the dinosaurs they would now be extinct. Was that a bad sign, a warning for Marnie to leave her emotions well alone or was she simply spending too much time with a palaeontologist, her imagination running amok?

'So, I just wanted to make up some exciting number sheets for Paislee so that she wants to do them and is interested in looking at them. I was thinking groups of dinosaurs that she can add up and maybe different number lines she can order. Smallest dinosaur to largest and things like that,' Marnie said, clearing her throat and pulling her attention back to the task at hand.

'Got it,' Nova said with a nod. Had she been thinking the same thing? There was a peachy blush on the apples of her cheeks and Marnie didn't miss that Nova's throat sounded croaky too. The living room was blanketed with a golden sunset that filled the room with that autumn warmth and vibe, but Marnie couldn't help wondering if the heat was anything to do with the sun and if she was ready to put her heart on the line again.

An hour later, Nova had updated Marnie on Canadian hockey teams, the best players to look out for and teams to support, while Marnie had given Nova tips on how to papier-mâché photo frames and small bowls. Many a doughnut had been consumed and Marnie felt a strong urge to grab her duvet from her bed and snuggle up on the couch, the business of the day catching up with her. Instead, she was pulling her white and red Canadian hoodie over her head, its softness only encouraging her tired eyes, and watching Nova lace up her black work boots.

'Where are we going?' Marnie asked, curiosity getting the better of her for the second time this evening. 'And, shouldn't it be me showing you around? You've only been here like a month,' she added, retrieving her yellow backpack from the floor by the front door.

'I like to explore. There's so much to see and do and I'm not telling you – it's a surprise,' Nova said, standing tall once done with her laces. She was a good half a head taller than Marnie so Marnie had to look up and Nova could see her scrunch her nose and playfully pout.

Nova chuckled and rolled her eyes in jest while Marnie saw to opening to the door. It wasn't lost on Marnie how at ease she felt with Nova. Nova had this ability to always look on the bright side and there was something incredibly endearing about it that made Marnie want to be around her and see life the way she did, but she knew for that she truly needed to let her guard down, not overthink for once and just be. However, with the ease also came a swarm of giddy and anxious butterflies that were hard to control, but was she supposed to control them?

'Will you wait there just a moment?' Nova turned to ask Marnie as they walked past The Glitter Emporium. With Marnie not knowing their destination, they had been walking in a comfortable silence because Marnie didn't want to interrupt Nova's concentration. Nova's eyes were narrowed and her tongue jutted out, making her bottom lip shine as she navigated the paths. Now though, she gave Marnie a bright smile and confidently ducked down the side alley next to Cameron's shop.

For a moment Marnie had gotten lost in Nova's enthusiastic grin, receiving it and returning her own without much thought, but standing alone on the pavement and staring into a dark shop, with all its lights turned off, made her curiosity grow stronger for what Nova had planned tonight. Since when was she in cahoots with Cameron?

Marnie didn't have to wait long. After five minutes Nova was back carrying a large backpack that wasn't easy to hide, yet she swung it onto her back nonchalantly, like she'd had it the entire time.

'Still no hints?' Marnie asked through a small chuckle.

'Nope,' Nova replied and took the lead walking, her concentrating face back on as she followed the cobbly streets, reading the street names and signposts and stopping ten minutes later when they reached the park.

Straight away Nova marched over to a large birch tree furthest away from the street lights, atop a small mound that overlooked the play area and the lake at the edge of the park; where the sun could be found hanging out above it. First, she whipped out a large blanket and spread it around the base of the tree with great skill, a skill that Marnie attributed to her days camping at digs. Nova looked content moving around the mat, pulling out lanterns and candles, a small cooler bag and then, making Marnie gasp, two medium-size rectangle canvases and two small square canvases followed by a couple of tubes of acrylic paint and paintbrushes.

Without hesitation Marnie flicked her pumps off and jumped onto the mat, squatting down to examine the paint. It had been a while since she had put paintbrush to canvas. After studying a tube of electric blue she looked up to see Nova watching her, her face bathed in the evening sunset. Her blonde hair shimmered under the fading rays and the flecks in her blue eyes looked like they were dancing with the happiness that radiated off her curved lips.

'This is amazing,' Marnie said, a little breathless. 'Thank you.'

Nova gave a gentle shrug as she unlaced her boots and crossed her legs. 'I see how hard you work at school. You have so much passion for the kids, I figured you might need a little you time.'

In that moment it was incredibly difficult for Marnie to keep her heart rate under control. It was like the cheeky muscle had a mind all of its own and was screaming at her to set it free and stop detaining it in its cage. She stumbled over her words.

'Thank you for helping me with Paislee's activities,' Marnie managed, reaching out and picking up the small canvas first.

'I loved it,' Nova replied and Marnie's legs instantly turned to jelly. The tingles and weightlessness made her feel grateful that she was sitting down. There was no bored or annoyed expression on Nova's face with the mention of said activities. Earlier, there had been no rush to get Paislee's activities done in order for Nova to bring Marnie to the park. Marnie got the impression that Nova would have sat with her on her living room floor for as long as it took to complete the worksheets and games without question, without any grumbling or impatience and that meant the world to her. By the tone in Nova's voice and the smile that she was currently blessing Marnie with, Marnie got the feeling Nova understood exactly how much it meant; that she understood her.

When it came to thinking about work, Marnie knew she needed to find a better balance. Josh's job had been demanding. When he worked, she worked, always finding something to do and always wanting to go above and beyond for the kids and do a good job. But when he switched off, he expected her to as well, like she had to occupy herself until he was ready for her. She'd been stuck in that routine for so long without even realising it. Canada had been a beautiful respite of making decisions and choosing things for herself and she needed to find that balance now that she was back working in a school, where she knew the children always found a way into her heart and became her everything. It helped that Nova hadn't called her crazy and that above all she had helped her, they had done it together and got the work stuff done quicker so they could enjoy this time now.

Marnie shook out her legs before crossing them and picking up a paintbrush. Nova had already made a mark on her canvas, choosing a forest green to create the outline of what Marnie could only assume was some sort of dinosaur. If Paislee was there she would no doubt know exactly which one and could whisper it to her so she didn't look silly. At the same time Marnie had the feeling Nova wouldn't think of her as silly and she would revel in getting to describe each dinosaur to her.

At least five minutes had passed where Marnie stared at her canvas. The slightly bumpy texture of the fabric shimmered in the dipping sun while she sat there with no idea of what to paint. She used to love creating from scratch, transforming nothing into something, but now she felt paralysed and stuck. She couldn't make a move and the fear that the canvas represented her life now engulfed her. She was thirty-five, she was starting over. The years of getting to know someone, the years of investing in someone, the years of building a relationship until you were happy, content, safe, ready and at ease with a person, she had to do it all again, start from scratch.

'Are you scared?' The question tumbled out of Marnie's mouth before she could catch it. She looked up as Nova did the same and met her gaze.

'OK, I might need a little more specifics,' Nova said, with another knee-buckling wink, the gentle tease in her tone making Marnie smirk despite her nerves. 'That dinosaurs could come back to life and roam the earth once more? No way, that would be magic. Of giant sink holes that come out of nowhere? Terrified,' she added playfully, causing Marnie to release a hearty laugh, that made the corners of her eyes crease.

Marnie sighed at the question whizzing through her mind yet her body loosened, finding that she wanted to ask Nova; she felt safe asking Nova.

'Of starting new relationships in your late thirties?' Marnie asked, tickling her canvas with a clean paintbrush.

'Yes and no,' Nova replied straight away. Marnie loved

that she didn't hesitate, that she was honest. Her words came out thoughtful. Her head was positioned low with a slight twist as her brush moved across her canvas confidently. The sunset grazed the fabric on her shoulders, highlighting her slender neck and making the delicate gold chain around it sparkle. 'Time can make it a scary prospect, like suddenly you think as you get older you're running out of time to take it slow, to do it right, but time has also been a great teacher. I feel like I know who I am more, that I can trust myself and my own judgements,' Nova said, wiping clean her brush on a cloth and dipping it into a sandy metallic brown shade.

Marnie's lips pursed together, she made a small 'hmmm' sound in agreement and could feel one side tugging upwards with a tiny grin.

'But what happens if you can't trust yourself? What happens if you suck at making decisions?' she asked after a beat, her canvas still empty.

Nova didn't look up. It was like her words came out dancing along the movement of her brush.

'Please tell me why you think you're bad at making decisions?' she asked gently.

Marnie glanced around the playground, settling her eyes on the curve of the setting sun that had now nearly completely disappeared behind the lake. Her words came out as slowly as the sun inched its way out of the sky.

'I made the decision to go into a relationship with Josh. I made the decision to plan a life with him. I chose him.' Marnie paused and absentmindedly dotted the canvas with a clean paintbrush. 'I chose someone who didn't choose me.' No tears came this time when she spoke. It no longer felt hard to talk about Josh and she didn't feel like she was going backwards, instead it felt like she was stating facts, facts that she needed to bring to light in order to move forward. She wanted to move forward, to let go of fear but fear was a sticky sucker, like a barnacle that latched on to the bottom of a ship and could brave the harshest of waves and storms.

This time Nova looked up from her painting. Her canvas was looking whimsical, her dinosaur getting lost in brushstrokes of every colour, some that looked like bones, others just swirly lines that made the beast pop depending on which way you caught it.

'We don't choose things knowing what the outcome is going to be. We have no way of knowing if something is going to be the best decision we've ever made or the worst. All we can place our bets on is that it will be an experience, something we can learn from and take into the next second, the next moment, the next day. If Josh hadn't done what he did, you might not have ever made it to Canada, to have the guts to say screw it and travel across the world on your own and then this—' Nova gestured over the blanket with a soft smile at her lips '—would not be happening right now.'

Marnie met her bewitching blue eyes. 'I like this,' Marnie said and before she could get lost in Nova's enchanting features she looked away and sighed at her canvas for a distraction. 'I don't know what to paint.'

Nova stretched out her legs, grazing her toes against Marnie's thigh and nudging them while she gave a small laugh. 'Course you do. Just go for it.'

Marnie felt a spark run through her veins at Nova's

touch. So much for not getting distracted she thought, but it seemed to electrify her to action with a jolt. She dipped her brush into the shimmering black acrylic and got lost in the tiny specks of glitter as her paintbrush caressed the canvas.

Marnie wasn't sure how long she had been painting but the goose bumps that ran up her arms gave her pause and the slight inclination that someone was watching her. When she looked up, lanterns ornamented the blanket and she realised that Nova was lying down on the mat, her head inches from Marnie's knee, her blonde hair sprawled out around her and her striking blues on Marnie. Her face wore a dreamy expression that made Marnie smile.

'OK, I think I've finished,' Marnie told Nova once she was able to pry her eyes away from Nova's relaxed body position.

'Let me see it,' Nova urged, enthusiastically, rolling onto her side and propping herself up with her elbow.

Marnie happily obliged, turning her canvas over for Nova to survey. Marnie was pleased with how it had turned out. Once she had made that first swish, the paintbrush took the lead and her brain focused on nothing but her wrist movements and the way the paint decorated the canvas.

'Is that Godzilla in space?' Nova asked, her eyes growing as wide as saucers.

'It most certainly is,' Marnie proudly replied. It was only a small shadow of Godzilla but Marnie thought it looked pretty cool. His metallic black body shimmered under the light of the lanterns.

'And you said my dinosaur underwear was nerdy

when you're harbouring a secret love of Godzilla.' Nova harrumphed playfully.

Marnie let out a bark of laughter. 'I knew it wasn't just the socks.' She felt a giddiness creep into her belly and a lightness wash over her chest.

21

Since Monday night and painting under the stars with Nova, Marnie had been walking around as if she were on roller skates. There was a certain glide and smoothness to her steps, like she wasn't constantly anxious about tripping up and instead just focused on going with the flow. Despite the hiccups lately, she felt that life was getting back on track. She hadn't been able to see Nova yesterday, Wednesday, as she had a busy day working at the museum and so Marnie had checked in with her dad with a phone call after work and popped in to see her mum. Tim had been there and it had been laid-back as he asked if she was excited about the upcoming ice-hockey season, suggesting she was welcome to come and watch with him if she had nothing else going on. Marnie had actually been rather touched by the offer until her mum piped up about online dating and asked if she had set up a profile yet and argued that she shouldn't be sat around in front of the telly when there were people to meet. A brief protest left her mum pouting and reasoning that Marnie seemed happy lately and that was a great sign to get back out there. And that had been Marnie's cue to leave.

There was rarely a day that went by where Marnie missed a visit to the bakery before and after work and life was making sense again. She still got the odd look from townsfolk that could stop her in her tracks and make her stomach queasy, like she and Josh had been on a dramatic episode of *Love Island* and their relationship was up for discussion, but it was getting easier to brush off when she thought about the good that had been achieved recently and the people who had entered her new space, mainly Paislee and Nova. Today was Thursday, which meant Nova would be in her class this afternoon and so Marnie found that no matter the stink-eye that Mr and Mrs Hamilton had just sent her way as she passed the corner shop, there was still air in her lungs and hope in her heart.

'OK, we've got five minutes, Paislee, and then Miss Clarke will be here and we can show her what you've made,' Marnie told Paislee. They were sat in their makeshift area in the corridor amongst a sea of tin foil that now mostly resembled jaws of dinosaurs, all different shapes and sizes. Marnie hadn't thought it possible to conjure a dinosaur skull out of a sandwich wrapper and had brought it to use for a floating and sinking experiment they had carried out earlier that morning. It was Paislee who had the idea to scrunch, fold, and carve the crinkly fabric into impressive structures.

Paislee was making dinosaur noises, pitting two heads against each other, forcing their jaws open wide, but Marnie knew she had heard her and smiled, enjoying watching the little girl's game. Leaving her to it for a few moments, Marnie made a neat pile of Paislee's books and retrieved a box from the classroom so they could place the foil toys inside.

As she bent down to pick up a small skull that had rolled off the table, her forearms heated and heart rate picked up. She didn't have to turn around to know who the footsteps creeping up behind her belonged to.

'Good afternoon, Miss Barnes,' came Nova's familiar Canadian twang.

It was totally normal and perfectly fine to get this excited over seeing a friend, surely? Marnie found herself thinking as she straightened her back and turned to greet Nova. Paislee stopped mid dinosaur attack, hopped off her chair and walked inside the classroom to get herself ready for Miss Clarke's lesson, leaving Marnie and Nova alone in the corridor.

'Hey,' Marnie replied, grinning so big that the tips of her ears blushed. Nova wore her long wavy hair in a loose pony today, the gold of her necklace twinkling under the fluorescent school lights just under her collar and she was carrying what appeared to be holographic pictures this week. Every time Nova moved slightly the T-Rex on the paper threatened to eat Marnie as its jaw suddenly opened wide. Paislee was going to love them, Marnie thought, grateful for the small distraction.

'I have some ideas for next week's lessons and I was wondering if you would be free to help?' Nova asked, her eyes averting from Marnie's for the briefest of seconds when she spoke.

Was Nova nervous? Marnie couldn't help ponder. It

wasn't often she saw Nova with her chin to her chest, her eyes wandering.

'Yes sure, is tonight OK?' Marnie said, shrugging her shoulders and trying to play it cool, though the butterflies that her belly was holding captive were fluttering obnoxiously.

'Great, thanks,' Nova replied, her eyes finding Marnie's more confidently now. It took Mr Matthews, the music teacher, to walk past for Marnie to snap her head away from Nova and remember where she was – Nova's eyes having some kind of enchanting effect. Marnie's cheeks blushed furiously as Mr Matthews gave them both a small nod, springing them into action.

Marnie shuffled the box of tin foil with her foot to push it neatly against the wall as Nova gave her a bright smile and headed into the classroom.

'I won't be a minute,' Marnie said quietly, needing a second to collect herself. She hadn't felt these fluttery feelings in a long time. Something about Nova made her feel like she had walked onto a Hallmark set but at the same time that terrified her and she wasn't quite sure what to do with all these emotions.

She took a deep breath and had to grab onto the table when she clipped the chair leg with her foot, making her stumble.

'Ouch,' she grunted.

Were the butterflies in her stomach that were spinning in some daredevil fashion telling her to open her heart again and tempt her next forever? She scrunched her nose and furrowed her brow. She wasn't entirely sure Nova's take on forever made any sense, but just thinking about it made her lips curve upward.

The table was well and truly tidy by the time Marnie processed her thoughts, not a single tiny shred of tin foil was there to be seen on the floor, so she entered the classroom and quietly took her seat next to Paislee. Paislee's eyes were wide, her brow slightly furrowed as she watched Nova flick through the pictures of the dinosaurs. Her hands were idly swishing the tail of the dinosaur model she and Marnie had made earlier in the week.

'One day there'll be no people left? We'll all die,' Paislee suddenly turned and said to Marnie.

Marnie leant forward, pursing her lips in thought. 'Hmm, no because people have babies and then they grow up and then they have babies and then they grow up, so people will always be here.'

'But if everyone stopped having babies, we'd be extinct, if there were no more babies,' Paislee returned matter-of-fact.

Marnie was stumped for a moment, wanting to be careful when talking about death. Children often didn't like hearing about when they were going to die or about the people close to them dying.

'Yes, I suppose if people stop having babies but people like babies, so we won't be extinct.' Marnie noted calmly, whispering so she didn't disrupt Nova.

'You're old,' Paislee stated, but Marnie had come to gather that it was a question and smiled.

'I'm thirty-five, not too old,' she responded.

'You're still young,' Paislee said, flicking her eyes back to Nova's next picture for a moment.

'Yes, that's not really old yet,' Marnie concurred.

'People die when they're old,' Paislee noted, poking at the googly eye on her model dinosaur.

'Yes, but people can live till they're one hundred or more,' Marnie explained trying to sound jovial not to scare Paislee, but the little girl didn't seem too fazed.

'I'll be sad when you're ninety-nine,' Paislee said after a moment's pause that was filled with Nova making a screech like a pterodactyl. In that moment, Marnie's heart was officially ripped open whether she allowed it or not. Paislee had forced her way in regardless of its stubborn, terrified and boarded-up state, and Marnie couldn't say she was all that sorry about it.

Twenty minutes later, Marnie and Nova were stood side by side waving the kids off one by one while Amber spoke with one of the parents. Paislee clutched on to her model dinosaur and gave a soft 'See you tomorrow, Miss Barnes' when her mum came to collect her and Marnie was certain that her heart had its own smiley face with googly eyes Pritt-sticked onto it.

Floating on her Paislee cloud, she turned to Nova with a lot less concern for who was around, which was another small win today, and nudged her shoulder.

'So, my place?' she asked with an outside grin that matched her insides.

The window in Marnie's living room was ajar and the curtains remained open. Surprisingly, this autumn so far had been more idyllic and crisp than miserable and wet. Dusty pink and orange hues swept over the horizon and was having a calming effect on Marnie's mind and body. There was a gentle breeze blowing through the open window, which lent itself to Marnie requiring more blankets and pillows to deck the floor, thus creating a cosy office for her and Nova to work in.

Marnie much preferred this kind of office, one where she could spread out her crafting supplies, cover her legs with fleecy fabric and not worry if a sprinkle or two from a plate towering with doughnuts snuck onto the rug beneath her.

'I love this idea,' Marnie told Nova, waving a piece of card covered in black paint in the air. The card had a piece of string attached to it in the shape of a dinosaur.

'The idea is to pull the string and be left with a different colour underneath. That one is a glow-in-the-dark Allosaurus but I was thinking of making a few more examples and then allowing the kids to have a go themselves. You start with one colour underneath, let it dry, put the string in place in whatever design or shape you want and then paint the whole page before pulling the string off,' Nova explained, pointing at a stack of card and different paints she had pulled from her shoulder bag.

'That's amazing,' Marnie said once more, looking forward to drawing dinosaurs with string. It was definitely going to test her art skills, which gave her a little thrill.

'For next week, I wanted to cut out different bones and skulls and then pair them off into groups to see if they can sort them out and make a dinosaur from the bones they get,' Nova said and Marnie couldn't help the tug at her lips at the way Nova's accent and otherworldliness came out when she said 'out'. She had gotten quite used to Nova's twang but every so often it rang more prominent and created a pitter-patter in Marnie's chest that was difficult to ignore.

'What are you smiling at?' Nova asked, but there was a knowing look in her baby blues.

Marnie could feel her cheeks grow hot under Nova's magnetic glare.

'You do know that to me the way you say "out" is cuter...' Nova said, absentmindedly sketching bones on a big sheet of cream paper. There was no stopping the fire in the apples of Marnie's cheeks now; she needed to pull herself together.

'...and fundamentally strange.' Nova finished with that teasing tone of hers and a wink as she looked up and caught Marnie's stare. This woman really needed to stop winking if Marnie was to pull herself together and restore her body temperature back to that of a human and not the inside of a vat of boiling maple syrup. Did Nova have any idea of the effect she was having on Marnie? Did Marnie need to tell her? But she couldn't tell her, not before she had figured it out herself first, surely? She couldn't risk their friendship.

'Waffles or pancakes?' Nova suddenly asked, while Marnie's brain was overthinking the dilemma messing with her heart. At least her heart was working again, which had to be a good thing she supposed, but then again it also meant that with a functioning heart, she could get hurt again.

Marnie blinked at the cream paper in front of her and picked up a pencil. Why was she thinking about her heart when right now all she needed to think about was answering Nova's very important question? She squinted her eyes as images of pancakes and waffles flooded her brain replacing those of her heart with googly eyes and a mischievous face.

'I'd take a stack of fluffy warm pancakes over waffles

every time,' she said, her mouth watering at the thought, so she picked up a doughnut and took a bite, trying not to get icing on her work.

'Same. I like your style,' Nova said nodding her head. 'Toast or French toast?'

'It's got to be French toast with tons of syrup,' Marnie answered. She could feel Nova's smile on her without looking up, as she focused on a particular tricky bone that she was sketching.

'Coffee or tea?' Nova then asked while she concentrated on the cutting out.

'Most definitely coffee,' Marnie replied.

'Sunrise or sunset?' came Nova's next question.

'Sunrise,' Marnie noted after a few moments' pause. She was definitely an early bird. She loved being up in time to wake with the day, but Canada had shown her some pretty spectacular sunsets that she had wanted to make it a point to occasionally stay up to witness them in Orion too. Work had tired her out these past few weeks though and she hadn't managed that quite yet.

'Summer or winter?' Nova was on a roll.

'Summer for the happy vibes; winter for the cosy ones and snow,' Marnie said with a smile. It was hard to pick between the seasons. There was something special about each one that she loved.

'Autumn or spring?' Nova questioned and Marnie couldn't help but chuckle and give her a quick glance. Nova's brow was furrowed, her tongue sticking out ever so slightly as she cut round a particular delicate dinosaur rib.

'Spring for the fresh starts, flowers and new beginnings. Autumn for the leaves, blankets and oversized jumpers,'

Marnie said with a nod. Just thinking about the slow goodbye to summer as autumn stepped in sent an excited shiver down her arms.

'Justin Bieber or Shawn Mendes?' came Nova's next question and this time Marnie's chuckle burst out into the living room as it transformed into a full-on laugh.

'Is that some sort of test? They're both Canadian right? Am I supposed to say both?' Marnie answered with a question once her laughter had subsided. When she caught Nova's eyes, they seemed to be dancing with amusement. Tiny gold flecks swayed as the sunset kissed her face. Marnie's throat caught but she forced a casual smile.

'No, you have to choose. It's an imperative question,' Nova noted, moving her eyes away from Marnie's and shaking her head just a hair, like she was pushing herself to concentrate.

'Erm, OK,' Marnie said, clearing her throat and getting back to shading in a dinosaur rib. 'Shawn Mendes – it's the guitar and the voice for me.'

'Congratulations, you passed. Though Justin Bieber's still a legend,' Nova said with a laugh, but she wasn't finished with her questioning and Marnie had to admit that she was rather enjoying the game. She felt relaxed and carefree and found it interesting to know what Nova thought important.

'Kids or no kids?' Marnie's knee twitched and she kicked out her legs in front of her, the question catching her off guard and causing her body to squirm.

She scanned the array of blankets and crafting supplies, feeling safe in her surroundings and then instead of shying away, she raised her head, finding that she liked Nova's abruptness. Getting to know her was addicting and Nova's openness only inspired it in herself.

'Kids. I've always known I want to be a mum,' she answered honestly.

'Me too.' Nova nodded. Again Marnie found their eyes locking, sending the world around her into a black hole where the only light that shone was Nova. That's all she could see, as though Nova was lighting up the galaxy. No one moved for a few moments until Marnie watched Nova's right cheek dimple and her lips part, prised open with a question.

'Men or women?' Nova's eyes were intense when she spoke. They burned a fiery cerulean, which made Marnie's heart hammer hard in her chest. This wasn't a hard question but it caught Marnie off guard for a moment and caused her brain to rattle. She supposed she'd never told Nova where her interests lay. It was not something she had thought about in a long time. Her family knew as did most of Orion. She'd been out since college and had been used to talking about both men and women. Naturally, some of the old-fashioned folks in town had questioned her at first, given her funny looks and expressed their opinion that she just needed to meet a nice man and that she was confused, but other than that, she had been pretty lucky and accepted, especially within her inner circle of Jovi, Antoni and Jackson. She and Antoni were two peas in a pod and so it was never a big deal when talking about who they liked or when they were obsessing over crushes of either the opposite sex or same sex.

'Both,' she replied with ease, but was it just her or did something shift in the atmosphere? Nova's shoulders visibly loosened and her eyes seemed to burn brighter and clearer as her peachy lips glistened with a smile. Would Nova now piece together all the times Marnie had looked at her with a dreamy look on her face? Had that been the one thing holding Marnie back? Had Marnie held on to that piece of information on purpose, knowing that if there was a slight chance that Nova thought she was straight, that Marnie's heart would be safe? Now in this moment, it felt like it was trying to leap from her chest and practically bounce in Nova's face waving a bisexual flag yelling: 'I'm interested.' And Marnie couldn't let it do that, could she?

'Cool,' Nova replied, looking away and getting back to her activity prep. In the brief silence between questions, Marnie felt a mix of rapturous joy and blissful excitement at the tiny door of possibility she might have just opened yet at the same time, it felt like a ferocious tiger was circling at the pit of her stomach wreaking havoc and terror on all her organs. It wasn't a pleasant mix, not least because she couldn't even look at the doughnuts anymore.

22

Somewhere in the distance Marnie could hear a frustrated alarm, almost like this wasn't the first time it was giving its signal. Her eyelids fluttered, opening a crack and then closing again, her back ached and there was a definite crick in her neck. She slowly twisted her body to a sitting position, rubbing the back of her head and patting down the bed head when she realised there were long limbs stretching over her hip bones and the tops of her thighs.

Marnie's eyes bugged, suddenly registering the weight and warmth of the limbs pressing against her body. Nova was stretched out in the other direction, her long blonde hair hiding her tired, heavy eyes. Her stomach was moving up and down with her gentle breathing. Marnie smiled at the thought of her being a deep sleeper having not heard her alarm either. She looked peaceful and cute when she slept. Marnie couldn't help but be mesmerised by the tanned skin and the way the tiger stripes on Nova's hip bones glistened in the sunrise streaming in through the window – her tee having rolled up a touch. Marnie couldn't look away and the longer she looked the more her initial panic of waking up on her living room floor under a fort of duvets and blankets, amongst art supplies and plates of doughnuts, and with Nova's body entangled with her own, ebbed away.

Last night had been fun. After Nova's get to know you game, where by Marnie found out that Nova too was a coffee person, enjoyed sunrises but tried to catch as many sunsets as she possibly could if she wasn't already fast asleep, was a fan of autumn and loved winter sports, dreamed of a family of her own one day, had seen Shawn Mendes live before he took the world by storm and she'd been out as a lesbian since the Spice Girls were adorning bedroom walls back in the Nineties, the conversation had flown and the hammering in Marnie's chest had eased into a pleasant tickle the more they chatted.

Once Nova's activities were complete, the evening had turned into a competition to see who could build the best dinosaur out of tin foil while watching a Shawn Mendes documentary in the background, stopping every now and again to sing their hearts out until they had come crashing down from the sugar high of the doughnuts and apparently fallen asleep in a heap under the alluring snuggling nest they had created. The last thing Marnie remembered was making cheese toasties and Nova saying something about being right that every town has its gems and that Marnie was one of Orion's.

Just thinking about Nova's accent and the way the words had causally emitted from her lips in a soft, tired drawl made Marnie's skin heat. This whole skin-heating thing was becoming a bit of a danger. Marnie needed her brain to understand that chilled was where it needed to be.

Nova's eyelids began to flutter and as if she could hear the battle going on in Marnie's brain, a dimple formed in her cheek but her face remained squished into the pillow. She stretched out her legs making Marnie increasingly aware of every inch of her body.

'Are you watching me sleep?' Nova asked playfully and there was no way Marnie could deny it. Chill would definitely not be looking away hastily and blushing, so her eyes stayed focused on the one of Nova's she could see and she chuckled.

'I had to ensure that you were still breathing after all the cheese and sugar.' Marnie shrugged nonchalantly, but a grin found its way on to her face with how easy it was to joke with Nova.

'I think there should be an age limit on cheese. Make the most of it when you're young, folks, as your body might start to reject it when you get old,' Nova said, turning onto her back and rubbing her stomach.

Marnie kept her gaze on Nova's face, ignoring the lines and contours of her stomach.

'In that case, you can use the bathroom first and I'll make the coffee,' Marnie said with a knowing grin.

Nova let out a bark of laughter and gently scooted her legs off Marnie's thighs.

'I'll get you some towels and show you my wardrobe, if you want a new outfit for today?' Marnie said, pushing herself up using the edge of the couch. Nova flipped her head forward and scrunched her knotted long hair into a messy bun atop her head.

'That would be great, thank you. Though I've got a long shift at the museum today, so I'm all right for clothes,' Nova noted, wiggling out of the duvets and stretching.

'OK, this way,' Marnie replied with a confident nod, standing up and walking towards her bedroom, ignoring the flutters in her chest at Nova following her, the only people to have entered her bedroom since Josh left being Jovi and Antoni. She collected towels from her wardrobe and placed them on the side of the bath. 'I'll leave you to it.'

'Thanks.' Nova looked around, a touch of rosiness to her cheeks from where they had been scrunched against the pillowcase. 'I like your place,' she added as Marnie walked towards the bedroom door to make coffee.

'Thank you,' Marnie said with a happy nod, somewhat feeling proud that Nova liked her humble abode.

In the kitchen, Marnie listened to the water from the shower hum as she busied herself making coffee. The aroma soon filled the small space which Marnie tried to concentrate on as she collected the dirty plates from the living room and returned the uneaten doughnuts to their bakery box. It was too early to pay her brain noise attention, though it was very much awake and buzzing.

This wasn't strange. Having Nova in her apartment, in her shower – it was not bizarre. If it was any random woman, then yes, weird it might be, but this wasn't a one-night stand or even a date, it was Nova, her friend and they were hanging out. Nova knew that just as much as Marnie did. Everything was fine. Except her brief pep talk did nothing to steady her heartbeat when Nova walked out of her bedroom, clothes a tad wrinkly from being slept in, her face make-up-free and her long hair wet and wavy.

Nova spoke first. 'Thanks for that.'

It took Marnie a minute to remind herself that she wasn't

in a romantic comedy and Nova wasn't walking in slow motion, then she nodded, cleared her throat and managed words.

'No problem, your coffee is in the kitchen. I'll just pop in, if you don't mind. Help yourself to anything in the fridge or cupboards.' She gave Nova a smile and quick marched into her bedroom, closing the door behind her as gently as her shaking limbs would allow.

By the time Marnie was throwing a light knit jumper over her own damp hair, the clock was ticking, and missing the first few alarms this morning meant she wouldn't have time to stop by the bakery. She had to make a move. When she walked out into the living room faffing with her backpack to keep herself grounded, she smiled to see that Nova had folded all the blankets and tidied away all the craft supplies. There was also toast on the coffee table, a plate for her and a plate for Nova. Nova was already through one piece of toast and looked up at her with a casual, warm smile that did nothing to silence the noise in Marnie's mind.

With a brain that felt like it was at some sort of rave – wide awake, alive and singing from the rooftops to be heard this morning – Marnie wandered over to the couch to join Nova.

'Are you free tonight?' Nova asked as Marnie took her first bite. Marnie swallowed hard, the rough edges of the toast scratching all the way down her throat.

'Tonight, erm tonight I have a thing with Antoni,' she lied. Why on earth was she lying? Nova's face remained cheerful and bright and Marnie couldn't help but stare at the way her lipstick-free lips looked naturally plump and glossy. 'But you should come to the Starcrossed Festival on

Sunday,' she added, torn between genuinely loving the idea and trying to put space between them for the next day or two while she collected her wandering and crazy thoughts.

'I'd love that,' Nova replied, licking her lips as she took her last bite of toast. Nova wiped her hands on a tissue and then stood, taking a few strides to the kitchen and washing her plate straight away in the sink and leaving it to drip dry on the side. 'I'd best be off, but thanks for all your help last night. I wouldn't have managed it all without you and I think the kids will love it.' She moved to the door to put on her boots. It was a few seconds before Marnie realised she had become mute and there was definitely a layer of awkwardness in the air. She swivelled her sitting position on the couch and looked over towards the door, where Nova was now standing with shoes and backpack on, readjusting her topknot so she could wear her signature cap. Mornings suited Nova.

'Oh gosh, yes, that was no problem. I appreciated all your help with mine. The kids will love it,' Marnie said, cringing at repeating Nova's last few words.

Nova chuckled and patted her arms down by her sides. 'Right, well I'll let myself out. Have a great day at work and I'll see you Sunday,' she said and Marnie wanted to get up, to hug her, to open the front door, to do something, but she was glued to the couch. How was she being this rude? She was appalled with herself, yet her limbs were taking no notice and did not spring into action; they remained locked and unmovable. Hugging Nova might lead her on, give her the wrong impression, but she had hugged her before. If she opened the door and walked her out, it might come across like a date and she'd stumble over some awkward goodbye, though this was plenty awkward, Marnie thought. Before she could reply and coerce her body to act, the front door closed and Nova was gone.

By the time Marnie had managed to get herself off the couch, there had been no time to call into the bakery and wish Antoni and Jovi a good morning, which she didn't think was such a bad thing knowing the two of them would be able to read her vibes as if they were Tyler Henry. Instead she had made a mad dash to get to work on time to set up Paislee's day.

The morning had been a blur of dinosaur maths and encouraging Paislee to write a sentence about a story they had been reading, but the atmosphere in the classroom had been a touch miserable; Marnie could sense something was up with Amber and it was enhancing her already strict demeanour. Despite Marnie's own mind feeling on edge and confused over Nova, her cheeks were starting to ache from smiling so much and trying to lighten the mood and support the kids through their work. With Amber and Marnie's lunch schedules being different to each other's, they hadn't had much time to talk today.

On the agenda for the afternoon was art and so Marnie had set up Paislee and Mason's table with paper, paints, glue and other crafty bits and pieces, along with a few dinosaur and space stickers. It was lovely to see Paislee working alongside Mason and the smile on Mason's face was blinding at working side by side with his new best friend.

Watching the concentration on Paislee's features as she

sought out which paint to use and brought the brush to the paper, drawing what only her mind could conjure, made all Marnie's confused feelings melt away. There was something about the innocence on the little girl's face and on Mason's face too, as he tried to copy Paislee's abstract dinosaur, that was almost like a stick-figure dinosaur yet looked detailed and intricate, that made Marnie scold herself for making things so complicated in her mind with Nova.

Why did adults do that? At what point did life become so frightening and at what point did love become so terrifying? Marnie's eyes grew misty staring at Paislee's painting. Six lines and Paislee had created the most awesome dinosaur Marnie had ever seen. It wasn't complicated, though Mason was having a hard time to get his to look anything like Paislee's, but that was perfectly OK because Mason's picture couldn't and shouldn't match Paislee's, for he had to find his own creative genius. The same could be said for Marnie and Jovi. Just because Jovi's life drawing looked one way, it didn't mean Marnie's had to match. Compared to Jovi, Marnie had had to dip her brush in many coloured paints and wasn't one thousand per cent certain yet if she had landed on the right colour, but if Mason's picture was anything to go by, his lines had now become different-coloured shapes making his dinosaur a rainbowsauraus and it looked magical.

If she gave up and let fear stop her from trying one more colour, then she would never know if there was more magic to unveil once the brush met the paper and dared to be something from a dash, a line, a shape, that transformed into something bigger: a dinosaur, a spaceship, a monster.

'Paislee, can you stop making that silly noise please.'

Marnie jumped so hard that she knocked over the water on Paislee's table as Miss Olsen's sharp, harsh shout met her eardrums. Marnie blinked back to reality where Paislee had frozen. Mason's hand was hovering over the little girl's shoulder, wondering whether or not to comfort her, as her eyes went from wide to thin, her fists balled and she let out a scream and ran out of the classroom.

Marnie could feel the blood rush to her head when she stood. She hadn't heard Paislee's humming or dinosaur noises but apparently whatever Amber was going through today meant that she had and she couldn't cope with the noise, which was far from OK. If Marnie were a superhero with laser eyes, Amber would have had to duck in that moment as she shot her a rather furious look before dashing out of the classroom to find Paislee.

The screaming and thuds from the library gave away Paislee's spot. This was her safe space with bean bags and pillows that she could hit and throw without hurting herself. Marnie slowly walked up to the door but remained quiet.

'Go away,' Paislee shouted.

'I'm here when you need me,' Marnie responded softly and stood off to the side a little to not loom over and intimidate her.

'I hate her. She's horrible,' Paislee said, the tears evident in her wobbly voice. Marnie's heart thudded faster as she tried to calm her own anger.

'I know, I understand,' she replied. 'Can I come in?'

There was no response, just crying, and when Marnie peeked her head around the door she could see Paislee's head buried in a pillow. They had been practising screaming into pillows just last week. Marnie had made Paislee laugh regaling a story about her childhood and how once Jovi had broken her favourite toy and Marnie had really wanted to hurt her but hadn't wanted to get into trouble and so she had screamed into a pillow. Paislee had thought it hilarious when Marnie demonstrated.

Now, Marnie edged into the room, slowly sat herself beside Paislee and began rubbing her back with a touch of pressure. She could feel Paislee's tears steadying with each stroke.

'Why? Why did she say that?' Paislee suddenly cried, lifting her head, tears streaming down her face, confusion in her blue eyes. 'She's an idiot.'

Marnie wiped away Paislee's tears with the back of her hand. Paislee grabbed Marnie's hand in response and wiped it over her face and over her hair a little harder. Marnie had noticed a few weeks into getting to know each other that if Paislee was sad, there were times when playing with her hands and squeezing her palms helped to calm her breathing. Paislee would then trace her fingers over Marnie's fingers or use Marnie's hand to cover her eyes or pull Marnie's arm around her neck like a hug.

'Sometimes grown-ups get angry too and they say things they don't mean,' Marnie explained.

'No, she said it. She's so mean,' Paislee replied, her voice loud and angry. Marnie rubbed her back with her hand that Paislee wasn't holding.

'I know and I think she is very sorry,' Marnie noted.

'I don't want to say sorry,' Paislee cried.

'You don't have to say sorry – you did nothing wrong. I think the classroom was too loud for Miss Olsen. She didn't want to shout,' Marnie said, feeling her heart crack. She understood teaching could be tough. Having a class of thirty kids all chattering away, classrooms were scarcely peaceful, but Marnie didn't believe that was an excuse. She wasn't a shouter. She didn't agree with shouting at or embarrassing kids. Talking it out, writing it down, drawing a picture, the one, two, three clap, the all eyes on me song, and occasionally the silent treatment were her favoured methods when dealing with problems or getting their attention. Ten years in the game and she had learnt early on that what was going on at home stayed at home. The moment she walked into the school building, the kids were her priority; their needs came first.

'I never want to see her again,' Paislee said, thumping the pillow with her free hand.

Marnie paused before responding. Paislee's feelings mattered and she would not dismiss them in haste to get her back in the classroom right away. Paislee would do that in her own time when her mind could make sense of what had happened.

'I think tonight Miss Olsen will go home and think about what she did,' Marnie started.

'She will be grounded? Her parents will shout at her?' Paislee interrupted, wanting to ask her question.

'I think she won't be allowed to watch TV tonight and that she will think about what she did this weekend, for two days,' Marnie replied, leaning into the bean bag a little more, the hard floor slightly uncomfortable.

'Her parents will be mad?' Paislee asked again.

'I think they will be disappointed. It's not nice to shout at people and I think Miss Olsen was just feeling sad and it was an accident,' Marnie told Paislee.

'They won't let her watch TV?' Paislee said, rubbing at her face again with Marnie's hand.

'No, she can't watch TV. She will have to think about what she did,' Marnie said, looking Paislee in the eye. Paislee let out a small whimper, sadness still evident in her eyes. Marnie would be having words with Amber once all the kids had gone home. 'Would you like to read a story? We only have ten minutes before home time,' Marnie noted.

'I don't want to see her again,' Paislee said, settling into the bean bag and placing Marnie's hand on her forehead. Marnie's reached over to grab one of the nearest books.

'Miss Olsen will go home and think about it and we can talk to her on Monday,' Marnie said, wriggling to make herself comfortable and lifting the book so Paislee could see it. 'Dinosaurs vs. Humans,' Marnie began.

Twenty minutes later, Paislee had given Miss Olsen an evil glare as she collected her bag for home and Marnie had explained what had happened to Paislee's mum, who had been incredibly understanding and said she would talk to Paislee at home, while Marnie said she would talk to Miss Olsen and have a plan for Monday so that Paislee wouldn't feel scared coming in. Now, Marnie was leaning against one of the small desks facing Amber who sat at her desk.

'I'm sorry, Marnie, it just came out,' Amber explained, the tips of her fingers against the bridge of her nose.

'Look I understand if you're having a bad day but that's not fair on Paislee. It's not OK to take it out on her. If you needed five minutes you should have told me and I could have watched the class, but it's never OK to shout and put her through that. You have control over how you speak and act. You can always pause and think for a moment. I know it can be difficult if you're going through stuff, but Paislee doesn't get the choice as to whether your shouting will affect her. It instantly hurts her, it scares her, it fills her body with fear and anger and it can take her a while to process what happened, which she will – she'll process it, but is it really so difficult for us to just be more considerate and kind as a society?' Marnie said along a deep sigh, her chest deflating at the thought of how the world so often believes that anyone who is a little different should learn to fit in with society's norms, that they have to adapt to the language, to the actions and to the way in which the world was built, when in reality she believed it to be quite the opposite.

Sure, kids can learn that grown-ups get angry too, that they have their frustrated days, sad days, moody days just like everyone else and that's fine. Marnie always talked to Paislee about that, about how she could get angry, how she and Jovi fought sometimes. It's not that Paislee didn't understand that, but that was just it: they talked. If Paislee said a bad word or dropped something on the floor, they would talk about it, discuss the rules and move on. But shouting, shouting did nothing but scare her, not allowing for any information other than fear to get into Paislee's mind.

There was a long drawn-out silence when Marnie finished speaking. The shadows under Amber's eyes, the concern in their brown hue and the crease in her brow told Marnie that she was sorry, that she understood what Marnie had said. Once Marnie felt content with that, she spoke again.

'Are you OK? You can talk to me if you'd like?' Marnie was aware they still weren't the best of friends and she had to admit that she felt a little on edge after this afternoon. It was taking her blood a little time to cool off. But she was also hopeful that she would be at this school for quite some time now and she knew she had to put herself out there and build friendships with those around her, for it wasn't pleasant to work with people you didn't get along with, as the first few weeks with Amber could attest.

Amber looked up and swiped a hand over her eyes, taking a deep breath.

'I'm sorry for this afternoon. Being strict is one thing but shouting is another thing entirely. They are a good class and Paislee doesn't ask for much. I shouldn't have shouted,' Amber started. Marnie nodded.

'It's so stupid as well. Seb mentioned something about Christmas with his family and booking flights when we have had no discussion about where we were going to have Christmas this year. We saw his family two years ago. Last year was my family, I know, but this year I was thinking it might just be the two of us, though I think that's partly because I miss my family Christmas. His traditions are so different to mine. He has such a big family; it can get loud. With him assuming, it just rubbed me the wrong way. I guess it was on my mind this afternoon, preparing for the talk when we get home.' Amber let out one long breath.

Marnie shuffled on the table. She remembered those first few years with Josh, the Christmas Day debates. In the early days they had accommodated each other and with her family living in town and his just two towns over, it hadn't been difficult to alternate between Christmas morning with one set of parents and Christmas dinner with Jovi and the gang. It had slowly become just the two of them in the past three years. When looking back now, Marnie realised Josh had slowly pushed everyone away, only interested in work and apparently her and his 'them against the world' mantra. She rubbed at the silver bangle on her wrist.

What would happen when Nova went back to Canada? Her whole family was in Canada, Marnie's in Orion. It would be another Christmas split, more compromises and disagreements. Marnie shook her head furiously, making Amber jump. 'Sorry,' she mumbled, clearing her throat. Where had that come from – thoughts of Nova and Christmas?

'Erm, I don't think I should be the one dispensing relation-ship advice.' She laughed, resorting to self-depreciation when she felt nervous. 'But I think talking about it is all you can do. Listening to each other, having the scary conversations, finding out what's important to you both and hopefully figuring out something that makes you both happy.' Again, a vision of Nova flashed through Marnie's brain. She'd only known her a few weeks and one beautiful day in Canada, but was it really time they had a talk? Did Marnie need to have the scary conversation about her feelings?

Marnie kicked her legs under the table, swinging them to bring the feeling back into them. Her whole body was tingling with that new mix of excited and totally freaked out; a concoction that only Nova provided.

'You're right,' Amber said, shuffling a stack of papers on her desk. 'And, Marnie, don't be so hard on yourself. I know I was very much a mean girl when you arrived, but what Josh did is no reflection on who you are, your worth and what you believe in and I appreciate the relationship advice.' Amber's tone was earnest. Marnie gave a small appreciative nod.

'How can I make it up to Paislee next week?' Amber asked. Marnie had to admit she liked this version of Amber, the one who was willing to listen and talk and see another person's perspective, though she wasn't keen on hearing her own advice out in the open when she felt somewhat of a hypocrite.

'She likes notes and for people to admit when they are sorry. If you say sorry and leave something on her desk, that might be nice, then just allow her to process it. She will accept it in her own time,' Marnie explained, smiling just thinking about Paislee's quirks and her love of notes and people being thoughtful.

'OK, I can do that. I really am sorry again for shouting but thank you for all your help today. I'm going to finish marking these books then get home to have a grown-up conversation,' Amber said with a small smile. 'You get off and enjoy your evening. Are you going to the Starcrossed Festival?'

Marnie nodded. 'Yes, I'll be there. Have a nice evening too.' There wasn't really much tidying left to be done but Marnie felt herself moving slowly. She had her own conversations to have and her own feelings to face once she walked out of the door and she didn't know if she was quite ready.

23

The bakery was packed when Marnie walked in, giving her chance to go unnoticed by both Jovi and Antoni but also giving her a little too much time to think of a way out. She didn't have to face them or face herself today, not if she didn't want to. If it wasn't for the lone cinnamon roll tempting her from an almost empty glass counter at the back of the bakery, she was certain to have darted, but it was like the pastry had eyes so intense they were flirting with her and she couldn't look away. Nerves were making her delirious – that and her sweet tooth.

So lost in thought, her own eyes glazed over, she hadn't seen Jovi walk over, take the pastry from the counter, wrap it in a napkin and pass it to her. It wasn't until the sticky icing touched the tip of her nose that she registered her sister in front of her.

'If I ask this time, you tell the truth, no holding back. I can't help you if you lie and that hurts me as much as it hurts you – you know it does because you would feel the exact same way if it was the other way around. Twins for life,' Jovi said sternly, but then she raised her fist at the end with great sarcasm for the joys of being a twin. Marnie smirked. She could not argue with her. No matter how much Marnie had tried to trick herself in the past, to hide her deepest fears from her sister so that Jovi would not feel pain, she knew the truth. If Marnie felt pain, Jovi felt it too. If something was off with Marnie, Jovi would always be able to tell, and Jovi would feel it. Not telling her what it was only made her feel double the pain. The least Marnie could do was be honest, especially since Jovi had forgiven her after her most recent outburst and confession and the fact that she fled to Canada without her for six months.

Marnie took a teeny bite of her roll and looked into her twin sister's eyes, eyes that were identical to her own, eyes that she could trust with her whole entire being. Though she knew that getting her words out was still hard.

To give herself a tad more time, she looked around the bakery, only now realising that it was empty and Antoni was pretending to not be listening by cleaning the top of a glass cabinet that was already shining and squeaking in protest for him to lay off the cleaning products.

'It's too soon. She lives in Canada. I like living alone. She's too pretty. She's way too nerdy and she makes my stomach hurt.' Marnie didn't stop for breath. If she stopped, she knew she would clam up and not get her words out and so they came out in a tumble, the cinnamon roll now feeling too sickly sweet on her taste buds. She could feel tears pooling in her tear ducts. This was a lot. She was feeling a lot. She hadn't felt a lot in a long time.

Suddenly, Antoni was next to her and guiding her towards the bar stools at the front of the shop and Jovi had swung the sign around to closed. The two of them didn't speak right away, giving Marnie chance to process all she had said. She was right – they had to agree. There were so many reasons she could not have feelings for Nova. It just wasn't going to work, not least because she didn't even know if Nova liked her as more than a friend but because of her exhaustive list of red flags.

Marnie took a seat on one of the stools and put her pastry down on the table. Jovi sat opposite her while Antoni threw his arms around Marnie's neck and stood behind her, resting his chin on her hair. Marnie's body relaxed into the familiar scent of him and his comforting safe arms.

'First off, life doesn't really come with a schedule. There's no too soon or too late. Everyone's journey is different,' Jovi said calmly, rubbing at Marnie's forearm.

'Secondly, Canada's good. We like Canada and Canadian products,' Antoni chimed in to Marnie's ear. She wanted to retort and say something funny about maple cream but it seemed Jovi had more to say.

'Thirdly, no one is saying you can't live on your own. People don't have to move in together right away,' Jovi said, matter-of-fact, helping herself to a nibble of Marnie's abandoned pastry. Marnie appreciated the casualness in the way her sister was talking and how Antoni was holding her. It made her feel less on the spot and imprisoned in the conversation.

'Fourthly, do people still say fourthly?' Antoni queried and Marnie could feel his smirk against her head, though she couldn't see his face. 'Never mind. Too pretty? I've got nothing for that one, Jo,' Antoni said and Marnie could feel his chin move away from her head as he shook his.

Jovi waved her hand to brush his words away. 'Fifthly, there's no such thing as too nerdy. What is a nerd anyway?

She's passionate, Marn. She probably has as many dinosaur fossils as you have glue guns.'

'Six…ly, OK that's definitely not how that goes,' Antoni began and this time Marnie couldn't help a small snort, which earnt Antoni a warm smile from Jovi. 'I'm pretty sure it's the swarm of butterflies you can feel fluttering in your belly and not wind.' This time it was Jovi who snorted through her laughter, which only made Marnie giggle. She enjoyed seeing her sister laugh and was always grateful for Antoni's humour.

'Anything else?' Jovi asked once she had composed herself.

Marnie wiped at the loose tears that had fallen through a mix of laughter and with the weight that had lifted off her chest from getting her emotions out and hearing her sister's and best friend's words.

'What happens if she doesn't like me like that?' Marnie mumbled, picking at the icing on the cinnamon roll but not eating it. Antoni's arms wrapped around her neck, squeezing tighter.

'Of all the museums in all the world that she could have transferred to,' Jovi said with a cheeky smile, picking up the roll and pushing it up to Marnie's lips. 'You need to eat,' she added, in her motherly voice.

'I'm not really hungry,' Marnie said, gently pushing away Jovi's hand.

'You'll offend the cinnamon roll,' Antoni said, mock aghast, giving her one more squeeze and then moving away to flip the sign on the door back to open. He spoke again as he strode. 'Marn, love can be scary, especially when you've been burned in the past but love can also be beautiful. No matter what happens, enjoy the butterflies, embrace those dizzy moments where you look at someone and can't stop the dizzying grin that forms on your face, revel in the joy that just thinking about them brings. Sure, be cautious, ask the right questions, communicate both your needs and figure out if you're the right fit, but don't push away the magic and those feelings of bliss. Even if they are just that, just moments in time and nothing more, be grateful for them.'

Marnie was too stunned for words as she took in what Antoni had said. It was so beautiful that her tears started up all over again. From the kid who loved making pretty things and putting glitter and pom-poms on everything to the woman that worked alongside kids, experiencing their thrill over the smallest treasures in life every day, to the woman who flew halfway across the world to get down and dirty in nature and to ogle mountain tops and a medley of trees, she loved seeing the beauty in life. Was she really going to let her fears keep taking that away?

Marnie wiped at her eyes with the back of her hand and jumped off her chair, striding up to Antoni and wrapping her arms around his waist. His arms draped once more around her neck as she breathed in the scent of him and nuzzled into her usual spot. Joy, that's what that was. Talking to Nova brought her that same joy and she was allowed to feel it.

'Nova sort of stayed the night last night.' The words slipped from her mouth, the contentment she felt buried in Antoni's chest making her reveal all her secrets. Antoni released one arm and Marnie heard the swoosh of the open/close sign flip back over. Jovi jumped off her chair and practically yanked Marnie out of Antoni's grip.

'Maybe you should have started with that. Did she hurt you? Are you OK? Did she pressure you into anything? She's too pretty for her own good. Oh my God, what am I saying? You can't date a nerd.' Jovi's words came out rapid fire, identical to how Marnie had spoken when she'd shared her fears earlier.

'Jeez, Jo, no. No, it wasn't like that,' Marnie said putting her hands up to get her sister to stop and breathe. Then she laughed. 'God, you backpedalled on Nova quick.' Marnie couldn't help but laugh.

'You take this at your own pace. You shouldn't feel rushed,' Jovi said, closing her eyes and taking deep breaths in through her nose and out through her mouth.

'There was no rushing. I just told you I don't know if she likes me like that. We were just working and then it got late, we'd had too much sugar and fell asleep. It was…nice.' Marnie was unable to stop the edges of her lips shooting upwards. 'But then this morning I froze. She was saying bye and I just sort of sat there, like I didn't walk her out, hug her or anything and I lied. I made an excuse not to see her tonight and I feel like she saw right through me.'

Jovi let out a sigh of relief but Marnie's lips were now forming a pout. She closed her eyes, cringing at the awkwardness of this morning. It was safe to say she didn't miss the hurt and confusion in Nova's expressive blue eyes.

'The order of these sentences could have gone differently,' Jovi noted. 'Right, so you've already had a sleepover – there's a way to break the ice. Look, Marn, I can't top Ant's epic speech, all I can say is that you should talk to her. If you bring each other happiness and you both like each other, you will figure out the finer details. Just go talk to her. She's

Sienna's favourite teacher – think of your niece,' Jovi added with a hint of teasing now in her tone.

Before Marnie could speak, someone knocked on the door, reminding them that the bakery was still open for another hour and that Jovi and Antoni had to get back to work. Marnie hugged them both as Antoni switched over the sign for the third time and then she bowed out of the bakery in need of a plan. Of course she could simply communicate, just call Nova and ask if they could talk. She'd just had a pretty successful conversation, but Nova was special and now that Marnie was finally admitting that to herself, she wanted to show Nova that. Rejection be damned. How often in life do you meet a woman with stars in her eyes and dinosaurs on her socks? Marnie concluded, very rarely, if ever. Nova was a one-of-a-kind species that gave her one-of-a-kind feelings. Was she really going to let their relationship become extinct before it had even had chance to roam?

Dashing onto the street, Marnie raced past the preparations for Sunday's festival without even a glance at the blow-up ghosts and pumpkins. She focused on putting one foot in front of the other and moving swiftly in the direction of The Glitter Emporium.

'Is everything all right, Marn?' came Cameron's voice upon hearing the door and Marnie wheezing slightly out of breath.

Marnie looked around, checking the aisles for customers, as she made her way towards the back of the shop, happy that the coast was clear and she could talk to Cameron freely.

'Yes, yes everything's fine, thank you,' she said, plonking

her bag on one of the craft chairs before disappearing back to the shelves to get some inspiration. She barely looked at Cameron but caught her in her periphery, head down over some Egyptian bust she was spray-painting gold. It made Marnie's skin simultaneously shiver and tingle thinking back to that day at the museum and how the mummies had scared Paislee and how Nova had been her knight in shining armour.

'Hey, Cameron,' Marnie said, tracing her fingers over the bottles of glitter, their dazzling specks seducing her, though she knew she had more than enough glitter at home that even Cameron would most likely cut her off if she tried to buy more.

'Yeah,' Cameron called back.

'How do you woo someone?' Marnie asked, narrowing her eyes over the clay sculptures.

Marnie heard wooden legs scrape across the wooden floorboards and then suddenly Cameron was peeking her head around the aisle Marnie was on. Marnie had to do a double take for Cameron never moved that fast – she was way too cool and chill.

'You want to woo someone?' Cameron asked, raising a neatly shaped bushy brow.

'Erm, yes,' Marnie said meekly, then her eyes caught sight of a box depicting a palaeontologist dig, complete with bones stuck in some sort of clay coating that children, ages seven plus, could chisel away at. 'Yes. Yes I do,' she said more confidently with an inspired nod.

'Well OK then. I like this new you. I agree with whatever Canada is putting in their water,' Cameron said, clapping her hands together, then throwing one arm around Marnie's shoulders. 'It's not always about grand romantic gestures, unless you know the person is into that kind of stuff. I'd say it's more the thought that counts, no matter how big or small. Think about what they're into, what they like and what's clear cut. You don't want to be confusing, you want to say: "Hey, I'm here and I like you, like you."'

Cameron was pulling Marnie into her like they were on a life-or-death secret mission, heads huddled together in a manner of urgency. Marnie's eyes were scrunched together listening to Cameron's every word with intent. She'd never been the one to take the lead before and put herself out there but she guessed there was always a first time for everything and with Nova only having another few days left in the country, it truly was now or never and the mission had to go without a hitch.

'Cameron,' Marnie said, standing tall and looking her friend dead in the eye.

'Yes,' Cameron said, gripping Marnie's shoulders.

'We're going to need lots of sand, a bunch of dinosaur bones, a shovel, maybe some biodegradable glitter...' Marnie tilted her head from side to side. Glitter wasn't a necessity but it just made everything that much prettier. Cameron gave her a knowing look at the glitter comment. 'OK... maybe ixnay on the glitter, but we do need colourful card and that poop emoji stress toy,' Marnie said decisively, pointing at the poop toy over Cameron's shoulder.

'Right, OK. Got it,' Cameron replied, not batting an eyelid at the craziness of Marnie's list.

'Right, good. I'm really doing this,' Marnie stated causing Cameron to shake her shoulders.

'That's right – you are.' Cameron nodded. 'I'm right in

saying you want fake dinosaur bones? We're not looking to break into the museum or something?' she added dubiously.

'No breaking and entering, though add clay to that list. We're going to make our own bones.' Marnie noted, before the two of them nodded at each other and went in search of all said items. With each step Marnie took she felt an overwhelming surge of adrenaline, like all the blood in her body was tingling at what she was about to do. She was owning her feelings and she wasn't going to run from them anymore. She hadn't expected to feel things for another human again, not when fear had taken over her entire being, making it difficult for like and love to even be considered, but then wasn't it the unexpected things in life that made life interesting, that made life fun?

24

'Where's the poop?' Marnie asked in a hushed tone as they reached the park on Saturday afternoon. The air was a beautiful late October crisp, no rain, with a slight breeze and a few remaining warm orange sunbeams still splintering through the pale blue sky. The park was busy for the Eve of the Starcrossed Festival. Marnie assumed everyone would be at home making last-minute adjustments to their costumes for Orion's trick-or-treating extravaganza tomorrow; occasionally Halloween would fall on the same day as the festival which was why it was a combined effort in celebrating all things Halloween and Autumn, it made it extra special and worked well for the kids when Halloween occurred during the week, but there were groups old and young swinging on swings and chasing each other down the slide. That was not going to do. It was a good job she had the poo, she thought as Cameron waved it in her direction.

Marnie got a few odd looks as she and Cameron walked towards the sandpit both armed with carrier bags filled with sticking-out bones, a shovel, a bucket and one tub of green biodegradable glitter that Marnie hadn't been able to resist. The first hurdle, Marnie noticed right away, was the two reception kids from her old school happily building castles in the sand, their parents all merrily chatting away on a nearby bench. Marnie had to move fast. She signalled to Cameron with a swift spy-like nod and Cameron launched the poo like a professional baseball pitcher into the pit when the kids weren't looking.

It was then time for Marnie to swing into action. She casually placed her bags down by the nearest tree and made like she was just having a stroll past the play area. Upon getting closer to the sandpit, she let out a gasp. Hurriedly, she walked over to the parents to explain the dreadful situation that she believed their children were playing in an unsafe environment, that cats had gotten there first and had been using it as a litter box. Marnie wasn't quite sure if the scowls she received were because the parents recognised her and deemed her evil thanks to Josh or because their chilled Saturday evening was now being replaced by having to think about how to clean, cleanse and purify their children. Either way, guilt lined her stomach as she watched them swoop up their kids and dash home.

'Stop it – you've no time to feel guilty. It's not like we used real cat poo and actually poisoned their kids. Come on. Have you texted Nova?' Cameron said, striding over to Marnie with the bags and nudging her in the shoulder. Marnie stopped looking after the kids and swung her backpack over her shoulder to retrieve her phone.

'Please can you meet me at the park in half an hour,' she typed out and then read aloud for approval from Cameron.

'Perfect. Let's do this,' Cameron said with an enthusiastic nod as she scooped up the emoji poo and laughed as she threw it back in her bag.

★

Marnie sat on her hands, to keep herself from fidgeting, at the base of a giant oak tree, hidden from view of the sandpit. She wanted Nova to experience her dig without the pressure of Marnie's eyes studying her and willing her to like it. Her response had to be authentic and real.

Not that Marnie wasn't going to peek to see Nova's reactions. She'd set up the sign instructing Nova on what to do at the gate of the park, it read: *New developments found this way. Palaeontologists (apprentices or other) needed this way.* And next to it she had left the bucket and small shovel where the start of a green glittered path began leading to the sandpit. She prayed it would ignite the nerd in Nova and that her giddiness when talking about all things dinosaur digs would be sparked and she would be way too curious to walk away.

A buzzing from her pocket indicated that Nova had arrived. It was Cameron's one last mission, spying from behind one of the cars in the car park and letting Marnie know of Nova's status before she headed home. Marnie didn't know if she could have put all this together so quickly without her and she quickly sent Cameron the cat-face emoji, just for giggles, and a couple of hearts. She would craft her something to say thank you in the coming days.

Peering around the large bark, Marnie saw Nova standing at the sign in black bicycle shorts underneath an oversized grey hoodie with NASA written across it. She had chunky black boots that Marnie didn't think should go with bicycle shorts but Nova definitely made it work and she was, of course, wearing her signature cap, her blonde hair pulled through in a ponytail at the back. Suddenly, Marnie had a visual of her little pink heart tearing out of her chest and skipping across the grass to attach itself to Nova. It was thumping so fast, making her head spin.

Nova was still for a few moments. Marnie saw a flicker of hesitation cross her golden features as her narrowed eyes read the sign, looked at the path of glitter and then around the park, presumably for signs of life. Quickly Marnie sat back and out of sight, not wanting to ruin her plan from the get-go. To Marnie's relief, she heard the crunch of autumn's fallen leaves and when she thought it safe enough to do so, she peered out once more to see that Nova had made it to the sandpit.

Now, kneeling on the grass and peering out from the other side of the tree, Marnie watched as Nova animatedly took to the sand. Marnie's heart skipped a couple of beats at how Nova didn't show a care nor concern about what anyone would think of a thirty-four-year-old Canadian digging up a child's sandpit alone on a dark night in a town that wasn't her home.

Upon finding the first bone, under the glow of the rising moonlight, Marnie witnessed Nova's lips curve upwards, parting to give way to a pearly white smile. It looked to be the bone Marnie had buried in the bottom-left corner of the square pit, which read: *You are Dino-Mite.*

Marnie couldn't take her eyes off Nova as she uncovered each bone, letting out a mix of squeals, giggles and snorts. Marnie felt rather proud of herself as she'd tried to keep each note light and playful while at the same time being direct and clear with her messaging. For example, you couldn't read: *You make my heart Saur*, without knowing that the person who had written the message was proposing some kind of interest, could you? Marnie shook off any doubt. Cameron had checked them and told her quite bluntly that if anyone had ever done this for her she would have one thousand per cent loved it and put a ring on it. As it stood, Esme had done something similar with candid photographs of Cameron with notes attached expressing how each picture made Esme feel. Marnie didn't believe Cameron was far off the ring part.

From her position behind the oak, Marnie tried to count Nova's laughs while trying to remember how many bones she had dropped into the bucket, wanting to know when it was her turn to make her move. But Nova was still crawling on her knees and having abandoned the shovel – it was kiddie sand after all and not sedimented layered rock and soil – looked to be having the time of her life sifting the sand through her fingertips.

'I loved us the moment I saurus,' came Nova's voice from across the park. 'I love that one,' she said with a booming laugh. Marnie chuckled to herself behind the tree, tipping her head back against the cool bark, her insides soaring. 'Are you going to come out now?' Nova then shouted and when Marnie peeked back around the tree, Nova was sat on her heels, her piercing blue eyes staring right at her, glowing cat-like in the deepening sky.

'Hey, how did you know?' Marnie mock moaned, shuffling to her feet and walking over to the sandpit.

'I could hear your bracelets jangling every time you moved and there are crunchy leaves everywhere,' Nova confessed.

'That's some *Llukalkan aliocranianus* hearing that is,' Marnie said, stepping into the sandpit and sitting next to Nova, who moved so she now sat cross-legged.

'Since when did you know so much about dinosaurs? That one's relatively new, not many people have heard about it,' Nova questioned, her eyes still penetrating Marnie's.

'There's this really cool dinosaur teacher who teaches the kids where I work. Total nerd about the prehistoric beasts, but she has this incredibly delicious voice that makes for easy listening,' Marnie explained. With Nova having completed the bespoke dig, Marnie was feeling brave for once, like she was truly putting it all on the line. It felt like she had nothing to lose but everything to lose at the same time, but she knew if she never went for it she'd be stuck forever in limbo and that wasn't a fun place to be.

'I like that, dinosaur teacher.' Nova snorted, turning the last bone over in her hands.

'I'm sorry about Friday morning and for lying about what I was doing Friday night and tonight. I panicked. All these feelings were rushing through my head and instead of talking to you about them I just pushed you away and that wasn't fair nor kind. I like you, Nova, a whole lot and it kind of came out of nowhere. I kept telling myself I couldn't like you because we live worlds apart, that it's all too soon, that I'm supposed to be on my own now because I can't picture living with someone again or integrating someone in my life because I've made it my own life now and I'm capable of being independent, that I'm not supposed to need anyone.

'It was all these things swirling around my brain at once but you came in to my life and sort of popped my cynical little bubble. You made me feel alive again, like I can still do all these things for me but also share them with another human. I spent so long picturing Josh in every aspect of my life that I stayed with him, waiting for the day that these pictures in my mind would become a reality, because they were supposed to, because he was supposed to be my forever. I couldn't picture the future with you, I couldn't see how it could possibly work, how this gorgeous Canadian would fit in to any part of my life, so I was scared to take a chance. I couldn't see forever with you and so I've been in my own head these past couple of days and holding back. But I realise that forever is made up of a bunch of todays and I like my todays with you.'

The words came out in a rush. Marnie's cheeks felt cold with a nervous chill that washed over her, having bared her deepest feelings to Nova.

She'd never been this bold before, never been the one to make the first move and face possible rejection and failure but somehow it felt good. She sucked in a deep breath, awaiting Nova's response while mentally going over anything else she had forgotten to say. Her pulse was beating hard in her left wrist; she placed her right hand over the top of it to calm it.

'No one ever really understands my take on forever,' Nova said with a smile so warm it instantly heated up Marnie's frozen cheeks. Then Nova reached out and replaced Marnie's right hand, gently placing her own over the top of Marnie's left wrist and stroking it with her thumb. It caused a shiver to scale Marnie's arm, but it wasn't uncomfortable; it felt thrilling. 'I appreciate all that you've been through and respect all your fears and doubts. I'm sorry if I came on too strong coming here. I just like you a whole lot too and couldn't get you out of my head. When work said Museum Borealis was looking to do an exchange, your name kept circling around in my mind and I guess the lure of you and a giant T-Rex fossil were hard to resist.'

Marnie let out a bark of laughter that echoed around the now-still park. A cat meowed in response as Nova scooted a touch closer so their knees were touching.

'I'll remember that, if I ever want you to do something I just have to seduce you with dinosaur artefacts,' Marnie said, immediately flushing at her use of the word *seduce*, but it didn't seem to faze Nova. Her hand found Marnie's cheek, doing nothing to cool the flames that Marnie felt burning inside them.

'Can I kiss you, Marnie?' Nova asked, her peachy lips glistening under the opal moon, her accent melting Marnie's insides so much that she could only respond with a grunt and a nod. It was enough. Nova's lips found hers. They were soft and full and gentle. As soon as Marnie's brain realised what it was doing and allowed her to embrace the moment and how long she had actually wanted and waited to do this, her lips worked a little faster, kissing Nova back with more urgency. Her hand found Nova's cap, which she slipped off in haste to put her fingers through Nova's blonde hair and pull her closer. Nova's hand was now caressing Marnie's collarbone under Marnie's jumper and their breathing was becoming increasingly heavy.

'Uh, Marnie, do you think we should maybe...' Nova started, her breathing ragged, her words falling out in dribs and drabs as her lips remained glued to Marnie's '...take this somewhere other than the kids' sandpit? I'm not sure about here.' She pulled away, though her hands stayed on Marnie's hips. 'But in Canada we'd probably get arrested for indecent PDA.' Her eyes were glistening with amusement and mischief.

Marnie looked around to give herself a minute to compose her mind and body. 'Oh yes, you're probably right. Between this and putting poop in the sandpit, I don't want to be arrested tonight,' she said absentmindedly making to collect the bucket and spade.

Nova jumped up. 'There's poop in here?'

For a moment Marnie felt stricken. She had completely just ruined the moment talking about poo. 'Oh God, sorry no. Ignore me, I'll explain tomorrow. My place?' she then asked in a more hopeful but probably still no way near sexy tone. Thankfully, Nova's face flashed with desire, her blue eyes widening, her hand taking Marnie's and tugging her out of the box as if remembering what they had been doing mere seconds ago and desperate to get back to it.

With that look there wasn't a single fear that attacked Marnie's brain. Only the thought of Nova in her bed and getting to see for herself if her dinosaur underwear was all just a tease or not.

Sunday morning's laid-back sun edged its way slowly into Marnie's bedroom, highlighting the silver picture frames that hung on the wall and making rainbows bounce from necklace to bracelet on her jewellery stand. She lay partly under the duvet, partly on top of the duvet and she had no idea where her pillow was. Nova's long limbs were wrapped around her hips, an arm across her stomach and one hand resting on her shoulder. Marnie couldn't feel one of her own arms, for it was draped under Nova's body, but her other was pressed under her head as she propped herself up slightly, grinning like she'd uncovered the fossils of the *Llukalkan aliocranianus* herself.

She was trying not to replay last night over and over in her mind, though the taste of Nova on her lips made it incredibly hard not to, but she wanted to be in the moment, for in the moment she felt blissfully content. No past, no future just a rather snug and cosy present.

'I like fish and chips,' Nova whispered, a little slurry as her eyes flickered open and she tilted her head to look up at Marnie. Marnie tilted her chin to meet her morning gaze. She didn't think she would ever tire of staring into those love-struck blues.

'I like poutine,' Marnie replied, a smirk playing at her lips.

'So, what do we do now?' Nova asked, suddenly sitting up and pulling the duvet up around her chest. Marnie had been used to seeing her with a broad smile across her face and with a fierce confidence since she had met her, but now her face grew solemn and Marnie felt the urge to be strong for both of them.

'Well, it's the Starcrossed Festival in town today. Its starts around one. So that gives us exactly five hours to make the most epic couples costume known to man or dinosaur, if you're in, that is?' Marnie questioned, scoring a smile from Nova. She sat up to kiss her nose. 'As far as the rest goes, we'll put it together one fossil at a time,' she added, brushing her lips against Nova's.

'Are you all about the dinosaur metaphors now? Is that

going to be your new thing?' Nova teased, a dimple forming in her right cheek before she gently bit Marnie's bottom lip.

'If it makes you smile like that, then yes, it will be my new thing.' Marnie confirmed, her lip tingling where Nova's teeth had been. She leant forward and drew Nova in for a deep kiss.

When she released her Nova breathed, 'I'm in.' To which Marnie dived off the bed in a rush of excitement.

'Right, five hours is nothing. Come on. To the craft box,' Marnie ordered, waving her hands in the air while stepping over Nova's T-Rex print bra and knickers.

25

The last stitch sped through Marnie's fingertips as the clock struck one. Antoni had popped in around eleven-thirty for long enough to deliver paninis and drop off his costume that he hadn't fixed since last year and needed Marnie to see to. He hadn't been able to stay long due to the bakes he, Jovi and the gang were making for the party. The bakery made the most scrumptious treats for the festival every year. They had become a tradition and town treasures: mini apple pie bites, pumpkin cheesecakes, chestnut loaves and this year the special edition of maple cream doughnuts. Marnie salivated at the thought.

Pulling the fabric out from under the foot of the sewing machine, Marnie called Nova over from where she was sitting in front of Marnie's bedroom mirror with Marnie's make-up displayed around her. Nova hadn't bothered nipping back to the Airbnb she was staying at. Her hands had been too otherwise entangled with fabric, pom-poms and Marnie's hair. Besides Marnie needed her to play mannequin as she sewed and stitched costumes from scratch.

This was to be their first Halloween together; they had to make it count. Nova scuttled over to where Marnie was standing with the fabric aloft, still with lip liner in hand and a pout on her face as she tried to finish the job she had started without looking in a mirror.

'You've missed a bit…' Marnie started then dropped a kiss on Nova's lips when she reached her. 'There.' She finished, slowly pulling away and touching a finger to Nova's lips where her own had just been smudging Nova's pretty work.

Nova merely winked, which caught Marnie off guard and made Marnie's seducing attempt seem weak in comparison. How did Nova do that to Marnie's body with such a simple thing as a wink? She needed lessons.

'Right, arms up please,' Marnie said clearing her throat. Nova did as she was told as Marnie dropped the silver dress over her head and let it fall over Nova's curves, stopping just below the knee. 'Perfect,' Marnie said. It wasn't too tight or too big; it settled over Nova's figure just right for a gathering that included kids and families. Besides this costume wasn't for them, it was for Sienna. Nova had come up with the idea after asking what everyone in Marnie's family dressed up as. Marnie had told her that Sienna went to the festival as an astronaut every year. Marnie had practically thrown herself at Nova at the thoughtfulness of her idea and Marnie had been even more ecstatic when looking in her craft box knowing she would be able to put the two costumes together with ease.

'It feels nice eh,' Nova commented, twirling around and watching the silver fabric float out an inch or two from her body. As Nova watched the dress, Marnie watched Nova. Her blonde hair, which was tied up into two space buns, caught the light, making it shine a little whiter. The rainbow glitter that Nova had sprinkled over her centre parting dazzled in the rays, making Nova sparkle brighter than any star Marnie had ever seen. 'I need to get your hair done, come on,' Nova said tugging Marnie's arm once she had stopped spinning and admiring her dress.

Marnie blinked back into the room, having felt like she had actually morphed into an alien from outer space that had been staring down at this precious human with great inquisitiveness and amazement. She took Nova's place at the dresser and let Nova work her hair magic. Marnie's buns weren't as big as Nova's with Marnie's hair being shorter and thinner, so Nova added thick rainbow scrunchies to give it more volume and Marnie had to admit she loved the look. She hadn't worn this much colour and glitter since Sienna's fourth space birthday.

Once all intergalactic hair and make-up had been achieved, Marnie fetched knee-high socks and bicycle shorts from her cupboard. Anytime she wore a dress she liked having shorts underneath for comfort, plus autumn was in full effect today and there was definitely a strong breeze in the air. She couldn't wait to be holding a warm mug of chai latte in one hand and Nova's hand with the other as she strolled Orion, admiring everyone's costumes this year.

'OK, I think I have everything. Are you ready to experience Orion's Halloween-Spooktacular-cum-Autumn-Festival?' Marnie said, flitting around her living room one last time, making sure that she did indeed have everything. Antoni's outfit, check. Sienna's alien plushie, check. Backpack, check, and Nova, check. She glanced over to the door where Nova was putting on her chunky black boots and wondered how on earth this woman made chunky black boots work with every outfit.

'What are you smiling at?' Nova asked. Her tone was playful but when their eyes met, an understanding passed between them. There was a charge in the air that connected the two of them in a shared moment of contentment, excitement, nerves, joy and gratitude for a person coming into your life.

'You,' Marnie said simply before skipping over to Nova, taking her hand and leading her out of the door merrily.

'Obb and Bob!! Obb and Bob!!' Sienna yelled making Marnie turn away from the riveting apple-dunking competition that was currently taking place. Violet was beating Harry by three apples with fifteen seconds left on the timer. It was hard to look away but the delight in Sienna's squeal was equally hard to ignore – that and the names that Sienna had given to Marnie and Nova upon being overjoyed about their costumes made Marnie snort.

Sienna's face had lit up like a star exploding when she had first laid eyes on Marnie and Nova. She had jumped up and down expressing that she didn't need her plushie alien this year, because she had two real ones. Marnie and Nova were stripped of their real names almost instantly, everyone having to refer to them as Obb and Bob for the remainder of the festival. To Marnie it was all worth it and the few strums on her heart that she felt for Nova had turned into a chorus at her having come up with the genius concept of alien costumes to complement Sienna's astronaut. Believe it or not, no one in the family had done that before. One year

Jackson had been the sun and Jovi the earth and Marnie had been a mix of Disney characters, always enjoying the looks on the kids' faces upon seeing her. Rapunzel had been a favourite – so much so she had cheated and been her three years in a row. As for Antoni, he was always a rasher of bacon. It had never occurred to Marnie to replace the plushie alien for an actual alien costume but she loved it.

'Yes, my little space cadet,' Marnie said, squatting down to greet Sienna.

'Will you and Bob come on the teacups with me, please? Mummy says it will make her sick,' Sienna asked, eyes as wide as saucers in full pleading effect. For a moment Marnie's brow furrowed. Jovi loved the teacups. It was one of her favourite things to do with Sienna every year at the festival. She'd have to find her soon and check if she was feeling OK. It was always a busy day for her and Antoni. She was usually ready to tag out by six p.m., having been baking all morning and getting Sienna ready. Jackson too had so much on his plate with building the stages and sheds for the event. Sienna would often sleep over at Marnie's or Antoni's to give them a night to themselves, though they would both protest that they didn't need it and missed their little girl whenever she stayed away. Jovi hadn't shown signs of extra stress when Marnie had talked to her earlier this afternoon and there had definitely been a glimmer of happiness in her eyes at seeing Marnie and Nova looking extra cosy together. She hadn't let on to feeling under the weather.

'Violet won by five apples,' Nova said, bouncing around to see where Marnie had got to. Marnie stood up just as Nova bent down. 'Hi, pumpkin. Are you having fun?' Nova asked Sienna.

'Will you come on the teacups with me please? They will make Mummy sick,' Sienna asked, politely.

Nova stood up and smiled at Marnie who offered a smile back and reached out her hand for Sienna to hold. Sienna took it and reached out her other hand for Nova. Nova gently took it in hers and Marnie's stomach did a triple backflip.

'Let's go ride some teacups,' she said enthusiastically, embracing the present with two of her favourite people.

What Marnie or Sienna failed to mention to Nova was that while Jovi loved the teacups and they were a tradition for her and her daughter, Marnie was not a fan. Getting all caught up in the moment of being there for her niece and the three of them doing something fun together, Marnie hadn't considered her dislike for the ride and was now breathing rather heavily with her eyes closed as Sienna and Nova hollered beside her as the teacup thrashed from side to side.

'Obb, open your eyes. Look at the colours,' Sienna screamed with glee in her voice. Marnie was sure that the colours of the festival were a wonderful sight to behold. The park had been transformed into an autumn dream. Everywhere you looked there were stacks of vibrant orange pumpkins, classic white pumpkins, hay bales for seating, inflatable ghosts and spooky witches and wooden huts with all sorts of games and treats. However, she couldn't quite take them in when they blurred together to make a murky brown as the teacup spun around.

'There's a reason your mum always brings you on the rides,' Marnie said softly back, trying not to let the queasiness in her belly reach her head to signal the need to be sick. Suddenly, soft fingers curled around her hands that were gripping on to the metal silver bar for dear life. Marnie slowly peeled open her eyes to see Nova's fingers curled around hers as Nova continued to scream and cheer with Sienna who was sat facing the two of them in the cup.

Even in her vulnerable state, Marnie didn't miss Sienna's eyes dart to her and Nova's interlaced hands. Worries began prickling the back of Marnie's neck. Would Sienna be upset? All she had ever known was Josh, not that he spent much time with her, but she had called him uncle. Would this be too much too soon?

Just as Marnie was about to pull her hand away from Nova's, Sienna's lips curved into a cheeky smirk.

'It's about time,' the little astronaut called out.

Marnie was dumbfounded. She was pretty certain her chin had just hit the metal bar. She swiped a hand over her sweaty face, not caring about streaking her colourful make-up.

'Oh yeah. What is that supposed to mean, munchkin?' The words were out before she had time to consider that she was talking to a six-year-old and that maybe Sienna was just repeating words she had heard her mum or dad say.

'Well, if I met a girl that liked dinosaurs and space and wore really cool hats, then I'd want her to be my girl-friend too,' Sienna informed Marnie quite matter-of-fact and casual. While Marnie collected her jaw off the floor, Nova reached out and gave Sienna a high five.

'I like you. You have good taste,' Nova noted as the ride came slowly to a stop.

The spinning in Marnie's head began to ease as her pulse slowly calmed its thudding in her neck.

'I like you too,' Sienna told Nova and Marnie loved the simplicity in how her niece spoke her truth.

Stepping off the ride with sea legs, Marnie reached for the nearest barrier and lifted her chin to the breeze to cool her face.

'That was fun, thank you, Obb, thank you, Bob,' Sienna said with a skip in her step. She was still holding on to Nova's hand giving Marnie a chance to collect herself.

The aroma of apple pie was active in the air. A rich cinnamon scent blew along the gentle wind, wrapping Marnie in a warm supportive blanket.

'Nova,' Marnie said, turning around and looking Nova straight in the eye, her stomach having now settled thanks to the solid ground.

'Yes,' Nova replied looking up from Sienna with her dreamy eyes filled with a childlike glee.

'Will you be my girlfriend?' Marnie asked. In her thirty-five years on the planet Marnie had never asked such a bold question, a question that could yield an answer that could potentially shatter her heart for a little while or make her feel like the luckiest woman in the world. Her breath caught somewhere in her throat and for the first time in her life the smell of sugar-glazed doughnuts was too sweet, causing her head to thump. Tonight was gifting a lot of firsts.

Nova's eyes transformed more luminescent than Marnie had had the pleasure of experiencing before. Her free hand cupped Marnie's cheek as she planted a flowery kiss on her lips before shouting, 'Yes, absolutely yes.' Sienna let out a whoop and the moment felt like utter bliss. For all Marnie knew there could have been fireworks exploding in the sky for all the stars that she was seeing in her eyes. Though they'd never had fireworks at the Starcrossed Festival before.

Marnie's insides were still buzzing as she took Nova's hand and started walking back towards the stalls and the doughnut stand. The aroma suddenly made Marnie feel ravenous. She could hardly keep up with her feelings right now, but that gentle kiss had felt like the start of a beautiful promise and an unpredictable adventure all rolled into one and for once Marnie didn't feel so scared.

Marnie hadn't missed the fact that Nova hadn't let go of Sienna's hand when she kissed her, which made Marnie's cheeks glow in a way that she had no doubt aliens would be the ones spotting her with great curiosity from outer space. She really, really liked this girl.

'So, what do we do now?' Nova asked Sienna, wiggling their hands and swaying them as they walked.

'I think I'm ready for pumpkins,' Sienna replied, looking up at the two of them. 'Do you want to carve a pumpkin with me?' she added, her large eyes twinkling under the street lamps.

'You know I do,' Nova enthusiastically answered as they meandered past the candy floss stand, the candy floss having been turned orange for the occasion, and the hot chocolate bar, which boasted ghost-shaped marshmallows and Halloween sprinkles dancing upon the whipped cream.

'There you guys are,' came Jovi's voice as both the doughnut stall and pumpkin-carving station came in to view. A small plot of grass had been cornered off with wooden fencing and was home to a selection of picnic tables covered in newspapers and cutting utensils and an array of pumpkins all different colours and sizes. 'I was trying to get a hold of you. We're all sold out, so we've closed the stall and are ready for some fun.' She waved her phone in Marnie's face as if to say, 'Why didn't you answer?' before scooping up her little girl and smothering her with kisses.

'Sorry, we were otherwise occupied on the teacups,' Marnie noted, giving her sister an apologetic smile while at the same time narrowing her eyes with an evil glare given the fact that Jovi knew Marnie hated rides.

'And kissing,' Sienna said loud enough for her family and passers-by to hear. A few people looked Marnie's way and for a second that queasy feeling of unease washed over her as she remembered the rumour Josh had spread. Would people think Nova was the other woman, the one Marnie had cheated on Josh with?

'Who's been kissing who, Si? We need details,' Antoni playfully demanded from Sienna, making Marnie's negative thoughts poof into the air like a cloud of smoke. He then looked at Marnie with his understanding brown eyes and his lips dancing with his dazzling smile and she knew that it didn't matter what anyone else thought. She could yell, she could shout, she could scream at Josh, she could argue with her neighbours, fight her case, but that would certainly require a lot of energy, energy that she would much rather put into her family and her new girlfriend.

The people who truly loved her knew her story, besides with Miss Rose being due very soon, most of the town understood what had happened. It need not worry Marnie anymore for Josh doing what he did hand sent Marnie on a path of learning to love herself, her journey and what made her who she was. The past nine months had brought her acceptance of things she couldn't control and confidence in taking the lead with things she could. Furthermore, it had brought Nova into her life and she couldn't have been more grateful for that.

'Obb and Bob,' Sienna answered innocently, causing them all to burst out laughing.

'No way.' Antoni gasped mock shocked, jumping forward and throwing an arm over Marnie and Nova's shoulders.

'Welcome to the family,' Jackson said, stepping forward to embrace Nova too. Marnie's arm got tugged in the crossfire and she wobbled on her feet, getting pulled towards Antoni and Jackson's Nova sandwich. Jovi snorted making Marnie look over to her and Marnie noticed she had tears in her eyes. Her no-nonsense twin sister was crying.

'OK, without meaning to sound like your doppelganger.' Marnie smirked at her own sarcasm and Jovi rolled her eyes as Sienna looked back and forth between the two of them. 'There's something you're not telling me. You never miss the teacups, you always have costumes for tonight, and unless I've caused trouble, you never cry.' Marnie eyed her sister pointedly.

Jackson stepped back and put an arm around his wife and little girl. Jovi went to speak, a slight look of hesitation passing over her features. Marnie's stomach flipped. Why was her sister scared of what she was about to say? Jovi could tell her anything – she wanted Jovi to be able to tell her anything.

'Mummy has a pumpkin in her belly,' Sienna piped up – another win for the innocence and honesty of children. But instead of Jovi and Jackson's faces beaming with joy and excitement over such news, they were looking at Marnie as if she might crack.

'Don't you dare give me that look, the both of you stop it now. This is amazing news. Congratulations. Oh my God!!' Marnie shouted, charging at her sister and brother-in-law with her arms outstretched and squashing Sienna in a big bear hug.

'Congratulations, guys,' Nova said, clapping her hands and going in for hugs too.

Antoni beamed, wrapping his arms around Jackson and scooping up Sienna, spinning her around and cheering that she was going to be a big sister.

'You're not mad?' Jovi mumbled, looking at Marnie through heavy lids. Marnie had never felt less mad in her entire life. But my gosh how much did it hit her now how much had changed over the last nine months, which seemed symbolic for the nine that were about to come for Jovi. She'd spent too long comparing her life to her twin sister's and it pained her to know that she had made Jovi feel scared to tell her such beautiful news.

'Jeez, Jovi, way to make me sound like a catch to my new girlfriend. Of course I'm not mad,' Marnie teased which made Jovi crack a smile. Silence descended on the group for a heartbeat, until Antoni spoke up.

'Nova, as it's your first time at the festival, you get to pick out the pumpkin.' Nova's smile tickled her stardust-covered ears and she leant over to kiss Marnie on the cheek, seemingly understanding that the family wanted to give the two sisters time to speak. And so, Jackson, Antoni, Sienna and Nova walked through the rickety gate to the pumpkin patch leaving Marnie and Jovi to talk.

'I'm sorry if I ever made you feel guilty for the life you have, Jovi, but you have to know that I am beyond thrilled that you and Jackson are expecting again. You have to know that. I love you more than life itself and all that you have, you've gone after, you've built it, you've made it happen and I am so ridiculously proud, even in the odd times when I've felt a touch jealous, I was still so stinking proud,' Marnie told her sister with an urgency in her voice.

'I know that, I do. Everyone always made out that everything would happen to us at the same time. Even Mum and Dad sometimes acted like our lives would run smoothly alongside each other's, that we'd do and achieve everything together. I know that was harder for you,' Jovi said, hooking her arm through Marnie's crooked elbow where she fiddled with the straps of her backpack for comfort.

'Yes but that was never your fault and I think I made you feel like it was so many times. It was like I wanted to have the direction you had, to fall in love, have the career, have the kids, have the house. It was like you were doing it all and I was just falling behind. Even when I found my feet as a TA, I guess I was willing everything to fall into place with Josh and it just never did, but now I know why,' Marnie explained.

'Yes you needed to become your badass self and take charge,' Jovi stated, thumping Marnie in the arm.

'Ouch,' Marnie said through a chuckle, rubbing at her bicep. 'You're right though, gosh I just needed to stop being so afraid and go after what I wanted. I was so mad at Mum and Dad, but look at them now, so happy in their own lives; having made huge changes. I'm ready to accept that my life doesn't really have a plan and the things that I would like might not always come to me in the ways I might have thought.'

'What, you never thought you would find happiness by flying halfway across the world and bumping into an ice-hockey-loving woman who has an obsession with dinosaurs, makes caps look like they should be *the* accessory on every cover of *Vogue* and who loves doughnuts as much as you do?' Jovi asked, shrugging nonchalantly.

'Surprisingly no,' Marnie replied, giving her sister a gentle shove. 'But you know this baby, right? It's like mine, yeah? I mean Mum and Dad always said we had to take turns, like one for you, one for me. We have an equal amount of everything, so you have one, that means I get this one?'

Jovi let out a bark of laughter. 'I have a feeling everything will work out, Marn.'

'Yeah? Me too,' Marnie replied, looking out towards the pumpkin patch as they circled back around, walking across the other side of the park and row of stalls, and heading towards where they had come from. Marnie could see Nova and Antoni at one of the picnic tables and another figure, dressed as a fried egg, sitting quite cosily next to Antoni. Even through the egg disguise he looked suspiciously enough like Jonathan from the fire station. All three of them were talking animatedly and grinning broadly. Marnie wasn't sure if they were talking about dinosaurs, food or about saving the mortals of Orion, but the image made her heart beat ferociously.

She wasn't sure if it was somewhere between Whistler and Vancouver, or when scooping up Nova off the ice rink or kissing her in the sandpit, but all the ideals Marnie had put into her head for how her life was supposed to go had disbanded. Now she wasn't waiting for the moments to come to her; she was creating the moments.

'So, when did Nova ask you to be her girlfriend?' Jovi asked, a squeal coming through in her words.

'She didn't ask me, I asked her,' Marnie said, her smile sparkling brighter than one hundred Siriuses in the night sky.

Epilogue

'That's terrible,' Paislee said, without taking her eyes off her own Blu-Tack model of a T-Rex.

'Oh come on, I'm trying,' Marnie said, playfully. It was the last day of the summer term. Marnie and Paislee were sat outside on the grass making objects out of Blu-Tack, or at least Paislee was making objects out of Blu-Tack and Marnie was doing her absolute utmost to keep up. But no matter how crafty Marnie was or the epic vision she had in her head of what she wanted the Blu-Tack to transform into, they never quite came to life like Paislee's did.

The little girl looked over and smiled, making eye contact and studying Marnie. She did this often and Marnie had never felt as seen as she did in those moments. Their relationship had gone from strength to strength over the past year. Paislee's love of school had grown as they had carried out many spectacular experiments and constructed numerous Jurassic worlds. They had even made their own movies and studied animation in great depth and Paislee had made progress in all areas of the curriculum.

Marnie had still had to fight the odd fight when people tried to enforce their beliefs that all children should follow the same rules and school routine. She would continue to fight in the hopes of creating a world more suitable for everyone, where everyone had an equal chance at succeeding.

'When is Miss Clarke coming back?' Paislee asked, sticking a pencil into the Blu-Tack to make the dinosaur's eyes.

'Not yet. She's in Canada now. That's where she lives,' Marnie said. They'd had this conversation many times over the last couple of months, for Paislee was sad when Miss Clarke had had to leave to go back home back at the beginning of November. But Marnie told her stories all the time about what she was up to as Paislee loved to know about Marnie's life. Marnie had even brought Paislee back a gift from Canada when she had visited over the Christmas holidays.

Occasionally, Nova sent pictures of any new artefacts that had been sent to the museum for Paislee to see and Marnie would print them out and show her.

'You didn't go to Canada too?' Paislee asked, twisting tiny pieces of the Blu-Tack to make fingers.

'I went to visit at Christmas, but I live here, this is my home,' Marnie told her, still trying to roll her Blu-Tack to give her dinosaur a tail as Paislee had done. It was trickier than Paislee made it look.

'Did you argue?' Paislee asked.

'No, we didn't argue but Miss Clarke has her job in Canada and a family and I have my job here and my family too. I want to be here,' Marnie replied finding that she was smiling. Long-distance wasn't easy but Marnie had found that so far it had been just right for her and Nova. She had felt a sense of calm over the last couple of months as they got to know each other and learn about each other through phone calls, video calls and parcels.

Whenever Nova found something that made her think of Marnie, she would pop it in the post. Marnie now had a shelf just for those special trinkets that ranged from handcrafted photo frames, a pack of pom-poms in the colours of the Canadian flag and Marnie's favourite, a little gold necklace with a pendant of two T-Rexes side by side. Marnie liked to send Nova things too, mostly things that she and Sienna had made, from a lollipop stick treasure box for Nova to put her dinosaur artefacts in, to a beaded bracelet depicting the solar system, to recipes in a jar that Jovi and Antoni helped with.

The time difference allowed for Marnie to continue working on herself as she had done in Canada. When Nova was at work or sleeping Marnie spent time with her family and had loved hanging out in her dad's workshop and watching ice-hockey games with her mum and Tim. She never missed a Sunday morning at the market and had attended many craft evenings that Cameron held.

'You want to stay here?' Paislee questioned, squashing her amazing Blu-Tack dinosaur in to a ball to start all over again. Marnie hadn't even figured out the tail yet.

'Yes, I want to stay here,' Marnie replied with a confident nod. She'd often heard the saying that you would get all the things you wanted in life, just not in the way you might have expected and right now she had never known that fact to be truer. She had a relationship that nourished her soul where her girlfriend listened to her, loved her and appreciated all the things that made her her and never made her feel bad for the things she wanted and who gave more time to her family even when she lived over four thousand miles away. And she had a job that she loved with all her heart where she got to spend her days with the most awesome kids.

'You want to stay here with me. You knew I needed a best friend and you needed a best friend too,' Paislee said, her voice ever so gentle and matter-of-fact as she took Marnie's Blu-Tack out of her hand and started rolling out the tail for Marnie. Within two rolls it already looked more like a T-Rex tail than Marnie had managed in the last twenty minutes.

Marnie's eyes threatened tears. Paislee couldn't have been more on point. Marnie had loved every child, every class she had worked with over the last ten years but there was something about her connection with Paislee that made her jump out of bed in the morning ready to deal with the still-new environment of Apollo Primary, the teachers that were only now warming to her and a life she couldn't always plan and predict.

'Yes, I wanted to stay with you and you're the best best friend I've ever had.' Marnie smiled broadly. Paislee nonchalantly passed her back the Blu-Tack for Marnie to finish now that the tail was improved upon.

'Don't make it terrible,' Paislee instructed.

Marnie laughed, 'I'll try not to,' she said as Paislee edged her chair a touch closer to Marnie's and leant her elbow on Marnie's knee as she began manipulating another ball of Blu-Tack. It was a welcome reminder to Marnie the universe would always put her in the place she needed to be – plan or no plan.

★

Amber pressed pause on *The Mitchells vs. the Machines* indicating that the summer holidays had finally arrived. Twenty-five humans carrying heavy bags full of teacher gifts, schoolbooks and water bottles shuffled to their feet. Paislee took a moment, glancing out of the window as Marnie stood up.

'I'll see you in three days.' She said, turning her head and tilting it to one side as she took in Marnie.

'No, you get to have some fun at home now and play with your toys. I will see you in thirty-five days,' Marnie told her, putting a hand through her hair. Paislee took Marnie's hand and pressed it harder to her forehead and then round her neck.

'Just three days,' the little girl said.

'A bit longer than three days, OK? You will have fun,' Marnie reassured her.

'I won't see you for the summer,' Paislee noted, squeezing Marnie's hand, her forearm now resting over Paislee's back.

'No, but you're going to do lots of wonderful things with your mum and grandma,' Marnie replied.

'I won't see you, but you will be in my heart,' Paislee said, pausing mid-spin, still holding Marnie's hand, and looking up at her. Marnie didn't know if she had ever met a more compassionate child, besides her niece. Sienna and Paislee shared so many similarities with their big hearts and love for others.

'Exactly. I'm always there,' Marnie said. For the second time today she was trying not to cry. Suddenly, five weeks away from the school seemed like too much time. What on earth was she supposed to do with all that time?

It turned out Marnie didn't have to worry about what

would be occupying her time during the summer holidays. When she walked outside she was greeted by not only Jovi and Sienna, but also by Jackson, holding two-month-old baby Katherine, as well as Antoni, Tim, Mum and Dad. They all remained quite still and quiet while Marnie said bye to Paislee and her mum and wished them a wonderful summer, but once the rest of her class had departed there came a cheerful 'Surprise' from the large gathering.

'I feel like I'm leaving Year Six all over again. What's going on? What's the special occasion?' Marnie asked, her nose scrunching up in confusion though it was conflicting with a grin that had formed upon seeing all her family stood together, which saw Tim and her dad actually standing side by side.

'Whatever do you mean? It's time for our traditional family vacation,' Antoni announced with his hands on his hips, a smirk on his lips and his sparkling eyes dizzying her with all the mischief that swam within them.

'I'm sorry, have I missed something? Since when is a family vacation a tradition for our family?' Marnie couldn't help but ask through a snort.

'Since your girlfriend lives in Canada, duh!!' Jovi announced, her features glowing, her round, rosy cheeks practically beaming. Marnie hoped that she would glow like that when she'd just had a baby, but if Marnie had learnt, and come to terms with anything over the last year, it was that there were some things twins simply didn't share and there was no crazy doubt in her mind that if she got pregnant during the summer months, she would be embracing a messy, messy bun and her natural, glowing sheen would be sweat. For some reason, that thought made her ridiculously giddy, especially as her mind immediately pictured Nova holding her hand and feeding her ice cream.

'Come on, love. The taxi's waiting, get your stuff. Our flight leaves in three hours,' her mum explained, marching forward merrily, waving at Amber and pushing Marnie back inside the school, snapping her out of her Nova trance. 'We haven't got long.' Marnie got the impression that her mum had waited her whole life to go on a family vacation but it had never been possible growing up. She couldn't imagine her mum wanted to be stuck in a foreign country arguing with her dad, or deserted together on a sandy beach disagreeing over where to position the sunlounges.

'Mum, am I right in saying that we're going to Canada?' Marnie asked, leaning in as Amber waved goodbye to everyone and opened the door for Marnie with a genuine happy smile plastered on her face.

'Yes, dear,' her mum answered with a chuckle and roll of her eyes.

'OK, just checking,' Marnie said, her stomach suddenly fizzing as if she had drunk a large bottle of champagne.

'Oh my God, how big is that thing?' Marnie asked gobsmacked, craning her neck to take in all the detail from the claws on the ground by their feet to the pointy teeth way up in the heavens.

'It stands at twenty-six point three metres high,' Nova answered without a beat in between, swinging Marnie's hand together in hers, her excitement palpable.

'You're practically vibrating,' Marnie noted, tiptoeing a touch to kiss her girlfriend on the nose.

They had spent the last week with Nova's mum in Vancouver, where the rest of the family currently were, with Nova showing the family around and getting acquainted with downtown Vancouver. Tim, Marnie and Nova had been to watch the hockey. They had taken Sienna ice-skating and Jovi, Antoni, Marnie and Nova had done a Vancouver doughnut trail, trying out the best doughnut hotspots in the city. After devouring one of Lucky's Lemon Meringue and Honeycomb doughnuts, Antoni had declared that he was moving to Canada.

The week so far had been an entirely different experience to Marnie's first week here last March. Then she had been a knot of nerves and a ball of anxiety unable to leave her hotel room at the thought of facing the world on her own. She had overcome those fears, gratefully, and had thoroughly enjoyed her expedition across Canada, particularly enjoying the smaller, quainter towns of Whistler and Revelstoke, the former of which they, as a family, would be venturing to next week, for their last week of vacation.

Now though she was humming with energy, Nova's vibes transferring to her through their interlocked hands, filling her with a glorious sense of being assertively present. Every inch of her felt alive and in the moment.

'Have you ever kissed a girl in the clutches of a T-Rex's jaw before?' Nova asked, tugging at Marnie's hand and sprinting over to the stairs at the base of the ginormous creature.

'You're going to be shocked by this answer and I may lose all my cool points, but no,' Marnie teased as they started climbing. Nova laughed while adjusting the cap on her head that today suitably bore a Stegosaurus. Her laugh reverberated off every corner of Marnie's heart, making her wobble on the steps, causing Nova to take one step down behind her, wrap her arms around Marnie's waist and rest her head on Marnie's shoulder. Marnie liked having a tall girlfriend. Though there was no doubt that they could not possibly walk one hundred and six steps in this position, she was thankful that the line was slow-moving so that she could savour it for a few moments longer.

Nova had taken last week off but had to work this week, so she could take off next week for the family cabin trip to Whistler. Marnie had made the trip to Alberta with her so they could have some alone time together and because Nova had been dying to show her around Drumheller. Nova had been talking about how they had to take a selfie with every dinosaur in Drumheller since Christmas. They had spent Marnie's week-long trip in December in Vancouver with Nova's mum and family and hadn't had chance to make the trek to Alberta, not that Marnie had wanted to as she had loved Nova's mum from the moment she'd met her and had instantaneously been absorbed into Nova's family Christmas traditions. She couldn't have borne to leave and miss any of it.

But now, they were twelve dinos down on their dinosaur selfie list and Nova had to be at work at noon. It had been a busy morning to say the least. They had woken before the sunrise to start their dinosaur walk in hopes of beating the summer crowds. They had managed it for a peaceful couple of hours, just the two of them, an Ankylosaurus and the rising orange orb transforming the navy blue sky into a kaleidoscope of baby blue, reds and yellows, but the buzz of people had grown stronger by nine a.m. The eight dinosaurs still left on their list would have to wait for another day and Marnie found herself looking forward to it. She needed a picture of her with a Triceratops for Paislee.

'So, I've been thinking,' Nova whispered into Marnie's neck, the line still at a standstill. Marnie's skin tingled pleasantly.

'Mmm, hmm,' she croaked.

'I think I'd like to spend more time in England. I loved working in the museum there – it was a welcome change of scenery. I had a blast working with the kids at your school and as much as I'd miss seeing this guy every day...' Marnie felt one of Nova's arms move and in her periphery saw her reach out and caress the steel structure around them, but she daren't say a word that would interrupt Nova's train of thought. 'I believe I'd much prefer seeing my girlfriend every day eh,' she finished.

Marnie spun around so fast she nearly sent Nova flying backwards into a smart-looking family of four, who wore matching outfits, but Marnie caught her by the shoulders, sent a quick nod and an apology towards the family who all smiled it off with a laid-back manner Marnie could only dream of having, and smiled so brightly that to those on the outside, waiting to start their ascent up the dinosaur, it might look like the sun was shining out of the T-Rex's butt.

'You're being serious?' Marnie asked, just wanting to double-check she had heard correctly with all the blood thumping in her ears.

'I've literally never been more serious in my life,' Nova said cupping Marnie's face and then, with such audacity, considering the problems these stairs had been causing for them, Nova winked. Winked.

But Marnie didn't have time for her knees to buckle, for the line was moving and by the looks on some people's faces, they were desperate to get this ordeal over with. The late morning had been growing increasingly warmer, therefore inside the belly of this beast was like an inferno. The backs of Marnie's knee were definitely soaked with sweat, even in her short linen dungarees.

At the top of the famed Tyra, Marnie welcomed the faint breeze. The landscape before them, beyond the red railings, glass panels and sharp acrylic dinosaur teeth, wasn't exactly Whistler mountain, but she embraced the car park, busy streets and fountain all the same, for right now she felt euphoric. Being the easy-going, polite and confident Canadian that she was, Nova took the lead in excusing them to the very front of the dinosaur's mouth, where they both took a moment to appreciate the unique view, before Nova's hands were cupping Marnie's cheeks once more.

'I'd still like to spend lots of time in Canada,' Nova noted, staring deep into Marnie's eyes.

'I have thirteen weeks off a year. I'll book all the flights to Canada now,' Marnie said, meaning it.

'OK, cool,' Nova said, glancing away and hiding a sudden hint of nerves in her eyes.

'Hey, look at me,' Marnie said, resting her hands on Nova's wrists. 'We're in this fifty-fifty you and me. I'll start practising the Canadian national anthem and I promise our kids will be bilingual,' Marnie said, a playfulness in her tone to try and take away the edge of fear in Nova's eyes. It worked. Nova's nose scrunched up as she let out a giggle. Kids had slipped into the conversation many times since their very first sleepover. Marnie was content in knowing they both wanted them, but it didn't stop a teeny sliver of anxiety bubble in her stomach at making such a bold statement. She felt miles away from the woman who let life happen to her instead of going after what she wanted, but that didn't stop the occasional bouts of anxiety from hitting her every now and again.

But she needn't have worried.

'Our first child is going to be called Rex, right?' Nova said with a twinkle in her eye.

Marnie rolled her eyes and spun the cap around on Nova's head. With every promise of the future Marnie felt hopeful and deliciously excited more than scared these days, for she knew that though it was fun to dream, it was the present moments, the magical minutes and the seconds that felt like forever that mattered the most. And so, in the jaws of a one-hundred-and-forty-six-thousand-pound dinosaur, she pulled Nova in close and kissed her with all that she had because in that moment she was all she had and it couldn't have been more unexpectedly perfectosaurus.

'That's not a dinosaur,' Nova breathed, her lips grazing Marnie's as they parted only slightly for air. Marnie smirked, not realising she had spoken her thoughts out loud.

'I've just discovered it,' Marnie whispered against Nova's lips, before kissing her gently once more.

Acknowledgments

Thank you so much to the wonderful team at Aria for making *Love Lessons in Starcross Valley* the best it can be. Thank you Thorne Ryan for your encouragement, guidance and advice, Lizz Burrell, Lauren Palmer, Bianca Gillam and Emily Reader for all your help and support, Jessie Price for the stunning cover design that makes me as giddy as can be every time I look at it and to the incredible Helena Newton for being amazing in every way and making sense of the thoughts in my head that have made their way on to the page. I appreciate you all greatly.

Thank you to every reader who has picked up a copy of one of my books, I truly struggle to find the words to really express my gratitude. Your support, encouragement and kind words never fail to inspire me and make me smile.

This book is incredibly special to me and I had a few doubts and worries when putting pen to paper and so I want to thank a few authors who made me feel like my voice mattered and that I had a place: Sophie Gonzales, Nic Stone, Becky Albertalli, Rod Pulido, Louise Willingham and Steven Salvatore.

Thank you to my wonderful friends who are always there

with positive words to keep me going, you are all superstars and I love you dearly.

Thank you to my best friend, your friendship inspired this story and is one of the most treasured and special relationships in my life. You are awesome in every way and I hope maybe this book might help the world to see that we are all unique and should be treated as such, because when we love each other without judgement and take the time to care and to understand one another, amazing things can happen. When we find those people that get us, that see us, that listen, we see what we are truly made of, that our dreams can be achieved and that we are capable of so much.

Thank you so much to my family, you rock, don't ever change... But seriously, thank you for everything you do day in and day out to support me. I love you with all my heart for always.

Last but not least, thank you to all the gorgeous, brave, courageous people around me who, out or not, label or no label, let their magic shine in their own incredible way and make the world such a beautiful place.

About the Author

LUCY KNOTT is a former professional wrestler with a passion for storytelling. Now, instead of telling her stories in the ring, she's putting pen to paper, fulfilling another lifelong dream in becoming an Author.

Inspired by her Italian Grandparents, when she is not writing you will most likely find her cooking, baking and devouring Italian food, in addition to learning Italian and daydreaming of trips to Italy.

Along with her twin sister, Kelly, Lucy runs TheBlossomTwins.com, where she enthusiastically shares her love for books, baking and Italy, with daily posts, reviews and recipes.